TIME CASTAWAYS
THE MONA LISA KEY

The Time Castaways series

The Mona Lisa Key
The Obsidian Compass

Time Castaways

THE MONA LISA KEY

LIESL SHURTLIFF

Katherine Tegen Books
An Imprint of HarperCollins Publishers

For my beautiful, brilliant children.
You are my greatest adventure.

Katherine Tegen Books is an imprint of HarperCollins Publishers.

Time Castaways #1: The Mona Lisa Key
Copyright © 2018 by HarperCollins Publishers

Library of Congress Cataloging-in-Publication Data
Names: Shurtliff, Liesl, author.
Title: The Mona Lisa key / Liesl Shurtliff.
Description: New York, NY : Katherine Tegen Books, 2018. | Series: Time castaways ; 1 | Summary: When Matt, Ruby, and Corey Hudson discover their subway train is actually a time-traveling eighteenth-century frigate captained by a mysterious pirate, they are thrown into a series of adventures that offer cryptic clues about their past and their future.
Identifiers: LCCN 2017057242 | ISBN 9780062568168 (paperback)
Subjects: | CYAC: Brothers and sisters—Fiction. | Time travel—Fiction. | Pirates—Fiction. | Adventure and adventurers—Fiction. | BISAC: JUVENILE FICTION / Action & Adventure / Pirates. | JUVENILE FICTION / Fantasy & Magic.
Classification: LCC PZ7.S559853 Mo 2018 | DDC [Fic]—dc23 LC record available at https://lccn.loc.gov/2017057242

Typography by Katie Fitch
19 20 21 22 23   PC/BRR   10 9 8 7 6 5 4 3 2 1
❖
First paperback edition, 2019

1

Probabilities

It was a typical afternoon in New York City—cars and taxis honking in the streets, pedestrians and pigeons crowding the sidewalks. Tourists took selfies and browsed the street vendors for cheap souvenirs, and the food carts lined all along Fifth Avenue spread their smells of meat, cheese, and grease. But Matt Hudson didn't notice any of it. He walked down the bustling street deep in concentration, as if he were in a completely different world altogether.

Matt was thinking about probabilities. For instance, what was the probability of someone winning the lottery? About a 1 in 150 million chance, according to the last one. And the probability of being struck by lightning—twice? Attacked by a shark or striking a gold mine? Very low, he thought. And yet, improbable things happened all the time to people all around the world. Therefore, Matt reasoned, improbable was not the same as uncommon, and he could reasonably expect improbable things to happen to *him* at any time, perhaps even today. And so Matt walked purposefully down the street with a rolled-up piece of paper in his hand. The paper was most certainly an improbability, he knew, but he was feeling quite optimistic anyway, at least until his brother and sister decided to throw in their two cents.

"I don't know why you're even bothering to ask," said his sister, Ruby. "They're going to say no."

"Oh come on, Ruby," said Corey from his right. "Don't be a killjoy. I give it a solid one percent chance."

"Mom and Dad barely let us walk to and from school by ourselves," said Ruby. "They wouldn't even let me ride the bus a mile by myself once a week to take judo classes."

"You know how they feel about us riding transit," said Matt. "And this is different from judo classes. It's education."

"Ooh, *education*," said Corey. "I've underestimated his chances, I think. I'm bumping it up to two percent."

"No chance. It's never going to happen," said Ruby.

Matt suddenly wished he had kept his grand plans to himself, but he had been so excited he couldn't help but spill it to Corey and Ruby right after school. He didn't really have anyone else to tell, and he had hoped his brother and sister would be excited for him, but they had been less than encouraging. Matt's optimism was starting to deflate. He began to absentmindedly rub his thumb over the stone on his bracelet, his nervous habit.

"Watch it!" Ruby yanked on Matt's arm, but it was too late. He'd stepped in a fresh pile of doggy doo-doo.

"Grooooss!" said Corey.

Matt scraped his shoe on the cement for the final block before they reached the Metropolitan Museum of Art. People were spread all over the steps, eating food and taking pictures in front of the museum with its stately columns and arched windows.

Matt hobbled over to the fountains at the side of the steps, pulled off his shoe, and swished it around in the water. He inspected the bottom. There was still poop stuck in all the grooves.

"Nope. No chances now," said Corey. "They're not even going to let you set foot in the office."

"Will you be quiet," said Matt. His head suddenly ached, a dull throb at his temple.

"We're not trying to be mean or anything, Matt," said Ruby. "We're just trying to prepare you for the inevitable. It seems even the universe is trying to warn you." She motioned to his shoe.

"Actually, maybe the universe is trying to encourage me," said Matt. "Do you know how unlikely it is that I should step in dog poop right here, right now? I mean, the chances are very low, but it happened, didn't it?"

Ruby scrunched up her face. She and Corey looked sideways at each other. He could almost hear their thoughts.

Our brother is crazy.

I know, but is there any point in telling him?

Though Corey and Ruby were twins, they rarely agreed on anything. They were opposites in nearly every way. When Corey joked, Ruby was serious. While Corey bounced, Ruby kept her feet firmly planted. But there was one thing they usually agreed on—the complete perplexity and misunderstanding of their (only slightly) older brother.

Matt knew he was a little different, and he knew that others noticed. He regularly got teased for talking to himself in the bathroom and hallways (he thought better out loud) and no one ever let him live it down that he was a Mets fan. In fact, just last week his Mets hat had been stolen out of his locker, a scribbled note left in its place that said *It's for the best*. Matt took this all in good stride. He couldn't care less what others thought about him, but when his own brother and sister pointed out his oddball tendencies it made him feel especially freakish and just a tad irritable.

"Just don't say anything," said Matt, slipping his smelly shoe back on. "I'll handle this myself." He stomped toward the museum steps and began to ascend. Corey and Ruby hurried after him.

"*Hola, niños!*" said Javier, one of the security guards usually on duty whenever the Hudsons came in.

"*Hola*, Javier," said Matt. He gave him a fist bump.

"*Cómo está?*"

"*Bien, gracias.*"

"Yeah, he's *muy bien*," said Corey. "He stepped in dog poop, so the universe is on his side."

Javier looked at Matt quizzically, almost as if he wasn't sure he understood Corey correctly and wanted Matt to translate. "Never mind him," said Matt. "Are our parents in my dad's office?"

"*Sí*," he said. "But be careful. Your *madre*'s got a whole bunch of swords back there. Ooh, she scares me sometimes!"

"Us too," said Ruby.

"Ha! I believe you, *niña!*"

"*Adiós*, Javier!"

They walked through the great hall, dodging meandering patrons walking around with their heads tipped toward the high ceiling, where light poured through the windows and skylights.

They turned right at the grand staircase and walked down a corridor that eventually opened up to the Arms and Armor exhibit. They passed the glass cases of swords, daggers, spears, and suits of armor from various countries and centuries, many of which their mother had curated or restored, but the Hudson children didn't even glance at them. They'd practically been raised in this museum and knew it almost as well as their own home.

Finally they came to a narrow hallway. Their father's office was the third door on the left—*Matthew B. Hudson, Director of Museum Archives*. Matt knocked lightly and opened the door.

Mr. Hudson sat in the chair behind his desk, tapping away on his computer. He was a little disheveled. His dark hair looked like it had been through a windstorm, he hadn't shaved in a couple of days, and he had the misty look of someone who was not totally present, a result of years of history research and obsessing over old maps. He didn't even look up when the children entered. Matt hoped he was in an agreeable mood, but for his current plans he was more concerned with his mom's mood.

Mrs. Hudson was standing to the side of her husband's desk, behind a folding table. She was a beautiful woman with long dark hair, tan skin, and warm, intelligent brown eyes that were now knit in fervent concentration as she sharpened an old dagger. She was indeed surrounded by swords and knives, just as Javier had said. As a renowned freelance art restorer and authenticator, Mrs. Hudson worked on anything from old paintings to antique furniture and valuable memorabilia, but weapons were her specialty and passion. She had a soft spot in her heart for sharp objects.

Mrs. Hudson finally paused in her knife sharpening and looked up. Her face instantly brightened at the sight of her children.

"*Bonjour, mes chéris! Comment était l'école?*"

"Fine," said Ruby.

"Boring," said Corey.

"*J'ai reçu un A sur mon test de mathématiques,*" said Matt.

"*Très bien,* Mateo!" said Mrs. Hudson.

"Suck-up," muttered Corey.

Matt shrugged. He'd take all the help he could get at the moment, and Mrs. Hudson always appreciated it when her children spoke whatever language she happened to spring upon them. She could speak half a dozen languages, and she was determined to make polyglots of all her children. Matt was the only one who had shown much aptitude for it. He could speak French and Spanish almost fluently, as his mother did, and he was getting pretty good at Arabic, too, and had even started to learn a little Chinese. He had a goal to learn a dozen languages by the time he was twenty-one (his 12/21 project, he called it). Ruby and Corey were not as enthusiastic. They could understand French well enough, but they weren't as comfortable speaking it, and they had hardly picked up on Arabic or any of the other languages at all.

"I'm hungry," said Corey. "Can we get snacks?"

Mrs. Hudson reached into her bag and pulled out a green apple. "Here."

Corey groaned. "Can't we go get something from the vending machines?"

"The vending machines? Why would you want any of that junk?"

"Because it tastes good," said Corey.

"I disagree. Nothing in those machines can come close to the fruits of Mother Nature." She tossed the apple and caught it in her hand, then pressed the dagger she'd been sharpening against the apple with a mischievous twinkle in her eye. "Nor can they perform the tricks of *this* mother."

Mrs. Hudson began to peel the apple, quickly and smoothly cutting the skin into one long, curly spiral. She tossed the apple and the knife into the air, spun around, and caught the knife just in time to spear the apple right through the core.

The three children clapped.

"I'm going to pretend I didn't see that," said Mr. Hudson, still typing. "Using valuable artifacts for kitchen cutlery . . ." He clicked his tongue and shook his head.

"Oh hush," said Mrs. Hudson, wiping the blade with a cloth. "A good blade appreciates being used every now and then. It'll display better for us now."

Ruby picked up the apple peel and bounced it like a yo-yo. "When are you going to teach me how to do that?" she asked.

"I'd prefer you keep all your limbs for just a few more years," said Mrs. Hudson.

"Who taught you?"

"My high school home ec teacher. She was brilliant with a knife."

"Come on, Mom. Seriously," said Ruby.

"Can't a mother keep some mystery about her?" Mrs.

Hudson deftly sliced the apple into thirds, cut out the core, and handed them each a piece. "If I spill all my secrets to you, you'll think I'm completely boring and you'll never listen to a thing I say. Take your father," she said, pointing the dagger in Mr. Hudson's direction. He was still deeply engaged with whatever he was typing on the computer, completely oblivious to the conversation or the blade now pointed at his chest. "I had him hanging on my every word, once upon a time, until I told him all my secrets and he hasn't listened to a thing I've said since."

"Hmm?" Mr. Hudson finished typing something, then looked up. His misty, faraway look instantly sharpened when he saw his wife pointing a knife at him. He shot back in his chair and held up his hands. "Whatever you want from me, I'll do it!"

"That's more like it," said Mrs. Hudson. "Now, teach your children something interesting. This one seems to think school is *boring*."

"Boring?" Mr. Hudson straightened his glasses on his nose. "Oh no, what are they teaching you in that school? I have just the remedy. I recently acquired a map from ancient Greece. Loads of interesting things. There's a spot that claims to be the Fountain of Youth. Shall we go have a look?"

"Uh . . . actually, I'd better get started on my homework," said Corey. "Lots to do. Don't want to fall behind."

"Me too," said Ruby. "We'll be in the cafeteria." She and

Corey shuffled out the door, leaving Matt alone in the office with his parents.

Mr. Hudson sighed. "I don't understand it. When I was their age I couldn't get enough of maps. My favorite book was the *Rand McNally World Atlas*."

"Take heart, dear," said Mrs. Hudson. "At least one of your children didn't abandon you."

Mr. Hudson turned his attention to Matt. "Mateo! Of course, my namesake."

Matt had been named Mateo partly to honor his father and partly to honor his heritage. Matt had been adopted as an infant from Colombia. He liked his name for both reasons. He especially enjoyed whenever his mom called "Matt?" and they'd both answer. For this reason she usually called Matt Mateo and her husband Matthew.

"Don't you have homework, too, Mateo?" his mom asked.

"I finished most of it at school," he said.

"Of course you did," said Mr. Hudson. "He's a good one, Bel. I'm glad we decided to keep him."

"Yes, our good-luck charm." Mrs. Hudson winked at Matt. She often referred to him as her good-luck charm. Mr. and Mrs. Hudson had tried for years to have children, to no avail, then tried for years to adopt, to no avail—until they got Mateo from Colombia. And much to their surprise, shortly after bringing him home Mrs. Hudson found out she was pregnant. With twins. How improbable was that?

Matt felt a small boost. The universe *was* on his side, and he felt it pushing him forward. *Carpe diem.* He rubbed at his bracelet once again, this time for luck.

"Actually, there's something I wanted to talk to you about," he said, trying to sound casual.

"Of course, *chéri*, what is it?" Mrs. Hudson picked up another antique sword and began to inspect it.

"There's this awesome summer program that I'm really interested in." Matt unrolled the flyer and flattened it out on the desk. "Did you know they have foreign exchange programs for middle school kids?"

"Oh really?" said Mrs. Hudson a little absentmindedly. She twisted the sword in her hand, then took down some notes on a pad.

"Yeah. You can go to a foreign country for an entire summer and live with a native family so you can immerse yourself in the language and really become fluent. They have host families all over the world, and there's a great program in Paris this summer, one specifically for science and innovation. Wouldn't that be perfect for me?"

"You already speak French," said Mrs. Hudson. "You're practically fluent now."

"But not *completely* fluent," said Matt. "I never speak with anyone but you. This way I'll get to speak French all the time with lots of people. Besides, that's only a bonus. The real benefit is the scientific opportunities. They'll have world-class scientists conducting experiments and lecturing, people who are at the forefront of scientific discovery. I would learn *tons*, and it would look really good on a college application." Mrs. Hudson raised her eyebrows at him. Matt tried to hide his smile. He was proud of that bargaining chip. His parents took college for their children very seriously.

Mrs. Hudson glanced at the flyer. It had a picture of the Eiffel Tower and the Musée de Louvre. That also felt like a sign to Matt. Mrs. Hudson loved the Louvre, mostly because she loved the *Mona Lisa*, though she'd never been herself. She hated to travel, got terrible motion sickness, which Matt thought was ironic considering all the languages she could speak. But that shouldn't keep *him* from going anywhere. . . .

"It is a nice idea, Mateo," Mrs. Hudson said. "And I do want you to have every opportunity to learn, but I just don't feel comfortable with you traveling on your own yet, not that far and for so long."

"But I wouldn't be alone," said Matt. "I would be staying with a family vetted by the program. They do background checks and everything, and you can interview them too if you want."

"Maybe in another year or two," said Mrs. Hudson.

"But—"

"We can look into some summer science camps here in New York," said Mrs. Hudson. "I'm sure there are ones every bit as good as the one in Paris. Right, Matthew?"

"Sure," said Mr. Hudson a little distractedly. "We can go to the science museum all you want. I'll bet they've got some good summer programs too."

Matt tried not to make a face. He'd explored the science museum inside and out by the time he'd entered kindergarten. And why did his parents always think *museums* were the ultimate place for learning? He didn't need another museum. He needed real field experience, real mentors, and he'd never been anywhere outside of New York, unless you counted his birth in Colombia, which he didn't.

Mrs. Hudson turned her attention back to her work, poured some smelly chemical on a cloth and started to polish the blade of the sword. Matt's dull headache suddenly intensified, the throbbing now penetrating his skull. He knew he was losing. His hopes were slowly deflating, like a sputtering balloon. *Don't give in! Sweeten the deal!*

"It could be my birthday present," he said desperately. He would be twelve in June. "I wouldn't ask for anything else. It could be my birthday present for the next ten years."

"Ten years?" said Mr. Hudson. "That's quite the bargain, Belamie. After that he'll be too old for presents anyway."

"Exactly," said Matt. "You'll get out of giving me presents forever."

Mrs. Hudson took a long breath. Matt held his own. He knew she was considering, reaching a final decision. He rubbed furiously at the stone of his bracelet until it felt hot to the touch. "I'm sorry, Mateo, but it's just not the right time."

"But—"

"Mateo." This time it was his dad who interjected. "No more arguments, bud. Go and do your homework. Your mother and I have work to finish before we go home."

Matt felt his heart squeeze in his chest. It was over. Once his parents were united in a decision there was no changing their minds.

Matt took the flyer and rolled it back up. He wasn't sure what to do now. This wasn't how things had played out in his mind. His head throbbed harder than ever. He felt slightly nauseated.

"What *is* that smell?" said Mrs. Hudson, sniffing the air.

"You're working with chemicals, hon," said Mr. Hudson.

"No, it's not that. I keep getting a whiff of something like . . . dog poop."

Matt sighed and took a few steps toward the door, then stopped, catching himself on a chair. The door was suddenly lopsided, and it seemed to be shrinking. He thought he'd better go through it before it disappeared altogether. He took a few more steps and swayed.

"Belamie," he heard his father say, but his voice was strange, a little distant and echoey, as though he were calling her name down a tunnel. The floor tilted beneath Matt's feet, and everything began to vibrate. Were they having an earthquake? Should he get under a table? He turned around and the room kept turning, even when he stopped.

"Mateo?" He barely heard his mother call his name before he blacked out.

At that very moment, across the city, a ship appeared in New York Harbor, silently sailing toward the East River and the Brooklyn Bridge. This would not be noteworthy except the ship was not your typical boat spotted in New York Harbor. It was a very old-fashioned ship, a seventeenth-century frigate, to be exact, black with gold trim, two tall masts, and a dozen white sails billowing in the breeze. At the very top of the crow's nest was a black flag with several white arrows crossed to form a compass star, except part of the star was emboldened in red to make a V.

It looked like the kind of ship you might see in a pirate movie, or at least it did at first.

As the ship sailed, the air surrounding it began to shimmer, like the ripples of heat on a humid day. The ship seemed to suddenly dissolve and fold in on itself, and the next moment there was a white yacht, modern, sleek, not at all like the old frigate that had been there a moment before, except that the compass star with the red V was now emblazoned on the side of the yacht.

No one seemed to notice this miraculous transformation. New York was a busy city, after all, full of busy people absorbed in their own work or phones or food. Things moved and changed so fast all around, the transforming ship seemed to simply blend with the rest of the chaos.

On the foredeck of the ship-now-yacht, there stood a raven-haired man dressed in a black waistcoat, black leather pants, and a pair of red Converse. Captain Vincent of the legendary yet completely secret ship *Vermillion* was a handsome man with a self-assured and commanding presence that was somehow simultaneously intimidating and endearing. This generally had the effect on his crew to do exactly what the captain ordered (or suggested) and feel it was their pleasure to do so. And indeed it was their pleasure, for certainly any who dared disobey the captain found little pleasure thereafter.

The captain held a compass in his right hand, black with a gold chain attached to his wrist, but his gaze was focused steadfastly toward the New York City skyline.

A hatch opened in the deck, and a man with wild, dirty-blond hair and a slightly dazed expression poked his head out, gazing around until he found the captain.

"Crikey, are we here *again*?" he asked.

"We are indeed, Brocco."

"What year this time?"

"About the same as usual," said the captain. "Early twenty-first century."

"Well, I suppose I'd better get my cape then, hadn't I? Or do they not wear those these days? Odd fashions in this place and time, always changing from year to year. Hard to keep it all straight."

"I've decided to send Wiley this time," said the captain. "On his own. You weren't so successful on the last mission, if you remember."

"I almost had 'em last mission!" said Brocco, clearly offended. "We'd never gotten so close before, and then that mad woman came and chased me with a bloody stick!"

"Yes, that was unfortunate," said the captain. "But we can't take any chances this time. We're running out of opportunities. We must succeed in our mission, or I fear all will be lost."

Brocco slumped a little. "Well, I'll get my cape anyway, just so I blend in a bit when they arrive."

"By all means, blend away," said the captain.

Brocco popped his head down and shut the hatch.

Captain Vincent remained at the helm, staring out at the city with a hungry, almost desperate look in his eyes. He held out the compass and turned a dial one notch to the right and another dial one notch to the left, then held fast to the bulwark. The water all around the yacht began to bubble and froth. The yacht seemed to brighten against the dimming sky, growing brighter and brighter, until it glowed. The V on the side of the ship looked as if it were on fire.

The water swirled then rushed up the sides of the boat. It creaked and groaned then suddenly plunged several feet into the water. A blinding flash of light ripped through the air, and the water shot up all around the yacht like a circle of geysers. When the light faded and the water calmed, the yacht was gone, along with the captain, leaving behind nothing but bubbles on the surface of the sea.

A biker on the Brooklyn Bridge swerved and nearly hit a teenage girl with pink hair texting on her phone. "Watch it, moron!" She jumped out of the way, the bike narrowly missing her. She shouted a few more choice words, but the biker didn't seem to hear her.

"Did you see that?" he said. He was squinting into the harbor where he could have sworn he'd just seen a yacht. . . .

"What?" said the girl.

"There was a boat. . . ."

The girl rolled her eyes. "Yeah, it's a river, genius." She walked away, shaking her head as she put her headphones back on.

The biker waited another moment, staring at the spot where the boat had been. Finally he got back on his bike and rode off, debating whether he needed to drink more coffee . . . or less.

2

Whispers in the Night

Matt snapped awake. He was on the floor, his head cradled in his mother's arms. Both his parents were looking down at him, their faces drained of color and creased with worry.

"I had an episode, didn't I?" he said.

Mrs. Hudson pressed her lips together and took a deep breath, as though she were trying not to cry.

"Good thing your mom is so quick," said Mr. Hudson. "You probably would have cracked your head open on this floor, but she caught you just in time. She even dropped a three-hundred-year-old sword for you!"

"Wow," said Matt. "She must *really* love me."

"I wish you wouldn't joke about this," she chastised. "It's not funny in the least. Maybe we should try another medication."

"No!" said Matt. He sat up a little too swiftly. The room swam, but he steadied himself. "I'm okay. And I don't want to try any medication. You know they don't work."

"Maybe the next one will," said his mom.

"Please don't make me," said Matt. He *hated* the anti-seizure medicines. They always made his brain slow and fuzzy, and though some of the pills did keep him from having seizures, or at least from fully blacking out, they often produced side effects that were far worse, like vomiting or a dangerously low heart rate, so what was the point?

"We'll discuss it later," said Mrs. Hudson. "Let's get you home. Can you stand?"

Matt nodded. He stood slowly.

"I'll go get the twins," said Mr. Hudson.

Mrs. Hudson called a taxi company and ordered a minivan to take them home. That was rare. Because of her motion sickness Mrs. Hudson hated transit of any kind, be it plane, train, boat, or car, so most of the time they walked. They lived only a few blocks from the museum anyway, but Mrs. Hudson didn't want Matt walking and he was grateful. He would never admit it, but he was still a bit light-headed.

When the minivan arrived, Mrs. Hudson checked the license plate, the driver's license, his picture and certificate.

It might have seemed excessive behavior, but she wasn't totally unjustified. Once, when they were no more than four or five, Matt, Corey, and Ruby had almost boarded an ice cream truck in Central Park, near a playground. The ice cream man had Popsicles for each of them. Cherry, lime, and grape, Matt remembered. The man was wearing a cape, just like a superhero. Corey had started climbing up onto the first step when Mrs. Hudson started screaming, which must have spooked the ice cream man because he dropped the Popsicles and drove off, nearly running little Corey over. Matt remembered they all cried at this, including Mrs. Hudson. She didn't let the children out of her sight for weeks after that, and this was the time when she and Mr. Hudson made a strict rule that the children were never to go near any kind of transit—no cars, buses, trucks, or trains—without a supervising adult. It made perfect sense at the time, Matt thought, but they weren't toddlers anymore. He certainly wasn't about to be lured into a stranger's car by candy or ice cream. He'd told his parents that most of the kids in his grade now rode the subway or bus by themselves, but they still showed no signs of letting up on this particular rule.

"Where are you from, Farid?" Mrs. Hudson asked the taxi driver.

"Belamie," said Mr. Hudson in an exasperated voice.

"What? I can get to know the person who is going to have all our lives in his hands, can't I?"

The driver smiled nervously. "Syria," he said.

Mrs. Hudson smiled and instantly switched to speaking Arabic. "*Marhabaan.* I'm sure you are a very good driver. May I take your picture, please?" She pulled out her phone.

The driver looked at Mrs. Hudson like she was crazy. He

glanced at Mr. Hudson.

"Belamie, let's go," said Mr. Hudson a little impatiently. He opened the door, and everyone piled in.

As they drove, Matt opened up his fist to find the flyer for the foreign exchange program crumpled and torn. He had built up so much energy planning and strategizing, only to have a seizure. He hadn't planned for that. It had been months since he'd had an episode, so he hadn't really thought about it, but if there was anything that would make his parents say no to the foreign exchange program, or any kind of travel, it was that.

They arrived home in less than five minutes. The Hudsons lived in a very old building that had no elevator (Mrs. Hudson didn't like elevators either) so they had to walk up three flights of stairs, which made Matt a little breathless, but he tried to hide it. Mr. Hudson wrestled with the keys in the door and complained once again that they should get the locks changed. Finally he managed to get the door open.

"Shoes off, backpacks and sweaters put away," said Mrs. Hudson. "Corey and Ruby, please set the table for dinner. Mateo, come with me."

"I'm fine, Mom," he said, but Mrs. Hudson sat him down on the couch in the living room. She took his temperature and blood pressure, then listened to his heart and lungs through a stethoscope. She had no formal medical training, but she'd learned enough over the years. Matt had started having seizures when he was six, quite out of the blue. Up until he was nine his parents had taken him to specialist after specialist (there were a lot of specialists in New York). He'd received every test and scan possible—MRI, fMRI, PET, EEG, CT, SPECT, and so much blood work he was amazed he had any left. And after all that, no one had been able to determine the cause of his seizures. Nothing seemed out of the ordinary. He wasn't epileptic, his brain had no tumors, lesions, or abnormalities, no heart disease or kidney failure, no poison or abnormal levels of anything in his blood. They couldn't even see where the seizures were happening in his brain when he had an episode while hooked up to wires and monitors, which prompted one doctor to declare that Matt was faking it for attention. He said it was probably because Matt felt "displaced" by the twins. Mrs. Hudson went ballistic. Matt remembered Mr. Hudson had to restrain her from physically attacking the doctor.

And that was the end of it. It had been a relief to Matt. All those hospital visits and tests made him feel like a lab rat. Mrs. Hudson began to monitor his condition at home and took him to regular check-ups with their family doctor.

Matt stared at the many swords and knives displayed on the wall right in front of him while Mrs. Hudson took his blood pressure. She looked to where Matt was staring.

"Did I ever tell you about the time the adoption agent told me to take those swords off the wall?"

Matt shook his head. "Why?" He loved the swords on the wall. It made their small home feel more . . . adventurous.

"She said they weren't 'child-safe.' I told her a child would be safer with me and a sword than any other woman with a butter knife!"

Matt laughed.

"Well, she didn't think I was so amusing," said Mrs. Hudson. "We didn't get selected as adoptive parents through that agency, nor any other in the country. Sour luck. So we decided to try international adoption."

"When you got me."

"When we got you," said Mrs. Hudson. "I braved two airplanes, three buses, and a train to get you in my arms. I was so sick I thought I might die."

"Was I worth it?"

"It was the happiest moment of my life, and your father's. We felt we would never wish or want for anything again. And then the twins came, and all I've ever wished for since is some sleep! Still haven't gotten that one yet."

Matt smiled. His heart lifted, wobbled, then dropped again, like an airplane in turbulence. (Not that he knew what that felt like exactly, having never flown on an airplane.) He did love his family, and he knew how much his parents had gone through to have children, how much they'd sacrificed just for him, so he felt a pinch of guilt at his desire to leave them, go out on his own, mixed with bitterness that his parents wouldn't let him.

"You'll get your chance, Mateo," said Mrs. Hudson, seeming to read his thoughts. "One day you'll unleash yourself on the world and then heaven help us all! It just can't be right now, okay?"

Matt nodded.

"Good boy. *Tu es un garçon sage.*" She brushed her hand over his cheek. "You're all clear. Go wash your hands for dinner and fill the water glasses."

It was quiet at dinner. Everyone kept glancing at Matt. The family was always a little weird after he had a seizure, like he might disappear on them or something, and it made Matt feel even worse. He picked at his plate. He wasn't particularly hungry, but the food wasn't that great either. The chicken was chewy, and the vegetables undercooked. Mrs. Hudson had thrown it all together in a rush. On a day like this most parents probably would have settled for mac 'n' cheese or takeout, but Mrs. Hudson was a bit of a health nut and never allowed any processed foods in the house, so when she was stressed or short on time it usually meant a mediocre meal. They seemed to be having a lot of those lately.

"So, anything new and interesting going on at school?" asked Mrs. Hudson, trying to get some conversation going. No one seemed to want to take the bait. "Corey, you have a math test tomorrow, don't you? Are you prepared?"

Corey kept his eyes on his plate, poking at a carrot. "Yeah, sure."

Mrs. Hudson's eyes narrowed. "Why don't you let Mateo help you study tonight? I'm sure he could help you get that grade up."

Corey glanced up briefly at Matt, but Matt looked away. This sort of suggestion rarely played out well for either of them. Matt was very good at math, but he was a terrible tutor. It came so naturally to him, he found it difficult to break down certain concepts in a way that made much sense. This always left Corey feeling like an idiot and Matt like an arrogant jerk. Matt looked to Ruby, pleading with his eyes for help.

Ruby got the hint. She cleared her throat. "I'm giving a presentation tomorrow on Queen Elizabeth, and I could really use some *expert* help."

"Ah, the Pirate Queen!" said Mr. Hudson. "I'd be delighted to offer my expertise. I've come across some top-notch sources, you know."

"Actually, I meant Mom's expertise," said Ruby.

"Me?" said Mrs. Hudson. "Your father's the historian. I know very little about Queen Elizabeth."

"But you have that jewelry box you say belonged to her. The one you keep in the safe? I was hoping I could bring it for the presentation. We get extra credit if we bring good props and visual aids."

There was a safe in the wall of the coat closet where Mrs.

Hudson often kept artifacts and collector's items clients brought for her expert authentication. Once she'd gotten a baseball that was supposedly signed by Babe Ruth, which had greatly excited Matt, but it had turned out to be a fake, much to both Matt's (and the client's) disappointment. But as items came and went over the years, there had been one item that was always in the safe for as long as Matt could remember—an old wooden box, intricately carved.

"It's only *rumored* to have belonged to Queen Elizabeth," said Mrs. Hudson. "It's impossible to trace it back to her."

"But it's still from her time, isn't it?" Ruby asked. "That's almost as good. Couldn't we take it to school?"

"I would if I could, Ruby, but you know it's not even mine. I'm only storing it until the client can retrieve it."

"But you've had it forever," said Ruby. "He can't care about it that much if he's left it for this long."

"I assure you he does," said Mrs. Hudson. "And there is no possible way I can take that box to your school. If anything happened to it, my reputation would be ruined. No one would trust me with their valuable possessions ever again."

"Fine," said Ruby, stabbing at a hunk of meat.

"Still willing to offer my own expertise," said Mr. Hudson.

"Yippee," said Ruby dully.

The family fell into another uncomfortable silence. Mrs. Hudson looked like she was going to turn on Corey again about his math test, so Matt intervened this time.

"Mets play this Friday," he said. "Could we get tickets maybe?"

"Sure!" said Mr. Hudson. "How about we all go as a family?"

"No thanks," said Ruby. "I'll stay home and knit or something."

"Oh, but I was going to throw hot dogs and soda into the deal," said Mr. Hudson with a conspiratorial smile. "Maybe even a little cotton candy, right under your mother's nose."

"Matthew Hudson," said Mrs. Hudson. Ruby smiled just a little. Their father loved to sneak junk food to the kids. It drove Mrs. Hudson bonkers, and that made it all the more fun. She treated sweets and junk food as though they were straight poison.

"Plus you don't want to miss my dancing that gets me on the jumbo screen," said Corey. "I'll give you a preview." Corey started shimmying in his chair.

"Oh, please no," said Ruby while Matt burst out laughing. Both reactions only egged Corey on. He stood up and started swinging his hips, and though Ruby had put her hand over her eyes she started laughing too.

"All right, Corey," said Mrs. Hudson, smiling and shaking her head. "Sit down before you break something." But Corey was really getting into it now. He flailed his arms and threw his body around as if he were deranged.

"Corey . . . ," Mrs. Hudson warned.

Corey bumped into the table and knocked over his full glass of water.

"Watch it!" Mrs. Hudson scrambled to remove her phone, while Mr. Hudson snatched away his papers he'd been reading.

"Whoops," said Corey. The water was spilling over the sides of the table.

"*Va chercher des serviettes*," said Mrs. Hudson.

"What?" said Corey.

"Towels," said Mr. Hudson, shaking off his papers.

Corey ran to the kitchen and came back with a couple of towels. Mrs. Hudson snatched them and started to mop up the mess. "*Mes enfants sont des singes*," she muttered.

"I'm not a monkey," said Corey, "and I said I was sorry. It was an *accident*."

"I told you to stop," said Mrs. Hudson. "Why do you always have to keep going until something explodes?"

"It's just water," Corey argued, but that did not placate Mrs. Hudson in the least.

"Just clean up this mess. Then go to bed."

"Bed?" said Corey. "It's not even eight!"

"Then you can study for your math test." Mrs. Hudson's voice was quiet but sharp as one of her swords. Corey actually flinched.

They cleaned up without talking, except Corey, who muttered under his breath that they lived in a museum and did they expect him to be a statue?

Mrs. Hudson hastily made the kids' lunches for the next day, then she and Mr. Hudson set up their computers and papers at the table, gearing up for another late night of work.

Matt was glad to go to bed early. He wasn't sleepy, but he was exhausted after the day's events: his rejection, his seizure. Corey didn't pull out his math to study. He sat in bed with a deck of playing cards, flicking them one at a time at the wall. The noise blended with the taps and clicks of his parents working on their computers, the murmurs of their hushed conversation. Matt heard his name a couple of times. They were probably talking about his seizures, placing more restrictions on what he could or couldn't do, what he could eat, where he could go. They'd probably call the school tomorrow and have someone keep an eye on him, make a classmate accompany him at all times, even to the bathroom. Eventually they'd just bind him in Bubble Wrap and stick him in a sterile room. He loved his parents, knew they loved him, but in some ways he agreed with Corey. His parents spent so much time at the museum, they seemed to forget that their children were living, breathing beings, not special artifacts that needed to be restored or preserved.

Sometimes Matt felt he would combust with all the energy he had building up inside him. Maybe that was the *cause* of his seizures. Pent-up desire and potential, bursting to get out. He wanted to make big discoveries, mind-blowing inventions, but he felt like his parents were constantly pulling him back. He was like one of those toy cars, all revved up and ready to speed down the track, only he kept getting blocked.

He picked up the closest issue of *Physics World* from his shelf. He flipped through and read an article about the ability atoms had to teleport information over long distances, which some scientists believed supported the theory that people could potentially be teleported, *Star Trek* style. That would be cool. Then Matt could teleport himself to Paris, or anywhere for that matter, and his parents would never know the difference.

"Mateo?"

Matt woke to someone calling his name. At least he thought he did. Maybe it was a dream. Through the crack of his door he saw the glow of the dining room lights and a flicker of a shadow as someone moved. He glanced at the clock: 4:03 a.m. Did his parents really stay up all night working? His mother's voice drifted through the door. She sounded a bit panicked.

"You're breaking up . . . Where are you?"

Through sleepy eyes, Matt could just make out his parents' silhouettes. Their backs were to him, but he could see his mother was on the phone. Who could she possibly be talking to on the phone at this hour?

"The museum? But . . . Hello? . . ." Mrs. Hudson lowered the phone and glanced up at Mr. Hudson. "Matt . . . is it . . .

I don't . . ." She didn't seem to be able to finish her thoughts out loud.

Matt saw Mr. Hudson turn sharply toward the huge map of the world hanging above the kitchen table. It was the map they'd hung to help the children learn states and capitals and countries for social studies. Mr. Hudson studied the map intently with his glasses at his mouth, which was the position he always took when he was concentrating. "Here," he said, pointing to a place on the map. "It's here."

"But . . . the children," said Mrs. Hudson, turning toward the bedrooms. "They're asleep in their beds."

A shadow fell over the crack in the door, and a moment later Mrs. Hudson pushed it open. Matt closed his eyes and pretended to be asleep.

"What's done is done, Belamie," said Mr. Hudson. "Or will be done. We have to go."

"But . . ."

"Now." Mr. Hudson had an uncharacteristically hard edge in his voice. "We can't afford to spare a moment."

The door closed. Matt heard a few more murmurs in the dining room, the soft creak of the front door opening, and the click of the lock.

Matt sat up in bed. Did his parents really just leave them alone in the middle of the night?

He climbed down from his bunk and went out to the living room. He padded to the window and looked down at the street. It was mostly empty, only a few cars, but a minute later he saw his parents fly out of the building in their pajamas and run as fast as they could down the street. They turned left on Eighty-Sixth and disappeared.

Matt turned around. From the dim light coming through the windows he could see that his parents' computers and papers were still spread out on the table. There must have been some kind of emergency at the museum, a burglary or a fire or something. They would never leave them in the middle of the night like that, not without waking them or at least leaving a note.

Matt went back to bed, but he couldn't fall asleep. He had this nagging feeling that something wasn't right, but he wasn't sure what he should do about it. Should he wake Corey and Ruby? Should they call the police? And say what? *Our parents left us in the middle of the night.* The police would probably come and take them down to the station. They'd be questioned, possibly put in foster care. No way.

His parents would come back soon. Or they'd call. Matt waited until he couldn't keep his eyes open anymore.

3

Rule Breakers

It seemed only minutes later that Matt was woken again, this time by shouting.

"Wake up! We're going to be late!"

Matt squinted as morning light flooded his room. Ruby was pulling up the blinds. He glanced at the clock: 7:37! He flung off his covers and hopped down from his bunk bed. Ruby was trying to wake Corey, but he swatted at her and turned over.

"Why didn't Mom wake us?" Ruby shrieked. "I'm supposed to give my presentation in first period!"

"Probably slept in themselves," said Matt, yawning, but then he remembered. His parents had left early in the morning. Or had he dreamed that?

"Oh, I give up!" said Ruby. "You wake him." She walked out to the kitchen.

"Get up, Corey," Matt said. "Rise and shine." Corey

groaned and pulled the covers over his head.

"Come on. We're going to be late." Matt pulled the covers off Corey, who shielded his eyes, then blew a big raspberry.

"Thanks for the shower," said Matt, wiping the slobber off his face. "That'll save some time."

He went to the kitchen. He half expected to see his mom in her robe and slippers, rushing to get them breakfast, but she wasn't there. Their dad wasn't there either. Matt checked their bedroom. The bed was neatly made, as if it hadn't been slept in at all. Their laptops and papers were still spread over the table. Ruby was reading something.

"Mom and Dad already left for work," said Ruby. "Figures." She slapped down a piece of paper on the table. Matt went to it. The note was in his mom's handwriting, hastily written.

> Had to run to the museum early for a small emergency. Take the cell phone and text when you get to school. Stick together always, no matter what.
> WE LOVE YOU!
> XO . . .

"I think they left in the middle of the night, actually," said Matt, and he told Ruby what he'd seen and heard that morning.

Ruby didn't seem all that concerned. "It's their new

schedule. Twenty-four/seven."

It was true. Their parents had been working an awful lot lately, seemingly around the clock. Sometimes his dad fell asleep in the living room and never made it to bed. Matt would wake to find him still there, a book on his chest and his glasses falling off his face, but this seemed a little more out of the ordinary. To leave them in the middle of the night . . . Matt studied the note again. It sounded weird somehow. *Stick together always, no matter what.* Like the kids were the ones in some kind of emergency.

"Let's hurry and get ready," said Ruby. "I can't be late today."

Matt rushed to get dressed. He was out of clean clothes, so he pulled a dirty T-shirt and jeans out of the laundry. He thought to wear his Mets hat to at least flatten his hair, then remembered it had been stolen. He'd just have to go mad-scientist style.

Corey, still in his pajamas, pounded on the bathroom door. "Hurry up, Ruby! It's an abuse of equal rights to hog the bathroom!"

"It's equal rights of time in proportion to length of hair," said Ruby.

"Matt, get me the scissors," said Corey. "Ruby's due for a trim."

"Don't even think about it!" shrieked Ruby.

When they were all dressed with teeth brushed and

hair somewhat combed, they rummaged in the kitchen for breakfast. All they could find was a few apples and a couple handfuls of homemade granola.

"Unbelievable," said Corey, pulling out the bag of granola and shoving a handful in his mouth. "We might as well be starving abandoned children."

"We'll take it to go," said Ruby. She grabbed her lunch and the cell phone off the counter and slid it into her back pocket. They gathered their backpacks out of the closet, then rushed out the door.

"Wait! I need a jacket," said Ruby. She rushed back inside and rummaged in the closet. "Where is my gray jacket? This closet's a disaster." Matt could hear her tearing through the closet.

"Ruby, just grab something," said Matt. "We have to go!"

"Oh fine, whatever." She grabbed one of Matt's old Mets hoodies.

"Hey, that's mine," Matt said.

"Well, I'm borrowing it. Ew, it smells. When's the last time you washed this thing?"

Matt shrugged. "I don't know. Never?"

"Gross." Ruby slammed the door behind her and locked the deadbolt.

The morning was cloudy and cool. They ran a few blocks until they turned on Lexington, and then Corey started to fall behind.

"Corey, hurry up!" said Ruby. "I can't be late today!"

"But I'm *starving*!" he said.

"Just eat some of your lunch," said Matt.

Corey grumbled and opened his backpack. "You have got to be kidding me!" he shouted. "Mom forgot to pack my lunch!"

"*Mom* forgot it?" said Ruby. "It was sitting right on the counter. Don't you mean *you* forgot to put it in your backpack?"

"I swear, it wasn't on the counter!" Corey exclaimed.

"It was too," said Ruby. "I saw it."

"It doesn't matter," said Matt. "It's too late to go back now. You'll have to eat school lunch."

"No way," said Corey. "That stuff is barf. I'm going back."

"Corey, I can't be late!" shrieked Ruby.

Corey waved her off and turned back in the direction of their apartment. Matt was about to go after him when a man came around the corner and ran right into Corey, knocking him down so his bag came undone and all his books went everywhere.

"Oh no, I am so terribly sorry, my friend," said the man. He was smoking a wooden pipe. It bobbed up and down as he spoke through his teeth. The man tried to help Corey up, but Corey brushed him aside and started gathering his spilled belongings. He muttered something about old people not watching where they were going, but the man was not old at all. He was actually a young black man, maybe twenty, but dressed in an old-fashioned brown-plaid suit and the kind of hat Matt had only seen characters in old gangster movies wear. You got all kinds in Manhattan.

The man didn't leave, but knelt down to help Corey pick up his books and papers. "Oh no," he said again. "I've gone and torn a hole in your trousers." Corey looked down. There was indeed a hole in the knee of Corey's jeans, but it had been there for several weeks now, worn down by his inclination to treat most places like a gymnasium.

"That's not right. Not right a'tall," said the man. He took his pipe out of his mouth and fished inside his suit jacket. He pulled out a twenty-dollar bill and held it out to Corey. "Here, you tell your mama I meant no harm." Corey froze, staring at the money like he'd never seen anything like it before. The Hudsons weren't poor, but Mr. and Mrs. Hudson certainly didn't hand out cash to their children to spend as they pleased. The man stuffed the money into Corey's math book and shoved the book in Corey's arms. "Have a grand day!" He tipped his hat, put his pipe back in his mouth, and hurried away, disappearing around the same corner from which he had come.

Corey opened his book and took out the money. He unfolded the bill and a MetroCard dropped out and fell to the ground. Corey picked it up.

"Hey! Mister!" he shouted. He ran to the street corner

where the man had turned, but he was nowhere to be seen. Corey looked between the MetroCard and the twenty. He licked his lips, and Matt knew exactly what he was thinking. Well, almost exactly. Corey made a sharp about-turn and started walking the opposite direction of school.

"Where are you going?" Matt asked as he and Ruby ran to catch up.

"Subway," said Corey, waving the MetroCard and the twenty in his hand. "If we ride the train, we'll have time to get churros! My treat. Or the clumsy pipe guy's."

Matt and Ruby stopped and stared at each other, then chased after Corey.

"You can't go on the subway," said Ruby. "Mom and Dad will *kill* you!"

"Well, I'm almost dead already, and it's Mom and Dad's fault for leaving us alone with no breakfast or lunch, so I don't think they'd begrudge my survival instincts." Corey reached the steps of the subway station and paused. Matt hoped he was reconsidering, but Corey just looked back at them, grinned, and plunged down the steps.

Ruby looked at Matt. "What do we do?"

Matt thought quickly. He knew all too well that when Corey set his mind to something it was almost impossible to dissuade him, no matter how reckless he was being. He could let Corey go on his own and suffer the consequences, which might be nothing, but what if something happened to him?

His mom's scribbled note flashed across his mind.

Stick together always, no matter what. Matt pressed his mouth into a hard line. "We have to go with him," he said.

Matt and Ruby raced down the steps. By the time they reached the bottom, Corey had already swiped the Metro-Card and gone through the turnstile.

"Come on," he said. "There's enough on this card for all of us!"

"Wait!" said Matt. "Let's make sure we're getting on the right train."

"This is the right train," said Corey. "It's the six train. Goes straight to the churro stand right around the corner from school."

That sounded right to Matt, but still . . .

"Come on. It's not that big a deal." Corey swiped the card again.

"This is a horrible idea," said Ruby.

"I know," said Matt, "but we can't let him go on his own." Matt reluctantly went through the turnstile. Corey swiped the card a third time, and Ruby finally followed, shaking her head.

Matt couldn't remember the last time he'd ridden the subway. His parents didn't care for public transit at all, but the subway seemed to be their least favorite, and he sort of understood why. It smelled musty, slightly like a dumpster in summer. Movie posters and graffiti decorated the walls and trash littered the ground. The platform was pretty crowded with morning commuters waiting for the train. Most of them were glued to their phones or had headphones on. A man in ragged clothes played his saxophone against the wall with the case open, a few coins scattered in it. If their parents had been there they would have tossed some spare change to him.

A minute later they heard the train screeching on the tracks and saw the headlights glowing from a distance. When it came to a stop the three children boarded together and found seats at the end of the train car.

"Churros, here I come," said Corey.

"If Mom grounds us for life because of this, I'm going to choke you with a churro," said Ruby.

"I didn't *make* you come," said Corey.

"Oh right," said Ruby. "Like we're really going to let you go on a train all by yourself."

"Shh," said Matt. "I'm trying to hear the train conductor tell us which stop is next."

The train conductor was saying something through the speakers, but it was intermittent with a lot of static feedback, so they couldn't understand a word.

"Relax," said Corey. "It's just a couple stops."

They went by several stops, but none were the station by their school, Matt was pretty sure. He took off his jacket. Even though the train was cool, he felt hot. With every stop, more and more passengers seemed to be getting off than on.

Finally the last few passengers exited the train, and the three Hudson children were alone.

Matt's chest pounded, and he started to sweat. Something wasn't right. He looked at the map that was on the wall and traced the stops they'd already hit. His heart plummeted to the bottom of his stomach.

"You guys," he said. "We're on the wrong train."

"What do you mean?" squeaked Ruby. "We got on the six train! You said that was the right train!"

"Yeah, but we're supposed to be on the uptown train," said Matt. "I'm pretty sure this is the downtown train."

There was a moment of silence as they all stared up at the map. Finally Ruby turned to Corey and punched him on the arm. "Corey!" she shouted. "You're such an idiot!"

"Why am I the idiot? You guys got on the train, same as me!"

"You just *had* to break all the rules and drag us on a train just so you could have churros."

"Because I'm *starving*."

"Because you forgot your lunch!" said Ruby. "Did it ever occur to you that this is exactly the reason Mom doesn't let us go on trains alone?"

"It's a mistake," said Corey, gritting his teeth. "It's not like we're lost or anything."

"But now we're for sure going to be late!"

"Stop!" shouted Matt, wedging himself between Corey

and Ruby, who looked ready to strangle one another. "This isn't helping. We just need to get off at the next stop and get on the right train and go to school."

"I'm still getting churros," said Corey.

"No you're not," Matt said. "We're going to school. Together."

"You can't make me," said Corey.

"Yes, I can," said Matt. "I'm the oldest."

"Blah, blah, blah, oldest!" said Corey. "You're not even a year older than us and somehow that makes you think *you're* in charge?"

Matt gritted his teeth. "I'm in charge because I'm the oldest *and* the smartest!"

Matt wished he could take the words back as soon as he'd said them. Ruby sucked in her breath, and Corey looked as though Matt had just slapped him across the face.

There was some static feedback coming from the intercom and the train slowed. "I think the train's about to stop," Ruby said quietly. The lights in the train car flickered and then turned off completely. They came to a screechy halt.

Matt tried to look out the train doors for a sign, but he couldn't see any. "I think we're at the end of the line," said Matt. The doors opened.

"Should we get off?" Ruby asked.

"I don't know," said Corey bitterly. "Ask Matt, since he's the *smartest*."

Matt winced, but he didn't apologize or take it back. It

wouldn't fix anything. He didn't really think he was smarter than Corey. Sure, math and science came easier for him, and he got better grades in school, but other things came easier for Corey, things that couldn't be graded, like making friends and making people laugh. In those ways Corey was a genius, and Matt, a complete dunce, but he didn't know how to say these things without sounding like he was just trying to do damage control.

"We'll have to get off here if we're going to switch to the uptown train," said Matt. They shuffled off the train, onto the platform, and as soon as they did the doors closed. The six train rattled off, curving around the tunnel until it disappeared, leaving the three Hudson children alone.

Matt rubbed at his bracelet. It didn't look like a regular subway stop. The walls were tiled in a herringbone pattern, and the ceilings were arched and ornately designed with green-and-white tile. Brass chandeliers hung from the ceilings, and there were big, beautiful skylights designed with geometric patterns. It looked like they'd stepped into a fancy ballroom rather than a subway station.

"This is really pretty," said Ruby. "What stop are we at?"

"I don't know," said Matt. There weren't any of the normal black-and-white signs with the different numbered or lettered circles to tell you where you were and show you which direction to go. There wasn't another person in sight, and it was eerily quiet.

"Oh, look!" Ruby said, pointing to the ceiling. Right in the center of one of the white-tiled arches were words formed with black tile.

"City Hall," said Corey. "That's a regular station, isn't it?"

"I know what this is!" said Ruby. "We came here on a field trip in fourth grade. Remember, Corey? This is the old station that got closed about a hundred years ago."

Matt vaguely remembered his father showing him a map of the old subway routes. There were many train tracks and stations that were no longer in use.

"I guess I remember," said Corey. "But why did the train bring us to a closed station?"

"I think we were supposed to get off before," said Ruby. "It must come through here to switch tracks or something."

"Great. So we're in an abandoned train station," said Corey. "How do we get back now?"

"We just need to find an exit," said Matt. "There'll be someone to help us."

They walked in one direction for a bit but didn't find any stairs. Matt's stomach started to knot up. He felt a headache coming on. He hoped he wasn't about to have another seizure. This would be the worst possible time for that. Not that there was ever a good time.

"Let's go back the other direction," said Ruby. "There has to be an exit somewhere."

So they went in the other direction, but before they got

more than a few steps they saw a dull light creep up on the wall.

Matt craned his neck to see down the tunnel. "I think a train's coming!" he said.

The light grew brighter every second until they could see glaring headlights coming down the tunnel. The train did not sound like a train. It was eerily quiet. Perhaps it was a very new train, Matt thought. But as it approached and slowed, it clearly did not look new. It looked like something that had risen from a swamp. Water dripped down the sides of the cars. Toward the bottom it had what looked like rotting leaves and barnacles growing on it, as though the train had been pulled from the bottom of the ocean. It even smelled a bit like the ocean, briny, fishy, with a faint aroma of . . .

"It smells like peanut butter," said Corey.

The windows were so caked with grime it was impossible to see inside. A symbol was posted in the window, a bunch of white arrows crossed to make a star, with part of it in bold red to make a V.

"Have either of you ever heard of a V line?" Ruby asked.

"I think so," said Matt. About a year ago Matt had memorized the subway lines and routes in an unsuccessful attempt to convince his parents that he should be allowed to ride transit on his own. He knew there was a V line, or at least there had been at some point, but if he remembered correctly he didn't think it served this end of town, and he'd never seen any subway line with a symbol quite like that. Maybe it was some new design or something.

The doors creaked open. There were people inside, but the train was too dim to make out their faces.

"We'd better get on before it leaves," said Corey, stepping toward the train, but Ruby held him back.

"But we don't know where this train is headed," said Ruby.

"It's going in the right direction," said Corey.

"Yeah, but what if it's an express train? Maybe we should just call Mom."

"Are you crazy?" said Corey. "Do you want to be on a leash for the rest of your life?"

Matt really did not want to call his mom. Even though this had all been Corey's doing, Matt would get plenty of heat for not taking charge and putting a stop to it, and in this scenario it was going to be a fiery furnace. He pictured his mom at the museum, sharpening an old sword.

"Let's just get on," said Matt. "It's going in the right direction. We can ask another passenger for help if we need it."

Ruby sighed. "Fine. But I want it on record that I objected to this whole mess from the beginning."

"Noted," said Matt.

"Don't worry. You'll still be their favorite daughter," said Corey.

Ruby rolled her eyes.

The Hudson children all boarded the train and the doors

shut behind them. As the train began to move in the right direction a knot loosened in Matt's stomach. Soon they'd be at school, a little late, but safe and sound, and hopefully their parents would be none the wiser.

But that is not at all what happened.

4

Unusual Passengers

8:24 a.m., April 26, 2019
New York, New York . . . at least at first . . .

The train smelled like tar and dirty socks and even stronger of peanut butter. Matt had ridden the subway enough to know that shouldn't be too alarming. Get a bunch of people crowded together in a small space and all their smells could mix into a peculiar perfume, but this subway car wasn't all that crowded. There were just five or six other people.

A pale, towheaded little girl, maybe six or seven, was crouched on the floor, picking at a knotted rope. Matt looked around for a parent or grown-up with the girl, but the two people sitting nearest to her were children themselves—a boy and a girl about his own age. A grown man was standing at the far end of the car, but he was oddly dressed, like he had picked random pieces out of a costume bin. He wore leather chaps, a red cape, and, to Matt's disgust, a Yankees cap. Definitely not trustworthy. He looked up at Matt and grinned. The light hit one of his teeth and it glared like a blinding camera flash. He started to amble toward the Hudson children as though he wanted to talk to them.

"I think we got on the Weirdo Express," whispered Corey.

"I think we should get off," said Ruby.

Matt agreed. Next stop, they'd get off.

As the strange man in the cape got closer, the three Hudsons backed up a little and promptly bumped into something behind them. They whirled around and were faced with another passenger, a man dressed in all black except for a pair of red Converse.

"Oh, hello there!" the man said in a British accent. "Welcome aboard the *Vermillion*. We're so glad you've decided to join us."

Matt looked around to see if he was maybe talking to someone else, but he was looking right at Matt. The man looked nice enough, and Matt didn't get a crazy vibe from him like he did the guy in the cape and chaps. He was just about to ask him for help when a little white nose and whiskers suddenly poked out of the collar of the man's shirt. A white rat crawled all the way out and perched on the man's shoulder. Ruby gave a little squeak as the rat looked right at the Hudson children with red eyes that seemed far too intelligent for a rodent. It sent a little shiver up Matt's spine. The rat hissed at them.

"Now, now, Santiago, that's not friendly. Smile at the children!"

The rat obeyed the man, spreading his mouth to show his large front teeth in what looked more like a menacing grimace than a smile. The children all took a step back.

"Please, sir," said Matt. "Could you help us? We accidentally got on the wrong train and then we got on *this* train, and we're hoping that it makes a stop near Eighty-Sixth or Ninety-Sixth maybe?"

The man rubbed at his beard. "Eighty-Sixth . . . Eighty-Sixth . . . No, I don't believe it is one of our stops."

"Okay . . . then could you tell us which stop is next, please? We have to get to school."

"*School?*" said the man, as though he'd never heard of such a thing. "I don't believe we have a stop for *School* either."

Matt glanced at Ruby and Corey. Ruby shook her head, and Matt felt the warning signals go off in his brain. *Something's not right*, he thought. If it were October, Matt would have thought this was some kind of Halloween prank. Maybe they were extending April Fools' Day? Or was this one of those flash mobs?

"So . . . where does this train stop next, exactly?" Matt asked.

The man smiled. "You'll see soon enough. I don't want to spoil the surprise! I'd hold on tight if I were you. This ride could get a little bumpy."

The man pulled out a shiny black object attached to a gold chain from inside his shirtsleeve. It looked like a watch, but whatever it was, it seemed to frighten the other passengers. They all suddenly dove and scrambled to various places on the train. The man in the cape wrapped his arms and legs around the nearest pole, while the children crawled beneath the seats. Even the rat leaped from the man's shoulder and wrapped its scaly tail around a post. It looked at the Hudson children expectantly.

A voice crackled over the loudspeaker. "Prepare for a quantum time leap."

"What did he just say?" Corey asked.

The knots in Matt's stomach suddenly returned, twisting up in ever-tightening coils. "We need to get off," said Matt. He looked around for an emergency pull, but didn't see any.

A train horn blew, but it seemed a little distant, like it was coming from somewhere up ahead. It blew again, louder this time.

"There's another train coming!" shouted Ruby. "We're going to crash!"

"Don't worry," said the captain cheerfully. "*Vermillion* knows what to do."

Matt closed his eyes and waited for impact, but it never came. The train picked up speed, faster and faster. It roared so loud Matt couldn't even hear his own voice. He covered his ears. The whole train was vibrating violently, and then it lurched forward with such a jolt that the three Hudsons toppled over each other and landed hard on the floor.

Ruby gasped. "The floor!" she said.

"What the . . . what?" said Corey.

Matt looked down. He could hardly believe his eyes. The floor appeared to be melting, morphing from the smooth worn floors of the subway car to cracked and rough wooden planks. A nail head poked at his hand. Matt looked up. All around him the train car was altering, growing, transforming. The walls expanded, and the windows shrank. Lacy curtains unfurled and crawled down the sides of the windows like fast-growing vines. The hard plastic benches of the subway swelled into plush chairs and tables with white tablecloths. The fluorescent lights on the ceiling contracted and then dropped, forming crystal chandeliers. A plush rug sprouted beneath him. It grew through the floor as though it were a carpet of grass pushing through dirt.

Matt picked himself up, then helped Corey and Ruby, who had somehow gotten tangled in the rug. It seemed to have grown up and around Ruby's wrists and ankles, as though it were trying to weave her into itself. Matt and Corey helped free her, and then Ruby yelped as the white rat leaped across their faces and landed on a little table. It pulled a match out of the table drawer with its tail, struck it against the wall, and began lighting lanterns and sconces, then the crystal chandeliers hanging from the ceiling, until the space was well lit once again. It was not at all like the train they had been in before. The subway car no longer looked like a subway at all. Rather, it looked like a very old-fashioned train, but one for rich passengers. First class.

"Whoa," said Corey.

The other passengers began to crawl out from beneath tables and chairs. The man dressed all in black stepped out of a corner and the rat leaped back onto his shoulder, his whiskers twitching in an eerily rhythmic fashion.

Matt grasped for some reasoning behind the elaborate change.

It's a dream, thought Matt. *That's the only logical, scientifically sound explanation. I've had a seizure. I've passed out. . . .*

But he'd never had a dream when he passed out, and never had his dreams felt so real, so vivid. He could feel the sway of the train, the carpet beneath his feet. He still got a faint whiff of fish and peanut butter, but it was overpowered by the buttery aroma of pastries and coffee. You couldn't smell in dreams.

"I dare say the *Vermillion* quite fancies you three!" said the man in black. "She rarely goes to such lengths for the rest of us."

"Ver-who?" said Corey.

A door opened behind them and a man in a plaid suit and fedora stepped out. "She's all set, Cap'n," said the man. "Almost there!"

"Thank you, Wiley," said the captain.

"Hey!" said Corey. "You knocked me over this morning!"

Matt's memory clicked into place. It *was* the very same man who had nearly bulldozed Corey on their way to school and gave him a twenty-dollar bill as reparation. The man did not seem at all surprised to see the children there. He smiled broadly at them.

"Good to see you again, my friend!" he said, tipping his hat, then stuck a wooden pipe in his mouth.

Matt felt all the more uneasy. The knots in his stomach tightened again. "What is going on?" said Matt, addressing the man in black. "Who are you?"

"Captain Vincent at your service!" He bowed formally at the waist. The white rat stared eerily down at them.

"*Captain*?" asked Corey. "Captain of what?"

"Why the ship, of course! The *Vermillion* is the finest ship in the world! There's not another one like her."

The three children looked at each other. They had definitely gotten on the crazy train, and Matt felt he would have to handle this situation delicately.

"Captain Vincent, sir," he said. "I'm afraid we've made a terrible mistake—"

The train suddenly lurched. Matt pitched forward and caught himself on a table.

"Ah, I do believe we are arriving," said the captain. He pulled back one of the lacy curtains from the window.

Matt looked outside and his heart did a little leap. He couldn't see all that well, but they were clearly above ground. The train was passing over a river lined with the dark silhouette of trees hanging over the riverbank. Maybe they had traveled upstate? This could be the Hudson River.

"I'm going to try to call Mom," Ruby whispered. She pulled the phone out of her bag, opened it, and groaned. "Rats! No reception."

The white rat hissed at Ruby. Apparently he didn't like to be used as an expletive.

"Turn it off so we don't drain the battery," said Matt.

Ruby pressed the power button and put the phone in her backpack.

The train slowed and eventually came to a stop. The doors opened, and all the passengers filed out. Captain Vincent motioned for them to follow. "Come on! You don't want to miss all the fun!"

"We'd better get off now," said Matt. "We can ditch these crazies and get a taxi. Corey might still have enough cash for that."

"So much for churros," Corey grumbled, and they all stepped off the train.

The air was balmy, warmer than it had been that morning, and the sky was a deep periwinkle. Not a trace of cloud. It was also incredibly quiet. It seemed impossible to Matt that this could be anywhere in Manhattan, which was always bustling no matter the day or hour. But how far could they have traveled in just a few minutes?

Ruby tugged on Matt's sleeve. "Where are we?" she whispered.

Matt tried to get his bearings. His father would tell him to look for familiar landmarks and numbered streets and businesses. You could always find your way home if you had a reference point, but he couldn't see any street signs.

A horse-drawn carriage rolled by them, the driver in tails and a top hat. Well, that wasn't so out of place. There were plenty of horse-drawn carriages in New York, for all the tourists, especially around Central Park, but they were usually open carriages, and this one was closed. Inside the carriage were several women speaking a foreign language. He listened a moment more and detected they were speaking French. He couldn't hear all the words, but something about a party and a certain madame's ugly dress. Their laughter bubbled out the window, and then one woman stuck out her head and directed the driver to take them to some hotel on a street he did not recognize at all. Her hair was done up in elaborate curls with a bushy feather sticking out the top. They must be going to a costume party, he thought, or maybe they were filming a historical movie.

Matt looked around at all the buildings, none of which were familiar, until his eyes landed on one tall tower that stood above all the rest, right in the middle of the city. It took him a moment for his brain to register what he was seeing. He knew that building well. He'd seen many pictures of it, but not anywhere in New York. Ruby saw it at the same time. Her eyes bugged out of their sockets, and her mouth formed a perfect O.

"Is that the Eiffel Tower?" said Corey.

"Clever lad," said Captain Vincent. "Welcome to Paris, year 1911!"

"Huh?" they all said at the same time.

Matt's mind raced. He had to be dreaming. No matter the year, there was no *way* they had traveled all the way to Paris! They would have had to cross the ocean at the speed of light.

The captain came up behind them and draped his arms over Corey and Matt and motioned for Ruby to come closer.

"Now," whispered Captain Vincent. "As this is your first mission, you won't be expected to do much. Just stay close to me and the crew, and I promise you'll have the time of your life."

"But *what* exactly are we doing?" Matt asked.

"Nearly time, Captain," said the man in the plaid suit and fedora, consulting a gold pocket watch on a chain.

"Thank you, Wiley. Brocco? Our supplies and disguises, if you please?"

The man in the cape and Yankees cap appeared at the train door, holding a bulging linen sack. He tossed it so it landed at the captain's feet. "Carry that, will you, Albert?" The captain addressed the boy about Matt's age. He was a bit on the pudgy side with round cheeks, an upturned nose, and wire-framed glasses that looked too small for his face, like he'd gotten them when he was half the size he was now.

"Me? Why not the new recruits?" said the boy. "You always say new recruits have to do the grunt work."

"Now, now, Albert," said the captain. "They're not new recruits yet, they're still our guests. Let's be polite, shall we? Show them a good time?"

Albert didn't move at first. He held his head high and his nostrils flared, making him look somewhat like a pig wearing glasses, but the captain waited, perfectly calm and still, until Albert finally dropped his head and said, "Yes, sir." He picked up the bundle and slung it over his shoulder. He seemed to sink under the weight of it.

"Thank you, Albert," the captain said. "I always know I can count on you."

Albert straightened a little and lifted his chin.

"Let's be off," said the captain. "Don't want to be late!"

"Late for what?" Corey asked, but no one answered, and Matt felt they had no choice but to follow.

Matt was still trying to figure out what they should do next when the girl who had been sitting next to Albert on the train walked up alongside Matt. She smiled at him. "Hi, I'm Jia," she whispered.

"Matt," said Matt.

"Nice to meet you, and don't worry. We'll be perfectly safe.

The captain knows what he's doing." She had a strange sort of accent, as though she had learned to speak English from several different dialects and accents. She was Asian, and Matt was pretty sure Chinese. He wondered if she spoke Mandarin. It would be good to get some practice with a native speaker, but he figured now was not the time.

The strange group walked quickly and quietly down cobblestoned streets lined with shops and buildings built tightly together, until the streets opened up to a large square with a magnificent structure—a castle. And not just any castle. Matt was sure it was the Louvre, except it did not have the glass pyramid he'd seen in so many pictures. *Yes, I'm dreaming*, he thought. *Only in a dream would I see the Louvre without the glass pyramid.*

"It's pretty, isn't it?" whispered Jia. "I've never been to this museum."

"Why are we here?" Matt asked.

"Because," said Jia, "we need to steal *la Joconde*."

La Joconde. It sounded familiar. He knew it was French, but Matt couldn't quite place it.

"*La* what?" Corey asked.

"Oh, that's not what they call it in English. I forget. Albert, what do they call *la Joconde* in English?"

"The *Mona Lisa*," said Albert.

"That's it. The *Mona Lisa*." Jia smiled at them and kept walking.

5

Stealing the Mona Lisa

The three Hudsons stared at Jia, not sure they had heard her correctly. *We're about to steal the* Mona Lisa? *The* Mona Lisa? She had spoken in such a matter-of-fact tone that belied no fear or apprehension, nor any sense that stealing one of the world's most famous paintings was in any way wrong.

"We're going to *what*?" Ruby squealed.

"*Shh!* If you keep blubbering we *will* fail the mission," hissed Albert. "And I for one don't want to spend the rest of my life in stinking Paris. Foul, dirty city."

"Step lightly, crew!" said the captain, and everyone followed him down the dark street.

"What do we do?" Ruby whispered in a frantic voice to Matt and Corey. What *could* be done? They could call the police, but their phone wasn't working. Of course if they really were in Paris in 1911, who could they call anyway? Matt was so confused and disoriented, but whether this was a dream or not, he knew he needed to think clearly and keep them all out of danger.

"Just go along with it," said Matt. "If anything happens . . ." He didn't have a plan for if anything happened. "If anything happens, we stick together." He held out his fist. Corey and Ruby both made one too, and they did their three-way fist bump.

A moment later they were huddled with the captain and crew in the shadows of one of the many arches of the museum. The captain took the sack from Albert and pulled out what looked like white smocks worn by artists or bakers.

"This is what the cleaning crew wears." He passed them out. Everyone pulled the smocks over their clothes and buttoned them. Corey's was a little short in the arms and Ruby's covered her hands, so they traded and then they fit just fine. Matt pulled a smock on as the captain passed around some feather dusters and rags. Lastly, the captain pulled a coil of rope out of the sack and swung it over his shoulder.

At that very moment, footsteps sounded on the cobbles and the captain pulled them deeper into the shadows. He put a finger to his lips and peered around the archway. Unable to hold in his curiosity, Matt craned his neck to get a glimpse. A man in a white smock much like theirs approached the museum.

"That's our man, Peruggia," whispered the captain.

"Who's he?" whispered Ruby.

"The mastermind criminal about to steal the *Mona Lisa*."

Matt didn't think the man looked like a mastermind criminal, though what a mastermind criminal was supposed to look like, he didn't know. Peruggia was a small man, probably not even as tall as Corey. He had dark hair, beady eyes, and a thick mustache that swept up either side of his cheeks. He looked to his right, his left, then behind him, and he finally approached a door just two arches away. He opened it and entered.

"All right, places, everyone," said the captain. Jia and Albert immediately sprang into action. They ran toward the entrance where Peruggia had just entered. The captain waited until they heard some kind of clicking noise, which must have been Jia's signal that the coast was clear. "You three," said the captain, pointing to the Hudsons, "come with me." The captain walked swiftly to the door.

"Maybe we should run now," said Ruby. "We can go to the police."

"And tell them what?" said Corey. "We accidentally got on the wrong train in New York and it took us to Paris instead of Central Park? Oh, and a hundred years too early."

"You don't honestly believe—"

"It doesn't matter," Matt whispered. "We're definitely not near home, and I think our best chance to get back is to follow this Captain Whoever."

"Captain Vincent," said Ruby. "He's waving for us to come."

Matt took a breath. This was all insane. "Let's go."

They ran to the door where Captain Vincent was waiting, then quietly slipped inside.

Matt had spent countless hours inside the Metropolitan Museum, but never after hours, with no other patrons. The Louvre was dimly lit and ghostly quiet. He felt as though he had entered a tomb full of sleeping things that might wake at the slightest noise. They passed beneath grand archways and corridors that seemed to extend for miles. The pale morning light filtered through the windows, casting long shadows on the walls and floors.

"Keep up," whispered the captain. They hurried up a staircase and turned right, entering a wide space filled with marble statues. They lined the walls and dotted the floor like sentinels in silent watch. Matt got goose bumps as he passed them, feeling their stone eyes were somehow following him.

The captain stopped them just before a wide marble staircase. He crouched behind one of the pillars and put his finger to his mouth. Peruggia was still ascending the stairs. When he reached the top, he looked over his shoulder then turned left. The captain motioned for them to follow. They turned left at the top of the stairs, turned left again, and then again. The captain held his hand out to stop them, then silently pointed to a doorway. They peered around the frame into a large room. Magnificent oil paintings hung from floor to ceiling, some huge murals that covered the expanse of the entire wall.

"There she is," the captain whispered, pointing to their left. In the middle of the wall was the *Mona Lisa*.

Somehow Matt had always imagined the *Mona Lisa* to be as big as he was, but compared to the rest, it seemed rather small and unassuming. The painting hung at the lowest point on the wall, just above some brass railings. There wasn't anything in front of it, no glass case or any kind of alarm. There were no guards around, or any other museum staff. Crazy, Matt thought. This would never happen at the Met, at least not in 2019. They wouldn't have been able to get one step into the building without setting off an alarm, and there would have been night guards for sure.

Peruggia was casually dusting the frames of other paintings until he came to the *Mona Lisa*. With a quick glance to his left and right, he very easily took the painting off the wall, placed it under one arm, and made a beeline in their direction. Captain Vincent pulled the children back. They hid behind another statue. Peruggia came out with the painting and went into a door just to the side of where they were hiding. Peruggia very quickly popped the painting out of its protective glass frame and hid it behind a bunch of other paintings stacked haphazardly against the wall. He then descended the stairs.

"What's he doing?" Ruby whispered.

"Trying to open the door at the bottom of the stairs," whispered the captain. "Our time has come. Quickly now."

Matt's heart pounded as they entered the stairway. Captain Vincent retrieved the painting and quickly shoved it into Matt's arms. Matt staggered back, trying to grasp it in some proper way. But what way was that? He was holding the *Mona Lisa*! He didn't think there *was* a proper way to hold the most famous painting in the world. He shouldn't be holding it at all!

Captain Vincent took the bag that had carried their smocks and pulled it over the painting, then took it back from Matt and swung it over his shoulder.

There was a clang from the bottom of the stairs.

"Stupido! Idiota!"

The captain motioned for them to move out. "Quickly now. Peruggia will come this way in just a moment." They left through the door from which they had entered. Matt could hear a racket behind him, the clatter of someone rifling through paintings and frames.

"Dov'è lei? Dov'è lei?"

Peruggia must be searching for the painting in the stack where he had left it. Matt glanced at it swinging over the captain's shoulders.

They had reached the staircase, but Matt, as usual, wasn't watching his step, so he missed the first stair. He called out as he went flying forward, toppled down the staircase, and finally stopped himself halfway down. There was a rush of footsteps behind him.

"Matt! Are you okay?" Ruby's voice echoed through the empty, quiet museum.

Matt sat up, wincing. He didn't think he'd hurt himself too badly.

"Can you stand?" said the captain, holding out his hand. "We must hurry." But it was too late. Peruggia had come running at the noise and was now looking down at them from the top of the staircase. He took in the scene and comprehended all in half a second. His dark eyes narrowed on the rectangular sack swinging from the captain's shoulder.

"Now we really must hurry." The captain pulled Matt by the arm and yanked him upright as he hurried down the steps. Matt barely got his feet underneath him in time to keep from falling again.

"*Ladro!* Stop!" called Peruggia behind him.

"This way!" the captain said, and instead of going straight back the way they had come he turned to the left down another corridor. Statues and paintings whirred past Matt's vision. His heart pummeled in his chest. He glanced back for a brief moment to see Peruggia in hot pursuit. He was small but fast. The captain made a turn at every opportunity, effectively getting themselves lost, but Peruggia managed to keep up. The captain finally came to a door and tried to open it, but it was locked. He swore under his breath.

"Stairs!" said Corey, pointing behind them. There was another marble staircase leading upward. The captain didn't hesitate for a moment. "Go!" He shoved Ruby, then Corey, then Matt toward the staircase. "Find a place to hide!" They all bolted up the staircase, Matt in the rear. He hung back just enough to see the captain swing the painting and hit Peruggia square in the jaw with a solid *thwack!* He kicked up his leg and shoved him in the chest. Peruggia staggered backward and fell as the captain surged up the staircase two steps at a time. "Go, go, go!"

They ran all the way to the top of the staircase until it ended and opened up to a spacious gallery with elaborate murals all over the walls and ceilings and bright, arched windows, but no statues or furniture that could possibly hide them.

Hurried footsteps echoed up the stairs. The captain ran his hands through his hair, looking in both directions of the corridor, but both seemingly led to nowhere.

"There!" Matt pointed. "That window is open!" The captain pushed them toward the window. He stuck his head out and looked right and left, then motioned for the children to crawl through. Matt hopped through the window onto a balcony lined with statues and a low stone railing.

Ruby and Corey came through the window, followed by the captain, who quickly pulled the window shut. Matt, Corey, and Ruby crouched low, pressing themselves against the outer wall of the museum. The captain, however, went right to the stone railing, swung the coil of rope off his shoulder, and began to tie one end of it around one of the pillars.

"What are you doing?" Matt whispered. He would be seen!

"That staircase is the only exit," said the captain. "And Peruggia knows it. Who wants to go first?" He held up a length of the rope.

"You mean . . . you can't possibly mean for us to climb down from here!" Ruby whispered frantically.

"Well, it's either that or face Peruggia," said the captain. "And it's best if we keep our interactions to a minimum, for reasons of time-travel safety, if nothing else."

"I'll go first!" said Corey. He crawled toward the captain, who deftly made a large loop at the end of the rope, then secured it around Corey's middle. "Now just hang on. I'll lower you down. I promise I won't drop you."

Corey jumped over to the other side of the balcony, clearly eager for this risky adventure of which their parents would never approve. For his birthday Corey once wanted to go skydiving. He didn't get any further in the negotiations than Matt did for the exchange program in Paris.

"Don't fall," said Ruby in a small voice, her eyes squeezed shut.

"It's all right," said the captain. "I've got him." The captain pulled the rope taut and braced himself with his foot against the balcony. "Here we go." Corey held on to the rope and stepped out into the open air. Matt gripped the edge of the balcony as he watched the captain lower him down, swiftly but with control. Still, it gave him a bit of vertigo. Matt did not love heights. He had never had any desire to go skydiving. He didn't even like standing at the top of the Empire State Building. In less than a minute Corey made it safely to the ground and gave them a thumbs-up. He took off the rope, and the captain quickly pulled it to the top.

"All right, who's next?"

Matt and Ruby looked at each other. As the older brother, Matt felt he should buck up and go next, but he felt paralyzed. Ruby seemed to know it too. She gritted her teeth and stepped forward. She slid the rope around her waist and climbed over the railing. The captain lowered her down with the same ease as he had done with Corey, perhaps a little too swiftly for Matt. All too soon Ruby was on the ground and the captain had pulled up the rope. He held out the loop for Matt to slip inside.

"Maybe Peruggia's gone now and we can just take the stairs?" said Matt, his voice cracking a little.

"Afraid of heights, are you?" said the captain with a little smile. He pulled the rope over Matt's head and tightened it around his waist. "I'm not too fond of them either. Just close your eyes. You'll be on the ground before you know it." He lifted Matt over the balcony like a sack of potatoes. Matt grasped the edge. The whole building seemed to sway.

"And I'd like you to carry her down with you." The captain picked up the sack carrying the *Mona Lisa* and held it out to Matt.

"Oh, I don't think—"

"I can't carry it and lower myself down safely. What if I dropped her? That would be a tragedy." The captain swung the painting over Matt's back and pressed the strings into his hands. His palms were suddenly sweaty.

"But what if *I* drop her?"

"You won't," said the captain. "I have the utmost faith in you, Mateo."

Suddenly the window burst open and Peruggia came hurtling through. The captain turned toward him, and in his surprise let the rope slide. Matt lost his balance and suddenly plummeted from the balcony. He fell for what felt like ages, jerking to a stop directly in front of a statue of a somber-looking man holding a sword. He looked down to see Corey looking up at him and Ruby peeking through her fingers over her eyes. Matt craned his head upward to see the captain struggling with Peruggia. Peruggia was much smaller than the captain, but he had the use of all his limbs, unlike the captain, who was holding on to the rope with one hand, bracing himself against the balcony to keep from dropping Matt. Peruggia swung at the captain. The captain reared back to dodge the blow but lost his grip on the rope again. Ruby screamed as Matt plummeted another ten feet, then jerked to a stop that cinched him hard around his middle.

"I got you!" said Corey, holding up his hands. "Don't worry, I'll catch you, bro."

Corey was a good catcher, but there was a big difference between catching a baseball in a glove and a human, plus the most valuable painting in the world. Matt looked up again. The captain was struggling to fend off Peruggia, who was fighting like a little pit bull, punching him in the ribs, pulling at his hair. The captain glanced down at Matt, dangling ten feet above the ground.

"I got him, Captain!" shouted Corey. "You can let go!"

"No!" shouted Matt.

Suddenly the white rat burst out of the captain's jacket and attacked Peruggia, biting him full on the nose. It scurried around his head and down his shirt. Peruggia yelped and stumbled away from the captain, but in the shift of power, the captain had lost his grip once again and Matt went hurtling toward the ground.

He crashed face-first into both Corey and Ruby, the painting slamming onto his back.

"*Oof!*" said Corey. "You're heavier than you look."

Matt turned over and looked up to see the captain swing himself over the balcony while Peruggia was doing a strange sort of dance.

"Come, Santiago," said the captain.

A moment later the rat popped out from between the

buttons of Peruggia's smock and leaped for the captain, who then jumped from the balcony and dropped down in five seconds. He hit the ground running.

"Let's go!" he said.

They all scrambled to their feet. Matt hoisted the painting over his shoulder and ran as fast as he could. He looked back just for a moment to see the rope fall. Peruggia slammed his hands against the balcony and ran back to the window.

They sprinted to the end of the Louvre and tucked themselves back into the alcove where they'd started. Matt tried to catch his breath and calm his racing heart. A minute later Peruggia burst out of the museum, gasping and wheezing. The captain pressed them all back into the shadows and held up a finger.

Peruggia staggered out of an archway and looked all around him, up and down the Louvre then out toward the open square and streets. He rapped on his head and tore at his mustache. A police officer with a baton in hand passed by, eyeing Peruggia warily. Matt's heart thrummed in his chest and ears.

"Do you think he'll go to the police?" Ruby whispered.

"No, it's too risky," said the captain. "The French don't generally trust Italians, and he shouldn't have been in the museum in the first place."

Sure enough, Peruggia quickly walked past the police officer, took one more glance back at the museum, then disappeared around a street corner.

The door behind them opened. Matt jumped and Ruby squeaked a little, until they saw it was Jia and Albert. Wiley came a moment later.

"All clear?" said the captain. They all nodded. "Very good. Move out, crew!"

They hurried across the open square, down the cobble-stoned streets, and finally slowed as more pedestrians and carriages crowded their path. Matt was still breathless, his heart still pounding. He was certain that at any moment the police would arrive, blowing whistles and brandishing batons, Peruggia at their heels, but no one came. No one seemed to notice them at all. The city was still quite sleepy. A shop owner swept the sidewalk. A woman walked a fussy infant in a baby carriage. She wore a long blue dress with a matching hat tilted to one side. Definitely not twenty-first-century fashion.

After they'd been walking a few minutes, Matt calmed down enough for his brain to register a few clear thoughts. First, he realized that his body was incredibly sore from his two falls, not to mention the rope burn around his middle. He winced as he felt a pain shoot in his ribs and his knee. He'd never felt pain in dreams before, and he'd never run so fast in them. In fact, he usually couldn't run at all in his dreams, which was always incredibly frustrating. He finally had to conclude that this was no dream. He was not going to suddenly wake up. He was wide awake, and what he'd just experienced, however improbable, happened. They had traveled to Paris, France, *time-traveled* to 1911, and they'd just stolen the *Mona Lisa* right out of the Louvre. Matt was still carrying it in the sack over his shoulder, walking down a public street, following the mysterious man who had orchestrated this entire heist. His head swam with questions. How had the captain done it? And why? What was his motive in all of this? he wondered. And why did he so readily allow Matt and his siblings to be so intimately involved in such an important mission? Matt had nearly ruined the whole thing, and yet this Captain Vincent, whoever he was, had not seemed the least bit angry or annoyed with him and had saved all their necks. But what did that make him? Good? Trustworthy? Matt watched Captain Vincent walk confidently down the cobblestoned street, a slight swagger in his step. He nodded at a woman crossing with a loaf of bread in her arms.

"*Bonjour, madame,*" he said. "*C'est une belle matinée, non?*" His French was flawless. Matt would have guessed he was actually from France.

"*Oui, monsieur,*" the woman replied.

An old man in dirty, ragged clothing with bare feet was crouched in the gutter, searching for something. An old-fashioned motorcar rumbled by and splashed muddy water all over him.

"Ah!" The man stumbled back, spitting. "*Imbécile! Idiot!*"

He shook a fist after the car and then slumped down on the side of the road.

"Oh, poor fellow," said the captain. He walked straight over to the man, and Matt watched as the captain pulled out a small leather pouch and pressed it into the man's hands. *"Pour vous, monsieur."*

The man looked inside, and his bedraggled, lined face instantly lifted in happy disbelief. He stared inside the little pouch, looked questioningly up at the captain, then back down at the pouch. Finally he grasped the captain's hands.

"Merci, monsieur! Merci beaucoup!"

The captain patted the man on the shoulder. He started to move away but then turned back. He slipped off his red Converse and held them out. The man looked perplexed at their modern design and bold color, yet he instantly slipped them onto his bare feet and tapped them on the cobbles, smiling cheerfully, showing crooked, yellow teeth, both hands clasped around the leather pouch.

The captain returned to the group, now barefoot, but also smiling.

"Why did you give him your shoes?" said Ruby. "It seemed like you gave him enough money to buy his own."

"He'd never be able to find such comfortable shoes in this day. Besides, I have another pair back on the *Vermillion*. We must always share our good fortune whenever possible."

Matt was suddenly reminded of his dad. Mr. Hudson

always gave spare change whenever he saw someone who needed it and said something very similar. "We must give what we can when we can," he'd say.

Matt followed after the captain, perhaps with a little more trust now. They turned on the same narrow street through which they had come. Ahead, a shiny black train with gold trim puffed steam. Matt recognized the star with the red V he'd seen on the side of the subway train now painted on the nose of the engine.

Brocco stuck his head out from the front window, still wearing his cape, but also an engineer's striped cap.

The train gave a high whistle and let off a cloud of steam. "All aboard!" called Brocco.

Matt quickened his pace. The *Mona Lisa* seemed twice as heavy now and only grew heavier with each step. The captain hopped onto the train, then reached back to help everyone else. When he pulled Matt on board, he clasped his shoulder and said, "Well done, Mateo!"

The doors closed. The train let out another puff of steam and began to chug forward. Matt finally breathed freely again, and it was only then that he realized something. He had never told Captain Vincent his name, had he?

6

Flummoxed

"Prepare for a quantum time leap!" said the captain as he pulled the watch out of his sleeve once again and began to turn the dials.

Matt was still a little discombobulated by all that had happened in the last however many hours, but he was a quick learner and took the example of the rest of the passengers. Corey and Ruby clearly had the same thought. They both held on to opposite ends of a table while Matt braced himself on one of the plush chairs, but as the train picked up speed, it began to vibrate so violently his teeth started to rattle. Faster and faster, louder and louder the train roared. Matt looked out the window to view the landscape rushing by—blurred buildings and trees, people that seemed to be whizzing past him on a speeding conveyor belt. The train was going at least a hundred miles an hour, he thought, maybe faster. There was a flash of bright light and then all the candles flickered out.

Once again, the train began to shift around them. The floors widened, the walls spread as though they were being stretched and pulled by some invisible force. The carpet retracted into the wooden planks and all the furniture went through a series of changes. Matt watched in awe as the chair he'd been clinging to shrank and grew and then shrank again, changing colors and materials, as if it were trying on different outfits at a shop, until it finally seemed to make up its mind and settled as an ornately carved oak chair lined with red velvet.

All the small tables shifted and combined like a Tetris game to become one long table, which nearly crushed Corey in the middle before he slipped beneath them. The chandeliers on the ceiling melded together to make a large silver chandelier with many candles.

Finally everything settled into place, and the train seemed to steady and quiet. Matt still braced himself on the chair, though. His heart was pounding very hard, his limbs were trembling, and he was slightly dizzy. He looked around for his brother and sister.

Corey crawled out from under the table and shook himself like a wet dog as he stood. "Crazy," he said.

"Where's Ruby?" Matt asked. The other passengers were emerging from various corners and furniture, but he didn't see her anywhere.

"Ruby?" Corey called. "You can come out now!"

"Help!" cried a muffled voice. They looked around until Matt spotted a chest with a brass latch that was rattling a bit. He ran over and opened it. There was Ruby, curled up with a pile of table linens covered in mothballs, her arms wrapped around a silver candelabra.

Matt and Corey reached down and helped her out. Her usually straight, dark hair was now a little frizzy and wild, her eyes wide with shock. She looked like someone who'd walked through a strong windstorm.

"That was . . . that was . . ." She searched for the words.

"That was awesome!" Corey shouted, and he punched the air.

Matt smiled a little. Now that the danger seemed to be past them, he had to admit it had been pretty exciting.

"I'm so glad you enjoyed yourselves," said the captain, sliding the black watch on the gold chain back inside his sleeve. "I must say you did an excellent job for your first mission. Incredible, really."

Ruby smiled but then knit her brow. "But . . . we just stole the *Mona Lisa*!"

"Actually, we just *saved* it from being stolen," said Albert, pushing his glasses up on his pudgy nose. "The *Mona Lisa* was going to get stolen anyway. We just intercepted the real thief, Vincenzo Peruggia."

He pronounced the name *Peru-gee-uh*. Matt had studied sufficient Italian to know it should have been *Peru-jah*. He had an itch to correct Albert, but Ruby spoke first.

"So that makes it okay, does it?" said Ruby. "We can steal it because someone else was going to steal it anyway?"

"Miss Ruby, you misunderstand our noble intentions," said the captain. "Peruggia eventually gets caught in 1913. So we will keep the painting for a while, enjoy its many virtues, then plant it back on the real thief when the time is right."

Matt's brain was whirling. "So . . . we stole the *Mona Lisa* before some other guy could steal it, and then we'll plant it back on the guy who didn't steal it, but would have if we hadn't, so he still takes the blame for us stealing it?"

"We call it out-crooking a real crook," said Jia, smiling.

"Exactly," said Captain Vincent. "It's difficult work, but quite rewarding. Mateo, the painting, if you please?" The captain held his hand out. Matt twitched a little as he remembered he was still clutching the sack that held the *Mona Lisa*. He carefully slid it off his shoulder and held it out to the captain, glad to be relieved of the burden.

Captain Vincent gently removed the painting from the sack and held it gingerly in his hands for all to see. Everyone crowded in to look at it, all of them still and quiet, like they were in the presence of a sacred relic.

Matt regarded the painting. He had never been much of an art enthusiast, but he had to admit the *Mona Lisa* was captivating, and far more interesting in real life, up close, than any pictures he'd seen of it in books or on the internet. The strokes of paint, the texture and colors, shapes and shadows . . . it was all at once simple but complex, ordinary yet marvelous. The work of a genius.

"Isn't she *dazzling*?" said the captain. "Such beauty and mystery."

Matt vaguely recalled a conversation between his parents and Ruby about this very painting. Ruby had asked what made certain pieces of art so famous and others less so. Mrs. Hudson replied that it was always the stories and mysteries about art that captivated people. "Take the *Mona Lisa*," she said. "It's not a particularly grand painting, just a picture of a woman, but her expression, her eyes . . . very mysterious. Da Vinci captured an expression that no one could quite read or translate, and the world treasures the mystery of her. She symbolizes all the secrets women hold within them that no one will ever be able to decode."

"She symbolizes why all women drive men mad," their father had said, to which their mother blew a big wet raspberry right in his face.

Matt smiled at the memory and then frowned. What would his parents say right now if they were here with them, staring at the *Mona Lisa*, which had just been stolen by their own children? The reality of what they'd done, what they were standing before, truly began to sink in . . . not to mention that they'd supposedly traveled through time and space, a hundred years in the past, thousands of miles in a matter of minutes. Impossible! No, Matt thought. *Improbable* maybe, but not impossible. He knew time travel was possible in theory. Einstein and other scientists had all made strong cases for why and how it could happen, but Matt had never heard of anyone bringing it from theory to reality. Until now. A hundred questions suddenly popped into his head.

"Excuse me, sir. Captain Vincent?" said Matt. "I'm still a little confused."

"Only a little?" said the captain. "That's impressive. Most are convinced they've gone mad after their first mission on the *Vermillion*. Brocco here was bashing his head against the wall for half a day."

"Thought I'd gone bloody insane!" said Brocco.

"I think he did," Corey muttered in Matt's ear.

"I was scared half to death," said Wiley. "Actually, I thought I *was* dead!"

"I thought I was dreaming," said Jia. "I was convinced I'd wake up any moment and be back in the orphanage in China. Albert thought he'd been bewitched, didn't you, Albert? He thought the captain was full of black magic."

"I didn't think he was full of *black* magic," said Albert, clearly annoyed. "I thought he was a great magician, that's all, like Merlin."

"Don't I wish I were!" said the captain. "Unfortunately I'm a regular bloke, not a magical bone in my body."

"But how did we just *do* all of that?" said Matt. "How did

we time-travel? What's that watch inside your sleeve? Is that what makes the train transform?"

Captain Vincent chuckled. "One question at a time, Mateo, if you please."

Matt stiffened, hair raising at the nape of his neck. "All right, here's *one* question: How do you know my name? I never told you my name was Mateo. No one calls me that."

The captain blinked, clearly caught off guard. "Don't they?"

"Just our parents," said Corey. "And sometimes teachers, but only if they don't like Matt. It doesn't happen too often."

Matt looked around at all the crew. No one looked him in the eye. Wiley put his pipe in his mouth and stared at the ceiling. Brocco tugged his cap lower over his head and his cape around his neck, as though the temperature had suddenly dropped. Albert and Jia gave each other a meaningful look while a little girl sat cross-legged on the floor, picking at her rope. Pictures and memories seemed to be flashing in Matt's brain. The ice cream truck they'd almost boarded when they were little . . . the driver had been wearing a cape just like Brocco's. Wiley running into Corey this morning . . .

"Have you been following us?"

"*Following* isn't quite the right word, no," said the captain. "I think *waiting* would be more accurate."

"Waiting? What do you mean? Why?"

Ruby sucked in her breath. "Have we been kidnapped?" she asked in a small voice.

"Kidnapped!" said the captain, aghast. "Oh no, no, no. We are not kidnappers. The *Vermillion* wouldn't stand for such things. She only allows those on board who come willingly. And worthily."

"Who is this *Vermillion*?" Corey asked. "Maybe we should be speaking with her."

The captain laughed. "I'm afraid she's not much of a conversationalist. The *Vermillion* is my ship."

"Don't you mean train?" said Matt.

"No, no. She may have looked like a train when you boarded her, but she's really a ship." The captain stomped his foot a couple of times on the floorboards. "Seventeenth-century frigate, though she's pretty timeless, as you've already witnessed. She can be a bit temperamental, doesn't always like to be told what to do, but truly she would never hold any passengers against their will. So I beg your pardon, I never would have set sail if I knew you didn't *want* to be here. But I *can* take you home at any time, this instant, if you wish." He gingerly set down the *Mona Lisa*, leaning it against a wall, and took the black watch on the gold chain out of his shirtsleeve once again. "I can take you back to the exact time we picked you up. You won't have missed a moment!" He moved as if to change a setting.

"Wait!" said Matt. The captain paused and looked up expectantly. "I'm sorry, it's just . . . it's a lot to take in."

"Quite understandable," said the captain. "You needn't

apologize. Shall we go then? Truly, I don't wish you to feel uncomfortable."

Matt hesitated. He did feel uncomfortable, there was definitely something strange going on, but he suddenly wasn't sure he wanted to go home. Not without answers. He'd just *time-traveled*. On a transforming ship. How often would he get this kind of opportunity? And he still had so many questions about how it was all done, how the ship worked, what that watch thing was in the captain's hand, and all the implications of traveling through time and space. What kind of scientist would he be if he didn't take the opportunity to explore and study this phenomenon, discover all the possibilities? How far into the past could they go? How far into the future? Could they travel into *his* future? Could he see himself in twenty or fifty years? If he went back in time and accidentally killed his grandmother, would he still be born?

"Could I have a minute alone with my brother and sister," Matt asked, "to talk things over?"

"Of course!" said the captain. "You take all the time you need. It's one thing we have in abundance!" He slipped the watch thing back into his sleeve and picked up the *Mona Lisa* again. "I'll be in my office if you need me."

"Shall I take the painting to the gallery, Captain?" said Albert, stepping forward as though to take it out of his hands.

"No thank you, Albert," said the captain. "I should like to

study her in private for a day or two, see what I can learn from Master da Vinci."

"But, sir!" said Albert. "Your office does not have the proper conditions for preservation. The light might damage her."

"I assure you she'll be perfectly safe, Albert. Santiago, door, please."

The white rat popped out of the captain's jacket with a key between his teeth. He scurried down the captain's leg, climbed a door, and, with his paws, inserted the key into a lock and turned it until it clicked and the door swung wide open.

"Thank you." The captain carried the *Mona Lisa* into the room. Matt caught a glimpse of an entire shelf full of red Converse and a sword leaning against an art easel before the captain turned around in the doorway, blocking his view.

"Feel free to explore the ship," said the captain. "I'm sure any of the crew would be happy to show you around. Oh, and you really must climb up to the crow's nest! Spectacular views up there. Not to be missed. It can really change your perspective." He smiled and winked at Matt, then withdrew into the room and placed the *Mona Lisa* on the art easel facing him. Matt felt as if she were staring right at him with a teasing sort of smile, like she knew a secret about him that he didn't even know about himself.

"Santiago, door, please." The white rat swiftly shut the

door with a whip of his scaly tail. A moment later the lock clicked, leaving the Hudsons feeling . . . What was Matt feeling?

"Well, I'm flummoxed," said Ruby.

That was it. Flummoxed.

7
Notes to Self

Matt stared at the door for a second then turned to Corey and Ruby. They both looked just as perplexed as he felt.

"That rat is super creepy," said Corey.

"And the captain," said Ruby. "He seems sort of . . ."

"Mysterious?" said a voice behind them. Matt jumped a little. He had forgotten that they weren't alone. Jia was still there, and Albert as well. The others—Wiley, Brocco, and the pale little girl—seemed to have slipped away at some point.

Ruby nodded. "Yes, very mysterious." Matt was certain Ruby was about to say the captain was crazy.

"Would you like me to show you around the ship?" said Jia. "If you need a bathroom, we have three flushing toilets!"

"Oh . . . really?" said Matt, not quite sure how to respond to this random information.

Jia nodded enthusiastically. "I installed modern plumbing last year, even real, working showers with hot water. Now I'm working on installing electricity, but I haven't quite figured that one out yet."

"Are you the ship's mechanic then?" Ruby asked.

"I'm the *Vermillion*'s Repair Master," said Jia with an air of great pride, though not conceited pride. It was rather endearing, Matt thought.

"Why would this ship need repairs?" Corey asked. "Isn't it, like, magic or something?"

"Kind of," said Jia, "but it's not a self-healing organism like us. Sometimes travel and transformations cause damage to the *Vermillion*—or Brocco blows something up—and someone has to fix it. I know how to fix anything from a cartwheel to an auto engine, but every crewmate has their expertise. Albert is *Vermillion*'s Keeper of Investments. He takes care of all the valuable things we bring on board and keeps them in good repair."

"And safe from untrustworthy passengers," Albert added, eyeing each of them with unmistakable dislike.

"Don't be rude, Albert," said Jia. "Of *course* they're trustworthy. The captain would not have let them stay on board if they weren't."

Albert gave a dubious snort, pushing his too-small spectacles up on his nose. "If you'll excuse me, I have important work to do." He turned around and left through another door.

"Gee, he's a real ray of sunshine, isn't he?" said Corey.

"Don't mind Albert," said Jia. "He's just a bit jealous."

"Of what?" asked Matt.

"Albert was the last one to come on board the *Vermillion*. He's been a special favorite of the captain's, and now he's afraid all the attention and special treatment will go to you."

"He shouldn't worry," said Ruby. "We're not going to stay."

"Won't you?" said Jia, seeming surprised.

"Our parents are probably really worried," said Ruby. "We should have been at school hours ago."

Jia looked confused. "You have parents?"

"Of course," said Ruby. "Don't you?"

Jia shook her head. "I'm an orphan. Everyone is on the *Vermillion*."

"Oh. Well, we're not," said Ruby.

"That's strange," said Jia. "You're very unique then."

"Tell me about it," said Corey. "Could I use one of those flushing toilets now? Nature calls."

Jia lit up. "Yes! There's one just down the hall! I'll show you."

Before any of them could use the bathroom, Jia gave them a formal tour of it. She pointed out the chain hanging from the ceiling that flushed the toilet and the turquoise sink with two brass faucets, one for cold and one for hot. She was clearly very proud of her work. Matt thought it was quite impressive, though he though it smelled oddly of peanut butter.

"Go on, try it!" she said eagerly.

"Uh . . . can I try it by myself, like with the door closed?" asked Corey.

"Oh yes, sorry!" said Jia, stepping out.

They all took turns using the bathroom. "Did it work okay?" Jia asked each of them as they came out. "Did it all go down?"

"Yeah," said Matt. "You built this all yourself?"

"Yes," said Jia, beaming. "It took some time and effort to figure it all out, especially with the *Vermillion* being a transforming ship. She didn't take right away to the plumbing. A few times all the pipes burst during a transformation. It was a disaster, but eventually I found the right materials and method to make it all work."

"What materials?" Matt asked, quite curious to know what would make metal pipes adapt to a transforming ship.

"A mixture of bubble gum and peanut butter," said Jia in a matter-of-fact tone, as though she'd just shared the ingredients for common glue.

"That's an unusual combination," said Matt.

"Yes, I thought so too at first, but the *Vermillion* seems to quite like it, slurps it up like a milkshake. I slather it on the pipes and they'll bend and stretch without bursting when the ship transforms. I use it a lot when I'm making upgrades or additions."

"You must go through a lot of bubble gum and peanut butter," said Corey.

Jia nodded. "It's one of the top reasons we have to travel to the twentieth century every so often. I tried to make a stockpile, but I found it all kept disappearing. I actually think the *Vermillion* eats it."

Jia took them on a small tour of the ship, sharing information about the *Vermillion* as they walked. "Like Captain Vincent said, this is the original form of the *Vermillion*. There are three levels and about two dozen rooms, but any or all could disappear in transformation and then reappear in a completely different area of the ship with things scattered all over and sometimes hidden. It makes it difficult to keep track of things sometimes. The *Vermillion* is always stealing my hammer. I think she thinks it's funny."

"You all talk about the ship as if she's a person," said Ruby.

"She almost is," said Jia.

Matt suddenly heard a voice nearby, someone singing. He cocked his ear to listen.

"What's that?" he asked.

"What?" said Jia.

"That singing. The *Vermillion* doesn't know how to sing, does she?"

Matt walked around until he came to a door. He smelled fresh baked bread, simmering meat, onions, and garlic. The singing was coming from there. He couldn't make out the words, but he was pretty sure it was French. He pushed the door open a little.

"Don't go in there!" Jia suddenly shouted.

The singing stopped abruptly and a giant metal pot came flying at Matt's face.

"*Va t'en! Va t'en, méchant, avant de vous couper la tête!*" yelled a shrill voice. Matt barely saw a knife come flying toward him before he pulled the door shut.

"What the . . . ," said Matt, brushing at his cheek where he'd been grazed by the pot.

"Did she just say she was going to chop off your head?" Ruby asked as Corey doubled over in a fit of laughter.

"It's not funny," said Matt. "She could have stabbed me!"

"Who *was* that?" Ruby asked.

"That's Agnes, the cook," said Jia. "I should have warned you before. She doesn't care for company. She's been here longer than any of us except the captain, and she's cranky as a wet cat."

"Well, I think she's got some serious psychological issues," said Matt.

"Yes, I'm sure the captain would have discarded her by now, but I think he's afraid she'll kill him if he tries. But she *is* a good cook, so maybe that's why the captain lets her stay."

"I guess that's a good redeeming quality," said Corey, "if you're insane."

Matt got a sudden wave of dizziness. He stumbled sideways a little.

"Are you okay?" said Ruby, catching him by the arm.

"I'm fine," said Matt. "Just lost my balance."

Ruby eyed him closely. Matt did not want her to think he was about to have a fainting spell or seizure. She'd probably insist they go home right away.

"I'm fine," he said. "Probably just the rocking of the ship. I'm not used to boats, you know."

"None of us are," said Ruby.

"How about we go above deck and get some fresh air?" Jia suggested.

"Yeah, that sounds good," said Matt. He pulled his arm away from Ruby and followed after Jia. He had to concentrate on walking with straight, steady steps.

He could feel Ruby watching him.

When they were above deck Matt took in a deep breath of fresh, salty air. A cool breeze rushed over him, and he felt a little better. No big deal, he told himself. He was probably just a bit motion sick.

"This is amazing," said Corey, gazing up at the big white sails, three tall masts of them billowing in the wind.

Ruby went to the side of the deck and looked out over the endless blue water. They were surrounded by ocean on all sides, no land in sight.

"Where are we?" said Ruby. "And when?"

"Nowhere in No Time," said Jia.

"Huh?" the Hudsons all said together.

Jia laughed. "We actually don't know where or when we are, so we call it Nowhere in No Time, but this is where we always come between missions. We can sail around for days and weeks and never come to any land at all or see another ship. It's like some kind of blank piece of time and space in the middle of the ocean."

"So how does the captain get here?" Matt asked.

Jia shrugged. "Some setting on the compass takes him here."

"It's a compass then?" said Matt. "And how does that work? Did the captain make it? And the ship? Which did he make first, the compass or the ship?"

Jia cocked her head and smiled. "Which came first? The chicken or the egg?"

Matt laughed. "Touché."

"The captain did not make the compass or the ship. He would be a better one to ask about that. I only know a little. The captain turns the dials to take us to whatever time and place we want, and the *Vermillion* transforms to whatever transportation is appropriate for the time—train, boat, car, bus—anything at all, really."

"Dang," said Corey. "Do you think it could turn into the Batmobile?"

Jia scrunched up her face. "What's that?"

Corey's eyes bulged in disbelief. "Only the coolest car ever."

Jia shrugged. "Sure. The *Vermillion*'s always trying out new forms, but you can't really tell her what to turn into. She has a mind of her own."

"Well, I want to see her transform again!" said Corey.

"When's your next mission? Where are we going?"

"Does that mean you'll stay?" Jia asked hopefully.

"You want us to?" Matt asked.

"Of course!" said Jia.

"Why?" Ruby asked. "What did the captain mean exactly when he said you'd been waiting for us? And how *did* he know Matt's real name was Mateo?"

Jia's smile faded. She fiddled with one of the flaps of her many bulging pockets.

"It's difficult to explain," said Jia. "I think it's better if you see for yourself."

"All right," said Matt. "How do we do that?"

Jia looked up toward the mainmast. "Climb up to the crow's nest," she said. "I think you'll understand then."

Matt looked up at the crow's nest, at the very top of the mainmast, and got a slight feeling of vertigo.

Corey, however, had no reservations. He was already at the base of the mast. "YOLO!" he shouted. "A pirate's life for me!" He began to climb the rope ladder.

"You can stay here," said Ruby, clearly sensing Matt's apprehension. "I'll go with Corey."

"No, I'm okay," said Matt. He wasn't about to admit he was afraid of heights in front of Jia. He also had the feeling that whatever it was she wanted them to see, he needed to see for himself.

Matt was careful not to look down as he climbed, and he

tried to ignore the queasy feeling in his stomach. His breathing got a little raspy the higher he went. When at last he reached the top, he had to flop onto the floor of the crow's nest.

"You okay?" said Ruby, helping him up.

"I'm fine," said Matt. He forced himself to stand and was almost knocked over by the wind. It was much stronger up here, whipping his hair in all directions. He grabbed on to the edge of the crow's nest. Just above his head was a black flag flapping in the wind. It had the same symbol he'd seen on the side of the subway and the nose of the steam engine: a star made of arrows with a red V in the middle. Matt suddenly realized it was a compass star.

"This is amazing!" said Corey.

The view was spectacular, as the captain had said. Matt could see for miles, the expanse of the ocean, the endless sky. The sun was starting to set, casting pink and gold over the water.

"What are we supposed to see, though?" said Ruby. "I don't see anything that would help us understand why these people have been looking for us."

"Waiting," said Matt. "He said they'd been waiting."

"Whatever. Big difference," said Ruby. "The point is, we did not just stumble onto this ship by accident, and Mom and Dad would never in a million years be okay with us staying."

"Who cares what Mom and Dad think?" said Corey.

"They're not here, and remember the captain said he could take us back right where and when we boarded. They won't even know we've been gone, so what's the big deal?"

"What's the big deal?" said Ruby. "What if one of us had gotten caught in Paris? What if we get lost or stuck in some other time, or in this Nowhere-in-No-Time place and we never get home? What if—"

Ruby was cut off midsentence as the ship suddenly lurched beneath a wave and the children all tipped inside the crow's nest. Corey clung to a rope while Ruby grasped the edge of the nest. Matt crouched low and wrapped his arms and legs around the mast. He closed his eyes until the ship steadied. When he opened his eyes he saw something very strange.

"Guys," he said. "I think I found what we're supposed to see up here."

Corey and Ruby crouched down by him.

"What the . . ."

Etched into the wood of the mast were three names.

MATEO

COREY

RUBY

Matt brushed his fingers over the letters.

"But . . . *how*?" said Ruby.

"I see only two possibilities," said Matt. "Either three other people with our same names carved their names on this mast, or . . ."

"Or?" said Corey.

"We carved them ourselves."

"But we didn't," said Ruby.

"But we could have," said Matt.

"Don't you think we'd remember if we'd been on a time-traveling ship?" said Ruby. "Or any ship at all, for that matter."

"Not if our future selves traveled to the past," said Matt. "Don't you see? We've already been to the past. What if we stay on the *Vermillion* and go into the past again? At some point in the future, we go to the past, and our future selves carve our names into the mast."

"Or someone on the crew could have just carved them here," said Ruby.

"Why would they do that?" Corey asked.

"To convince us to stay!" said Ruby. "To manipulate us."

"I don't think that's it," said Matt. "Look. That's my *M*. How would they know to make my *M* like that?" Matt always made the *M* in his name with crisscrossing lines and it was carved exactly like that in the mast. This must have been how the captain knew his name, why he called him Mateo instead of Matt.

"This is so weird," said Corey.

Ruby brushed her thumb over it. "But what does it *mean*?"

"I think it means that we stay," said Matt. "We're supposed to stay." He felt sure of it now, deep in his gut. He didn't know why they were supposed to stay, but staring at his name in the mast, so clearly carved by himself, was enough to convince him.

"But Mom and Dad—" Ruby protested.

"Mom and Dad will never know," said Matt. "If the captain can take us back before we boarded the train, it won't matter."

"Exactly," said Corey. "Come on, Ruby. Two to one. Remember Mom and Dad told us to stick together, no matter what? Our future selves clearly did." He gestured to their names.

Ruby continued to stare at the names, then took a deep breath. "All right, we'll stay."

Corey whooped and jumped into the air, then grasped one of the ropes before he went toppling over the edge of the nest.

"But not for too long," said Ruby. "And we really need to be careful. Even if the captain can take us right back to where and when we left, it won't matter if one of us gets lost or Corey falls to his death. Just because we carved our names here at some point in the future doesn't mean our future selves don't get into trouble."

"If we die in the past though," said Corey, "wouldn't we be nonexistent in the future? And if we don't exist in the future, we couldn't have boarded the *Vermillion* and traveled in the past, so we never would have come on board this ship. So we must survive."

Ruby shook her head. "Stop, you're making me dizzy."

It made Matt dizzy, too, and sent a shiver up his spine. He still hadn't thought through all the implications of time travel, but the more he thought about it the more it seemed a very dizzying, delicate thing. "We'll be careful," he said. "But let's go down now." Corey and Ruby began to climb down, but Matt held back for just a moment. He had a strange feeling that he could only describe as déjà vu. Of course he had déjà vu. He'd been here before, apparently, sometime in the future. And now his future self was circling back to him, whispering in the back of his mind. It told him he was not here by chance.

8

The Crew and the Compass

Matt climbed carefully down the mast and was grateful to have his feet on the deck of the ship.

"Did you see it?" Jia asked, looking concerned yet hopeful.

Matt opened his mouth to answer but suddenly lost his balance and stumbled right into Jia, nearly knocking her over. She wrapped her arms around him, stumbled backward a few steps, and stopped them both from falling.

"Are you okay?" she asked.

"Yeah, sorry," said Matt.

"Ah! Bonding already," said the captain. He was coming up the stairs onto the deck, the white rat sitting on his shoulder. He beamed at Jia and Matt, who looked like they were embracing. Matt felt his cheeks warm as he untangled himself from Jia and stepped away. She didn't seem at all embarrassed.

"The Hudsons just climbed up to the crow's nest, sir," said Jia.

"Did you?" said the captain, clearly intrigued. "And how did you find the view?"

"It was spectacular," said Matt. "Just as you said." The captain's eyes flashed, and Matt was certain he knew exactly what was carved on the mast.

"I'm very glad to hear it," said Captain Vincent. "And I hope you're all hungry. I've ordered a feast in your honor. May I escort the young lady to the dining room?" The captain offered his arm to Ruby, and she regarded it warily, a hint of disgust on her face.

"Oh no, Captain," said Corey. "Ruby doesn't like stuff like that."

"Doesn't she?" said the captain.

"She's a *feminist*, sir," said Corey in a loud whisper. "That means she's a girl who likes to be in charge and doesn't like to depend upon men for anything."

"Is that so?" said the captain, who seemed thoroughly amused.

Ruby scowled at Corey. "I like good manners just fine," she said, taking Captain Vincent's arm. "What I *don't* like is boys telling me what I do and don't like."

The captain gave a hearty laugh. "Miss Ruby, what a fine time pirate you will make! I think we shall get on splendidly."

Matt smelled the food before he saw it—meat and garlic and onions and cheese. When they reached the dining room an enormous feast was spread over the table. It looked to be mainly French fare—soufflé, coq au vin, green beans with shallots, cucumber salad, and more pastries, cheese, fruit, and plenty of wine.

The captain sat at the head of the table. He invited Matt to sit on his right, Ruby on his left, and Corey next to Ruby. However traditionally French the food was, the table settings were rather eclectic. Each place setting was unique—different patterned bone china, pewter plates, silver bowls, and hand-crafted stoneware. There were various crystal goblets, pewter mugs, champagne flutes, and a large tin tankard. Matt's setting was an odd pairing of a plastic plate with a picture of Darth Vader and a delicate china teacup with pink rosebuds.

Jia sat next to Matt, and the little blond girl with the rope sat next to her. She peered around Jia and stared at Matt. She had the palest gray eyes he'd ever seen, and he felt as though she was seeing right into him.

"Have you met Matt yet, Pike?" said Jia. The little girl went back to her rope, picking at the knots. Matt noticed that it was actually tied around her waist, cinching up what looked like a pillowcase with holes cut for her arms and head. Along the neckline and hemline hung safety pins, hairpins, and old-fashioned hatpins, like she was trying to create a metallic sort of fringe from the contents of an old lady's sewing box.

"Pike doesn't talk," said Jia, "but she's really sweet. She likes to tie and untie knots."

"Where's she from?"

"We haven't a clue, actually," said Jia. "I found her one day in one of the food pantries, wearing nothing but a sugar sack and a rope and eating the pile of sugar she'd dumped on the floor. Poor thing! We never could figure out where or when she's from, but she really is very sweet. She helps me around the ship sometimes."

Brocco came bursting into the room, followed by Wiley, talking in a loud, brassy voice. "What do you mean, books are more powerful than guns?" said Brocco. "My guns could blast your books to smithereens!"

"The books perhaps," said Wiley, his pipe bouncing up and down in his mouth, "but never the words, my friend. Words are forever. Words can pierce the heart sharper than any sword or bullet."

"Right then," said Brocco. "You bring your books and I'll bring my guns, and we'll see whose heart gets pierced first." Brocco sat down next to Corey. He was still wearing the red cape, but he'd taken his hat off, making his features much more noticeable, the most prominent being his hair. It was dark blond and very wild, with long, crooked clumps sticking out in all directions like a bunch of crab legs. His skin was tan and weathered, and his teeth were crooked and slightly yellow, all except for one top tooth on the side that was remarkably clear and sparkly, like crystal or diamond.

"That's my seat."

Matt jumped a little and looked up to see Albert staring down at him, nostrils flared.

"Oh," said Matt. "Sorry." He started to rise, but the captain held up his hand.

"Albert," said the captain. "It's impolite to ask guests to move."

"It's all right," said Matt. "I don't mind."

"Please find another seat, Albert," said the captain quietly but with finality.

Albert blinked, clearly taken aback, but he did not argue. He pushed up his glasses on his nose, walked to the other end of the table, and plopped sulkily in the chair next to Wiley. Matt tried to offer an apologetic smile, but Albert seemed to think he was gloating and only glared in return. Matt flinched and looked away.

"I like your bracelet," said Jia. "Is it special?"

Matt looked down. He hadn't realized he'd been rubbing his thumb over it. "Oh, thanks. No. It's just something I've always worn, sort of a good-luck charm, I guess."

When Matt was little he had frequent, recurring nightmares, often about someone coming and taking him away, though he could never see the face of his kidnapper. He'd wake up screaming, and his mom or dad had to rush into the room and hold him until he fell asleep. Then one day, while walking down Fifth Avenue with his mom on their way to the museum, Matt spotted a street vendor selling crystals and jewelry with a sign written in fancy, loopy letters.

Positive Energy Crystals and Stones
Erase bad thoughts.
Calm fears.
Stop nightmares.

Matt begged and pleaded with his mother to buy him one. He was certain it would help his nightmares because the sign said so. (He was still at a stage where he believed everything he read.) Mrs. Hudson said no and pulled him along, but Matt threw a temper tantrum, which was very unlike him, and then the man offered to sell one for only a dollar, and so Mrs. Hudson, exasperated, bought it, thrust it in Matt's hand and dragged him down the street. Matt was thrilled. The stone was somewhat metallic, dark, and smooth, with a slight sparkle that seemed to shift like grains of sand in an hourglass whenever he moved it. He put it on that day and had worn it ever since. Strangely, he never did have the same nightmare again, and it had almost become as much a part of Matt as his eyes or ears.

"Do you know what the symbol means?" Jia asked.

"What?"

"The symbol. It looks Chinese."

"Oh," said Matt, rubbing his finger over the bracelet, feeling the grooves in the stone. "I always just thought it was a random design."

Jia shrugged. "Maybe it is. I never did learn the writing

system, and I can barely speak Chinese anymore." She seemed ashamed of this.

"I've studied a little Chinese," said Matt. "Did you speak Mandarin or Cantonese, or some other dialect?"

Jia shook her head. "I'm not sure. I never went to school or anything."

"Maybe you could speak with me and it would bring it back to your memory," said Matt.

Jia smiled. "Yes, I'd like that."

The captain tapped his knife to his crystal goblet. Everyone quieted their chatter and stilled. They all looked to the captain, waiting. Matt wondered if they were going to say grace. Almost. The captain recited what Matt thought was a mix between a prayer and a poem.

We drift on the sea
And rest from our noble work
To stuff our faces.

He speared a chunk of meat from one of the dishes and stuffed it in his mouth.

"The captain always recites a haiku before dinner," Jia whispered to Matt. "And we don't eat until he finishes his first bite."

The crew all watched the captain's every chew with rapt attention, but as soon as the captain swallowed, everyone converged on the food all at once, attacking it like a mass of starved piranhas.

The Hudsons all looked at each other, not quite sure what to do. Their parents had always been very particular about their manners at the dinner table, and especially coached them for when they were guests, either in other people's homes or a restaurant.

Corey shrugged and leaned into the fray, heaping food onto his plate. Ruby had to sit back to avoid his elbow, but then she shoved him out of the way and began to dish up her own food.

"Mmm . . . this is delicious," said Corey, shoveling food into his mouth. Matt was sorry he wasn't feeling particularly hungry. His queasiness had only gotten worse since the crow's nest, and now that they were sitting down, the last dregs of his adrenaline rush seemed to drain and exhaustion set in. He barely had the energy to lift a fork.

"You'll get used to it," said Jia. "The food, I mean. It was very different for me when I first came on board the *Vermillion*. I didn't like it at all. So much flavor and variety! At the orphanage all we ate was rice and cabbage."

Matt felt a little sheepish that he'd appeared to be so finicky. He dished himself up a bit of coq au vin and some potatoes, nibbling bites every now and then, but his stomach curdled. He wondered if Corey and Ruby were feeling off at all, but they were both eating hearty amounts of food.

As they ate, the crew told them where and when they were from. Brocco was from Australia, born in 1851, and had apparently been a part of a gang of bank robbers when he met the captain.

"I mean, he comes in right after we've robbed the bloody bank, steals all the money right out of our hands, and the bloody rogue had the gall to wink at me!"

"I always know a fellow time pirate when I spot one," said the captain with a smile and a wink.

"What about you, Wiley?" Ruby asked.

"I was born in Alabama," said Wiley. "Don't know what year exactly. The good captain picked me up in 1925, but I was in Chicago by then."

"You don't know what year you were born?" said Ruby.

"Well, I suppose it was somewhere around 1910. My parents both died when I was pretty young. Don't even know my own birthday!"

"How did you survive?" said Ruby.

"Begging on the streets when I was little. Pickin' pockets when I got a little older."

"You mean you stole from people? Couldn't you get a job?" Ruby asked, trying but not totally succeeding in withholding the judgment from her voice.

"No, ma'am. Weren't no paying work for a raggedy homeless illiterate black boy like me," said Wiley. "It was either steal or starve. After my mama and papa died I hitched a train to Chicago, made out pretty well for a time, and then I made the brilliant move of trying to steal from the captain! Ha-ha! There weren't no foolin' him. He caught me by the hand the instant I went for his pocket. I was scared out of my skin, thought I was going to the slammer for sho', but the good captain had pity. He saw how young and scared I was, and he hauled me on the *Vermillion* and that was that. Made me a part of the crew, taught me to read and write, and made an honest man out of me."

"Oh," said Ruby. "That's . . . nice."

"Well, I didn't have to steal my way onto the ship," said Albert, pushing his glasses up on his nose. "I was chosen by Captain Vincent to be a member of the crew. He said he'd been looking for someone like me. Right, Captain?"

"I did indeed, Albert," said the captain. "You are invaluable to our crew. I don't know what we'd do without you. Ah! See, you even inspire rhyming poetry!"

Albert beamed.

"What happened to your parents?" asked Ruby.

"My mother died when I was a baby," said Albert, "and my father was killed in your traitorous war." It took Matt a moment to realize what he was talking about, and then it hit him. Of course. Albert's father had fought for England during the American Revolution. A decidedly awkward silence followed. Matt squirmed in his chair, trying to think what he could possibly say when the captain came to the rescue.

"Yes, a sad loss," said the captain, "but luckily Albert found a new home and family just at the right time. Didn't you, Albert?"

Albert nodded and straightened in his chair.

"We're all orphans and vagabonds in one way or another," said the captain. "But on the *Vermillion* we are family, bonded by our noble cause."

"And what is your cause, exactly?" Ruby asked—a bit pointedly, Matt thought. "You call yourselves time pirates? Isn't *pirate* just another name for thief?"

"Time pirate is more of a silly nickname," said the captain. "It would be more accurate to call ourselves *time venture capitalists*, but that's not nearly as fun to say, is it?"

"So what do you invest in?" Matt asked.

"Why, having a grand time with time!" said the captain. "Time is the most precious commodity in the world, wouldn't you agree? One can always accumulate more wealth and power, but eventually everyone runs out of time and can never get more. We time pirates of the *Vermillion* are determined to live every moment to the fullest."

"Hear, hear!" said Wiley, raising his goblet. "To Captain Vincent and the *Vermillion*!" They all lifted their goblets, glasses, or mugs and drank to the captain.

The captain beamed. He was idly swinging the black compass back and forth on its chain. Matt's attention zeroed in on it. It was no bigger than Matt's palm and it was not made of metal, as Matt had supposed at first, but what looked like polished, sparkling black stone. There were three layers of dials all surrounded by symbols, numerals, and notches etched into the rock and inlaid with gold. It was stunning. It almost looked more like a piece of jewelry than a navigation tool, and yet Matt could almost detect a deep and powerful energy swirling around it, pulsing inside of it, though perhaps that was in his head. He did have a slight pulsing at his temples. Matt squinted at the markings surrounding the dials. Some were Roman numerals, but others were foreign to him. "What do these symbols mean? Is that pi?" He pointed, and the captain jerked the compass away. Matt flinched.

"You mustn't touch," said the captain sharply, all warmth and friendliness suddenly gone.

"Sorry," said Matt a little sheepishly.

The captain softened and smiled. "It's perfectly all right. It's natural to be curious about such a powerful object, but the compass, like the ship, can be very temperamental and takes years of training to use properly. If you were to turn the dials willy-nilly you could send us into someplace we might never wish to go—like in the middle of a battle!"

"Hear, hear!" said Brocco. "Let's go to a bloody battle! I could use a good brawl." He took a big gulp out of the tin tankard. His face was a bit red now.

"Not me," said Wiley. "I prefer peace and books, thank you. And a good pipe." He patted his suit pocket where the top of his wooden pipe was sticking out.

"What's the compass made of?" Matt asked. "Is that onyx?"

"Obsidian," said the captain, tucking the compass back into his sleeve. Matt wished he could look at it some more.

"So how does it work?" Matt asked. "Where did the compass come from? Did you make it? And the ship? How does the ship transform? I mean, what's the power source and the chemical makeup? Is it a cellular organism or a machine or both?"

Captain Vincent chuckled and rubbed at his beard. "I'm afraid some of your questions are above my intelligence."

"He can't help it," said Corey. "Matt's above most people's intelligence most of the time."

Matt looked away, his cheeks warming a bit. He knew he could come off as a bit of a know-it-all sometimes, even if he wasn't trying to be. It was one of the reasons he had so few friends.

"Well, that's certainly nothing to be ashamed of," said the captain. "I'm sure Mateo will do great things. Now to answer *some* of your questions, I built neither the Obsidian Compass nor the *Vermillion*," said the captain. "The *Vermillion* started out as a normal ship, a naval ship in the British Navy, but she developed a special relationship with the Obsidian Compass not entirely understood by myself. They're almost like an old married couple, if you will. Sometimes they get along, and other times they have their squabbles and don't always cooperate with each other, which never bodes well for the rest of us. You have to treat them both very gently." He patted the table as though he were trying to placate a tantrum-prone two-year-old.

"And the compass?" Ruby asked. "Who made it?" She sounded much more casual than Matt, but he was glad someone else was asking questions.

"That is actually a great mystery," said the captain. "No one knows. At least, no one on board the *Vermillion* knows."

"How did you get it?" Corey asked, his cheeks bulging with food like a chipmunk. Their parents would have been so embarrassed. "Did you steal it?"

"Corey . . . ," said Ruby.

"No, no, it's a fair question," said the captain. "There are certainly many who would steal it, if they could. No, I did not steal it. I inherited it from another time pirate," said Captain Vincent, "one of the first, and the greatest time pirate I ever knew."

"What happened to him?" asked Corey.

A hush came over the table. Brocco froze with a whole chicken thigh in his mouth.

"Her," said the captain. "What happened to *her*." There was such intensity in the captain's voice and something told Matt they were on delicate ground, but Corey didn't always pick up on those kinds of signals.

"Sorry. What happened to her?"

"She's dead," said the captain in a hollow voice.

There was an awkward, heavy silence. Matt definitely sensed that this was not a subject the crew spoke of openly at dinner, but he couldn't help himself.

"I'm sorry," he blurted. "But if you can travel through time, can't you go back to a time when she was alive and simply save her life, like you did with the *Mona Lisa*?"

"If only," said the captain. "While the compass can lead this ship to nearly any time or place in this world, there are certain limitations to what we can actually do, especially when it comes to people. Once certain events occur at any given time, it's very difficult, often dangerous, to try to change them. I can't just go back and find someone from my past as if they were a painting."

"Why not?" Ruby asked.

"Because they're a living thing, and so am I, and that makes everything so much more complicated. The interaction of living things, especially interactions between humans, in the space-time continuum is a delicate, intricate web, the disturbance of which can cause any number of disasters. There are many risks to time travel, many potential pitfalls, one of the most dangerous being seeing yourself in the past."

"What happens if you see yourself in the past?" Matt asked.

"Hmm. It's easier to show you than just use words." He looked around. "Jia, do you have any thread?"

Jia reached into one of her many bulging pockets and

pulled out a small spool of black thread.

"Thank you." Captain Vincent unraveled the thread and wrapped one end around Matt's finger and the other around Ruby's, across the table. "Time is more like a circle, or a sphere even, like the world. It *bends*, you see, and eventually meets at the other side. But for our purposes we're going to pretend time is a straight line. Hold steady, please." The captain opened his jacket and whipped out a dagger. Matt flinched a little, and Ruby gasped and jumped in her seat. The captain, however, gently placed the knife on the string. "Now let's say you exist along a certain portion of the string—born in, what, 2007?"

"I was," said Matt. "The twins were born in 2008."

"Close enough. We'll say the point of your birth is here." He pointed with his finger at a random place on the thread. "Let's say you're now here." He moved the knife a few inches down, "and you'll die in . . . well, who knows? Let's say 2099." He moved the knife to another place almost at the end of the thread.

"If you go back to the time when you were born and see yourself as an infant, you're far enough apart on the time line that it won't matter much. You might experience some strange side effects, dizziness or a little nausea, but nothing cataclysmic will occur. But if you see yourself in the not-so-distant past, like we traveled back to yesterday and we got the timing wrong and you saw yourself as you are now, then . . ."

He moved his finger and the knife right next to each other and the thread snapped. "You've put too much weight on the delicate thread. You create a fracture in the timeline, one that can cause any number of calamities. You could destroy yourself, quite literally. Or you could cause a natural disaster that could potentially harm others. It could be something as simple as a bolt of lightning, or a cloudburst, and no harm done. Or you could cause some real damage with an earthquake or a tornado."

"A tornado?" said Matt. "A tornado is caused by warm winds from the south colliding with cold air from the north. I created one during the science fair in fourth grade with a plastic bottle and dry ice." He'd also taken first place, but he didn't mention that.

"Brilliant!" said Captain Vincent. "You prove my words with your own! *You* created the tornado! What creates a tornado in the real world, or an earthquake, or hurricane, or tsunami? Shifts in the space-time continuum can shift winds, water, and land. It's all connected, and believe me, it's not something to trifle with. You could destroy not just yourself but an entire village or city, perhaps the world. It could all just collapse like a castle of cards."

Matt shivered a little. He didn't have the courage to ask if the captain and his crew had ever caused some terrible disasters with their time-traveling. He remembered seeing an earthquake in South America on the news a couple of years ago that killed hundreds and injured thousands. Could it have been caused by this compass? Or some other group of time travelers? How many could actually do this?

"What if one of us had been left behind in Paris?" Ruby asked. "Would you have just left us there?"

"For a few weeks perhaps," said the captain. "We couldn't risk going to a time where we'd already been. We'd have to come back a little later than that. But rest assured we would come for you. Unless you'd done something terrible, of course. Then it would be *au revoir.*" He grinned at them. Matt wasn't quite sure if he was joking or not.

"But what about taking us home?" said Ruby. "You said you could take us to the exact time and place you'd found us. Isn't that a risk?"

"No, no, no, that's an entirely different matter," said the captain quickly. "Because it was the first time you boarded the *Vermillion*, we can take you back right where we found you with very little consequence. It's only when you start to time-travel a good deal that things get complicated. We have to keep very good track of all our missions and travels. Wiley keeps a very thorough record."

"Yes, it's in my library," said Wiley, lighting his pipe and taking a puff. "Come see it and I'll find good books for all of you!"

Matt's brain was spinning, trying to take in all the information. It didn't answer all his questions, but he didn't think he could absorb any more just now. His universe had just expanded. Suddenly the world was full of possibilities so much bigger than he ever thought possible. He suddenly felt hot and dizzy.

"So what's next?" Corey finally asked. "Do you have another mission planned? Can we come? Where are we going? And when?"

Matt smiled. Even Corey couldn't help pestering now.

"We don't have another mission planned quite yet," said the captain. "I'm still working out the details, but we would be delighted for you three to come along, if you wish it."

"Sounds good to me," said Corey.

"And you, Miss Ruby?"

"I guess if we can get back home right when we left we can afford to stay for a little while," said Ruby.

"And Mateo?"

"I think . . . ," said Matt, but he couldn't finish his sentence. A wave of nausea suddenly hit him hard.

"You okay, bro?" Corey asked.

Matt's stomach twisted. "I think . . . I just need . . ." Matt tried to stand. He needed to run to the bathroom, but it was too late. He leaned over and vomited right onto his plate. There wasn't much in his stomach, but what was there came out.

"Ew," said Corey, leaning away.

"I'm okay," said Matt. He tried again to stand but collapsed right back in his chair. He was not okay.

9

Time Sick

Matt closed his eyes, trying to still the spinning of the room. The captain leaned over and placed his hand on Matt's forehead, then lifted his eyelids like a doctor might to inspect his pupils.

"Ah. I was wondering when one of you would come down with it," said the captain. "A little sooner than I would have thought."

"Is he seasick?" Ruby asked.

"No, he's time sick."

"Time sick?" said Corey. "You mean he's sick from time-traveling?"

"Of course," said the captain. "You can't expect to travel miles and years in such a short time and not expect some physical effects, or even mental ones, for that matter. Mateo came down with it a little sooner than most, but the time sickness usually visits all of us at some point or other. Pike, go and fetch some of the American food in the storeroom for Mateo, some of the things we picked up in New York. Quick now."

Pike hopped off her chair and scampered away, pins tinkling along the bottom of her pillowcase dress.

"I don't think he should eat anything," said Ruby. "He'll just throw up again."

Matt opened his mouth to agree, but he couldn't get any words out. He heaved again.

"No, no," said Captain Vincent. "Believe me, this is the best remedy. To eat something from your own time and country can help stabilize your brain and body, put them back in harmony with each other."

In a few minutes Pike returned with a box of crackers, a can of Cheez Whiz, and a bottle of Coke. The captain tore open the box, squirted a glob of cheese on a cracker, and brought it to Matt's mouth.

"Come on, Mateo, eat up," he coaxed. Matt shook his head. He was certain that would only make him sicker. "I promise it will make you feel better," said the captain. Reluctantly, Matt opened his mouth. The captain shoved the cracker in, and he chewed. "There we are," said the captain. "Have another." He shoved in another cracker before Matt could refuse. The captain opened the bottle of Coke, and Matt took a large, fizzy gulp that burned down his throat and chest. He'd never thought he'd see the day when he was forced to eat junk food in order to feel better, but it did work somewhat. He was still shaky, but at least he didn't feel like he was going to throw up anymore.

"So . . . when will I get sick?" Corey asked eagerly. "And do you have any Cool Ranch Doritos, by chance?"

"Hard to predict," said the captain. "You might get sick tomorrow, or it could take years of travel before you start to feel any effects, and the symptoms can vary. It's different for everyone, but food from your particular era and country seems to help in most cases. We try to keep stores for all the crew. You're lucky we just happened to pick up some food in New York at the time you came aboard."

"When I start to feel a little time sick I find reading books from around the time I was born helps," said Wiley. "A little W. E. B. Du Bois or Winnie-the-Pooh! That's a grand book."

"Or just change your clothes," said Brocco. "Every time I start to feel the time sickness I get a new pair of shoes." He clicked his heels together two times. His shoes were bright floral oxfords.

"I think we need to go home," said Ruby. "Matt doesn't have the best health, Captain. He sometimes has seizures."

"I'm not having a seizure," said Matt, trying to muster up some energy. "And we're not going home."

"It's not advisable to travel when you're time sick anyway," said the captain. "I think it best we stay put for now, let Matt get his time-traveling legs beneath him before we go any-where."

"But what if he does have a seizure?" said Ruby. "Or what if he gets worse? Is one of you a doctor?"

"We did have a doctor once," said Wiley, "but he ran away with a belly dancer in Egypt, and we never saw him again."

"Bloody idiot," said Brocco. "Never liked him anyway."

"I don't need a doctor," said Matt. "Or a hospital. I'm fine."

"But—"

"I'm *fine*." Matt sat up straight. The room was still spin-ning a little, but he forced himself to look his sister fiercely in the eye. He was more determined than ever. He was *not* going home. Not now, anyway. How many opportunities like this would come his way? If they went home they might never get a second chance to be on the *Vermillion*, and he still had so many questions about the compass and the ship, how it all worked, all the places they had traveled and would travel, their missions, and a thousand other things. And he kept see-ing his name on the mast. He was supposed to be here.

Ruby and Corey shared a look. Even Corey looked a little worried. "You sure you're okay, bro?"

"Yes. Honestly, I already feel better." He ate another cracker with cheese and forced a smile.

"It's been a long, eventful day," said the captain. "A bit of rest will help the time sickness as well. I'm sure you're all exhausted."

"Where will we sleep?" Ruby asked.

"Can we sleep in the crow's nest?" Corey asked.

Matt groaned. He nearly vomited thinking about climbing up there right now.

"I would say yes if I trusted *Vermillion* to behave," said the captain, "but the truth is she can be a bit of a trickster at times. She's been known to transform without warning, and the crow's nest is probably not the safest place for that. I had Santiago prepare a room in case you *did* decide to stay, even if just for a night or two."

"Santiago?" asked Ruby. "You mean the *rat* prepared our room?"

"It's nothing so fancy," said the captain. "But Santiago's a very domestic and hospitable rat. He quite enjoys housekeeping and making things comfortable for us. Santiago, why don't you scurry ahead and light the lanterns, will you?"

Santiago squeaked and popped out of the captain's jacket. He skittered down his side and paused at the top of the stairs leading to the lower decks. He turned around and beckoned with his tail for them to follow, like a rodent bellboy leading some guests to their hotel room.

"Follow the tail!" said the captain.

Their room was on the second deck, about midway down the ship. When the captain opened the door, Santiago scurried up the wall with a match between his teeth. He struck the match and lit a sconce, illuminating a small room that reminded Matt of an old person's attic. Three hammocks hung in the corners. On one side of the room stood a small wooden table with a Delft pottery pitcher and washbasin. A gilded mirror hung above it. Paintings hung on the walls, landscapes and portraits, modern art that didn't look like anything. There were old trunks and chests. One of them was open and full of seashells and sand. "Ooh, these are pretty." Ruby reached for one of the big, swirly pink seashells when a claw suddenly shot out, snapping at Ruby's fingers. She screamed and tossed the shell back into the trunk, which made some of the sand spill onto the floor.

"What the . . . ," said Corey as the claw retreated back into the shell and Santiago scurried over to sweep the sand up with his tail, glaring at Ruby.

"Pardon the surprise," said the captain. "The *Vermillion* has somewhat of a habit of taking in live creatures on some of our travels. She seems to think they're her pets."

"Oh . . . really?" said Ruby. "What else has she brought on board? Anything very wild or . . . or dangerous?" She looked around cautiously, as though a lion might burst out and attack her.

"No, no, usually harmless creatures," said the captain. "Stray kittens and bunnies mostly, though once when we went to Africa she somehow brought a baby elephant on board! It was a real disaster. Poor Jia was repairing the ship for weeks."

"That's awesome," said Corey. "Can I get a pet too?" Corey

was always begging their parents for a pet—a puppy, a ferret, a snake. But the answer was always a firm no. They wouldn't even allow a goldfish.

"Of course!" said the captain. "I think everyone should know the delights of animal companionship. Santiago is a great friend to me. Come, Santiago, these children need their rest." The rat swept up one more bit of sand with his tail, climbed up the captain, and tucked himself inside his jacket.

"If you ever need anything don't hesitate to come and see me. I am at your service. We are very glad you've come aboard the *Vermillion*. Good night!" He gave a short bow and shut the door, leaving the Hudsons alone.

"What a day, huh?" said Corey, sinking into one of the hammocks.

"It felt more like years," said Ruby.

"Well, it was, wasn't it?" said Corey. "We traveled over a century!"

"I wonder where else he'll take us," said Ruby. "Where would you like to go?"

"I don't know," said Corey. "We've never been anywhere, so it all sounds good to me. Maybe we could travel to the dinosaur age and I can get a baby woolly mammoth for a pet!"

"Wrong age," said Matt a little sleepily.

"What?" said Corey.

"Dinosaurs lived like a hundred million years ago, in the

Mesozoic Era. The woolly mammoth lived like ten thousand years ago, in the Ice Age."

"You're such a nerd," Corey grumbled.

Matt was too exhausted to reply or care. He kicked off his shoes and climbed into the hammock. It enveloped him like a cocoon and rocked him back and forth. Corey and Ruby continued their conversation about where they would go and when, what they'd like to see and who they would want to meet, but Matt couldn't process their conversation in his mushed-up, scrambled brain. Within moments he was fast asleep. He dreamed about stealing the *Mona Lisa* while riding a woolly mammoth being chased by a T. rex inside the Metropolitan Museum of Art. He knew it made no sense, but he couldn't make his brain correct the mistakes. Oh well.

10

The Vermillion

Matt woke to the smell of cinnamon and bacon and a loud *bang*! He shot out of sleep, flailed all his limbs at once, and flipped out of his hammock, landing hard on the wooden floor. It took him a minute to figure out where he was.

I'm on a ship, he remembered. *A time-traveling ship. I just traveled to Paris in 1911 and stole the* Mona Lisa *from the Louvre.*

"Careful there, bro," said Corey, laughing. He was swinging in his own hammock with his legs sticking out.

"Are you okay?" Ruby asked. She was standing in front of the mirror, braiding her hair.

"I'm fine," said Matt, picking himself up. He teetered a little but stabilized himself against the wall.

"How are you feeling?" Ruby asked.

"Better, I think. Just hungry." The smell of cinnamon and bacon hit his nose again, and his stomach grumbled loudly.

He was starving, which he supposed was a good sign.

"Me too," said Corey. "I've been smelling breakfast for the last hour, but Ruby said we couldn't leave the room without you."

"How would you have felt if you'd woken up in this room all alone?"

Corey shrugged. "Like I had a little breathing room for once."

Bang! The explosion was followed by what Matt thought was laughter. "What is that?"

"No idea, but it woke me up this morning," said Ruby a little grumpily.

"Maybe they're shooting cannons," said Corey. "Maybe they've spotted an enemy ship!"

"Who's the enemy in Nowhere in No Time?" said Ruby.

"Other time pirates? Come on, I really need to pee. Ruby wouldn't let me do that either." He hopped out of his hammock and strode for the door. When he opened it, Jia was standing right there.

"Good morning!" she said brightly.

"Ah!" Corey shouted, and stumbled back.

"Sorry, I didn't mean to scare you! Captain Vincent wanted me to check on you and see if you needed anything."

"Yes," said Corey. "I could use your amazing flushing toilet again, pronto."

"Of course!" said Jia. "I'll show you the one closest to your room. It has a shower, too, if you want. And after breakfast Brocco wants to measure you all for clothes and costumes for future missions."

"Do we have another mission planned?" Corey asked eagerly.

"Not yet," said Jia. "Our last mission did some damage to the rudder, apparently. I'll need to make some repairs before we can travel again. But don't worry, there's plenty to do on the *Vermillion*. You won't be bored for a moment!"

After they'd all used the bathroom they went to the dining hall where they'd eaten dinner the night before. The table was now spread with a huge breakfast buffet—warm cinnamon rolls, boiled eggs, fresh-squeezed orange juice, fruit, pastries, and a mound of crisp bacon and plump sausages. There were also some Pop-Tarts and a few boxes of cold cereal—Lucky Charms and Froot Loops, and a box of some cereal called "Sugaroos" that Matt thought had to be from the 1960s.

"Medicine," said Corey, reaching for the Lucky Charms.

"You're not even sick," said Ruby.

"It's preventive."

Mrs. Hudson never bought cold cereal, not even plain, healthy kinds. She would have regarded these as candy rather than a decent breakfast, but Matt poured himself a little bowl of Froot Loops and also dished up a bit of everything else.

BANG! The explosion was much louder now, and it was followed by a high-pitched, somewhat maniacal laugh.

"What *is* that?" said Ruby.

"That's Brocco," said Jia. "He's doing target practice."

"With guns?" said Corey. "Can we do it too?"

"Sure, Brocco loves to teach people how to shoot and explode things. It's one of his special skills. That and clothes. He's our Weapons and Disguise Master."

"Excellent," said Corey, rubbing his hands together. "I've always wanted to shoot a gun."

"Mom would go ballistic," said Ruby.

"I know!" said Corey, delighted. He took a huge bite of Lucky Charms and chewed with his mouth open.

After they'd finished breakfast, Jia led them above deck. The first thing Matt saw was Brocco standing in the middle of the deck holding a gun. He was wearing a completely new outfit this morning, perhaps even wackier than the one he'd been wearing yesterday—a fur vest, blue-and-yellow-striped bellbottoms, and pointy purple boots with gold buckles. Around his forehead he wore a thick gold headband that pushed all his hair upward so that it spilled over the sides, making his hair looked like a hairy plant growing out of a pot.

Brocco reached into a crate, tossed something up in the air, and shot it with his gun.

BANG!

The object exploded and rained down over the deck. Matt thought it was a dish or something, but it didn't make that much noise when it fell.

"Oh no, Brocco stole the vegetables again," said Jia, shaking her head. "Agnes will not be amused."

Brocco pulled out another object from a crate and tossed it high up into the air. It looked like a head of lettuce or cabbage. He shot his gun and leafy chunks rained down on the deck.

Brocco finally noticed them all watching. He smiled and waved.

"Want a turn?" Brocco asked, holding out the gun.

Corey practically ran toward Brocco, hands outstretched. Brocco set a large pumpkin on the edge of the ship then showed Corey how to hold the gun and cock it. Corey, being just a little overeager, pulled the trigger right away and was knocked back like he'd shot himself.

Ruby yelped and covered her eyes.

"He's all right," said Jia. "Just a little backfire. I'm going to go check out that rudder now. I'll see you around!"

Brocco picked up the gun and helped Corey up. Corey was a little more hesitant this time, but he took the gun in his hands and Brocco stood behind him to give him some extra support. Corey aimed the gun, and cocked it, focusing on the pumpkin. Ruby plugged her ears and turned her head while Corey pulled the trigger.

BANG!

The pumpkin exploded and sprayed all over the deck.

"Woo-hoo!" Brocco crowed, and did a little jig.

Corey grinned. "Can I do it again?"

"Sure, you can," said Brocco. "What's your least favorite vegetable?"

"Eggplant," he said.

"Let me see . . ." Brocco pulled out a big purple eggplant and set it on the side of the deck. Corey set himself up this time, but Brocco still stood behind him for support. He shot and the eggplant was no more.

"He's a natural!" said Brocco. "A little bullet himself."

Corey grinned.

"Do you think this is safe?" Matt whispered to Ruby. "Mom and Dad would never in a million years let us handle a gun."

But Ruby wasn't listening to him. She wasn't even watching Corey anymore. Her gaze had moved to the other end of the ship where Captain Vincent was swinging around a sword, slashing at a wooden post. His focus was razor sharp. He was clearly a master swordsman, and Ruby watched, mesmerized, until the captain finally noticed them and paused. He wiped the sweat from his brow.

"Good morning!" he said. "How are you feeling, Mateo?"

"Fine," said Matt. "Better."

"Very good. Glad we don't have to feed you to the sharks! And Miss Ruby? Did you sleep well?"

She nodded, still staring at the captain's sword.

"This is only my practice sword," he said. "It isn't sharp. Would you like to try?"

Ruby grew suddenly shy. She looked at Matt as though she needed someone else's permission.

"Go ahead," said Matt, smirking a little.

Ruby stepped forward. She gingerly took the sword from the captain's outstretched hand.

"It's a little big for you, but I'm sure Brocco can find you a proper fit."

Ruby rotated the sword in her hand, admiring it.

The captain showed Ruby how to grip the sword, the proper posture and stance, and then took her through a series of simple movements to get used to the feel and weight of it in her hands. Soon he was adding footwork, simple steps forward and back while they moved the sword up and down and back and forth. Ruby moved fluidly, her feet weaving smoothly over the deck as she moved the sword up and down and side to side.

"Good! Very good," said the captain. "You look as though you've done this before."

"Our mom is an expert on swords," said Ruby proudly. "She has a really big collection from all over the world."

"Really?" said the captain, brows raised. "Your mother must be a fascinating woman. Has she taught you how to use the sword, then?"

Ruby shook her head. "She's not that kind of an expert. We're not allowed to touch any of her swords. But I've always wanted to learn."

This was news to Matt. Ruby was always so calm and practical, it was surprising to see her get excited about anything associated with violence.

"Well, on the *Vermillion* a sword is a tool and dueling is an art! I would be honored to teach you."

Ruby beamed, and her cheeks flushed. Matt couldn't remember the last time he'd seen her this excited.

"Now, Mateo," said the captain. "It seems your brother has a passion for guns, and your sister for swords."

"It's not so surprising," said Matt. "Corey's always been a bit explosive, and Ruby's a lot like our mom."

"Am not," said Ruby, jabbing the captain's sword at one of the masts. "Mom would never pick up a sword except to carbon-date it."

The captain laughed as Ruby started making circles around them, swiping the sword. "So what will be your passion, Mateo, as a time pirate?"

"I don't know, sir." He didn't have any desire to pick up a sword or a gun.

"Come now, everyone has something they're passionate about. What sorts of things do you like?"

Matt shrugged and shoved his hands in his pockets. What he was really interested in on this ship was the Obsidian Compass. He wouldn't mind getting a closer look, figuring out how it worked, but he doubted the captain would be willing to teach him how to use it in the same way he was teaching

Ruby how to use a sword. He seemed very protective of it.

"I like baseball," he blurted.

"Baseball?" Clearly that was not the answer the captain was expecting. Matt wasn't even sure why he said it.

Matt nodded. "Yeah, I mean, I'm not very good at playing it. I just like watching the games, I guess, and studying all the statistics and things. It's a very strategic game, and there's always more going on than meets the eye."

The captain cocked his head at Matt, clearly amused. "Strategy can be a very useful skill on the *Vermillion.* We always need good planning for our missions. Perhaps you will be able to assist me."

Matt nodded. "I'd like that."

Just then Jia poked her head above the wheel of the ship, a screwdriver in one hand and a bit of metal in the other. Her hands and face were smudged with oil, but she was smiling.

"I think I found the problem, Captain!" said Jia, waving something in the air. "Some of the train got stuck in the axle."

"Ah! I should have known," said the captain, smiling and shaking his head.

"The train?" Matt asked.

"Sometimes that happens during transformation," said Captain Vincent. "A few pieces of whatever the *Vermillion* turned into get stuck in parts of the ship as it changes back. Most of the time it doesn't make a difference, but sometimes it can cause damage that keeps us from traveling until it's fixed."

"So we can travel again now?" said Matt.

"Yes, though we'll want to take it easy," said the captain. "You could still experience some time sickness, or your brother or sister could come down with it too."

"Hey!" shouted Corey, waving at them from the other end of the ship. "Come on! Brocco wants to fit us for new clothes in his shop!"

Ruby reluctantly handed the captain back his sword. "Can I have another lesson tomorrow?"

"Of course!" said the captain. "I will expect you to train very hard during your time here on the *Vermillion*!"

"Can I join you in the shop?" said Jia, coming down the steps from the wheel. "I'm looking for some pants with more pockets. I'm running out of space in my vest."

"'Course you can, Li'l Hammerhead!" said Brocco. "If we don't find anything, I'll make it for you."

"Hammerhead?" Matt asked.

Jia smiled. "That's his nickname for me. Because of my tools." She patted her pocketed vest.

"And because she's smart as a shark," said Brocco. "I'll have nicknames for all of you soon enough, once I get to know you a bit. I've already dubbed your brother Li'l Bullet, and I think your sister should be Li'l Blade. There! Bullet and Blade, how about that?"

"If the name fits, wear it!" said the captain. "Enjoy Brocco's shop. You'll never see another like it!"

That was an understatement, Matt thought. Brocco's "shop" was perhaps the greatest paradox Matt had ever seen. It looked like the backroom of a runway fashion show mixed with an artillery room. One side of the room held shelves stacked floor to ceiling with colorful fabric, thread, yarn, and baskets of sewing materials and tools. Movable clothes racks hung full with dresses, coats, and shirts. On the other side of the room there hung swords, daggers, spears, axes, guns, and a number of other weapons that looked to be from all different eras and countries. From the ceiling hung a collection of hats—wide brimmed hats and bonnets with flowers and lace, ribbons and feathers, little cloches with netted veils, top hats, fedoras, golf caps, and sailor hats. Dangling between the hats were what looked like cannon balls, hand grenades, and bundles of dynamite.

"Wouldn't Mom love to get her hands on some of those swords?" said Ruby, her neck craned upward at all the swords on the wall.

"Of course! Li'l Blade's gonna need her own sword. Let me see if we can find a good size for you." Brocco browsed the swords and pulled a smaller one down. "There! That should be a right fit!"

Ruby rotated the sword in her hand, admiring it.

"Now all we need to do is find you the proper outfit. A good weapon is always nice to have, but never underestimate the power of good fashion when facing enemies." With lightning speed, Brocco drew his pistol and cocked it. Ruby yelped and dropped the sword. Matt jumped, and Corey raised his hands, backing away.

"He-he-he-he!" Brocco laughed, high-pitched and hysterical. "You look ready to wet yourselves! Don't worry. It's not loaded. I always practice good gun safety." He raised the gun to the ceiling and pulled the trigger. There was a huge blast. Brocco fell backward over his chair and his legs went over his head. Ruby screamed and crouched to the floor as debris fell from the ceiling and smoked filled the room. Matt coughed and waved it away.

Brocco stood up, brushing himself off. "Oopsie daisies! Guess I left one in there."

"Brocco!" shouted a voice above them. "You just destroyed a very valuable ceramic pot from twelfth-century Rome!"

Brocco winced. "Sorry, Al! I'll make you a new dinner jacket if you want. Or would you like a gun?"

"Don't call me Al! You know I hate that name!"

"Well, you didn't like Bert either. How about Bertie? Bertie Beans? You like beans, don't you? He never takes to the nicknames," Brocco whispered to Matt.

"I'll be up to repair the damage in the floor, Albert!" called Jia.

Only a growl came as a response.

"Let's get started on our new crewmates!" Brocco pulled a measuring tape from around his neck and without warning wrapped it around Matt's head, then his waist, stretching it down his arms and legs and across his shoulders. He measured Corey and then Ruby, too, and then marked it all down in pencil inside a little leather notebook.

"Now we'll need to get you some new outfits," said Brocco. "Can't have you running around in the same clothes all the time, can we?" He started rifling through the clothes racks.

Matt was a little concerned, based on Brocco's fashion tastes. He looked like he put all fashion eras in a blender with the lid off. But they *did* need clothes besides what they were wearing if they were going to stay for more than a day or two. It wasn't as though they had packed for this adventure.

Corey seemed to find it all very entertaining and tried on all sorts of weird outfits—a baggy pinstripe suit and bowler hat, a velvet smoking jacket with breeches, a kimono, leather chaps, lederhosen, and finally a kilt and Glengarry cap with a giant red pom-pom on top. "Look at me! Ain't I a bonnie lad?" He put his hands on his hips and did a little jig.

Matt laughed. "Definitely keep that one."

Brocco kept trying to throw sparkly, frilly dresses to Ruby, which she politely but firmly refused.

Brocco sighed. "One day the *Vermillion* will pick up a dress-wearing girl."

"But I can't swordfight in a dress, can I?" said Ruby, waving her sword in the air.

"True, true," said Brocco. "I suppose we'll have to

compromise." In the end Matt thought Ruby compromised a great deal by taking some sparkly, sequined shirts, a pair of floral pants, and a frilly pink nightgown, which Matt could tell disgusted Ruby, but seemed to appease Brocco somewhat in the dress department.

Finally Brocco turned his attention to Matt. "And what shall we put on you?"

Matt suddenly felt a bit panicked. "I don't need anything fancy," he said. "Something plain and simple will work just fine for me."

"Plain?" said Brocco, as though Matt had just said a dirty word. "Simple? Where's the fun in that? Have some sense, boy. We have to be plain and simple often enough. I say take every opportunity to express a little personality." In Matt's opinion, Brocco went way above and beyond personality.

Matt's heart lurched as Brocco pulled out a gold sequined jacket and held it up to Matt's chest. "No, not at all your color." Brocco tossed the jacket aside. He spent the better part of an hour making Matt try on outlandish jackets, frilly blouses, and feathered hats. He was never satisfied and tossed clothing all around. In the end Matt was outfitted in what he felt was an awkward Halloween costume. He wore white knee breeches, blue-and-red-striped socks and mustard-yellow oxfords, a violet My Little Pony T-shirt (with pink sparkles), and a long waistcoat, much like the captain's, only it was navy blue with brass buttons, instead of black.

"Ah, now that's more like it!" said Brocco, beaming.

Matt had never cared much about his looks or fashion, but this just went to show that even he could be embarrassed by an outfit. Corey and Ruby were in fits of silent laughter while Matt looked longingly at his pile of clothes on the floor.

"Just needs a final touch." Brocco brought out a Yankees cap, but this was where Matt drew a hard line. He ducked out of the way.

"I can't wear that," he said.

"But everyone wears these in New York!" said Brocco, waving the Yankees hat. "It's the one fashion I can get behind in that crazy city."

"Not me. I'm a Mets fan." He really wished he had his Mets hat with him now. Stupid locker thief.

"Come on, don't be stubborn. Just try it on and see how it looks." Brocco tried to push the hat on Matt's head, but he ducked out of the way and hid behind one of the clothing racks.

"Give it up, Brocco," said Corey, laughing. "He'd sooner eat that thing than wear it."

"Fine," said Brocco, tossing the hat aside. "But you look unfinished, and I think you should reconsider."

"That is probably true," said Corey. "We all know the Mets don't have a chance of winning."

"It's not about winning," said Matt. "It's about loyalty."

"Ah!" said Brocco. "Now that *is* a fashion we can all

appreciate, especially the captain. Nothing's so important on the *Vermillion* as loyalty. If we can't trust each other, we can't be a real crew, you know. First lesson as a time pirate. Second is to always pick the right footwear. Who wants some new shoes? Look, these are lots of fun!" He pulled out some orange scuba-diving flippers. Matt felt it wise to keep hidden a while longer.

"Is he a bit . . . crazy?" Corey asked Jia, pointing his thumb back when they'd left Brocco's shop, their arms stacked with several changes of clothes.

"Brocco?" said Jia. "No. He's just . . . what's that word? Eccentric. We all are, I suppose. I mean, when you travel to as many places and times as us, you start to realize that 'normal' is a very relative matter."

Matt guessed that was true. He hadn't thought too much about how his environment and culture had shaped who he was, but then he wondered how different he would be if he'd been left in the orphanage in Colombia, never adopted by his parents or anyone else.

"I have to go up to the gallery," said Jia. "Albert's probably having a fit right now."

"Is that where you keep all the stuff you steal?" said Corey. "Can we come too?"

Jia hesitated. "You can, but just a warning, Albert's *really* picky about all the investments up there. You can't touch anything. Better yet, try not to even breathe."

"Don't worry," said Matt. "We practically grew up in a museum. We know the drill."

"I need to go get some tools and supplies. Why don't you go put your clothes away and I'll meet you right back here."

When they returned a few minutes later, Jia was waiting for them with a toolbox, a fresh plank of wood, and a jar of peanut butter.

Indeed, when they arrived at the gallery, Albert eyed them all with deep mistrust. "Don't touch anything," he said.

"We won't," said Matt politely. "We'll be very careful."

Albert curled his lip at Matt but let them inside.

"Where's the damage?" said Jia. Albert pointed toward the back wall of the room.

"I've already cleaned up the pot and made a full report for the captain," said Albert. "Brocco ought to be discarded for such behavior."

"You know the captain won't do that," said Jia, kneeling down where the gunshot had blown out a good chunk of the floor.

"He could have killed me!"

Jia took out a saw and began to cut a piece of wood from the fresh plank she'd brought with her.

Matt glanced all around the room, mesmerized by its contents. Paintings and tapestries covered the walls. Sculptures and pottery were stacked all over, and there were glass cases filled with crowns, jewelry, and old pocket watches.

Albert was standing in front of an oil painting on an easel, a brush in hand, though he wasn't painting, Matt knew. He was restoring. He had a tray with several bottles of solvents to safely remove debris and old varnish. It was a familiar sight and smell to Matt, as he'd seen their own mother with very similar supplies.

Ruby came closer to inspect the painting. It was of a man and two little girls. She let out a little gasp. "That's a Degas," she said in a near whisper.

"I *know*," said Albert, clearly annoyed. "It's called *Count Lepic and His Daughters*. We rescued it from thieves in Switzerland in 2008, and it will be returned in Serbia in 2012."

Ruby watched him as he brushed over the painting, and then her attention was caught by something else. "Wow," she said. "What is that?" She had her face up against a tall glass case. Inside was the most stunning piece of jewelry Matt had ever seen. Several enormous diamonds the size of Matt's nose were all connected by a web of more diamonds and rubies.

"That's the Patiala necklace," said Albert. "Nearly three thousand diamonds, and that large one, the 'DeBeers,' is two hundred and thirty-five carats."

"I think Captain Vincent stole it for the old captain, before she died," whispered Jia. "I think the captain was in love with her."

"How did she die?" Ruby asked, also in a whisper. It seemed this subject required it.

"It's somewhat of a mystery," said Jia. "The captain hardly ever speaks of her. All I know is she died in a tragic accident on one of their missions. A fire or explosion of some kind."

"That's so sad," said Ruby.

"What was her name?" Matt asked.

"Captain Bonnaire," said Jia.

"But I wouldn't say that name in front of the captain if I were you," said Albert. "He doesn't like it."

"Captain Vincent went mad with grief when she died," said Jia. "He tried to go back in time again and again to save her, but he couldn't, and he almost destroyed himself and the ship while trying."

"No one knows that for sure," said Albert.

"They do. Wiley told me," said Jia.

"And how would Wiley know? He wasn't on board the *Vermillion* when it happened."

"Do you get some of this treasure too?" said Corey, gazing at an open chest full of gold and silver coins. "I mean, you do some of the work, right? So you should get a share."

"We get our share," said Albert. "We get food and shelter and a life of adventure."

"But you can take some if you want, right?"

"Do you mean *steal* it from the captain?" said Albert in an accusing voice.

"That's not what he meant," said Matt defensively.

Albert walked over to Corey and snapped the chest shut. Corey barely had time to remove his fingers. "These are all the captain's *investments*," hissed Albert. "No one touches anything except me, and no one takes any of it out of this room, not unless you want to get discarded."

"Jeez, sorry," said Corey. "I was just asking."

"What does that mean? Discarded?" Matt asked.

"It means the captain takes you someplace far from your time or home," said Jia, "and leaves you there. Forever."

"Has he done that before?" Ruby asked, clearly alarmed.

"He certainly has," said Albert. "All the crew before us was discarded."

"The whole crew?" Matt asked. "Why?"

"Well, there was a change in command, wasn't there?" said Albert. "The old captain before Captain Vincent had gathered her own crew that was very loyal to her, but when she died and Captain Vincent took charge, some weren't loyal to him. A few even plotted to steal the compass from him, even though the old captain had clearly left it to him. Captain Vincent didn't know who he could trust, so he had no choice but to discard all of the old crew, and then he gathered his own loyal crew."

"That's us!" said Jia. "We are *very* loyal to Captain Vincent."

"And we're quite perceptive when we sense those who *aren't* loyal to the captain," said Albert, looking directly at Corey.

Corey lifted up his hands. "I'm cool, bro."

Albert sniffed, clearly still suspicious. "If the captain were to even get the slightest *sense* that you were stealing from him . . ."

"What? He'd discard us in the Sahara a thousand years ago?" said Ruby, a slight edge to her voice.

"Of course he wouldn't!" said Jia. "The captain's not a barbarian. Honestly, Albert, you really need to lighten up."

Albert looked as though he were about to make some kind of retort when a bell suddenly began to ring.

"What's that?" Ruby asked.

"That's the bell for travel!" said Jia. "We're going on another mission!"

"Yes!" said Corey, pumping his fist in the air.

Albert frowned, rinsing and drying off his brushes. "The captain didn't say anything about going on another mission today. We just got back!"

"The captain doesn't have to tell you everything, Albert," said Jia.

"But he still hasn't given me the *Mona Lisa*! It's not safe to travel when it's not in the gallery."

"Why not?" Matt asked.

"Because the *Vermillion* always changes the rooms around between transformations, and things are always going missing," said Albert. "The gallery is one of the few places the ship knows to leave alone."

"And the captain's cabin," said Jia. "You know the *Vermillion* never messes around with his stuff. The *Mona Lisa* is perfectly safe. Come on!"

11

Game Changers

"Where are we going?" Matt asked as soon as they reached the captain in the dining hall. He had the Obsidian Compass in hand with Santiago perched on his shoulder.

"What's the mission?" asked Corey. "Is it dangerous? Do we get to steal treasure from robbers again?"

"This mission will be slightly different than our usual," said the captain. "I thought we might take a little test trip, travel someplace not too far from your time and home and see how Matt does with his time sickness. I believe I have thought of just the thing."

"What is it?" Matt asked.

"Let's see how quickly you can guess," said the captain. "I never like to spoil the surprise!"

"Sir," said Albert in a whiny voice. "I really think you should allow me to take the *Mona Lisa* to the gallery before we travel. It isn't safe—"

"I assure you the *Mona Lisa* is perfectly safe, Albert, thank you. Crew! Prepare for a quantum time leap!"

All the crew scrambled to find furniture to hide behind or beams to hold on to, but Matt strategically placed himself just behind the captain so he had a clear view of the compass.

The captain first turned the inner dial to the left and then the right, then the middle dial, also to the left and then right, and finally the outer dial, left, right, then left again. It was like a three-tiered combination lock, Matt decided. Each layer had to unlock some specific pathway of time and space, but he was clueless as to when or where they were going. There wasn't enough time to figure out what all the symbols and numerals meant.

The candles and lanterns flickered, and the ship immediately began to shift. It seemed to be shrinking. The walls were moving in, the ceiling pushing down. The furniture split and combined against either side of the *Vermillion*. Matt was jostled until he was forced to sit on a smooth black leather seat.

"Sweet!" said Corey. "Are we in a limo?"

"Once again, the *Vermillion* is determined to impress you three," said Captain Vincent. "She's clearly pleased you've decided to stay."

"And I made a new hat just for the occasion!" said Brocco, who was driving the limo wearing what looked like a classic chauffeur's uniform, except the hat had a band of purple sequins, which matched his purple sequin jacket.

"Wait, where's Ruby?" said Matt. Everyone looked around. The whole crew was there except Ruby. "Where did she go?" Matt started to panic. It wasn't as though there were many places she could hide in this vehicle.

"Don't worry, I'm sure she's here somewhere," said the captain. "Wait, listen."

They all grew quiet. There was a thumping sound coming from somewhere and a muffled yell. "I think she must be inside the seats somewhere," said Jia. "Yes, look!"

At the very back of the limo the seats were moving slightly with the thumps. "She's in the trunk!" said Corey. Matt scrambled to the back of the limo and pulled on the seats. The middle section came forward and an arm shot out.

"Get me out of here!" shouted Ruby. Matt grabbed her hand and pulled. Ruby flopped onto the seat, her face red, her eyes a little stunned. "Am I doing something wrong?" she asked.

"It can take a little time to learn where best to stand during transformation," said the captain. "But don't worry. The *Vermillion* will never harm you."

"That's reassuring," said Ruby. "So where are we?"

Matt looked out the windows. They were driving along a bridge over a large body of water. In the distance he could see buildings and skyscrapers that looked very familiar.

"Hey," said Corey. "What are we doing in New York?"

"You're not taking us home, are you?" said Ruby. Matt

thought it was interesting how quickly she'd warmed up to the idea of staying. He suspected the sword lesson had something to do with it.

"We're not home," said Matt.

"What do you mean?" said Corey. "That's New York! I can see the Statue of Liberty!"

"Yes," said Matt, "but this has to be New York years before we were born. See the Twin Towers?" Across the water were two towers that Matt recognized from old pictures of New York but knew no longer existed, not since September 11, 2001, almost six years before Matt was even born. His parents had taken all of them to the 9/11 Memorial and Museum and often tried to convey the horrors of that day, how it changed everyone and everything, but Matt never knew what things were like before, so it had always seemed somewhat removed from him. Now, seeing the towers with his own eyes, he felt a strange closeness to those events.

"Still, how come we're in New York?" Corey asked. "We've lived here all our lives, remember? I thought you were going to take us someplace exciting."

"Trust me, this will be very exciting," said the captain. "It's not always about location, you know, but certain events going on at the time of travel."

"What year did we travel to?" Matt asked.

"Nineteen eighty-six!" said the captain.

"And the date?"

"October twenty-fifth."

It sounded familiar to Matt for some reason, but he couldn't put his finger on what it was.

Brocco drove the limo through the streets at what Matt thought was probably an unsafe speed. He wondered what they'd do if the police tried to pull them over. Did the *Vermillion* provide Brocco with a driver's license? Did he even really know how to drive? It didn't appear so. He ran a red light and nearly hit a woman crossing the street with her dog. Cars honked and slammed on their breaks. Everyone was squished together as he took a corner very fast and knocked over a metal garbage can.

Jia closed her eyes and grimaced. "That's going to cause some damage," she said.

"Where does everything go?" Matt asked. "All the stuff on the ship, I mean." The limo was quite spacious and fit all of them comfortably, but still, there was no way all the things they'd been carrying in the ship could somehow fit inside of this vehicle.

"You know, I haven't the foggiest," said the captain, as though he'd never given it a thought before. "I assume it all goes *somewhere* as it always reappears, at least most of the time. A few things do tend to go missing every now and then."

"Like my hammer," said Jia bitterly.

"Santiago is quite good at finding things after transformation, though," said the captain. "So if you need assistance finding anything, just ask him." Santiago came out of the captain's pocket and climbed onto his shoulder.

"What is with that rat?" asked Corey. "I mean, is he like a super-rodent or something?"

"Something like that," said the captain. "He's been on the ship even longer than I have, I believe. He's very useful."

"What about that crazy cook?" Matt asked.

"Agnes?" said the captain.

"Yeah, where's she? Was she in the trunk with you, Ruby?"

Ruby shrugged. "I don't think so, but I couldn't see anything."

"You know, I've no idea where Agnes goes either," said the captain.

"Could she shrink somehow?" Ruby asked.

"Maybe she anatomically disassembles when we travel," said Matt, "and then reassembles when we return."

"Maybe that's why she's so cranky all the time," said Jia. "She gets blown into bits whenever we travel."

"I believe Agnes was simply born that way," said the captain. "Though it does make one curious . . ."

Matt almost wanted to experiment with going to different parts of the ship when they traveled the next time, just to find out, but then he thought maybe that wouldn't be wise. Whether he shrank or disintegrated, it would probably be extremely uncomfortable.

Matt looked through the windows again, almost feeling

that they were back home in New York and nothing was different at all, until he saw it and his heart skipped a few beats.

"Is that . . ." Matt squinted and then his eyes widened. "Is that *Shea Stadium*?"

Shea Stadium was the old Mets stadium. It had been torn down when Matt was just a baby. His dad had managed to snag a couple of the old stadium seats, which were now in his and Corey's room.

But now Shea Stadium stood intact and towering. Matt thought it sort of looked like a giant blue metal Oreo cookie. It gave him the strangest feeling, even stranger than traveling to Paris in 1911. It was like reliving an old memory.

"October 25, 1986," said Matt. His heart started to beat a little faster as he realized where they were going, what they were about to see. He looked to Corey. Corey didn't seem to understand.

"What?" he asked.

"I thought a familiar activity might also help with your brother's time sickness," said the captain. "And since he's so passionate about baseball . . ."

Ruby groaned. "Oh brother, we're going to a baseball game?"

"It's Game Six of the 1986 World Series!" said Matt.

"Whaaaaaat?" said Corey. "Game Six?! *The* Game Six? No way! No freaking way!"

"So?" said Ruby.

"Dude, it's the greatest baseball game of all time!" said Corey.

"First of all, I'm not a dude," said Ruby. "Second of all, it's lame."

"I agree with Ruby," said Albert. "I read about baseball in a book once. It sounds like a poor, lazy imitation of cricket."

Ruby, clearly disliking the idea of being in agreement with Albert, glared at him. "You can't judge a sport by *reading* about it," she said. "I've at least given it a fair chance."

Albert's cheeks turned pink. He pushed his glasses up his nose and looked out the window.

"How did you know?" Matt asked.

"Well, Brocco asked if we could take another trip to New York to get you a certain baseball cap," said the captain. "Said you needed it for your new wardrobe."

"I told him you were too stubborn to take the other," huffed Brocco, "and you look unfinished."

"So, knowing you cheer for this particular team," said Captain Vincent, "I asked Wiley to do a little research, find out when a good game would happen."

"It was no trouble," said Wiley. "I searched my library, did a little digging in some of my books from the future, and boom! Number one Mets game of all time, no argument, was October 25, 1986! Must be an exciting game."

"It is!" said Matt. "It's the game where they're tied and they go into extra innings and then Bill Buckner—"

"Don't spoil it for us!" said Wiley. "I didn't read all the details, and I'm not from the future, remember? Let us be surprised a little."

Matt was thrown to the right as Brocco took a sharp left and swerved through the crowds of people. He pulled over to the side, driving the front wheels on the curb. A traffic regulator started walking toward them, shaking his head, and waving his glowing stick for them to move. "Everyone out!" said Brocco. "I have to avoid the constable!"

They opened the doors, and everyone piled out of the car. As soon as the captain shut the door, Brocco pulled away, just as the traffic person tapped him on the hood.

"How will he know where to find us?" Matt asked.

"The *Vermillion* will find us. The compass is like a magnet to her." He patted his shirtsleeve.

Matt felt swallowed up by the crowd as he moved toward the stadium.

"Nice shirt," a guy walking next to him said, and his friend snorted with laughter. It was only then that Matt realized with sickening horror he was still wearing the clothes Brocco had put on him earlier that day. Here he was at the greatest Mets game of all time and he was wearing a My Little Pony T-shirt! He glanced at Ruby, who was still wearing his Mets hoodie that she'd taken from the closet the morning they left. He almost demanded that she give it back to him, but it was chilly and he didn't think she'd want to part with it.

Wiley split off from them and disappeared in the crowd.

"Where's Wiley going?" Matt asked.

"To procure our tickets and uniforms," said the captain.

"Oh," said Matt. In all the excitement he hadn't thought of that detail. Tickets to this game had to be very difficult to get and expensive at this point, maybe even impossible. "If he's not able to get them, it's no big deal," said Matt. "I just think it's awesome that we're even here."

"I have complete confidence that Wiley won't disappoint," said the captain.

Crowds of people streamed toward the entrances in their Mets or Red Sox shirts and hats, with painted faces and signs.

They passed a man sitting by a light pole, shaking a McDonald's cup. The captain reached in his pocket, took out two twenty-dollar bills and stuffed them in the man's cup.

"Thank you, Mister! God bless!"

"You're quite welcome," said the captain. "God bless."

When Wiley returned, not only had he managed to get tickets, but also jerseys, jackets, hats, flags, and a sign that said Go METS! It's your TIME! Matt quickly grabbed a jacket and zipped it over his T-shirt. He slipped on a hat, too, wishing once again that he had his old one. It fit him just right. This one was stiff and squeezed his head a little, but he was glad to have it anyway.

"Can I see the tickets?" Matt asked.

Wiley pulled them out of his inner pocket and held them out to Matt. He gaped at them.

WORLD SERIES
1986
Mets
VS.
AMERICAN LEAGUE CHAMPIONS
GAME 6

He was going to see Game Six! It was like it was his birthday, only it was happening before he was ever born. Matt thought about all the games his father had taken him to *on* his actual birthday, but none of them were nearly so exciting. Matt felt a shot of guilt just then. He shouldn't be belittling his parents' gifts. If the Mets had been in the World Series his dad probably would have found a way to get them tickets. It wasn't his fault he couldn't time-travel.

They entered the stadium. The tickets weren't scanned like they did in their time. Instead they were simply checked over with a flashlight to make sure they weren't duplicates or fakes. The attendant waved them in.

The smells of hot dogs, pizza, and cotton candy drifted beneath Matt's nose. He sniffed deeply and smiled. It was all so familiar and yet new and bewildering. Ruby held on to

Matt's jacket as they pushed their way through a sea of bodies that seemed to be going every direction but the one they were.

Their seats were incredible. Second row. Right behind first base. They had to be sitting around some movie stars or other celebrities, but Matt was too young to know who they might be.

"How much do you think these seats cost?" Corey whispered to Matt.

"Thousands. Each one," he muttered.

"It's kind of nice traveling with rich time pirates, isn't it?" Corey whispered to Matt.

Matt agreed there were definite perks.

"Which team are we wanting to win again?" said Jia. "Oh yeah, the Mets." She pointed to Matt's new hat. Matt took it off as everyone stood for the National Anthem. Paul Simon sang in a high, slightly nasally voice without any embellishment or variation.

Albert snorted at the performance. "He's supposed to be a famous singer? Americans certainly have strange taste."

"You really need to stop commenting about things you know nothing about," said Ruby. "Paul Simon is an American icon and quite famous throughout the world."

Matt smiled at his sister. He knew she didn't care for Paul Simon any more than she did baseball, but he felt like she was defending their family and country's culture. Matt's parents *loved* Simon and Garfunkel. Mr. Hudson especially. He had gone to one of their concerts in Central Park when he was just about Matt's age. He said it made him want to be a rock star, which the whole family thought was hilarious as Mr. Hudson was hopelessly tone deaf. He couldn't even sing "Happy Birthday" in tune.

Finally the game started. Matt knew how Game Six played out, inning by inning, so while he watched he explained to Jia and the captain what was going on, the rules and strategies of the game. The captain seemed mildly interested, but Jia concentrated on the game very hard and asked a lot of questions.

"There! He hit the ball, why didn't he run to the base?"

"It was a foul ball," said Matt. "It has to stay inside the lines."

Matt knew neither team scored in the third or fourth innings, so they used that time to go get concessions and use the restrooms.

The captain doled out twenty-dollar bills to all of them like they were just plain slips of paper, and they were allowed to order whatever they wanted—hot dogs, burgers, pizza, popcorn, candy, drinks, and ice cream. Matt ordered a hot dog, licorice rope, Cracker Jack, and a root beer. He wrapped the rope around his neck and carried the Cracker Jack beneath his arm. They worked their way back to their seats, except on the way Matt was jostled by someone in the crowd and he dropped his drink. Root beer splashed up his pant leg and all over his shoes.

"Oh man, I'm so sorry, little dude." The guy quickly swept up his drink. "What is this, root beer? Here, let me get you another one. Nick, man, go get a root beer, will you?"

"It's okay," said Matt, "It's no big—"

Matt froze. The man in front of him, the one he had bumped into . . .

It was his dad, a teenage version, only a few years older than Matt was now, but it was definitely Matthew Hudson.

Ruby gasped beside him. Corey, in a barely audible voice, said, "Dad."

"What's that?" said their dad. "You looking for your dad?" He looked around to see any adult who might be with them. They'd been separated from Captain Vincent and the rest, but somehow the Hudson children had remained together and now they were standing right in front of their teenage father, who had no idea who they were. Matt studied this younger version of his dad. He was wearing tight jeans with holes in the knees and a new Mets jersey that Matt knew was still hanging in his closet, even though it didn't fit him any-more. His hair was classic eighties style, poofy on top and a curly mullet in the back. He had a playful glimmer in his eyes that reminded Matt of Corey.

"Are your parents nearby?" said the young Mr. Hudson, still looking around.

Corey laughed, but Ruby elbowed him in the ribs so he

turned it into a cough.

"Yeah," said Matt. "Our dad's here. And we know where our seats are, so it's no big deal."

"Okay, I'll just wait with you until your dad gets here," said their dad. "I'm really sorry about your drink."

The kids all looked at each other, none of them quite sure what to do. Their dad's friend returned with a large cup in one hand and an ice cream in the other. Mr. Hudson took both and held them out to Matt. "Here you go!" he said. "Have an ice cream too. It's on us." Matt struggled to get both in his hands with all the other stuff he was carrying.

"There you are! We've been looking for you everywhere!" Matt turned to see Jia pressing through the crowd, the captain right behind her with a cotton candy in his hand.

"I was getting worried!" said the captain. "Thought we'd lost you in this madness." He caught sight of their father. He looked at him quizzically, like he was wondering what he was doing there.

Their dad shifted uncomfortably. "Hey, sorry. I accidentally knocked into your kid and spilled his drink." The captain said nothing. Matt thought his expression was not so friendly. His dad seemed to think so too because he added quickly, "I got him a new one though, so no harm done? Well, have fun, enjoy the game."

"Go Mets!" said their dad's friend, and they hurried away, disappearing in the crowd. The captain kept staring after him, his brow creased in confusion.

"That was our dad," said Matt.

The captain started from his stupor. "Really? You don't say. How very . . . interesting."

"Weird is what it was," said Corey.

"Did Dad ever tell you he was at this game?" Ruby asked.

Matt tried to think. Had he? His dad had told him so much about the Mets and had described so many games, it was hard to remember which ones he had actually been to. But he would have remembered his dad being at Game Six! It was *the* game. "He must have," said Matt. "I guess I just don't remember him telling me. It won't matter though, right, Captain? It's not like he recognized us or anything, and it's years before we were born, so it won't cause any problems with the timeline, will it?"

The captain shrugged. "Who knows? Even small things like that can cause a ripple or a glitch. We'll just have to see." He brushed a hand through his hair and frowned. Matt thought he was maybe a bit angry they hadn't known his dad was at this game. Maybe he wouldn't have brought them if he had known.

When they sat down again the Mets were at bat at the bottom of the fourth. They all watched happily, eating their hot dogs and treats. Santiago scurried around their feet, picking up their mess. He seemed more concerned with keeping their area clean than eating their leftovers, but he did nibble on some of Matt's spilled Cracker Jack and seemed to like it quite a bit, until it started to rain. Santiago quickly gathered up the rest of the Cracker Jack in his paws and scurried up into the captain's jacket.

"It rained in Game Six?" Corey asked.

Matt shrugged. "Apparently." He didn't remember that detail, but it must not have been noteworthy. It was only a drizzle. They certainly didn't cancel the game over it, and it didn't seem to change anything. Boston didn't score in the top of the fifth. As the Mets came up to bat, Matt geared up for the two runs that would come. Strawberry walked. Then Knight was up to bat.

"Now watch this," said Matt. "Strawberry's going to steal second on this next pitch."

"Don't tell me!" said Jia.

"Sorry!" said Matt, smiling. Jia was on the edge of her seat, watching.

The pitcher wound up and threw and . . .

"Hey, you trickster, you said he was going to steal second!" said Jia.

Matt's face fell. He stared, dumbfounded.

"Apparently not," said Jia. "It's not so important, is it?"

But it was important. Without Strawberry stealing second, he didn't score on Knight's single. He scored on the next play, when Wilson singled, but then Knight didn't score a run on Heep's double play.

"This is a disaster," said Matt. "We were supposed to score two runs. We only scored one."

"Maybe you're getting the plays mixed up," said Corey.

"No," said Matt.

Matt knew that wasn't right. His dad had replayed this game a hundred times for him. He'd watched recordings of the game at least a dozen times. He knew exactly what runs happened in which innings.

"Captain, could, uh, running into our dad have changed the game?" Matt asked.

Captain Vincent shrugged. "Certainly. I told you something like that could cause a small ripple or a glitch. Small changes, but nothing catastrophic."

Nothing catastrophic? "I think we changed the game," said Matt.

"What?" said Corey.

Matt swallowed. His throat was dry. He could barely speak the words. "I think we may have messed it up somehow."

"So the Mets are going to lose the World Series just because you knocked into Dad?" said Ruby. "Some good-luck charm you are."

Albert snorted, but Matt couldn't muster the will to shoot him a dirty look.

He felt sick. He wished they hadn't come. "Can we turn back time and not come to the game?" he asked.

"No, no," said Captain Vincent. "What's done is done. A

ripple in the timeline has been created and going back won't change that. You're here now, and from now on, moving both forward and backward, you will always have been here. No, we can only go on I'm afraid, and hope for the best."

Matt felt a pit in his stomach, and it only got bigger as the game went on. It played out much as he remembered, but that one change of Strawberry not stealing second messed up everything. In the bottom of the eighth the Mets scored a run, as they should have, but the score was only 3–2, not 3–3, as it should have been. Unless the Mets scored an unanticipated run in the bottom of the ninth, they were going to lose Game Six. And the entire series. Matt started to nervously rub his thumb over the stone of his bracelet.

The Red Sox didn't score in the top of the ninth. Finally, in the bottom of the ninth the Mets scored a run to tie the game 3–3 and send it to extra innings.

"See?" said Corey. "It's fine. It's not a big deal."

But Matt couldn't rest so easy. Things were different. Nothing was for certain.

The Red Sox scored two runs in the top of the tenth: 5–3 Red Sox.

It was the bottom of the tenth inning. The Mets were supposed to win here, but would they? The Mets should never have won this game in the first place. Everyone knew that. They only did because of a crazy error on the part of the Red Sox, where Bill Buckner lets a grounder go right through his legs. It was one of the most famous moments in all of baseball history, but what if it didn't happen tonight?

Backman hit a pop fly to left. Out.

Hernandez hit a fly to center. Out.

The Red Sox were one out away from winning the World Series.

Carter hit a single to left field, then Mitchell singled. Two men on base. Knight was the next batter up. The first pitch was called a strike. He fouled the next pitch into the stands.

Schiraldi wound up, pitched, and Knight hit a line drive to center field. Carter scored, and Mitchell ran to third! 5–4 Red Sox!

"Now here comes the wild pitch," said Matt. The Red Sox replaced Schiraldi with Bob Stanley, who threw a wild pitch, allowing Mitchell to score and tie the game.

The crowd went wild. Matt and Corey were jumping up and down screaming. Even Ruby was up from her seat, clapping and shouting, "Go, Mets!"

"That's how it's supposed to go!" said Corey. "All we need is Buckner to miss the ball when Wilson grounds to first and we're golden!"

Yes! That was all that was needed! Just for the inevitable to happen!

Foul.

Ball.

Ball.

Foul.

There was a time-out from the Red Sox. The Boston coach went to the mound to talk to Stanley, the pitcher.

"It's okay," said Corey. "We've still got one more."

But Matt's heart was hammering in his chest now. His head began to throb. He could barely breathe. His thumb was raw from rubbing his bracelet so much. He started twisting the stone. He pulled at it so hard it broke off of his wrist. He clutched it in his fist.

The coach left the mound and then Stanley dug his feet into the dirt, turning the ball over in his hand. He wiped sweat off his forehead, looking toward the batter at home plate.

"Come on," said Matt. The pitcher wound up. He threw. Wilson swung.

Crack! The ball rolled toward first.

"Go! Go! Go!" Matt pumped his fist in the air as Wilson ran for first. And then everything started to slow. The whole stadium seemed to tilt.

No, thought Matt. *Not now!*

The shouts of the crowd dulled to a low roar. The players, everyone around Matt, all seemed to go into slow motion. Matt braced himself on the seat in front of him. He couldn't miss this moment because of a stupid seizure! He forced himself to look toward the field, even though it appeared to be sideways.

The ball bounced and rolled right to first. Bill Buckner was there, his glove on the ground. He was definitely going to catch the ball and get the batter out, but suddenly there was a shudder, a slight tremor in the ground. The stadium lights dimmed just for a moment, and Matt could have sworn he saw the air around him pulse and flicker, almost like a television screen with bad reception. It might have all been mistaken for flashing cameras, but Matt knew it wasn't that. It was as if the whole field had shifted a few inches to the left, right beneath the player's feet. The ball seemed to realign itself, just to the left of Buckner's glove. It rolled right through his legs.

And then, as though someone had pressed the play button on a remote, everything clicked back to normal speed. The volume was turned up. Matt collapsed in his seat as the entire stadium exploded, screaming, jumping up and down, waving their arms. Wilson made it safe to first, and Knight ran from third to score the winning run.

"Mets win!" Corey pumped his fists in the air and jumped onto his seat. The people in front of Matt were hugging each other, pouring beer over each other's heads. The team tackled each other on the field. Even Ruby was standing and clapping her hands, her cheeks flushed. No one could resist getting caught up in the excitement.

But Matt barely noticed any of it. He barely heard anything going on around him. Everything seemed to be checkered, like a pixelated screen.

"Dude," said Corey. "Are you okay?"

"What?" Matt looked up and blinked at his brother. His face sort of looked like a Minecraft character.

"The game!" he said. "We won! Just like it was supposed to be."

"Oh, yeah. Amazing," he said. He shook his head, trying to clear his vision and mind. Had he just had a seizure? Or was he about to have one? He wasn't sure.

"I am afraid we may have exhausted Mateo with so much excitement," said Captain Vincent.

"Oh, Matt, you look pale," said Ruby. "Are you okay?"

"I'm fine," he said. "I think maybe I ate a little too much junk as medicine." He tried to laugh.

"Let's get back to the *Vermillion*," said Captain Vincent. "Brocco will be waiting for us."

"If he didn't get himself arrested," Jia whispered to Matt.

"Has that happened before?"

"Oh yes," said Jia. "The captain has to bail him out regularly."

When they got to the street, the limo was at the curb right where it had dropped them off. Brocco honked the horn at them, then got out and opened the doors for them all to get inside. When they were all seated, Brocco drove away, speeding and swerving in and out of traffic and pedestrians. A police car flashed its lights and turned on its siren briefly, but the captain had already begun to turn the dials of the compass. The pedestrians and lights blurred outside their window, and a moment later the limo started to transform, the floor stretching, the seats melding from leather to wood and fabric, until the *Vermillion* was a ship again, back to Nowhere in No Time.

"That was the best night ever," said Corey.

"I quite enjoyed it as well," said the captain. "Such a delightful game!"

"The captain just called baseball delightful," Corey whispered in Matt's ear. Matt laughed, then realized he was still clutching his broken bracelet. He stuffed it in his pocket and forgot about it.

"I love baseball!" said Jia. "We should have a victory dance, shouldn't we?"

"Oh yes!" said Brocco. "I'll get my fiddle!"

Brocco was a pretty awful musician, but that almost made it all the more fun as none of the Hudsons were very good dancers, so they felt perfectly fine stomping and swinging around to his scratchy, off-key playing. Matt hooked elbows with Jia, and they swung around each other, stomping their feet while Corey and Ruby did somersaults over each other's backs. Wiley, however, delighted them all with his dancing. He was the absolute worst dancer in the very best way. As off-key as Brocco was on the violin, Wiley was off-rhythm, awkward and wacky in his movements. He tapped his feet and swung his arms all over the place with his eyes closed, so the others had to frequently duck and dodge his flailing limbs.

"Dancin' is poetry of the body," he said, smiling with his pipe bouncing between his teeth.

Matt looked around to see if the captain would be a good dancer or just as awful, but he wasn't dancing at all. Matt saw him slipping into his cabin, Santiago perched on his shoulder. Maybe he didn't care for music or dancing.

After they were all sweaty and tired from dancing they decided to go above deck for some fresh air. Matt gazed out at the ocean, so smooth and glassy it mirrored the waning gibbous moon and the stars. There were so many stars, and they were so much brighter than Matt could ever recall seeing in New York. It was like he had been looking at the sky his entire life with a great screen over it, and now the screen had been removed to reveal a vibrant, majestic night sky.

"What a night," said Corey.

"Can you believe we saw Dad?" said Ruby. "He couldn't have been more than fifteen."

"Sixteen," said Matt. "He was born in 1970."

"I cannot wait to tease him about his hair!" said Corey. "Did you see that thing? It almost looked alive!"

"Do you think he'll remember us?" Ruby asked.

"Probably not," said Corey. "He was probably too distracted by the game. That last play . . . so cool to see it in person. I almost thought Bill Buckner was really going to catch the ball, and then there it went, right between his legs."

Matt replayed that particular moment in his mind again and again. What had happened, exactly? That's what everyone had always asked about that game. It was one of the plays that made it so famous. Not even Bill Buckner, the Red Sox first baseman who didn't field the ball, could fully explain it. He'd said in an interview that it had something to do with his glove, that he wasn't used to it, but now Matt had a different theory. No one else had seemed to notice the strange slowing of time, the slight shift in space. Was it because they were there at the same time as their dad? Had the captain accidentally jostled the compass somehow, causing some kind of glitch in the space-time continuum?

Matt slumped into his hammock that night, exhausted but happy. He absentmindedly reached for his bracelet, and then remembered it was in his pocket. He pulled it out and brushed his finger over the stone, studying the marks and grooves. It did look like a Chinese character, he realized. He'd have to figure out what it meant. Later. He tied the twine back together, slid the bracelet on his wrist, and fell asleep.

12

The Eyes Hold the Key

Matt woke in the middle of the night, needing to use the bathroom. That's why he'd woken up, he realized. He flopped out of his hammock and padded quietly down the dark hall. He opened the door he thought was the bathroom, only to have a bunch of baseballs, bats, gloves, and hats tumble out on him. He scrambled to snatch up the baseballs before they all rolled away. The rooms had apparently changed after their last transformation from limo back to ship. Matt gazed around, trying to guess where the bathroom might be now.

Only a small lantern gave any light. He didn't want to just start opening doors.

He came to the bottom of the stairs leading to the upper deck, where the dining hall and the captain's quarters were. He noticed a faint glow spilling over the floor. He went up the steps and peered into the dining hall. The captain's door was slightly ajar, and the weak light of a lantern shone through the gap. If the captain were awake he'd tell him where the bathroom was.

Matt tiptoed quietly to the door and peeked around the frame. He had a much better view of the room this time. There was the row of red Converse and the art easel with the sword leaning against it. What he hadn't noticed before was the hundreds of paintings and drawings both hanging on the walls and layered in piles on the floor. Matt could only vaguely tell what some of the paintings were, as most of them had a series of slashes through them, but after a moment he realized that most of them were portraits of women, or the same woman, perhaps. It was difficult to tell. They all appeared to have long black hair, but most of them had their eyes gouged out, or faces slashed or stabbed in several places.

Captain Vincent was standing in front of the art easel that held the *Mona Lisa*. He was looking at her very closely through a magnifying glass. He appeared to be alone, except for Santiago, who sat on his shoulder, squeaking in his ear.

"Yes, I know, Santiago. This was our Bonbon's favorite painting. Do you remember? She said it was a masterpiece beyond compare, but I must say I never quite understood her fascination with it. I always thought my own paintings of our Bonbon were much better, but *she* never thought so. She said I never got the eyes right. The eyes . . . the eyes . . . the eyes hold the key . . ." The captain took a knife out of his jacket, a small dagger, the blade thin and pointy. Matt let out an involuntary, strangled gasp. He covered his mouth, but too late. Santiago looked right at him with his red eyes and hissed.

Matt stepped away from the door. He wanted to run back to his hammock, but before he knew what was happening the door flew open and a hand grabbed him by the collar and pulled him inside the room. Captain Vincent shoved Matt against the desk and pointed the knife right at his throat.

"I'm sorry! I'm sorry!" Matt shrieked. He closed his eyes, waiting for the knife to sink into his neck. But it didn't. Matt dared to open his eyes. The captain's snarl softened.

"No. It is I who am sorry, Mateo." The captain relaxed and dropped the knife on the desk. "I'm afraid you caught me off guard." He released Matt, then helped him up, straightening his shirt. The captain smiled a little, but Santiago hopped down from his shoulder and squeaked and hissed right in Matt's face.

"You needn't reprimand him, Santiago," said the captain. "I'm sure Mateo has a very good explanation for why he came to see us." Captain Vincent looked at Matt expectantly, clearly waiting for him to explain himself.

Matt swallowed. Somehow saying he'd gotten lost while looking for the bathroom seemed a very pitiful excuse in this situation. "I . . . I didn't mean to . . ."

"Spy?" said the captain.

Matt flinched. He had been spying, hadn't he?

"Don't be frightened," said the captain. "I'm not angry."

"You're not?"

The captain smiled gently. "A little spying can be a valuable skill for a time pirate. We might need to work on your technique, though."

Matt looked away, and then his gaze fell on the *Mona Lisa*. "I just thought you were going to . . . you know." He looked at the knife, now sitting on the captain's desk, and glanced at all the other ruined paintings.

"I assure you I will not damage her," said the captain. "These are all my own paltry attempts at art." He gestured at all the ruined paintings and sketches. "I am never satisfied with them, and so they become my victims in battle instead. The *Mona Lisa* is an entirely different matter. But I think it's provident that you are here, actually. I could use your sound intelligence, and you are, in fact, the reason I have the *Mona Lisa* in the first place."

"Me?" said Matt. "I didn't do all that much, sir. I mean, I almost ruined the whole mission."

"I don't mean the mission," said the captain. "I'm talking about your message."

"My message?" said Matt, confused.

The captain regarded Matt. He seemed to be calculating how much he should tell him, or perhaps wondering how much Matt already knew. But Matt's ignorance must have been believable. The captain pulled open a drawer and took out a hat. And not just any hat. It was his Mets hat. The very one that had been stolen out of his locker last week. It had the exact fraying, the fabric curling back from the plastic of the brim.

"Hey! Where did you get that?"

"From you, Mateo," said the captain. "You gave it to me, about a week before you boarded the *Vermillion*."

"No I didn't! Someone stole it out of my locker!"

Captain Vincent twirled the hat around his finger. "I'm not surprised you don't remember. You do look younger now than when you gave me the hat."

"What are you talking about?" asked Matt. "I never gave you my hat."

"Not yet, anyway," said the captain.

"You're not making any sense," said Matt.

Captain Vincent smiled, clearly amused. "It's a common conundrum of time travel. At this present moment, I've met you before, but you haven't met me before, but when you gave me the hat last week it was just the opposite. You'd met me already, but I had yet to meet you."

Matt shook his head. He felt like the captain was speaking in riddles.

"Let me see if I can simplify," said Captain Vincent. "At your present, you are just beginning on your time-travel journeys, while I have already traveled extensively, but it appears you travel a great deal in your future, perhaps even more than myself, and you seemed to have a keen interest in our missions."

Matt gaped at the captain as this information sunk in. He would time-travel more in his future? He would travel back to his past and steal his own hat and give it to Captain Vincent, all for reasons he couldn't fathom.

"Sorry, but it's all still a little confusing. Why did I give you my hat?"

"To send a message," said the captain, "or rather to send multiple messages. I believe you were letting me know that the time was drawing near for you to board the *Vermillion*, and when you did it would be time to take the *Mona Lisa*."

"How did you know that?"

Captain Vincent tossed the hat on the desk so it landed upside down. "Take a look inside the hat."

Matt looked. "I don't see anything."

"Look *inside*." Captain Vincent tapped on the brim. Matt picked up the hat and brushed his thumb over the frayed fabric and noticed a grayish corner poking out. He pulled on it with his fingers and a folded-up piece of paper slid out. He unfolded it. It was an old newspaper article from France, *Le Petit Parisien,* and the headline article was the theft of *la Joconde.* He glanced down the article, reading the events of the famous heist he had been a part of not days ago. But that wasn't the really interesting part. Written across the paper in blocky, uneven, eerily familiar handwriting were the words:

LES YEUX TIENNENT LA CLE.

The eyes hold the key.

"That's my handwriting," said Matt.

"If anyone would know, it would be you, wouldn't it?" said the captain.

"But I don't remember writing this."

"No you wouldn't, would you? Not if your future self wrote it."

Matt stared at the paper and message, utterly perplexed. "So . . . you think I gave you my hat with this newspaper and message, to tell you to steal the *Mona Lisa* and somehow get some message from her eyes?"

"Something like that," said the captain. "I've been studying her, convinced that there must be some hidden message in her eyes. There are theories that Da Vinci himself placed some kind of secret code in her eyes, and while you can see things that might look like numbers and letters, there was nothing that made any real sense. So I'm curious to know if you might have an idea of what you meant, seeing as you wrote the message?"

"How could I?" said Matt. "Like you said, I wrote it in the future."

"Yes, but you know the way you think, the way your brain works, and you are connected to your future self, even if you haven't yet experienced all the same things. That's another interesting thing about time travel. We may travel to our past or future, but if you time-travel enough, eventually there is no past or future. It all just becomes one round. You may not always be conscious of the things you've done in the future or the past, but it is all there, and so, even though it is impossible for you to *re*-member, I believe there is a way for you to access what your future self meant, even if it's just a general feeling or a hunch. I call it *fore*member."

Matt recalled that feeling of déjà vu he'd gotten after he'd seen his name in the mast. Was that what that was? Was he *foremembering* his future self doing that?

Captain Vincent held the magnifying glass to Matt. "Why don't you take a look and see what you think?"

Matt took it and the captain turned the painting toward him. Matt focused on the eyes. He saw specks of paint that could be seen as numbers or letters, but nothing jumped out at him. He got no magical feeling. Matt looked up at the captain and shook his head.

"Hmm," said the captain. "I wonder . . . try taking a look at the back." He turned the painting over so the wood panel faced Matt. "Take a look right about here." He tapped near the middle of the wood. Matt gazed into the magnifying glass. At first he didn't see anything. Just the grain of the wood. But then he caught it. There were very faint lines in the wood, straight grooves that went against the grain. They formed a rectangle. "It looks like a piece was cut out of the wood and then glued back in," said Matt.

"Exactly," said the captain. "And see where it's located on

the painting? Right behind the eyes!"

Matt nodded. "That makes more sense. I've always been pretty literal." It was a problem in English sometimes. He didn't always get all the metaphors and similes. Why anyone would compare a laugh to a ray of sunshine or say his love was a burning flame, he had no idea.

"See? You're beginning to feel it, I think," said the captain, "that connection to your future self."

"So there's something *inside* the painting then?" said Matt. "Right there?"

"Only one way to find out." Captain Vincent picked up the knife he'd held to Matt's throat only minutes before.

Matt had a sudden impulse to knock the knife out of the captain's hand, grab the painting, and run. But he also wanted to know what, if anything, was inside the painting. Another message? Would it be from his future self again?

Matt nodded. Captain Vincent pressed his knife into the wood. Matt winced. He had to remind himself it was just a painting, just wood. It almost felt like a real person. The captain drew his knife slowly in a small rectangle. He went over the spot a few times, going a little deeper each time, then gently pried the wood upward, revealing a small hollow in the panel.

"Ah!" He pulled something out and held it up in the light of the lantern. It was a small gold key. "So your message was doubly literal."

"What does it unlock?" Matt asked.

"Another thing I was hoping you might know," said the captain.

Matt shook his head. He couldn't remember—or *fore*member—doing such a thing.

"Well, no matter. We can sort that out. Ah! Look, there's an inscription." Captain Vincent picked up his magnifying glass and placed the gold key beneath it. "Take a look," he said, handing it over to Matt.

Matt leaned forward and gazed into the magnifying glass. Along the handle of the key were three words.

VIDEO ET TACEO

"It's Latin," he said. Latin was not one of his 12/21 project languages, but he had studied it because he knew it would give him a good base for learning many other languages. "*Video* means 'I see.' I'm not certain what *taceo* means."

"I see and say nothing," said the captain. "How clever."

"What does it mean?"

"Haven't the foggiest, but it's a clue, I believe, telling us where we should go next to fulfill the mission."

"Sir, if you don't mind my asking, what *is* the mission? I mean, where do you think this all leads? And why am I giving you messages from the future?"

The captain cocked his head, regarding Matt. "That is a

mystery even to myself. I've asked that question a few times. It's unclear exactly what your motives are, whether you're really trying to help me or serve your own ends."

Matt shifted uncomfortably. He couldn't help but feel he was on some sort of trial here. "I . . . I can't speak for my future self, not yet anyway, but it looks like I'm trying to help, doesn't it? I mean, I do want to help now." Which was perfectly true. His curiosity had been piqued to the point where he knew there was no going back.

Captain Vincent smiled gently. "I believe you. You are a great time pirate, Mateo, or you will be someday. Perhaps the greatest of them all."

These words sent a thrill through Matt's veins. "So . . . what's the mission then? I mean, you must have some idea where this key leads, why it's important."

"I do have an idea," said the captain. "The truth is, I've been having a bit of trouble with the compass lately. It doesn't always function properly. I know how to use it well enough, and we can travel nearly anywhere and to any time, but there are . . . glitches, shall we say, times and places I cannot access, and it only seems to be getting worse."

"Like it's losing power," said Matt.

"Something like that," said the captain.

"So that's bad," said Matt. He knew he sounded like an idiot.

"It's inconvenient for now," said the captain, "but it could be catastrophic in the future. Our future, I mean."

"How?"

"What if the compass were to stop working while we were on a mission? Or what if it happened right now? We'd be stuck in Nowhere in No Time. Or worse, it could malfunction in the midst of travel and transformation, and we'd be stuck in a kind of limbo. Don't be frightened, I don't think it's nearly to that point yet, but . . . I do believe it is along that path, slowly declining, eroding our timeline for travel."

"Sorry," said Matt, "but if the compass is really at risk of breaking down in the middle of travel, why travel at all? It seems like flying on a malfunctioning airplane. No one would take that kind of risk. So why don't we all just go home and live our lives out normally?"

"Your logic is sound, Mateo, except I'm afraid it no longer applies to our situation. You see, we've all time-traveled already, which means 'normal' no longer exists for us as it does for others. We're not living our lives on straight lines, we're in a circular web, and who knows how many threads we've all touched? I at least have some idea of what I've done so far, but in the future there's clearly much more, at least for you, Mateo. The rest of us seem to be somewhat . . . invisible."

Matt suddenly became alarmed. "You think you're all going to die?"

"I'm afraid it's worse than that," said Captain Vincent. "It's more like we cease to exist."

"Is that what happened to Captain Bonnaire?" said Matt. "Did she cease to exist?"

Matt winced under the captain's sudden, sharp look. He remembered what Albert had said about never mentioning that name in front of the captain. "Sorry," he muttered.

"Don't apologize," said the captain. "I know what the crew whispers behind my back. No, she died under different circumstances. Though perhaps it would have been better if she had ceased to exist. Maybe that way I could have a hope of bringing her back, if we were to fix the compass." He gazed at the slashed paintings of the dark-haired woman.

"So what do we do now?"

"We must find whatever it is this key unlocks," said the captain. "This *video et taceo* might be a clue. Or not. With time travel things can come from anywhere."

"I can do some research," said Matt. "I do have a knack for finding information others can't."

"I'm sure you do," said the captain, twirling the gold key between his fingers. "But we will likely have to travel a great deal to find what we're looking for, and I can't pretend this doesn't concern me. You're clearly very sensitive to time travel."

"I'm okay," said Matt. "I can handle it, I promise." Even though he still wasn't feeling completely well, he was eager to travel again, to begin the search for whatever the key unlocked, and he didn't want the captain to hold back just because he had a weak stomach.

"We will monitor your condition closely, and we'll go gradually at first, not too far, to hopefully condition your brain and body to travel," said the captain. "Our missions could be strenuous, and I need you to be at your best. Now it's very late. You should get back to bed."

Matt nodded. He was feeling a bit dizzy again, though he wasn't sure whether that was due to time sickness or simply the information he'd just received.

"Can I take this?" he said, pointing to his Mets hat.

"Of course," said the captain. "It is yours, after all."

"Thank you." Matt took the hat and turned to leave.

"Mateo?" said the captain.

"Yes?"

"I would ask you to please not tell the rest of the crew what we have discussed here this night."

"They don't know?" said Matt.

"They know their way of life is at risk, but not the full extent. I cannot afford for them to be consumed by fear. You may of course share with your brother and sister. I'll leave that up to you."

Matt considered this, wondering if it was really fair that the crew not know, but then what could they really do about it? The captain was right. Sometimes ignorance really is bliss. "I won't tell," he said.

"You must think me quite a villain," said the captain, "allowing you and your siblings to board the *Vermillion*, knowing what I know. My only defense is that I do believe you may be the real key to fixing all of this. In the future at least, you seem to know something that can be of help. Still, if you feel this is too much for you, if you truly wish to have no part in this, I will take you home as I said I would."

Matt considered. Strangely he felt no sense of betrayal or malice toward the captain. Yes, it appeared that he had lured them on board the *Vermillion*, but it also seemed that they were supposed to go, and now he finally understood why. He had to save the ship and the compass. He didn't know how, but he would figure it out. He felt the challenge settling in, and the desire to get to work.

"No, I want to stay," said Matt. "I want to help. I think Corey and Ruby will too."

The captain nodded. "Very well. I'll see you in the morning."

Matt padded out of the captain's office. Santiago followed closely at his heels and shut the door after him. A moment later the lock clicked and Matt was left alone in the dark.

He felt his way along the walls back to his room and flopped into his hammock. It was only then he realized that he never did find the bathroom, but he didn't dare get out of bed again. He imagined taking another wrong turn and Brocco pulling a gun on him. Matt might not be so lucky in that case. So he lay in his hammock, wide awake, his mind buzzing with all that had just happened and been said. It was a long night.

13

Wiley's World City of Books

"He did *what* to the *Mona Lisa*?" Ruby shrieked and dropped her sword. She'd been slashing at the air when Matt had woken up and began to tell her and Corey the events of the previous night, but he hadn't really felt he had her attention until now. Corey had brought breakfast into their room, if you could call it breakfast. He was stuffing his face with a Twinkie and nearly choked at Ruby's outburst.

"Shh!" said Matt, looking toward the doorway of their room. "Be quiet. I don't want anyone else to hear." Matt had resolved to tell Corey and Ruby everything, but now he was having second thoughts. He hadn't even gotten to the part where they could potentially cease to exist. But Matt knew he needed to tell them. He took a breath and plunged in.

Matt explained about the key inside the *Mona Lisa*, his message from his future self, the mission to save the compass, and the consequences if they failed. Corey paled slightly as he spoke. Ruby's expression shifted between fear and horror.

"So unless we figure out how to fix the compass, we'll never get home?"

"Or worse," said Matt. "We could go home and then one day not exist anymore."

"Like *poof*, we're gone?" said Corey, a glob of Twinkie cream filling at the corner of his mouth.

"Something like that," said Matt.

"What does the key go to?" Corey asked. "What does it unlock?"

"I don't know, and the captain doesn't either, but the captain thinks it has something to do with the compass, like it will lead us to something that can fix it."

"So what do we do now?" said Ruby.

"Well, I told the captain we'd help him," said Matt. "We don't have to, though. He did say he'd take us home if we didn't want to take the risk."

Matt half expected Ruby to say they should go home, that this was far too dangerous, but to his surprise Ruby pressed her lips together in a firm line and said, "No, I think we need to stay and help. It's like you said before, what good will it do to go home if we suddenly disappear? And it looks like our future selves are trying to help, or at least future Matt is. That's enough for me."

Matt looked to Corey, who ironically looked a little less certain. He had been keen on staying when it had been a fun, carefree adventure, with no expectations or strings attached. But now things had taken a serious turn, and Corey never did cope well with serious things.

"Yeah," he said. "I guess this is what we have to do."

"Take heart," said Matt. "Think of all the Twinkies and Pop-Tarts you'll get."

Ruby rolled her eyes. "Okay, so we're all in." She held out her fist. Matt put his in and then Corey.

Matt was ready to get started right away and wanted to make a visit to the library after breakfast to see if they could find out what *video et taceo* meant, but Ruby was supposed to have a fencing lesson with the captain, and Corey said Brocco was going to teach him how to make his own fireworks. Matt got the sense they weren't feeling quite the urgency that he was, but he didn't want to go searching without them, and he had told Jia that he would help her with her electricity project, so *video et taceo* would have to wait. Corey and Ruby ran above deck, and Matt set off to find Jia.

Jia's room was just two doors down from the room he shared with Corey and Ruby, but he hadn't been inside yet. He knew it had to be Jia's room by the door handle. Instead of a standard knob or handle, there was a hammer. When he knocked, the door swung open right away and Jia beamed. "Come in!" she said, pulling him by the arm. "I was just working on the electricity, but it's being stubborn."

Matt couldn't decide if Jia's room looked more like a workshop or a toy shop. There were buckets and crates of tools and stacks of instruction manuals. Saws, screwdrivers, chisels, and pliers all hung on the wall, while dangling from the ceiling were fancy models of cars, trains, boats, ships, helicopters, and airplanes.

"Can the *Vermillion* really turn into all these things?" Matt asked, looking up at all the models dangling from the ceiling. "Even an airplane?"

"Sure," said Jia. "Airplanes are rare, but it can happen. It's only happened once since I've been on board, and it was terrifying! No one knew exactly how to fly it, and we almost crashed. I've been trying to learn more about aviation. It's incredible. It's still hard to believe that something so big and heavy can fly."

In the very center of the room was a table where there sat a big, beautiful model of the *Vermillion* as a frigate ship, sliced in half, so you could see all the rooms and cabins inside. Matt peered closer, astonished by all the fine detail, the furniture and light fixtures. There were even miniature models of the captain and crew, but it didn't give him any further clue as to how it all worked.

The door creaked open, and Pike stepped inside. She froze when she saw Matt.

"Hi," said Matt. She just stared at him.

"Hello, Pike," said Jia. "Don't worry, you can come in.

Matt's just here to help me with something."

Pike padded silently across the room, still staring at Matt. She skittered to the back corner of the room where there was a small bed that looked to be made out of old crates with a tie quilt spread on top, all the ties untied. A small metal box with a lock sat next to the bed. Pike crouched down and began fiddling with the lock, looking over her shoulder at Matt every couple of seconds. There was a click and the box popped open. Pike reached inside and pulled out a tangled ball of yarn, quickly shut the box, then skittered out of the room, taking one last look at Matt before shutting the door.

"I don't think she likes me being in her room," said Matt.

"Oh, she doesn't mind," said Jia. "Pike's just very shy, but she'll warm up to you."

"What's her position on the crew?" Matt asked.

"She doesn't have one yet," said Jia. "She's still a bit young, and all she really seems to want to do is untie knots. Anything that's knotted up and tangled seems to fascinate her. I'm sure the captain will find a good use for even that skill and give her an official position eventually. He'll train you and your brother and sister, too, if you want. You can choose whatever you want to do on the *Vermillion*, whatever you're good at and like to do, and the captain will find a way to make it useful."

Matt felt a little awkward just then. The captain had given him a task, but he didn't think he could explain it to Jia without telling her things the captain had asked him not to. It was disappointing because he felt Jia really was someone he could confide in, and she was smart. She could probably help. But he would respect the captain's request to not tell the rest of the crew.

"So . . . ," said Matt. "Where's your electricity project?"

"It's over here," said Jia. She went to the opposite back corner of Pike's bed, where a hammock hung, almost as an afterthought to the rest of the room. Underneath the hammock was a box full of electrical wires, power boxes, light bulbs, and sockets. A power box was already attached to the wall with a light socket just above it. "I've been fascinated with electricity ever since I first saw it, and I'm determined to bring it to the *Vermillion*, just like I did the plumbing. It would be nice to flip a switch and have light instead of lighting candles or lanterns, wouldn't it?

"I've read all about Thomas Edison and the invention of electricity, and I've been trying and trying to make it work here, but I'm beginning to think it's a lost cause. I can't even get a buzz out of the wires, even though I'm sure I've got the right ones."

"Where's your power source?" Matt asked.

Jia knit her brow. "What do you mean?"

"You need a source of energy for the electricity to work, you know, like a generator? You have to either burn coal or use wind or water to generate the power for the electricity to work."

"Oh," said Jia. "I just assumed the *Vermillion* was the power source. It *is* full of energy, you know. It couldn't transform and travel the way it does if it weren't. And things tend to work a little differently on the *Vermillion*. Shall we experiment?"

"You can't know until you try," said Matt, though he highly doubted it would work.

"Exactly," said Jia. "Here, help me untangle these." They began to pull apart the piles of wires. Jia grouped a few together and wrapped them tightly around a beam. "I just need to get the right combination. If we cross these two wires, we should get a little buzz." She crossed the two wires. Nothing happened. Matt wasn't surprised, but Jia seemed genuinely disappointed.

"Is the ship the real source of energy?" Matt asked. "Or is it the compass?"

"I suppose it's the compass," said Jia, "but really they're so connected they're pretty much one and the same, so we should get *something*."

Matt didn't want to tell her that this was never going to work, so he decided to humor her. "Electric wires are usually connected physically to the power source," he said. "Maybe the wires need to be *in* the ship."

"Oh! I never thought of that. Good idea," said Jia. She looked all around her room, deciding where she should place the wires. "The floors are always the first thing to change during travel," she said. "Let's try putting them in there." She went to her table full of tools and got a hammer and screwdriver. She came back to the corner and pounded a hole in the floor beneath her hammock. She threaded the wires through the hole, then took the other two ends and held them apart from each other. Matt felt the hair on his head tingle. A light but distinct vibration buzzed in the floorboards.

"Here goes," said Jia.

She touched the wires, and they zapped her so hard she fell back on her bottom. Her hair started to float outward.

Matt stifled a laugh. "Are you okay?" He held a hand out to her. When she took it, it shocked him so thoroughly he stumbled backward and fell into a bucket of tools. He winced as a screwdriver poked him.

"Sorry!" said Jia.

Matt just laughed. "Hey, we got it to work!"

"Well, we've figured out how to access power," said Jia. "Or *you* figured it out at least. Now we need to see if we can get it to actually light a bulb."

They connected the wires to one of the sockets and screwed in a light bulb. It buzzed to life almost immediately, but it also burned Matt's hand and then exploded. Matt yelped, jumping out of the way just in time.

"It got hot really quick!" He shook out his hand. It was a little red, but he didn't think it was too bad.

Jia ran to the other corner of the room where she had a

small sink. She got a cloth wet with cold water and pressed it over Matt's palm.

"I'm so sorry, I should have given you some gloves and glasses before screwing that in. I'm never very good about safety."

"It seems the *Vermillion* is almost *too* powerful of an energy source," said Matt.

"We just need to figure out a way to harness the energy properly," said Jia. "But isn't this fun? I mean, I don't really like getting electrocuted so much, but I've never had anyone else to work with on projects before."

"Did you have a family before?" Matt asked. "I mean . . . sorry, you don't have to talk about it if you don't want to."

"Oh, that's all right," said Jia. "I never knew my parents. I was left at an orphanage in China when I was just a baby."

"Me too!" said Matt.

"You were?"

Matt nodded. "Well, not in China. I was born in Colombia."

"So it's almost like you're an orphan like the rest of us."

"Sort of. My parents adopted me when I was three months old. I don't remember anything except my life in New York."

"You're lucky," Jia said. Matt agreed. As unlucky as he had felt in some ways, he had always felt very lucky in that way.

"But it's almost like the captain adopted you, too, isn't it?" Matt asked.

Jia scrunched up her face. "I'm more like his . . . what's the word . . . his ward? He has charge of me and we get along, but I don't think he's my father like your father is your father, and the crew aren't quite like brothers and sisters, I don't think. But I'm happy here. Of course I would rather live anywhere than the orphanage." She shivered a little, as though shaking some terrible memories from her mind. Mateo wondered what awful things she'd had to endure at such a young age, but he knew it would be impolite to ask.

"Do you still want to learn Chinese with me?" Matt asked hopefully.

"Yes," said Jia. "We'll be able to learn better together."

While they worked and continued to electrocute themselves, Jia tried to teach Matt a little Chinese. Matt picked it all up very quickly, and they were able to have some short conversations, but Jia exhausted all her knowledge within twenty minutes.

Matt asked Jia about all the places she'd traveled, what was the farthest in the past she had gone and what was the farthest in the future. Coincidentally it was the day Matt and Corey and Ruby had boarded the *Vermillion*.

"But you could go farther, couldn't you? I mean, the compass could take us farther into the future, couldn't it?" Matt had been a bit envious when he realized that everyone on the *Vermillion* had traveled well into the future, according to the time they were born, not just the past. They didn't just see things that had already happened before they were born, they also got to see how the world changed long after they should have died. Wouldn't it be cool if Matt could go a century or more beyond his time and see all that had happened? The new inventions? He could see the iPhone 20. Maybe they'd have flying cars, like in *Back to the Future*, and maybe there was a time when they really *had* figured out how to teleport. In a hundred years humans could have colonized other planets, traveled to other galaxies. And maybe, just maybe, they could find a future year when the Mets win the World Series again.

But Jia shook her head. "I'm pretty sure the captain has tried many times, but we always get yanked back here to Nowhere in No Time. It's a little jarring, actually."

Matt crinkled up his face. The captain hadn't told him that, and it seemed significant. What could that mean? Why would the compass stop working right after the time he, Corey, and Ruby boarded the *Vermillion*? Did they all cease to exist? Did the world end?

"It's not so unusual, really," said Jia. "There have been other times and places we haven't been able to travel, sort of pockets of times and places where we are unable to go. The 1940s is a big spot, actually, almost everywhere in the world. Wiley says it's probably something to do with a big war he read about in one of his future books."

"World War Two," said Matt.

"Yes, that's the one. It sounds awful."

"But you can travel *after* that particular decade," said Matt.

"But not beyond my time at all, right? So that's different."

Jia just shrugged. "It could be any number of things—a natural disaster, or someone else causing a glitch in the space-time continuum. Who knows?"

"You mean there are others who can time-travel?"

"I don't know," said Jia. "I've never heard of anyone else, but it's possible. After all, the captain didn't make the compass, and who knows if the inventor created more than one or some other person has figured out a way to time-travel."

"I wonder who *did* invent the compass," said Matt. "The captain really doesn't know?"

"No," said Jia. "Captain Bonnaire, the captain before him, had some clue, I think, but she kept it very secret, even from Captain Vincent, and then she died."

Matt wondered if this was what the key was supposed to lead them toward, the maker of the compass. Surely if anyone would know how to fix it, it would be him. Or her.

"Okay, I switched some wires," said Jia. "Let's try just one more time, shall we? Then we can go to lunch."

They both got zapped again.

"Oh well," said Jia. "I guess today is not the day." They unplugged their wires, coiled them up, and headed to the dining hall.

"What happened to you two?" said Corey, laughing as Matt and Jia appeared with their hair looking like masses of tumbleweed.

"Electricity," said Jia.

"Oh good," said Ruby. "I thought maybe Brocco had started a hair salon or something."

After lunch, Matt, Ruby, and Corey made their way to the lower deck, where Wiley said the library was located. He was delighted when they told him they wanted to pay a visit and said he'd help them find some books.

"What's the phrase again?" Ruby asked.

"*Video et taceo*," said Matt. "It translates to 'I see and say nothing,' but I don't know what that's supposed to mean."

"You know, it does sound familiar for some reason," said Ruby, "but I can't think why."

"Probably because it sounds like *videos and tacos*," said Corey. "Maybe we're supposed to go to dinner and a movie somewhere, instead of the library." Corey was dragging his feet on this particular mission. He had never had a great relationship with libraries or librarians. He was always too loud and rowdy and thought all the books the librarian kept pushing into his hands were boring.

Matt opened the door at the end of the hall and was hit with the smell of old leather and oil, paper and pipe smoke. It smelled much like a library, he thought, but when they entered he very soon found that this wasn't your typical library. Yes, there were books, lots of them, but they were not lined in neat rows on straight shelves. Instead they were stacked in towers all around the room, each in the shape of a famous building, many of which Matt recognized. There was the Empire State Building, the Colosseum, an Egyptian pyramid, and a tall tower of books that seemed to be miraculously leaning without toppling over—the Leaning Tower of Pisa. It was a world city made of books.

"Whoa," said Corey.

"Wow," said Ruby.

"Yeah," said Matt.

A head poked out from behind the Empire State Building. "Good day, my friends!" said Wiley, a huge smile on his face. "Come in, come in!" He sat in a worn leather chair with his feet resting on an old lobster trap (filled with more books). He held a large leather-bound book in his lap. His pipe was between his teeth, and he wore wire-framed spectacles that made him look very scholarly.

"Welcome to the *Vermillion* library!" said Wiley. "I am your humble librarian, at your service. You kids like to read?"

"Yes," said Ruby and Matt nodded, still taking in everything.

"And how about you, young man?" Wiley asked, turning to Corey. "Got any favorite books?"

Corey shrugged. "I like comics," he said. "But I know that's not real reading."

Wiley raised his eyebrows. "And who told you that?"

"My teacher," said Corey. "She said there are too many

pictures and it's not enough of a challenge for my brain."

"Well, with all due respect to your teacher, who I am sure is fine educator, I disagree," said Wiley. "Pictures are no less powerful than words, and words no more powerful than pictures. They each tell us a story. And what happens when you put the two together? A symphony in the mind, like lobster and butter. People who read pictures and words at the same time are smart people in my book, yes, sir."

Corey, who probably hadn't been referred to as smart in quite some time, seemed to grow two inches in two seconds, and it made Matt want to hug Wiley.

Wiley set his own book down on the lobster crate. "Now let's see if we can't find something right for you, my young friend. No book is for everyone, but for everyone there is a book!" Wiley guided Corey around the library until they found a stack of comics in the middle of one of the towers (that big clock tower in London, maybe?). Corey tried to pull them out carefully but ended up toppling half the tower.

Corey sagged. "Sorry," he said.

"No apology necessary," said Wiley. "I always look forward to a good toppling so I can stack it into something else. I was thinking of making an Eiffel Book Tower. I liked that tower. What do you think?"

"That'd be cool. I can help." Corey crouched down, hurrying to pick up the stacks. "No way, this is, like, a vintage Batman! And Dr. Strange!"

"Let's let him have some time," whispered Ruby.

Matt nodded in agreement. Watching Corey be enthusiastic in a library was like watching a tiger cuddle with a bunny rabbit. Do not disturb.

Matt wandered around with Ruby, browsing all the different towers, reading their spines. Some of the books looked quite modern, while others looked ancient. There were old medical and science books, philosophy books, and stacks of books in various languages. There were leather-bound books with no titles on the spines and a wagon stacked with stone tablets.

"Those look like they could come from the days of Moses," said Ruby. Matt agreed.

From the rafters hung fishing nets bulging with more books, and a brass birdcage hung right above his head, filled with scrolls. Curious, Matt reached up and opened the birdcage and took out a scroll. He unraveled it carefully.

"Careful, those are real old," said Wiley. He'd snuck up behind Matt.

"This is Greek," said Matt. He couldn't read it, but he recognized the different alphabet.

"Ain't it fancy?" said Wiley. "They're from the great library of Alexandria."

Matt froze. Real old? These scrolls were ancient and supposedly completely destroyed.

"Dad would *kill* for some of those," said Ruby.

Matt suddenly wasn't sure what to do. He shouldn't be touching these. At the very least he should be wearing gloves.

"Have you read them?" Matt asked.

"Don't I wish I could!" said Wiley. "Learning to read in English was a big enough feat for me. I didn't learn until I was about your age, just after I boarded the *Vermillion*."

"You didn't go to school before then?" said Ruby.

"No, ma'am. I was born in the days of Jim Crow."

"Who's that?"

Matt wanted to tell Ruby to hush, but Wiley didn't skip a beat.

"Jim Crow Laws," he said. "Laws that tell black people they can't go certain places or do certain things, like use a certain toilet or go to school with the white kids. Weren't no school for me within ten miles."

"Oh," said Ruby. Wiley hadn't spoken with any kind of bitterness, just matter-of-fact, but still, Matt felt a bit awkward. He could tell Ruby did, too, and neither of them was sure what to say. Matt had learned about Jim Crow in social studies and read some books from that era in language arts, like *Roll of Thunder, Hear My Cry*, but just like the Twin Towers, it had almost felt like a myth, or some prehistoric animal, distant and extinct. Now, talking with Wiley, a person who had lived it, it all seemed so close and real and terrible, and Matt felt a sudden and intense shame that he'd thought of it so casually, never stopping to consider how it had really affected people and still did. Matt had always considered himself pretty smart, but he decided there was nothing like being around a bunch of people not only from different places, but also from different centuries and decades to make you feel like a complete ignoramus.

Matt rolled up the scroll and carefully placed it back into the birdcage.

"And what kind of books do you two like to read?" said Wiley. "Adventure? Mystery? I've got the full collection of Hardy Boys and Nancy Drew!"

"Actually, we're interested in some Latin books," said Matt, remembering why he was here. "Or history books of Latin-speaking countries?"

"Huh," said Wiley. He put his pipe in his mouth. "I would not have guessed that."

"I like studying different languages and cultures," said Matt. "Ruby does too."

"But I'll take some Nancy Drew books," said Ruby.

Wiley helped them search for some Latin books. They found quite a few tucked into the columns of the Colosseum, including a language and phrase book, books on the Roman Empire, and one Matt thought looked particularly promising, called *Decoding Latin: The Living Messages Inside the Dead Language*.

Corey came around a tower with a stack of comics. "Can I take all these, Wiley?"

"Sure thing, my friend," said Wiley. "You take as many as you like as often as you like. There are no reading limits here."

Wiley brought the stack of Latin books around the towers and set them on the lobster crate next to the book he'd been reading. Matt glanced at it casually, curious to know the kinds of books Wiley read. It was spread open and Matt saw that it wasn't any kind of novel or manual, but a record book, with columns and rows all filled in with neat, precise ink.

"Are those all the places the *Vermillion* has traveled?" Matt asked.

"Indeed it is," said Wiley. "I was just entering our last mission when you came in."

"Can I look at it?"

"Sure, sure! Go ahead!"

Matt skimmed down the open page, mesmerized at all the times and places the *Vermillion* had traveled. On just one page he saw Russia, Italy, China, Madagascar, Australia, Switzerland, Spain, Angola, Scotland, Brazil, and, in at least a dozen rows fairly close together, *New York City, NY.* That must have been the time the captain had been looking, or waiting, for them. The last entry was for the Mets game.

Matt flipped the pages farther back, skimming the dates and places.

"Hatfield, Hertfordshire, England, 1558!" said Ruby, pointing. "That's when Queen Elizabeth I became queen! And look—there's Westminster Abbey, Greenwich, London, the Tower of London, all of them during her reign!"

"Yes," said Wiley. "Those would have been old missions, before my time on the *Vermillion*. I believe the previous captain was friends with that queen."

"Captain Vincent would have been, too, then, wouldn't he?"

"Don't think the captain was quite as friendly with the queen. Anyhow, we've never traveled there."

"But maybe we could travel there, do you think?" said Ruby. "I'm doing a report on Queen Elizabeth at school!"

Corey groaned. "Ruby, are you honestly going to do homework while we're on this ship?"

"Why wouldn't I take the opportunity to see her?" said Ruby. "What better source for a report than the source itself! Do you think the captain would take us there?" Ruby asked Wiley again.

Wiley stuck his pipe in his mouth. "You could ask the captain," said Wiley, "but I wouldn't get my hopes up too high if I was you. Captain Vincent has never sailed to England any time since I've been on board the *Vermillion*. I don't think he likes it, particularly. Probably bad memories from childhood."

"What years is the captain from?" Matt asked.

"Oh, somewhere around 1750. He was the son of some rich lord in Cornwall, and as I understand it he was treated quite unfairly by his older brother after his parents died. He ran away from home when he wasn't more than sixteen or seventeen. That's when he met up with Captain Bonnaire and the *Vermillion.*"

"That's sad," said Ruby. "But Queen Elizabeth is so long before he was born, over a century, so maybe he'd be willing to go there."

"You can surely ask," said Wiley. "But if all else fails, I have some fine books on that queen, ones you won't find in any other library."

They searched the Latin books all afternoon. It was slow work, since some of the books were completely in Latin and the print was not always easy to read. Matt also didn't totally trust Ruby and Corey to not miss something of significance, so he ended up reading everything they read as well, which Corey and Ruby found as a reason to stop searching with him and do their own thing.

At dinner, Captain Vincent tapped his glass for silence and offered his haiku.

> *Birds and plants of earth*
> *You are rich and beautiful*
> *On our plates and tongues.*

Tonight the food was more traditionally Chinese—roasted duck, rice, noodles, and egg drop soup—but there was also macaroni and cheese that Matt was sure came from a box, Cup Noodles, granola bars, cheese puffs, and bottles of soda. Corey was about to reach for the cheese puffs when Santiago came scurrying over, snatched one right out of the bag, and started munching on it like corn on the cob. He then opened a bottle of root beer, guzzled half the bottle in ten seconds, and let out a hearty belch. Matt couldn't decide if he was impressed or disgusted. Corey didn't eat the cheese puffs.

"Any luck today, Mateo?" the captain asked Matt quietly.

"Not yet," said Matt, "but I haven't searched all that much. I think we'll find something."

"I'm sure you will," said the captain, and Matt felt an added weight resting on his shoulders. He knew the captain was counting on him, but what if he failed? What if they never discovered what the *Mona Lisa* key opened or learned how to fix the compass?

14

Within the Walls

Matt searched for days for anything having to do with the *Mona Lisa* key or the phrase *video et taceo*, but he found nothing even remotely helpful. He practically turned Wiley's library upside down, nearly dismantling the entire Colosseum and the Leaning Tower of Pisa in search of the information. He looked in Latin history and language books, French history books, art history books, books and articles about the *Mona Lisa*, articles about famous keys, but nothing surfaced.

The captain didn't seem too worried, though, however much it worried Matt, and he continued to use the compass as though no danger were imminent. Ruby asked if they could go see Queen Elizabeth, but Captain Vincent said it was best that they travel back in time a little more gradually, in order to help Matt adjust to travel and combat time sickness. Ruby was sorely disappointed but didn't argue. She had grown to respect the captain a great deal, perhaps the most out of any of them. She continued to practice the sword every day and had gotten so good that Matt had to admit he was starting to become a little bit intimidated by her.

And so the *Vermillion* traveled, mostly within the United States and the twentieth century, moving back a decade or two at a time. Sometimes their time travels involved a mission, like disrupting a train or bank robbery or rescuing passengers off a sinking ship. They even intercepted a store robbery in a small town in Texas by the famous Bonnie and Clyde! The manager was so grateful he gave them all free sarsaparilla, which Matt learned was a drink that tasted a lot like root beer.

The *Vermillion*'s transformations were always a surprise and always trapped or tricked Ruby in one way or another. When the *Vermillion* transformed into a little red roadster, she ended up on the windshield, clinging for dear life as Wiley swerved and slammed on the brakes, and when it turned into a tugboat, she somehow ended up on top of the mast.

"I don't think the *Vermillion* likes me all that much," said Ruby after she'd ended up in the coal bunker of a steam engine and came out completely covered in soot.

"Oh, she's just teasing you, Miss Ruby," said the captain. "She has a sense of humor, you know."

"Does she?" said Ruby. "Well, she needs to work on her comedic timing, in my opinion."

The captain laughed. "I'm sure she'll make a note and try

to improve herself next time."

Matt sort of appreciated the *Vermillion*'s antics and almost believed it was for his benefit, not to entertain him necessarily, though it certainly did, but to hide his time sickness. He still struggled with dizzy spells and nausea, usually right after travel, though it could hit at any time, and he didn't want the others to notice. He didn't want the captain to think he couldn't handle the missions.

Sometimes they had no mission and just went places—many of which were as foreign as Paris or any other country for three city kids who had barely traveled beyond their own state lines. They explored the Grand Canyon, hiking through the majestic red rock ravines, climbing the rocks, and even jumping off some waterfalls. They went to Yellowstone National Park, where they saw hot springs and geysers like Old Faithful, and plenty of wildlife—bears, wolves, buffalo, and elk. Matt read in one of Wiley's books that the entire park was a volcano that could destroy half of North America if it were to explode in full force.

"Now that's one big firecracker," said Brocco. "Maybe we should learn how to create our own volcano, eh, Li'l Bullet?"

"Yes!" said Corey.

"Maybe Li'l Professor here can teach us the right way to do it."

"Li'l Professor" was Brocco's chosen nickname for Matt. He'd finally settled on it after Matt continually spouted facts and corrected others' misinformation, like when Albert suggested that Matt needed to be bled to cure him of his time sickness and Matt told him how that wasn't actually a remedy for anything and doctors from his era actually knew very little about safe or effective medical procedures.

"It's part of the reason why so many people in your era died before the age of forty," said Matt.

Albert paled at this. "The other reason is they were murdered by filthy traitors," he said, his voice shaking, and he turned away and left.

"His father was a physician," said Jia quietly. "He attended to his mother before she died, and Albert said he always blamed himself for her death, that he didn't know how to save her."

Matt could have kicked himself. How could he have been so insensitive? He'd forgotten about Albert's parents, how his mother died when he was a baby and his father died in the Revolutionary War, fighting for the British.

Matt tried to apologize to Albert later, but he wouldn't even hear him out. "I don't need your pity," he said, sneering. "At least my parents wanted me. They didn't abandon me like some stray dog."

Matt was confused for a moment, and then he realized what Albert was referring to. It shocked him more than it hurt, that Albert would even assume he'd been abandoned when Matt had always believed his biological parents had both died. For a brief moment Matt thought of his own parents back in New York and got another twinge of guilt. He hadn't thought about them too much lately. He'd been so consumed with their missions and traveling and searching for clues to the *Mona Lisa* key that his parents and home had been pushed to the recesses of his memory. He almost couldn't pull up their faces.

As annoying and inconvenient as it was, it was actually Matt's time sickness that led him to the information he needed. They had just returned from traveling to someplace in Iowa, in the late 1800s, having intercepted a train robbery by the famous Jesse James. It was the farthest back in time they had traveled yet, and when they returned and the *Vermillion* transformed back to a ship, a wave of vertigo hit Matt so violently he completely lost his balance and had to grab on to one of the sconces on the wall, which ripped right off and took some of the wall with it. Albert laughed as Matt stood helplessly with the light fixture in hand.

"Are you okay?" Jia asked.

"I—I'm sorry," he stuttered, still feeling the room spin a bit.

"Don't worry," said Jia. "I can fix it."

The captain came right away and inspected Matt, checking his forehead and pupils. "I'm sorry, Mateo, I may have pushed you a little farther than I should have."

"I'm okay," said Matt.

"Better get you some food."

"I'll get it!" said Corey. "Want some Twinkies, Matt? Pudding cups? Oreos?"

"Whatever," said Matt.

"Ooh! Look there!" Wiley called and ran toward the wall that Matt had just destroyed. Matt shook his head to clear it and turned to see what Wiley was so excited about. To his surprise, he had uncovered a small cavern within the ship, full of odd items—a coil of rope, a few dusty books, and a hammer.

"My book!" Wiley picked up one of the books and held it like it was a sacred treasure. "This is the book that learned me to read! I thought it was lost forever!" Wiley flipped through the pages. There were illustrations throughout of a boy and girl, both blond and blue-eyed, playing with a ball, a dog, a rope. "Listen to this, listen to this!" Wiley started to read one of the pages aloud. "'Come, Jane, let's swing. Do you want to swing?' 'Yes, Dick, I want to swing. Will you push me?' *He-he-ha!*" Wiley continued to read about Dick and Jane out loud as he walked out of the dining hall.

"Hey, my hammer!" said Jia. She reached in the wall and pulled out a small hammer with a leather handle. "I've been looking for this! Thanks, Matt!" She attacked him with a hug, accidentally knocking his head with the hammer. "Oh, sorry!"

And that wasn't all. Pike suddenly jumped up, reached

over Matt's head, and grabbed a rope inside the wall. It was dirty, worn, and frayed at the ends, but Pike hugged it against her chest, like she'd found a beloved stuffed animal.

"Your rope!" said Jia. "How clever of Matt to find it. Say thank you."

Pike gave Matt a rare smile and then immediately began to tie elaborate knots in the rope.

"She's been searching for that rope for ages," said Jia. "I think it might be the only thing she had with her when she came on board, and she almost always carried it with her, but it disappeared during a mission. She was devastated. You saved the day!"

"Look, there's something else in here," said Ruby. She reached in and took out a thick, rectangular piece of paper, or maybe it was a thin piece of wood. It looked very old and brittle, and it had writing on it in a foreign language. Matt's heart leaped, thinking it might be Latin, but as he looked closer he realized the alphabet was different. He didn't even recognize it.

"That's a palm leaf document," said Albert knowledgeably. "We have some in the gallery from India. They're usually bound together. How did that one get in there?" Matt almost felt Albert was accusing him of stealing and hiding it.

"Same way everything else got in there," said Ruby.

"Do you know what language this is?" Matt asked.

"Sanskrit, most likely," said Albert. "Here, I'd better take it back to the gallery. It's probably been damaged already."

Matt didn't readily hand it over. He had a feeling. Was it foremembering? He wasn't sure. He just felt that he hadn't found this by chance, that it meant something.

"I'd like to take this to the library," said Matt. "If I can find some books in the library I could translate it. Could I, Captain?" He looked meaningfully at the captain. He seemed to understand.

"Yes, I'd be very interested to know what it says. Go ahead, Mateo. Translate away."

"But—" Albert began to protest, but the captain cut him off.

"Albert, why don't you come into my cabin and take the *Mona Lisa* with you to the gallery? I do believe she's in need of your expert care." This seemed to appease Albert. The captain winked at Matt as he led Albert to his cabin.

Matt went to the library right away. Wiley was more than happy to assist him and found some books on Sanskrit, as well as some sources about India and palm leaves and their uses in writing, including a scholarly article that said in some parts of India, palm leaves were often used to record horoscopes and Ayurvedic astrology, which really excited Matt. He dug into translating. It took him nearly half the night, but the message was short and eventually he had what he felt was a decent enough translation. It made his heart beat a little faster.

What you seek lies within the walls of the temple, but beware the serpents who guard the sacred vaults.

Matt did a little more digging about temples in India. There were several that mentioned snakes, but only one that mentioned snakes guarding any vaults.

The only thing he didn't find was any mention of a key or the *Mona Lisa* or *video et taceo*. Not that he was expecting it. It could be that these connections were never recorded in history, and the message seemed too clear and pronounced to ignore.

What you seek lies within the walls of the temple . . .

And he'd even found the message in the walls of the *Vermillion*! It couldn't be a coincidence. Someone was giving them a clue.

15

Treasures and Snakes

"Say that again?" Corey asked as they were preparing for travel. "Where are we going?"

"Kerala, India," said Matt, "to the Sree Padmanabhaswamy Temple."

"Say that fast ten times," said Corey. He tried and by the end of it he was saying something like "Free-pad-mah-swampy Temple."

"What year are we traveling to?" Ruby asked.

"Seventeen fifty-one," said the captain. Matt felt a little dizzy. Nearly three hundred years from his time!

"It's a much bigger leap than I would have liked," said the captain, "but the truth is, the vaults of these temples were frequently burglarized in the later centuries. I think it's necessary that we go as early as possible in order to find what we're looking for."

Captain Vincent had been delighted at Matt's discovery. As it happened, the captain was quite familiar with the Sree Padmanabhaswamy Temple. He'd been there several times before with Captain Bonnaire, which seemed to make him feel it was more likely that whatever the *Mona Lisa* key unlocked might be there. "She may have hidden it there herself!" said the captain.

"I love India!" exclaimed Brocco. "Fantastic colors. And perhaps we could ride some elephants! Have you ridden an elephant before, Li'l Bullet?"

Corey shook his head. "They don't have elephants in the Central Park Zoo."

"Think Li'l Bullet and I might have time for some elephants, Captain?"

"There will be time for elephants and other pleasures," said the captain. "But our main mission is the temple. It holds massive amounts of gold and treasure in secret vaults."

"I like treasure too," said Brocco.

"So do I!" said Corey.

"Is someone going to steal the treasure?" Ruby asked.

"Someone is *always* stealing that treasure," said the captain. "There are hoards of gold, jewels, and many sacred relics in the vaults, which are not very well protected. Thieves are constantly breaking in to steal it. The *Vermillion* has traveled there several times before, and we take what we can to keep it safe from the petty thieves."

"Time pirates to the rescue!" said Wiley.

"Very good, then. Shall we prepare for travel? Brocco, have you prepared us proper costumes?"

"I have," said Brocco. He lifted a bulging bag and brought out several simple tunics and headdresses that didn't look much different from what Matt saw some Indian people wearing around modern New York. They easily pulled them over their regular clothes.

"So what are our positions?" Albert asked. "Do you need me to stand guard this time?"

"Actually, I would like you and Jia to remain on the *Vermillion* with Pike this time," said the captain. "Wiley and Brocco can stand guard, and I need the Hudsons' skills for this mission, particularly Mateo's."

"Me?" said Matt, feeling a little self-conscious, particularly since Albert was scowling at him. "What do you need me to do?"

The captain bent down and lowered his voice. "The key, Mateo. I'm hoping you might sense whatever it is that it will unlock."

"You mean foremember?"

"Precisely," said Captain Vincent.

Matt nodded. "I'll try my best."

The captain clapped him on the shoulder and shook him a little. "That's my boy!" He straightened up and pulled the compass out of his sleeve. "All right, crew! Prepare for a quantum time leap!"

The crew positioned themselves. Corey took hold of the

end of the table. Ruby first held on to a chair, then changed to a wall, and finally settled for crouching right in the center of the floor. She was clearly trying to choose the area where she'd be least likely to get trapped in a trunk or something.

The ship was shrinking fast, almost as if it were eager for this particular mission. The floor planks swelled slightly, then quickly shrank smaller than before, as though they were elastic or rubber. The top of the ship opened up like a convertible and rolled down the sides. The captain's cabin door split open for a moment, revealing all that was inside—his bed and desk, the slashed paintings—and then all folded in on itself like a collapsing pop-up book. Matt found himself seated in a simple rowboat, grasping an oar. The boat rocked violently from side to side for a few moments until it finally settled.

"That was weird," said Corey. He shook his head and then looked around. "Where did Ruby end up this time?"

"Get your feet off my face!"

Matt looked down and realized that his feet were resting right on Ruby's head, smashing in her cheek. Somehow she had ended up at the very bottom of the rowboat, beneath all the benches. Matt quickly lifted his feet, and he and Corey helped Ruby up. She rocked the boat a little until she finally sat down on a bench, muttering curses under her breath that Matt was certain their mother would punish by washing her mouth out with soap.

"Let's row, crew!" said Captain Vincent. They all began to

row the little boat toward the shore. It was lined with small cottages all surrounding a golden temple that rose above everything else. It looked like a giant treasure chest, a gleaming tiered tower of gold, ornately and intricately designed.

The sun was low in the sky. Matt guessed it was early evening. There seemed to be a great deal of motion and excitement on the shore, throngs of people and a procession of elephants elaborately decorated and painted.

"Ooh! Look at the elephants!" said Brocco. "And there's people riding them!"

The people atop the elephants were also elaborately dressed, wearing gold headdresses and beaded gowns and tunics. They were riding the elephants toward the water.

"That's the royal family atop the elephants," said the captain.

"What's going on?" Matt asked.

"It's the Painkuni festival," said the captain. "This is the tenth day of the festival where they will perform the *arattu*, or 'holy bath.' They bring idols out of the temple and bathe them in the sea. It's very sacred, but it's also a good time for thieves to get into the vaults of the temple as it won't be so heavily guarded."

They hit sand, and the captain and Brocco hopped out and pulled the boat onto the shore. Pike tied the boat around a wooden pole stuck in the sand, knotting it as expertly as any sailor.

"Albert, Jia, Pike, you'll remain here," said the captain.

"Yes, sir," said Jia. "We'll keep the *Vermillion* safe, won't we, Albert?"

Albert folded his arms and kicked his feet into the sand. Some of it sprayed up onto Matt's tunic.

They headed up the beach, and soon they were pushing their way through the crowds moving in the opposite direction. The air was spicy and earthy. Matt was pressed between bodies. A woman carrying a smelly bucket of fish with flies all over it knocked into him. Animals seemed to be loose everywhere. Stray dogs chased chickens and goats. There were monkeys, too, running along the thatched roofs and swinging in and out of windows. Some even hopped onto the shoulders of people, using them for a ride, or in some cases, stealing hats or food.

There were beggars, too, which wasn't shocking to Matt. He had seen plenty of people begging on the streets of New York, huddled against storefronts and subways, holding signs or shaking cups of change, but those people seemed practically well-off compared to the beggars here. Some of them were younger than Matt. A little beggar girl who couldn't have been more than five or six moved through the crowds with hands outstretched. She was filthy and barefooted. As she approached them, the captain reached inside his jacket and pulled out a few coins, dropping them into the girl's cupped hands. She immediately clasped her hands together and without a word or even a grateful smile scampered away. Matt understood why soon enough. His small act of generosity quickly attracted the attention of other beggars, like sharks to blood. Soon there were dozens of outstretched hands in front of the captain. The captain tossed coins into hands until he was quite out, but the mob only seemed to grow more desperate, pressing in on them. Finally Brocco lifted his gun and shot into the air, and the people scattered, creating a clear path for them.

"So much need here," said the captain, seemingly not at all disturbed, "and that temple is full of riches that could feed the entire country."

"So why don't they?" Matt asked.

"It's supposed to be for their gods," said the captain. "To take it, even to feed the hungry, would be sacrilege and incur their wrath."

"But we're about to take the treasure," said Ruby. "Will we incur their wrath?"

"That depends. Do you believe in their gods?"

The temple loomed in front of them, and as they came closer, Matt could make out the many statues on every layer, seemingly holding up the entire structure. Stone steps led up to a large archway where uniformed men with long sticks stood guard.

"How are we going to get inside?" Ruby asked. "They don't just let anyone in there, do they?"

"Oh no," said the captain. "And that's not where we want to go anyway. We have a different entrance."

"How many times have you been here?" Ruby asked.

"A few," said the captain. "Though not since I became captain of the *Vermillion*. It was a favorite place of Captain Bonnaire's."

They walked around the temple and then beyond it where things became quieter. They went through a village with dusty streets and rickety homes, a few lanterns flickering in windows as the sun in the sky lowered. The captain took out a piece of paper, a map, Matt realized, and consulted it. They walked a bit farther and finally stopped in front of a small hut. It was lit by a single candle. A man opened the door and beckoned them forward. The captain whispered, "No one speak. He believes we are gods come for our treasure."

The man was old, frail, and tiny, shorter than Matt, even. He spoke in a language Matt did not recognize at all, which annoyed Matt. It was like there was a part of his brain that itched to understand and he couldn't scratch it. Next language for his 12/21 project, perhaps.

The captain said nothing to the man. He didn't have to. The captain simply showed him the Obsidian Compass, and his face suddenly grew awed and fearful. He bowed deeply to the captain and beckoned him and all the crew to come inside. He kept his head down, not looking at any of them.

The house was warm and full of pungent, spicy odors—

curry, cinnamon, and jasmine. The man motioned toward the table and began to shift it. Brocco assisted him, and then the man lifted a rug that uncovered a square wooden grate. He lifted the grate and made a way for them to enter.

The captain went first. The man held out his lantern. The captain took it without saying a word and descended a narrow set of crumbling stone steps. Brocco followed after the captain, and then Wiley, each of them disappearing into the darkness.

"This doesn't seem at all safe," whispered Ruby.

"The captain wouldn't lead us into any real danger," said Corey, and he stepped down. Ruby went next, and Matt followed after her, stepping carefully down the crumbling, uneven steps. When they reached the bottom, they each took out flashlights and moved them around the space. They were in a narrow, shallow tunnel that clearly hadn't been used in many years. Cobwebs brushed their heads. (At least Matt hoped they were cobwebs.) The tunnel was fairly straight, and after about ten minutes of walking they came to a stone door.

"That was it?" said Corey. "There weren't any booby traps or anything."

"Patience, Corey," said the captain. "We haven't opened the door yet."

The captain pushed on it. It opened easily, revealing what looked like an ancient underground palace. Huge pillars and archways made various tunnels and paths. The captain stepped out of the doorway and into the space. Matt waited, his eyes half closed, waiting for something terrible to happen, but nothing did. The captain consulted his map again. "There are six vaults," he said. "Each has incredible amounts of treasure, but we are looking for a very specific vault. Of course some of them are cursed."

"Cursed?" said Ruby. "What kind of curse?"

"Oh, the usual. Seven years of bad luck or a plague on all your family. Something like that." The captain didn't seem to think this was anything to worry about. He forged ahead into one of the tunnels. Matt kept waiting for something to attack them, a mummy or a giant ax, but all was quiet and calm. They walked in a maze of tunnels until finally they came to a door. It was large and had what looked like brass snakes all over it.

Beware the snakes . . . The warning from the palm leaf rang in his ears.

"Cobras," said the captain, brushing his hands over the serpents. "They are believed to be the guardians of the sacred treasure inside the *karllaras*, the vaults. This is a different vault than I've been to in the past. I'm not sure exactly how it opens . . ." The captain reached up and pulled, but nothing happened. He looked and felt around all over the door.

"Maybe the key is to open the door," Matt said quietly.

"Yes, but where?" said the captain. "I see no keyhole.

There's not even a doorknob or latch."

Matt studied the door, zeroing in on the snakes and how they were placed. He imagined how they would move if they were really alive. Right now they were sideways, some of their bodies broken apart. If they were shifted upright . . . "Here," said Matt. He reached up and turned one of the snakes clockwise, then another counterclockwise. He did the same again, shifting the snakes until they were in their proper positions. After the fourth snake the door make a loud click. The captain pushed on the door and it opened.

"Mateo, you genius!" the captain beamed. "It would have taken me ages to figure that out."

The captain lifted the lantern into the cavern, illuminating the space. Matt gasped. The cavern was stacked floor to ceiling with gold and treasure—stacks of gold bars, piles of gold coins, pottery, jewelry, gems of all colors, shapes, and sizes, some as big as Matt's thumbnail. A suit of gold body armor was strewn across the dusty floor, cobwebs between the arms and legs. A little farther back, on a high pedestal, a life-size gold statue of a man in an elaborate headdress sat on top of a jewel-encrusted throne. The pedestal was dark, so it looked to Matt like the idol was levitating and made a chill run down his spine. Matt wondered if it was one of the temple gods standing guard over all the treasure. What would happen when they crossed the threshold? He imagined the god incinerating them on the spot, or cutting off their air supply.

The captain stepped inside the vault, but nothing happened. He brushed his hands over a pile of gold, scooping up a handful of coins and dropping them again.

"Should we start loading up, Captain?" said Brocco eagerly.

"Yes," said the captain absentmindedly. He was gazing all around the room. Matt could tell he was searching. "Take as much as you can carry. We don't want this to fall into the hands of petty thieves."

They all set to work, filling their packs with as much gold and jewels as they could carry. Ruby layered the bottom of her pack with gold bars, then coins and handfuls of diamonds, rubies, emeralds, and sapphires. Corey's eyes shone like jewels themselves as he stuffed more in his pockets.

But the captain gathered no treasure. He was looking around the vault, searching with a careful eye. Matt remembered his purpose on this mission. He was supposed to be looking for the thing the *Mona Lisa* key might unlock. He was supposed to recognize it, *foremember* it. He walked around the vault slowly. He had read that there was supposed to be a special kind of energy, a "spiritual charge" in the vaults that one could feel only if they were very lucky. But if it was disturbed, disaster would follow. It wasn't clear what that disaster might be, and Matt wasn't sure if he could feel the "special energy," but he decided it was best to err on the side of caution and try not to disturb it.

Matt moved quietly and cautiously, weaving in and out

of the mounds of treasure. He saw a few interesting things, a gold bow and arrow, a flute that looked to be made of an ivory tusk, but he saw nothing that the *Mona Lisa* key might unlock. There were plenty of chests full of treasure, but most of them were open, and if they did have a keyhole it was too big for what he knew they were looking for.

He came to the gold statue of the god on the pedestal. He was sitting cross-legged on the jewel encrusted throne, staring out with blank eyes. There were snakes wrapped around his neck.

Beware the snakes . . .

He noticed the snake heads were resting on the statue's stomach, facing downward. The statue's hands were cupped at the level of his stomach. He was holding something. A gold, circular box. It was small and ornate, about two inches high and maybe six inches wide, and it had a small keyhole in the center. Matt stared at the box. It was resting just beneath the heads of the snakes, and his heart began to pound. Could this be it? Was he foremembering?

"Captain?" said Matt.

The captain came over to him and inspected. He smiled. "Well spotted, Mateo. Now I'm going to lift you up on my shoulders so you can reach it, all right?"

Matt nodded. The captain crouched down, and Matt sat on his shoulders. He wobbled a little as the captain lifted him up. He looked at the blank eyes of the idol, the heads of the snakes. He hesitated. It felt wrong somehow, like he wasn't supposed to take this. *Don't be a scaredy-cat*, he told himself. This was the mission! He was supposed to find whatever the key unlocked. He took a breath, reached out, and gently removed the box from the hands of the statue.

The captain lowered him down. "Very good," said the captain, taking the box from Matt's hands, trading it for the lantern. "Now we'd better—"

A hiss interrupted the captain. Matt stumbled back as two giant snakes rose up behind the golden statue. They coiled around the golden body, over the golden snakes, slithered across the stomach and over the hands and dropped to the floor right at their feet. The snakes rose up, flaps of skin extended at their necks. King cobras. They both hissed, showing their fangs. The first one lashed out at the captain. The captain jumped back, clutching the box to his stomach. Matt slowly retreated in the other direction, his breath growing short, heart hammering in his chest.

Wiley yelped and hid behind a large chest of gold. Ruby whimpered and backed away.

"I got 'em, Captain," said Brocco, slowly approaching the snakes from behind. He drew out his gun and aimed, but as soon as he cocked it, one of the snakes turned and lashed out at Brocco. He yelped, dropped the gun, and tumbled backward, landing in a heap of gold coins. The cobra curled around the gun and pulled it into his coils.

"Well, hot dang," said Wiley. "That was a fancy steal, don't you think?"

"Bloody snakes," said Brocco. He was sweating bullets. But the snakes had turned their focus back on the captain, who now had his sword out and was waving it at the cobras. One cobra attacked, and the captain swiped and jumped to the side, clutching the golden box in one arm. The other cobra came to the other side and struck at the captain's leg while the captain slashed his sword again. The snakes retreated a bit, hissing and circling the captain. They were in a deadly dance.

Corey slowly made his way over to Matt. "Give me the lantern," he said.

"Why?"

"Just trust me."

Matt handed the lantern over to Corey, who reached in his pocket and took out a small packet.

"Captain," said Corey. "On the count of three, you should jump back from the snakes and get behind something."

"What are you doing?" said the captain sharply.

"Just trust me," said Corey calmly. "One." Corey opened the door of the lantern. "Two." He put the packet inside and shut the door. "Three!" Corey threw the lantern at the snakes. Everyone jumped back and scrambled for cover. Matt crouched behind a statue. Corey grabbed Ruby and dove behind a pile of gold coins while Brocco tried to close himself inside a chest. Captain Vincent barely had time to launch himself before the lantern exploded. Smoke filled the cavern. The snakes hissed madly, and when the smoke cleared they were gone.

The captain rose from his crouched position, still clutching the box, and carefully stepped in the space where the snakes had been. Matt looked all around, but it appeared the snakes really were gone and they were safe. The captain whistled and motioned for everyone to come out of hiding. Brocco went and retrieved his gun. He picked up the smoking lantern and quickly dropped it, shaking his hand.

"Bloody snakes. Li'l Bullet, that was bloody brilliant!"

"Indeed," Captain Vincent said. "I believe you just saved us all!"

Corey beamed.

"Taught him everything he knows!" said Brocco.

A sudden crash made them all jump. The pedestal on which the golden god rested crumbled. A stone pillar to Matt's right cracked, and the golden god toppled to the ground and rolled until it was facing outward, staring at them with empty eyes. Matt was guessing that the special energy had now been disturbed.

"I think we'd better take our leave," said the captain. "Quickly now."

They all hustled as fast as they could with their loads of treasure, dust and rock trickling down on their heads. Matt was glad he was unburdened so he could get out faster. When everyone was out of the vault, the captain slammed the doors shut. The snakes automatically clicked back into place, locking the doors, which trembled. It sounded like the ceiling was caving inside the vault. Matt looked up and saw the ceiling above him begin to crack.

"Everybody run," said Captain Vincent.

They ran. One of the giant pillars started to crumble and archways cracked. Matt ran as fast as he could, just behind the captain.

"Wait!" Ruby cried. Matt turned around. Ruby and Corey were trying to haul their treasure as they ran, but it was too heavy for them. Stones began to fall. They were getting bigger.

"Just drop it!" shouted Matt. Ruby did so, but Corey clung to his. "Corey! Let go!"

The archway under which Corey was standing started to crumble. A stone hit him in the side of the head.

"Corey!" Ruby shouted. She shoved him out of the way. Corey dropped his pack and got out of the way just as the archway came tumbling down.

"Go! Go!" Matt shouted. They ran down the tunnels. Finally they got to the end where the captain was waiting for them at the bottom of the steps. They ran up them.

When they emerged above the floor and shut the latch, the ground trembled slightly beneath their feet. The little man stared at all of them in an awed silence. He bowed deeply to them and then spoke rapidly. He seemed to be asking for something. He pointed to the candle in his window and then to the captain.

"I think he wants the lantern back," Matt whispered.

"Oops," said Corey.

The captain took out his flashlight, held it out to the man and clicked it on. The old man jumped back. He reached out hesitantly and took the flashlight. He clicked it on and off again and again. He started laughing and bowed over and over to the captain and the rest of them.

When they were a ways away from the house, Matt looked back and saw the little window light up then wink out over and over.

"He'll be so disappointed when the batteries run out," said Ruby.

"Not as disappointed as I am," said Corey. "I can't believe you made me drop my bag!"

"Excuse me," said Ruby. "Did you want to get buried alive?"

"All that treasure," said Corey, "and we didn't get any!"

"The important thing is you're all safe," said the captain. "And we didn't come out empty-handed. Brocco and Wiley still have their treasure."

"Crikey, it's a load. Ah, but look! The elephants are coming back this way!" said Brocco, pointing. "Can Li'l Bullet and I go take a ride now, Captain?"

"Yes! Can we?" Corey asked.

"Yes, go on," said the captain. "We'll get the treasure back to the *Vermillion*. Don't take too long."

"I'd like to go too," said Wiley. "I never have seen an elephant." He dropped his sack down at the captain's feet.

"Do you want to come too, Matt and Ruby?" Corey asked.

"No thanks," said Matt. "I'll stay and help the captain with the treasure."

"Me too," said Ruby.

As soon as Corey, Brocco, and Wiley were out of eyesight, the captain reached into his jacket and took out the little golden box. "Speaking of treasure . . . ," he said, holding it in the palm of his hand. The box glistened in the fading sunlight.

"What's inside, do you think?" Ruby asked.

"Who knows?" said the captain. "Another clue perhaps, or the answer to the compass. Let's find out, shall we?" The captain reached into his jacket again and took out the *Mona Lisa* key. He stuck it in the keyhole. He turned it both ways, but it didn't open. The captain wriggled it for another minute, growing a little more frustrated with each attempt. Finally he threw the box to the ground where it burst open. Gems spilled over the dusty ground, rubies and diamonds, sapphires and emeralds. Matt stared at them. They sparkled in the sunlight.

The captain swore under his breath. He growled and kicked at the gems, then tore at his hair and twisted his face in a kind of frenzied anguish. He finally released himself and just stood there, breathing hard.

Matt didn't know what to do or say. He felt this was all his fault. He'd been mistaken. Perhaps that palm leaf clue wasn't really a clue at all. Just a distraction, a wild-goose chase. Or snake chase, it seemed. He'd gotten excited over nothing.

Finally Ruby walked up to the captain and took his hand. He looked down at her, surprised. "We'll find it," she said. "It's not hopeless yet. We still have time."

The captain smiled weakly and patted Ruby's hand. "Thank you," he said. "I am not always the most patient man."

Ruby reached down and grabbed Brocco's sack of treasure, slinging it up on her shoulder. She took the captain's hand again and led him toward the *Vermillion*. Matt lifted the other sack of treasure and followed. They left the little golden box and the gems in the dust.

16

Video et Taceo

When the *Vermillion* returned to Nowhere in No Time, they barely paused for breath before they traveled again. They traveled nearly every day without pause between missions at all. They didn't seem to have any rhyme or reason for where they went, though it was clear the captain was searching. He did not seem interested in waiting for clues from future Matt or anywhere else. He apparently decided to take things into his own hands and follow his own whims and hunches. They hopped centuries and countries like a giant game of checkers. Italy, Egypt, China, Spain, Mexico; 1503, 1922, 1708, 1403, 1891. Matt started to lose track.

The *Vermillion* transformed into a gondola, a streetcar, a train, and various ships and boats. They did not explore or enjoy any sites. They raided museums, libraries, and palaces, perused curio shops and pawnshops, even broke into vaults and safes and more sacred temples. They stole famous art, books, money, relics, gold, and jewels. Matt wasn't even sure they were saving these things from other robbers. It didn't seem like it, especially when he saw Wiley picking pockets in a little village in Spain, or Brocco stealing shoes from a cobbler shop in Italy, and he still hadn't seen anyone return any of the "investments" aboard the *Vermillion*.

"Have you ever seen the captain return anything since you've come aboard?" he asked Jia, after they'd taken a good haul of gold from a group of explorers in Mexico. (Captain Vincent had said they were pirates—the bad kind.)

"Not exactly," said Jia, and then seeing Matt's dismayed expression hurried to explain. "But he will, eventually. You know it doesn't really matter when we return anything, because we can always go back to exactly the time we need."

"I guess," said Matt, "but what if you couldn't?"

"What do you mean?" said Jia. "Why couldn't we?"

"I mean what if something were to happen to the thing before you could return it, like it gets damaged or stolen?"

Jia shook her head vigorously. "That could never happen. Albert is far too protective of all the investments to let any harm come to them."

"Well, what if you couldn't travel back to the time or place you needed to go to return it, like how you can't travel past my time?"

Jia shrugged. "That might stop us for a little while but not forever. The captain would find a way. He always does."

Matt didn't disagree with Jia. The captain seemed very determined to always get what he wanted. He just wasn't sure he understood what he wanted, exactly.

The captain kept Matt close to him on all the missions. He was constantly asking him if he recognized or felt anything, if any objects sparked his memory, or *forememory*. Matt tried the best he could. He strained to listen, to feel something special or magical, but nothing called out to him. He occasionally pointed to possible objects, little boxes or cabinets, but they never turned out to be what the captain was looking for, and Matt could sense his disappointment deepening, his impatience growing with each failed mission. He grew sullen and despondent. His dinner haikus became somewhat depressing.

We are all adrift
Wandering the world alone
Never to arrive.

And sometimes they were more like a reprimand.

What use is a key
If no one can find the thing
It needs to unlock?

Matt couldn't help but feel that this one was directed toward him. After all, no one else on the crew even knew about the key, except Corey and Ruby, but Matt didn't feel the captain expected quite as much from them as he did Matt. Matt was plenty used to failure. That came with the territory of being a scientist, he knew. But he didn't have much experience with disappointing people who had put their trust in him. He had always been the type to rise to whatever challenge was thrown his way, often exceeding expectations, but now he felt the full force of failure weighing down on him. He didn't like it at all.

But his failure to find whatever went with the *Mona Lisa* key wasn't Matt's only shortcoming. His time sickness steadily worsened with each mission, and it became harder and harder to manage. He did all the recommended things— ate cheese puffs and potato chips and drank soda as often as he could, but it seemed to take the edge off for only a little while. He changed his shoes, as Brocco suggested, which did nothing as far as he could tell. He tried to read some books that were relatively close to his time, as Wiley had suggested. It was a distraction if nothing else, but the *Vermillion* seemed to have a strange habit of hiding his books during transformations so he rarely got to read one all the way through. He was almost always dizzy and nauseated.

"Not everyone is meant to be a time pirate," said Albert one day, after they'd just pillaged an Aztec temple in Mexico City. Matt couldn't remember what year or even the century. He had run behind some bushes to be sick. He kept it from

Corey and Ruby and the rest of the crew, but Albert had noticed and was waiting for him when he returned.

"I'm fine," said Matt.

"We've had passengers like you before," said Albert, "weaklings who couldn't stomach the travel. The captain was eventually forced to discard them."

Matt's patience was all dried up. He was used to being teased and laughed at for his oddities, but Matt had never met anyone who showed outright hatred for no apparent reason. He was done being polite. Done trying to make peace with Albert.

"You know, I wouldn't be surprised if we had to discard you sooner or later, Albert," said Matt. "No one seems to be able to stomach your sour personality."

Albert looked taken aback at first, and then he pushed up his glasses and sneered. "You may think the captain favors you," he said. "But just wait until he realizes you aren't good for anything. You'll see then."

Matt had no retort for this. He had the growing fear that Albert was right. He was never going to find whatever it was the *Mona Lisa* key unlocked. He'd exhausted all sources at the library. He'd turned over the phrase *video et taceo* over and over again in his mind, trying to think what it might mean, where it might lead. He was constantly trying to *fore-member,* but nothing came.

"I still think I've seen it somewhere, 'video et taceo,'" said

Ruby as they pored over more history and Latin books in their room.

"Maybe you're foremembering," said Corey. Matt had told them all about what the captain said about time travel and foremembering, and they'd all become quite fascinated by the idea. Any time they had a half-formed thought or hazy memory they wondered if they were foremembering something from their future.

"Maybe," said Ruby. "Or maybe I saw it in one of the exhibits at the Met?"

"Well, we're not going there," said Matt.

"Why not?" asked Ruby. "We could go before Mom and Dad started to work there. Might be good for you." She eyed him closely and he knew what she was thinking.

"I'm fine," he said, even though his head was aching.

"You're not," said Ruby. "Everyone can tell you're time sick, and it doesn't appear to be getting better."

"I'm managing it," said Matt, skimming another page in a book about Julius Caesar.

"We could ask the captain to slow down a bit," said Ruby, "take us to New York for a little while, and we can do research there."

"Yeah, you know this would all probably go a lot faster if we had the internet," said Corey. "Books are way slow." He shut the book he'd been searching and set it aside.

"We're not going home," said Matt. "Not yet."

"I didn't say we should go home," said Ruby. "I just think you need a break."

Matt didn't want to ask the captain for a break. He couldn't. What if he threw another fit and really did discard Matt for being worthless?

"How long do you think we've been gone anyway?" Corey asked. "A week?"

"I think it's been more like two or three weeks based on how much we've traveled," said Ruby.

Matt was sure it had been longer than that. Even though time travel made it so they didn't always have a normal twenty-four-hour day, they all slept fairly regularly, and if he had to guess he'd say they'd been gone over a month, maybe two.

"I wonder if we'll look different to Mom and Dad when we get home," said Ruby. "Both of your hair is longer. Do you think they'll suspect anything?"

"That we've been time-traveling for weeks while no time has passed for them?" said Corey. "No. Mom and Dad couldn't even imagine such a thing. They're too boring and practical."

"Well we really shouldn't stay too much longer," said Ruby.

"It's fine for now," said Corey. "We can afford to stay a bit longer."

"Maybe another week or two," said Ruby. "But not longer. Mom and Dad will have to imagine something odd happened if you return home with a beard."

Corey rubbed at his jaw and grinned. "That would be awesome."

Matt kept skimming the pages, trying to ignore his headache. He didn't want to talk about home or their parents. He didn't want to think about his time sickness or taking breaks. He needed to focus on their mission, on the *Mona Lisa* key.

It was the *Vermillion*, however, that finally put a stop to their travels. The captain said he wanted to travel to twelfth-century Constantinople, during the Roman Empire. Matt felt dizzy already. There was no way he could travel that far. He'd fall apart. He was ready to have a meltdown. But when the captain went to use the compass, the *Vermillion* also seemed to have a meltdown. She began to transform, and then she suddenly shuddered to a stop. The ship seemed to groan in protest and popped back into her original form. The captain tried again. Again the ship began to transform, but stopped even sooner this time, and when the ship popped back into place it rocked violently from side to side. Matt braced himself as the captain turned the dials again, but the *Vermillion* flatly refused this time, and as though she were sending a final message, a beam in the ceiling came crashing down through the floor, narrowly missing the captain.

"Crikey!" said Brocco. "I think she as good as spit in your eye, Captain."

"Is it broken?" Matt asked. "Are we stuck?"

Jia shook her head. "The *Vermillion* is exhausted," she said. "She's demanding a break."

The captain didn't say anything. He simply kicked the fallen beam, then went into his cabin and slammed the door. The lock clicked. Matt slumped against the side of the ship. He patted the floors, grateful for the *Vermillion*'s sudden stubbornness.

While Matt was relieved to have a break from traveling, he also couldn't take his mind off the key. Why couldn't his future self give him some more clues? Why couldn't he be clear in the first place and just say where the thing was that the key unlocked? Or just tell them what they needed to know to fix the compass? Why lead them through all the trouble to retrieve a key that didn't appear to unlock anything?

Matt discussed this with Corey and Ruby alone in their room, though they didn't seem nearly as concerned. "Maybe you couldn't send more messages," said Ruby. "What if it caused a glitch somehow? Your future self must know you can figure it out with what you've got."

"I'm beginning to think maybe I overestimated myself," said Matt.

The captain remained scarce for the next few days. He didn't emerge for meals. Not even for supper. Jia brought trays of food to him, but the crew seemed a little unsure what to do without his traditional haiku. It seemed like it would be sacrilegious for anyone else to offer it, so after a long silence they finally just started eating.

Matt kept himself busy by helping Jia with repairs on the ship. The fallen beam was not the only thing that needed fixing. After so many transformations there was quite a bit of work to be done—holes to patch up, tears in the sails that needed stitching, jammed pulleys and levers, bits of metal stuck here and there. They went through a lot of bubble gum and peanut butter, and Matt thought it was little wonder that the *Vermillion* had refused to travel anymore.

Corey was back to target practice with Brocco. Matt noticed that he was using some of his schoolbooks for targets this time. He seemed to take particular delight in shooting holes in his math book, then placed one of his homework assignments in an old vase and dropped a small explosive inside. He chucked it overboard right before it popped and shattered.

Ruby tried to get the captain out of his room to practice swords with her, but he didn't answer any of her knocks. She tried to practice on her own, but it wasn't nearly as satisfying. Finally she gave up and started the books Wiley had given her on Queen Elizabeth. She had asked the captain again if they could go there, now that they'd been traveling in a wider range, but the captain had so far put off her request.

It was Ruby who found it. They were all above deck, each at their respective tasks, when Ruby suddenly gasped.

"What?" said Matt. "What's wrong?"

Ruby was pale. She was staring at her book as though something had just jumped out of the pages and grabbed her. "I found it," she said.

"Found what?"

"*Video et taceo*. I found it!"

Matt ran over to Ruby. She pointed to the passage.

The motto of Queen Elizabeth I. Video et taceo, Latin for "I see and keep silent." This could have several meanings. One, that she often listened more than she spoke, something that actually worked to her advantage as a female monarch. When she did speak, people tended to listen well, not just because she was queen, but because they knew she chose her words wisely.

Queen Elizabeth was also known to have a wide network of spies who worked silently, but effectively, to carry out missions as well as protect her secrets, of which it is rumored that she had many. We will never unlock them all.

Unlock . . . "That's it," said Matt. "Queen Elizabeth has what the *Mona Lisa* key opens!"

"We need to show this to the captain right away," said Ruby. She jumped up and ran down the steps with the book in her arms. Corey and Matt followed closely behind. She went directly to the captain's office and pounded on the door. No one answered. She pounded again and kept pounding until finally it unlocked.

The captain opened the door, and Ruby let out a small gasp. Matt stepped back a little. The captain looked awful. His eyes were sunken with dark circles beneath them, his clothes rumpled, and his hair was in all directions, like he'd been attempting to pull it out. Even Santiago, perched on his shoulder, looked a little sickly. His whiskers drooped, and Matt could see bald patches where he'd lost fur.

"Captain, we know where we need to go," Matt said. "We found *video et taceo*!"

"I found it," said Ruby, a little huffily.

"Yes, yes, Ruby found it. Look!" He snatched the book out of her hands and held it out to the captain. The captain stared blankly down at the book.

"Queen Elizabeth!" said Ruby. "We need to travel to see her!"

The captain didn't answer. He kept staring at the book. His face seemed to grow paler than it already was.

"Captain?" said Matt. He finally looked up at Matt.

"We can't go there," said the captain.

"Why not? The queen has what we're looking for!" said Matt. "She must have whatever the *Mona Lisa* key unlocks!"

The captain shook his head. "She'll never give it to me."

"Why not?" said Matt. "You have plenty of treasure, right? I mean, she'd make a trade if the deal was good enough."

"Especially if we get to her earlier in her reign," said Ruby knowledgeably. "It's well known that the royal finances were drained while fighting off Spain. She'd probably welcome a chest of gold."

"You don't understand," said the captain. "She won't give it to me at any price. She'd rather see my head on a pike."

"Why?" Ruby asked. "I thought you were friends."

Captain Vincent shook his head. "She and Captain Bonnaire were great friends at one time. Captain Bonnaire was the one who led the charge on stealing gold from all those Spanish ships, not Sir Francis Drake, whatever the history books say. Captain Bonnaire even called Queen Elizabeth the Pirate Queen. Oh, Queen Elizabeth loved it, but soon she began to desire an additional title. She wanted to be the *Time Pirate Queen*."

"She wants the compass," said Matt.

"She knows about it?" said Ruby.

"Of course she does!" said Captain Vincent. "And she always resented that Captain Bonnaire left it to me and not her. She'll stop at nothing to get it. She believes the compass is her royal, God-given right. The minute she spots me she'll have my neck in a noose." He rubbed at his throat, as though he could feel the rope tightening around him already.

Matt's mind raced. There had to be a way.

"What if we go to the queen instead?" said Matt. "Corey and Ruby and I. We can go to the queen and make her believe we have the compass, or that we can get it for her, if she gives us what we want."

The captain shook his head. "She's too smart for such tactics. She won't give you what you want unless she has the compass in her hands. And she wouldn't believe you have it anyway. The only people she's seen with the compass are myself and Captain Bonnaire. Captain Bonnaire is the only time pirate she ever trusted, and she's dead."

Matt thought some more. "What if," said Matt, "we said we were the children of Captain Bonnaire?"

The captain opened his mouth, presumably to say why that wouldn't work, and then paused.

"Will that work?" Ruby asked. "I mean, do we look anything like her?"

The captain gazed at each of them, first Matt, then Corey, then Ruby. "It's not so unbelievable," he said. "Granted, Captain Bonnaire was never the mothering type, but it's not *impossible*. She was a beautiful, dark-haired woman. Any man would have fallen at her feet to have her. I rather think it made the queen a bit jealous, in fact. That alone might make her believe it."

"We could say our mother meant to leave us the compass," Matt continued, "but *you* stole it from her before she died."

The captain rubbed at his chin. "She'll definitely believe that," he said.

"We'll tell her our mother also left us the *Mona Lisa* key, without your knowledge. She told us that Queen Elizabeth would have what the key unlocks, that it would help us get back the compass."

"And we can tell her we'll let her use the compass every now and then," said Corey, "If she gives us whatever the key unlocks. You know, like share it?"

The captain shook his head. "Not good enough. She won't share with you. She'll want the compass all to herself."

"Maybe she wouldn't share," said Matt, "but maybe she'll believe *we* are naïve enough to think she would. We're only kids, after all. We're no match for her, a queen. If she believes we're the children of Captain Bonnaire and can get the compass, she might believe she has the opportunity to get the compass for herself, if she helps us."

The captain considered. A smile slowly grew on his pale face. "That's good, Mateo. You do have a tactical mind. As crazy as it all sounds, it might work if we play our cards just right."

"So we can go?" Ruby asked hopefully. "We'll get to meet the queen?"

"It will take some preparation," said the captain. "It will not be easy, but I do believe this is the only way."

Ruby let out an uncharacteristic squeal and clapped her hands. "Oh my gosh, I wonder if I could interview her. Can you imagine if I had actual firsthand quotes from Queen

Elizabeth in my report?"

"Not to be a downer, sis," said Corey, "but it's probably gonna be hard to convince your teacher that you actually spoke to her."

"It doesn't matter," said Ruby. "It will still give me insight I wouldn't have had before. Oh my goodness, what are we going to wear? Does Brocco have clothes for us? I mean, I'll need a gown from that era."

"I'm sure Brocco will be thrilled to outfit you for the mission," said the captain, "but that is only a small portion of our preparations. There will be many pieces to this mission, each one as vital as the next. You must pay close attention or you may just find your heads in a noose, or on the tip of a sword."

Matt swallowed. He hadn't been considering any of the dangers of this mission, only the rewards.

"We can do it," said Ruby confidently.

"I have no doubt," said the captain.

17

The Pirate Queen

"Bow at the waist," said Albert. "No, no, that's all wrong. Keep your back straight and put your chin down. You're not supposed to look at the queen. Abase yourself!"

The Hudsons had been practicing their court manners for hours. They had to make sure they were presentable in every way, not only in their clothing, but in speech, address, and manners. Wiley had brought out a stack of books on Elizabethan customs and manners and was spouting off things about titles and rules and certain phrases they should say, words like *anon* and *verily* and *thee* and *thou*.

"Instead of saying 'excuse me' you should say 'pray pardon me,'" said Wilcy, "and you don't say 'How are you?' but 'How fare thee?' Ooh, that sounds fancy, don't it?"

They hadn't made much progress. Matt's brain buzzed with all the titles and phrases to remember.

"These tights are killing me," complained Corey. He pulled

off his poofy, feathered hat and scratched his left leg with his right, pulling the stocking down. "Can't I just go without?"

"No," said Albert. "And you have to wear the hat, too, or the whole court will think you're nothing but a pickpocketing urchin."

"Only you'd be called a 'cutpurse,'" said Wiley. "That's the proper word for a thief, it says right here."

"What should I care what they think?" said Corey. "It's all stupid anyway."

"Do as you like," said Albert. "I don't care if the queen chops off your head just because you can't manage to bow and dress properly."

"I'll chop off your head," Corey grumbled, shoving the hat back on.

"Oh, and lookie here," said Wiley. "Instead of calling someone a drunkard you'd call them a 'tosspot.' Ooh, I like that one. Brocco, you tosspot! *He-he-ha!*"

"I'll toss your pot," muttered Brocco.

Ruby had been quite excited to wear her costume, until she had to try it on. It was a full-length gray gown trimmed with pearls. "How do people breathe in these things?" said Ruby, pulling at her stiff bodice.

"High fashion comes with a price, Li'l Blade," said Brocco.

"Barbaric," Ruby grumbled. Matt wondered if she was having second thoughts about this trip, if the torture of the clothes was worth seeing one of her historic heroines.

"I'd happily suffer right along with you if I could come too," said Jia with a sigh.

It had been decided that only the Hudsons would go to the queen and hopefully be convincing as the children of Captain Bonnaire. Captain Vincent would escort them only to the outer gates of the palace and would wait for them in hiding until they returned, hopefully with their treasure in hand.

Just then Captain Vincent appeared. He looked a little more rested than he had before. At least some color had come back to his face and his hair was combed. He was dressed in a black suit with puffy sleeves and a white ruff around the neck, a brimmed hat on his head.

"You look like Shakespeare!" exclaimed Ruby.

The captain smiled, took off his hat, and bowed. Matt tried to watch how he did it so well. "Do you think we could see one of Shakespeare's plays while we're there?" Ruby asked.

"Oh no," Corey muttered.

"Perhaps," said the captain. "But it all depends on how things go with the queen, and you must put all your focus on her. She is a magnificent woman: intelligent, bold, exceedingly handsome, and extremely proud. She would have made an excellent time pirate. It's unfortunate she'd sooner have my head than call me Captain."

"Why does she hate you so much?" Ruby asked.

The captain sighed. "She believes I made an attempt on

her life, which is untrue. She's rather paranoid, not that I blame her. There have been plenty of attempts on her life. In any case, it's impossible for me to visit the queen at any time, so you three are vital in this mission."

Ruby nodded resolutely. "We won't let you down."

The captain smiled down at Ruby. "You know," he said. "I can almost believe you to be the children of Captain Bonnaire myself. Especially you, Miss Ruby. You have her passion and strength of spirit."

Ruby beamed at the compliment. They all knew how much Captain Bonnaire meant to him.

The captain reached inside his sleeve and pulled out the compass. "Let's hope the *Vermillion* cooperates this time. Ready, crew? Prepare for a quantum time leap!"

Matt held on to a beam as the ship began to transform. The sides pressed in, and the floors narrowed. The ceiling lowered, then split and rolled around the edges, much as it had when they'd become a rowboat in India, only it didn't shrink nearly so much. The dining table and chairs folded in on themselves and pressed themselves to the side, while the door to the captain's cabin split open and the whole of it sank down into the floor and sealed itself off. The air went from warm and balmy to a bitter chill within a few moments. Matt shivered, and they all pulled on the cloaks that Brocco had provided for them.

"Finally!" said Ruby. "The ship didn't try to kill me during a transformation!" She made to walk and promptly tripped and fell over. Her ankles were entirely knotted up in ropes.

"Spoke too soon!" Corey said, laughing.

Pike ran over to Ruby and immediately started untying the ropes, freeing her within minutes.

They all stood on the deck of a long, narrow river barge with a single large white sail, the *Vermillion*'s flag waving at the top, floating down a river. Sheets of ice were floating through the steely gray water.

"The River Thames," said the captain.

They passed little sailboats and fishing boats and a few other barges. Along the frosty banks were little cottages and fields, empty for the winter. As they went farther downstream the fields disappeared and the buildings drew tighter together. Towers and steeples peaked up between small houses and shops all pressed together, their rooftops white with snow and with icicles hanging down. They looked like rows of gingerbread houses.

They passed beneath a bridge and when they came out the other side Matt spotted the palace.

"Richmond Palace," said Captain Vincent. "One of the queen's favorite residences and the place of her death."

"It's beautiful," said Ruby. She gazed fixedly on the palace, completely mesmerized. It was magnificent, Matt had to admit. Built right on the banks of the river, the castle was a bright grouping of dozens of towers and turrets with spiked domes on top that looked like giant Hershey's Kisses, frosted with ice and snow. It looked like something out of a fairy tale.

"It was built in 1501 by King Henry VII," said Albert in his usual pompous tone. "It's no longer standing in your time."

"What year are we?" said Ruby.

"February 1603," said the captain.

"Oh! But that's only a month before the queen dies!" said Ruby. She seemed quite disappointed.

"Yes," said the captain, "and she knows her death is imminent. She'll be more desperate than ever for the compass and more likely to give us what we need."

"But the compass can't stop her death, can it?" said Matt.

"No, but she doesn't know that," said Captain Vincent. "As far as she's concerned it can grant immortality, and who knows? It's possible that it can. I certainly haven't unlocked all its secrets."

Brocco steered the barge toward the bank, a ways before the castle, where they could be well hidden by the thick, frosted brush. The captain jumped down and helped Matt, Corey, and Ruby off the barge. The rest remained behind.

"Good luck!" said Jia.

"Keep your hat and tights on!" said Albert.

"And if you don't understand someone or don't know what to say," said Wiley, "just say 'Forsooth!' and leave."

"We will go on foot through the village," said the captain.

"When we reach the palace you will have to be on your own."

Matt turned his head every which way, trying to take in all the sights: the tall gabled buildings with tiled and thatched roofs, the merchant stands selling everything from fish to medicines to amulets to protect against witchcraft. He kept his nose plugged against the smells. Though it was cold, the odors were still quite strong. Clearly bathing was not a priority at this particular time, and he knew plumbing was also not developed, so it smelled like a combination of teenage boy's gym bag, rotting compost, and sewage. He hated to imagine what it smelled like in summer.

A woman poured the contents of a chamber pot out of a window, which splashed mere feet from them. Steam curled up from the frozen ground.

"Gross," said Ruby. It seemed her romantic visions of this period in time were beginning to fade with the starkness of reality.

Matt met eyes with a boy about his age, his clothes so dirty and full of holes he could see his bony shoulders poking through. His cheeks were sunken. His eyes were big in his skull and looked more animal than human. He stared at them, unblinking, as they passed. Matt expected the captain to reach into his pockets and give the boy a sack of money, as he had done for all the other poor beggars they'd encountered, but he walked right by without even looking at the boy. He's just nervous and distracted, Matt thought.

"This is as far as I dare go," said the captain. He placed himself between two buildings. "I will wait here for you. You will be all right without me?" He seemed nervous.

"We'll be fine," said Ruby. "We know what to do."

"Very well. Good luck."

As they approached the palace Matt had a strange sense of foreboding, and it only grew as the towers loomed over them. *Just nerves,* he told himself. It was their first mission on their own, without the captain or any of the crew. And there was so much riding on this one. They needed to be convincing. They needed the queen to trust them. They needed to succeed.

As they reached the gate, Matt started to feel a bit nauseated. He should have brought some chips or cookies with him or something. He'd been so focused on what they had to do with this mission, he hadn't thought about managing his time sickness.

Ruby and Corey approached the gate before they realized Matt wasn't with them.

"You okay, Matt?" said Ruby.

"Pray pardon me, wench," said Corey. "Methinks you meant to say, 'How fare thee, brother?'"

"Oh, by your leave, brother!" said Ruby, taking a curtsy.

Matt laughed and joined them at the gate. "I'm fine," he said. "I mean, I feel wondrous well."

"Excellent," said Corey. "We don't want the queen thinking you're a tosspot!"

They all laughed, and Matt did feel a little better.

It wasn't so hard to get into the palace. Children weren't seen as such a threat and they were dressed well enough that they were at least allowed inside. Matt was eager to get in from the cold, but the palace was not much warmer on the inside than outside, and they found getting an audience with the queen would be much more difficult than entering the palace.

After speaking with several servants, they were led to a small room where a man met them. He was short, slightly hunched, with a pointed beard and watery eyes with puffy pouches underneath. He wore a white ruff about his neck and looked rather surly at them as they entered.

"I am Sir Robert Cecil, Earl of Salisbury and advisor to Her Majesty the Queen," he said. "And you are the children of whom?"

"Captain Bonnaire, my lord," said Ruby with a curtsy, "who was acquainted with the queen some time ago, before we were born. We have brought Her Majesty some news we think will be of interest to her."

"Regarding?"

They all paused, not sure if they should mention the compass to anyone but the queen. Who knew who else might know of it and be after it as well?

"Pray pardon me, my lord," said Matt. "It is a very private matter between Captain Bonnaire, our mother, and the good queen."

Sir Robert stiffened a little. His dark eyes narrowed. Matt could sense his annoyance and distrust of them. "This *captain* you say is your mother? A woman? Captain of what, pray?"

"Of the ship *Vermillion*," said Matt.

"I've never heard of such a ship, nor of a woman captain on any ship," said Sir Robert.

"Well, our mother was one of a kind," said Corey. He laughed a little, until Sir Robert turned his gaze on him. Corey started to scratch at his tights. Matt fidgeted with the buttons on his vest. He couldn't help but feel they had started off on the wrong foot.

"It all may seem rather, er, strange," said Ruby. "But I promise Her Majesty will understand and be quite keen to see us, when you give her the name of Captain Bonnaire."

"I will see if she can be persuaded," said Sir Robert, "but Her Majesty has not been well of late and rarely takes visitors, especially children." He sneered down at them as though they were filthy dogs instead of human beings. He left them to wait in the room with a man standing guard at the door.

They waited and waited. None of them spoke or hardly moved, not even Corey, except to scratch at his tights. A fire was blazing in the hearth, and Matt was starting to feel extra warm now. He pulled off his cloak. The man standing guard at the door didn't look in their direction or in any way acknowledge their presence. He didn't even move, but

Matt got the sense he noticed their every breath and twitch. He felt himself growing increasingly nervous, panic rising in his chest with every minute they waited. It had been at least an hour. What was taking so long? Had they been forgotten? If the queen wouldn't see them, would they be arrested? Thrown in a dungeon?

Finally Sir Robert returned. "The queen will give you a brief audience," he said. Ruby let out an audible breath. The Hudsons followed Sir Robert to a large set of doors. Two guards were placed on either side of the doors, each wearing red tunics and red tights, a white ruff at the neck, and black flat-topped hats with red-and-white rosettes around them. They stood stiffly and silently at attention with long, sharp-looking spears.

Sir Robert opened the doors to a stately sitting room with lavish furniture and tall, arched windows that overlooked the river. Matt squinted to see if the *Vermillion* might be visible, but the windows were so warped and bubbly it was hard to make out anything. It was cold again in this room, though a fire had recently been lit. Matt thought regulating comfortable temperatures in these giant castles must be impossible.

A figure suddenly moved near the windows. Matt hadn't noticed her, but as she turned slowly around he wondered at how anyone could *not* notice her.

"Her Majesty, Queen Elizabeth of England," said Sir Robert.

The Hudsons all bowed low. Matt only stumbled a little bit. When they came up they were face-to-face with none other than Queen Elizabeth, the Virgin Queen, Good Queen Bess, Gloriana, and, as Captain Bonnaire had named her, the Pirate Queen.

The queen was quite intimidating and severe-looking, Matt thought. She was a tall, slender woman in her late fifties or early sixties. She wore a black gown embroidered with gold, a large hoop around her hips to make the dress shape into a sort of cylinder around her legs, and a white collar that extended up and around her head. Her skin was powdered white, while her lips were painted crimson. She wore a dark-red wig, curling around her face and decorated with pearls. She must have been wearing a lot of perfume, because Matt could smell her from across the room.

The queen eyed each of the children in turn, studying their faces intently, first Matt, then Corey, and finally rested and lingered on Ruby. Ruby seemed to be holding her breath beneath the queen's piercing gaze.

"You may leave us, Sir Robert," said the queen. As she spoke Matt noticed that her teeth were quite gray and rotted, which wasn't something he expected in royalty, but then they probably didn't have the best dental care in this time.

Sir Robert bowed, gave the children one last suspicious look, and left the room.

"You are the children of Captain Bonnaire?" said the

queen when they were alone. Her voice was high and a bit shrill, as though she was used to shouting demands and yelling to large crowds.

"Er, yes," said Matt. He winced at his poor speech. With the queen's entrance, all the fancy words and manners he was supposed to have learned fled from his mind. The queen's nostrils flared a little, as though she could smell fraud, and then her eyes rested on Ruby, and she seemed to soften.

"And you, young lady, what is your name?" the queen asked.

Ruby curtsied again as she spoke. "My name is Ruby, Your Majesty, and this is my twin brother, Corey, and our eldest brother, Mateo. We are the children of Captain Bonnaire."

The queen appraised them. Matt hoped they looked enough like her to be believable. At least they all had dark hair. "Captain Bonnaire did not strike me as a woman with much desire to bear children," said the queen. "She certainly never mentioned you to me."

Matt shifted uncomfortably, not quite sure how to respond.

"But she was always a rash, unpredictable woman," the queen said. "I much admired her for it, except when it came to that abominable rogue who was always with her. I suppose he is your father?"

The children all looked to each other, none of them sure what to say. They hadn't discussed who was supposed to be their father. Somehow that detail had been overlooked. "You mean Captain Vincent?" Corey blurted.

"*Captain* Vincent? And how is *he* captain? Did he come here with you?"

"No, no," said Corey, suddenly realizing his mistake. "He's definitely not our father, and we have nothing to do with him. We hold him responsible, you see."

"Responsible for what, pray tell?"

Corey's voice suddenly became a bit wobbly. "For our mother's death." He dropped his head and sniffled a little. Matt had to give it to Corey. He was a good actor.

"Her death?" said the queen. "You mean she is . . ." The queen became very still, and then her face slowly darkened. "I warned her," she said. "I told her that man would bring her to no good. I should have beheaded him while I had the chance."

"It would give us nothing but pleasure to see it done," said Ruby. "Captain Vincent used our mother most ill, and cheated us of our birthright."

"Yeah, we *hate* that tosspot," Corey added.

The queen's pale brow rose, crinkling into folds.

Now Matt thought Corey was probably overdoing it a bit. Ruby clearly thought the same. She furtively stepped on Corey's foot and glanced at Matt, nodding slightly for him to speak.

"If it pleases you, Your Majesty," said Matt, "we bring you news of something our mother told us would interest you—the Obsidian Compass."

The queen looked surprised. "The Obsidian Compass? You have it?"

"No," said Ruby. "In truth, Captain Vincent stole it from our mother before she died, even though our mother meant for us to have it."

"Yes," said the queen, "I am not surprised. I always sensed his greed for it."

"She did, however, leave us a message, telling us that you could help us to retrieve it."

"Did she now?" said the queen. "Pray tell, how did your mother say this was to be accomplished?"

"She told us you have something in your safekeeping, something that would give us information about the compass that Captain Vincent doesn't have."

"Indeed," said Queen Elizabeth. "Captain Bonnaire did leave something with me of that nature."

Matt's heart skipped a few beats. "If you give it to us," he said, "we promise we will come back when we've gotten the compass from Captain Vincent, and we'll let you use it whenever you need."

"That is generous," said the queen shortly, and Matt's hopes rose until the queen's next words. "But I'm afraid I no longer have what you seek."

"Y-you don't?" stuttered Matt.

"The object you seek was retrieved by another, just days ago."

"But . . . *who*?" said Ruby, real panic starting to reach her voice.

"In truth, he didn't give a name. Rather mysterious man, not sure I trusted him myself, but he *did* have convincing evidence that made me believe I should give to him what he asked for."

"What evidence?" said Matt.

"Why, he had the Obsidian Compass," said the queen. "He wore it round his neck, just like Captain Bonnaire used to wear."

Matt was stunned. "And . . . it wasn't Captain Vincent?"

"Oh no, this man didn't look a thing like Captain Vincent. I would have known him at any age, and I would never have let him escape my presence alive. A powerful object such as the Obsidian Compass should never be in the hands of a man like that. I confess it probably shouldn't be in the hands of *any* man, for what man is to be trusted with such power? Or woman, for that matter?"

"But . . . don't you want the compass?" said Matt.

The queen looked down at him and spoke a little more gently. "There may have been a time when I did desire it. I thought the compass would bring me all I ever wanted, but when you've lived as long as I have, and seen all that I have seen, you don't wish for more time. You see the value of endings."

Matt felt truly nauseated now. How had things gone so

horribly wrong? They'd missed what they were after by just days. Perhaps they could try again, come at an earlier date, before this other mysterious man came.

"Ah! I've just remembered," said the queen. She moved toward a secretary in the corner of the room with many drawers. She opened a small drawer at the bottom and retrieved something. "This curious stranger *did* leave a letter in my care, should anyone else come to collect what he took. He seemed to believe that a rather likely event. I had hoped, even expected, it would be Captain Vincent, but alas, no one gets everything, not even a queen." She held out an envelope toward them. No one moved at first. Finally Matt reached out and took it.

"I am sorry your visit was in vain," said the queen. "I hope that letter, whatever it contains, will be of some comfort to you. Now you must leave me. I am old and tired and my time is precious." She held out her hand and waited expectantly. Finally Matt remembered that they were supposed to bow and kiss her royal ring if she offered it. Matt stepped forward and reached for her hand, then paused because the queen wore several rings, and he wasn't sure which one he was supposed to kiss.

"On the right," the queen whispered.

Matt felt his face burn. He quickly kissed the ring and backed away. Corey and Ruby followed.

"Can I see the secret locket?" Ruby asked after she'd kissed the queen's royal ring.

The queen withdrew her hand. "How did you know about that?" she barked.

"Forgive me," said Ruby, cowering a little. "My mother. She told me about it."

"Of course," said the queen, softening. "She was one of the few whom I trusted enough to share such a treasure." She unclasped her royal ring and opened it, revealing a tiny portrait of a young woman. "My mother, Anne Boleyn. She died when I was barely three, beheaded by my own father for treason." The queen snapped the ring shut. "So we share something in common. Both our mothers caught the eye of the wrong man, I'm afraid. You and I must be wiser than our unfortunate mothers and not make the same mistake."

Ruby nodded, and then the door opened and Sir Robert entered. Matt suddenly felt eager to leave. He gave another bow to the queen. "Thank you, Your Majesty." Corey and Ruby did the same and then they moved toward the door, but before they left Ruby suddenly turned back. "Your Majesty?"

"Yes?"

"What's it like? To be queen?"

The queen's steely eyes seemed to soften with a touch of sadness. "Lonely," she said. "And a burden I wouldn't wish on anyone, but then it was always mine to bear and I have carried it the best I could. Still, I shall not complain when it is lifted. Farewell, children of Captain Bonnaire."

* * *

Matt, Corey, and Ruby were escorted out of the palace by a servant. Matt was glad it wasn't Sir Robert. That man gave him the creeps. The sky had darkened and sleet was now falling, stinging Matt's nose and cheeks. Matt tightened his cloak around his neck. None of them spoke as they walked down the long path toward the gate. With each step Matt felt his heart sinking farther into his stomach, and his stomach twisting up in knots. They'd come too late. They'd failed the mission. Again.

"She was a bit scary, wasn't she?" said Corey as soon as they were outside the gates. "Let me see the letter." Matt realized he was still clutching the envelope. A few drops of sleet had splashed on the paper.

"I think we should give it to the captain first," said Ruby. "It's sealed, and he might not like it if we read it before him."

"Whatever," said Corey. "We're the ones who just put our necks on the line, and I want to know what it says." He tried to grab the letter from Matt, but Matt pulled it away and tucked it inside the back of his pants, tightening the strings to make sure it was secure.

"What are we going to tell the captain?" said Ruby.

"The truth. What else can we tell him?" said Matt, though the thought sickened him.

"Do you think we should mention that the man had the compass, though?" Ruby asked. "I mean, if that's true, it means at some point the captain doesn't have it. That might really worry him."

"Unless it was a *different* compass," said Corey. "There could be more than one."

"Or it could be before the captain ever got it," said Matt.

"The inventor!" said Ruby. "Do you think?"

"Maybe . . . ," said Matt. "Let's just give the captain the letter. For all we know it explains everything."

The sleet began to fall harder. The streets were a mixture of ice and mud. People were running for cover, pulling in laundry that was hanging out of their windows and closing the shutters. The little beggar boy was still crouched up against a building, seemingly not at all bothered by the poor weather, but when he saw them, he dashed away, which Matt thought was odd. Did they frighten him somehow?

The captain was waiting right where they'd left him. He eagerly waved for them to join him between the buildings.

"Did you get it? Where is it? *What* is it?" he asked excitedly.

Matt started to reach for the letter, but then the captain put a hand up. "Wait," he said, his body suddenly tense. He squinted out into the drizzling sleet and snow. Matt turned around. The streets were quite empty now, except for a burly man standing stock-still in the rain, looking right toward them. About twenty feet away from that man, Matt saw another man. He was handing something to the beggar boy. The boy closed his outstretched hand and scampered away. Matt squinted and drew in a sharp breath. "That man was guarding us at the palace," said Matt.

"Let's move this way," said the captain, pulling them between the buildings to the other side.

They moved through the streets quickly, dodging stray dogs, slipping on muddy slush and ice. Matt looked over his shoulder to find both men following them. The hairs on the back of his neck lifted and he got goose bumps on his arms that he knew had nothing to do with the cold.

"Captain," said Matt.

The captain glanced behind him. "Let's move faster," he said.

They started to run, but as they neared the end of the village, another man rounded a building, short and hunch-backed. Sir Robert Cecil.

"Her Majesty, Queen Elizabeth, desires an audience with you, *Captain* Vincent," he said, a grim smile on his face. "Your charming children are also requested."

The captain didn't reply, except to draw his sword, but just as he did so, an arrow came whirring past and stuck in the ground, mere feet from where the captain stood.

Ruby screamed and covered her head. Matt looked up and spotted a man with a bow and arrow on a rooftop. He was nocking another arrow in his bow, taking aim.

Captain Vincent saw it as well. He shoved Sir Robert hard, knocking him to the ground. "Run!" he shouted.

Matt didn't hesitate for a moment. They ran, though it was difficult on the icy, muddy roads. Ruby was further encumbered by her dress. She began to fall behind, but the captain wasn't slowing down. He was running as fast as he could toward the river, where the *Vermillion* was waiting. They weren't too far now, but the men were gaining on them. There were at least three of them, maybe more, and they all had weapons—bows and arrows, swords and daggers.

Matt spotted the barge ahead. They were almost there. He could see the rest of the crew watching for them from the deck. Brocco had placed a wide plank between the barge and the riverbank. The captain leaped over it completely and landed. He immediately took out the compass.

"Run, Mateo!" the captain called. He was already starting to turn the dials, before the rest of them got on board.

"Hurry!" said Matt. He pushed Ruby ahead of him. She lifted her skirt and ran along the plank. Brocco grabbed her by the arm and helped her aboard. Corey went next, teetering a little before making a final jump to safety. Matt took one glance over his shoulder. The burly man was almost to him. Matt jumped onto the plank, but just as he did he saw Albert lower a stick and give a quick shove off the bank. The plank slid from the barge and Matt fell, hitting his chin on the board as he toppled into the icy river.

Ruby screamed.

"Matt!" Corey shouted. "He's in the water! He's not on the boat!"

Matt flailed his arms, sputtering from the shock of

the cold. The water around the barge began to churn like whitewater rapids. The barge stretched and widened. It was transforming.

"Help him!" Ruby screamed.

Someone dropped down a rope. He grabbed it, just as someone else grabbed his collar.

"I got one!"

Matt clung to the rope, wrapped his legs around it, and then the roiling water shot up all around the barge like a dozen fire hoses. There was a bright flash of light, and then, with the force of a rocket, Matt shot down into the ice-cold water.

18

The Letter

Hold on to the rope.

That was the only thought in Matt's brain. There wasn't room for anything else, and yet he seemed to be feeling everything all at once. He felt as though he were being flushed down a toilet. He was being squeezed inside a narrow pipe. He was compressed on all sides, crunched down like an empty soda can and then stretched in all directions. He was pulled and squished all at once. He was freezing cold and then he was boiling hot. There was light and then darkness. And then there was nothing—no sound, no space, no air, no feeling. There was only his one thought.

Hold on to the rope.

He couldn't feel the rope anymore, but in the deepest recesses of his brain he was holding it.

And then he was born again. First there was water. He could feel it again, the cold. He could feel his lungs burning, too, desperate for air. Then there was light, only a pinprick, but it drew closer, or he drew closer, and the light spread and diffused, and he wasn't sure what he should do. He was still clinging to the rope. That was all he knew how to do. The rope was pulling him up and up until he finally broke through the barrier and there was air.

He gasped.

"Hold on, Matt!" said a voice. He wasn't sure whose it was, though it sounded vaguely familiar. He wasn't sure who Matt was either. Was that supposed to be him?

He held on to the rope. He was pulled up and out of the water, and then grabbed by several hands and hauled over the side of a ship. He flopped onto the deck.

"Give him space," said a deep voice. Captain Vincent.

He coughed and vomited water, breathed some more. He blinked a few times and opened his eyes. Above him was a gray, cloudy sky. A cool breeze brushed his face, and he shivered with cold. For one panicked moment he thought they might still be in England, but then he noticed the many white sails of the ship, the topmost black flag of the star and V of the *Vermillion*. They were back on the frigate in Nowhere in No Time.

"It's all right, Mateo," said the captain. He was leaning over him. "You're safe now. You can let go of the rope."

Matt realized he was still clinging to it for life. He had to concentrate on prying his frozen fingers off of it. He turned his head and saw Ruby and Corey kneeling next to him. Ruby was clutching Corey's arm and crying. Corey was pale, his expression shocked and worried.

"And I thought I was the reckless one," said Corey. "What did you go and do that for, bro? You crazy?"

Matt lifted a fist in the air. "YOLO," he croaked.

Ruby sputtered a laugh through her tears.

Matt started to sit up. He winced.

"Your chin is bleeding," said Ruby. "It looks like you need stitches."

He touched his chin. It stung, but the pain of it brought back his memory more fully. He remembered trying to leap for the boat. He remembered Albert . . .

Matt looked around. He found Albert staring at him with wide, fearful eyes. A surge of anger rose in him. "You . . . ," he started to say, but his voice caught in his throat.

Albert backed away. "I didn't mean to!" he squeaked. "It was an accident!"

"What do you mean, an accident?" said Ruby. "What happened?"

"You pushed him off, didn't you?" said Corey.

"No!" said Albert.

"You've hated us ever since we came on board," said Corey. "You almost got Matt killed!"

"Albert," Jia gasped. "How could you?"

Captain Vincent didn't speak at all. He took action, swift and strong.

He hauled Albert up by the collar. Even with Albert's considerable bulk, the captain swung him over the side of the ship as though he were nothing more than a fish on a string.

"You want to throw someone's life away? Throw away your own." He lowered Albert, and Albert started squealing like an animal about to be slaughtered.

The captain's eyes were two black holes in his head, void of all feeling. It reminded Matt of the black, bottomless nothing he'd felt when he'd been dragged beneath the *Vermillion*. He couldn't bear it. The air was being pressed out of his lungs and wouldn't inflate again. This wasn't right, even if it was Albert. Even if he did try to leave him behind.

"It wasn't his fault!" shouted Matt.

The captain looked over at Matt. Albert stopped flailing.

"What do you mean?" said the captain.

Matt tried to think quickly. "Albert was trying to help me," he said. "He lowered a stick for me to grab on to, but . . . the stick snapped and I fell."

"I don't believe you," said the captain. His eyes were still dark, so cold and empty, and Matt wondered if he was now looking at the real captain, if the smiles and seemingly generous nature had been a carefully crafted mask. His chest tightened even more, constricting his heart.

"But that's what happened," said Matt. "Ask Albert. He'll tell you."

"Yes, yes!" Albert squeaked. "I was trying to help!"

The captain looked at Matt for another moment, still holding Albert by the neck over the side of the ship. Matt knew he didn't believe him, but that didn't matter. What mattered was keeping Albert alive, and the captain wouldn't kill him if Matt said he was innocent.

Captain Vincent flung Albert onto the deck. Albert scrambled on hands and knees to the side of the ship. He curled up in a ball, covered his head, and whimpered. "I didn't, I didn't," he continued to say, until Captain Vincent gave him a rough kick.

"You've got some nerve," he said, then he turned sharply back to Matt. "Well? Let's have it then."

Matt blinked, unsure what the captain meant. And then he remembered the letter. He'd been about to hand it over to the captain when they'd noticed the queen's spy. Matt pulled out the letter. It was wet, probably unreadable now. The captain stared down at it.

"That's it?" he said, clearly disappointed.

"I'm sorry," said Matt. "Someone had already come, and the queen . . ."

The captain just stared at the letter in Matt's outstretched hand. Finally he took it and tore open the soggy envelope. Matt could see that the ink was smeared but still legible apparently, because the captain feverishly read the letter. His face dropped with every line. When he reached the bottom his eyes twitched a little, and then he crumpled the letter in his hand and stormed away without a word.

Brocco and Wiley followed the captain. Jia then took Pike's hand and led her away, leaving the Hudsons and Albert alone.

"You should have let the captain discard him," said Corey. "He deserved it."

"Why did you lie?" said Ruby. "I mean, he did try to lose you, didn't he?"

Matt nodded.

"Then why?"

Matt looked over at Albert. He was still huddled against the side of the ship, crying. "If you had experienced what I just had," said Matt, "you wouldn't wish it on your worst enemy."

The gray sky rumbled, and it started to rain. It seemed the gloomy weather had followed them from England.

"Come on, let's leave this loser to himself," said Corey. He held a hand out to Matt and helped him up. He winced as he stood. Everything hurt, his head, his arms, his hands, his shins. As they descended the steps Matt glanced back at Albert, and guessed that he was probably hurting more.

The *Vermillion* was quiet and subdued for the rest of the day. The loudest sound was the rain and wind lashing against the ship, the creaks and groans as it rocked on the waves. Matt was now shaking with cold. Ruby told him he needed to change before he got hypothermia, so he made his way to their room. The pain of all his cuts and bruises really began to sink in. His chin was still bleeding. It had dripped and smeared all over his freezing, soaking-wet clothes. He peeled them off, leaving them in a heap beneath his hammock, and put on his clothes from home, his Mets hoodie and hat, and as soon as he did he had a sudden and sharp longing for home, for his mom and dad. He wished they were here with him right now. He wanted his mom to fret over him, check his heartbeat, his blood pressure and temperature. He wanted to watch a baseball game with his dad, hear one of his corny jokes, or just see him asleep in his chair with a book lying open on his chest.

There was a knock on the door. "Come in," said Matt.

Jia stepped in carrying a shoe box. "I've brought you some medicine and bandages," she said. She set the box down on one of the crates. It was full of bandages, antiseptics, and some other medicines, some in old-fashioned tins and jars with droppers, and others the traditional orange pill bottles of a modern pharmacy.

"Thanks," said Matt. Jia stood awkwardly. She looked around and finally sat on the floor. Matt sat with her, wincing a bit. He was very sore. Time-traveling outside of a vessel was ill advised, he decided. Maybe he'd write that in a book someday.

"You need to make sure the wound is clean first," said Jia. She took a bottle of antiseptic and poured it onto some cotton. She held it out to Matt. He dabbed it on his chin and sucked in a breath.

"Sorry," said Jia. "I should have warned you it would sting."

"No, it's okay. I knew it would." He pressed the cotton ball on his chin until it stopped burning. Jia gently placed two butterfly bandages on the wound. "Try not to smile," she said, and of course Matt couldn't help but smile. "Stop! You'll pull the bandages off."

"Sorry," said Matt. He had to bite his cheeks to keep from smiling. He could tell Jia was doing the same.

"There's some salve, too, for your rope burns." She took one of the old-looking jars and pulled off the lid. "It's an old Chinese medicine." A very pleasant aroma was released, floral and minty. Matt took some of the cream and rubbed it on his hands. It cooled and soothed the pain immediately.

"Thank you," he said.

"I was really scared," said Jia in a small voice.

"Me too," said Matt.

"I thought you were going to die."

"Me too."

"Are you going to leave?"

The question caught Matt off guard. He wasn't sure how to answer. Jia was his friend, and he didn't want to hurt her, but he also knew it would be worse to lie. "I haven't talked to Corey and Ruby about it," said Matt, "or the captain, but we'll probably have to sometime soon. We have our parents, you know, and they'd be devastated if something happened to any of us."

Jia nodded but didn't meet his eyes. "There's something I think I need to show you." Jia reached inside one of her many pockets and pulled out a wrinkled piece of paper with smeared ink. It was the letter.

"Where did you get that?" he asked.

Jia looked around, almost to make absolutely sure they were alone.

"I found it in the captain's office," she whispered, "when I was bringing him some coffee and food. I didn't know what it was, exactly. I wouldn't have thought anything of it except I saw . . ." She didn't seem to be able to articulate what exactly she saw. She handed the letter to Matt.

Matt took the paper and unfolded it. It was difficult to read with the smeared ink, and the handwriting wasn't exactly neat anyway, but he was able to read and comprehend it well enough.

DEAR CAPTAIN VINCENT,

YOU THINK YOU CAN SHOW UP WHEREVER, WHENEVER TO TAKE WHATEVER AND NO ONE WILL BE THE WISER, BUT IF YOU ARE READING THIS LETTER, YOU KNOW I'VE GOT MY EYE ON YOU AT ALL TIMES. MOST RECENTLY (OR NOT SO RECENTLY) MY MAPS SHOWED THE VERMILLION AT THE SIEGE OF ASCALON. ISN'T WAR A THIEVES' PARADISE? SO MUCH GOES MISSING

WITHOUT A TRACE. NO DOUBT YOU MADE FRIENDS WITH THE
KNIGHTS TEMPLAR.

YOU MAY POSSESS THE OBSIDIAN COMPASS FOR NOW, AND I
KNOW YOU THINK IT WILL MAKE YOU IN-VINCE-IBLE (HA!),
BUT YOU DO NOT UNDERSTAND ITS FULL POWER. AND THOUGH
YOU MAY POSE A THREAT TO MY FAMILY, I WILL NEVER
LET HARM COME TO THEM BY YOU OR ANY OTHER. I UNDER-
STAND YOU FEEL YOU'VE BEEN ROBBED, BUT HOW CAN ANYONE
STEAL SOMETHING THAT BELONGS TO NO ONE? YOUR POSSES-
SIVE NATURE HAS ALWAYS BEEN YOUR DOWNFALL, VINCE, AND
SHOULD YOU CONTINUE YOUR CRUSADE FOR THAT WHICH WAS
NEVER YOURS, IT WILL PROVE YOUR FULL DESTRUCTION.
SINCERELY AND WITH NO REGRETS,
M. B. HUDSON

Matt read the letter a second time and then a third.

"Matt?" said Jia. He looked up. He'd almost forgotten she
was there.

"It's from my dad," he said.

"Your father?" asked Jia. "Are you sure?"

"I think so," said Matt, even though he couldn't quite wrap
his mind around it all. The ink was smeared, making the
writing a bit blurry, but the untidy handwriting was familiar
enough, and the mention of maps made it all the more likely.

"But how does he know the captain?" Jia asked.

"I don't know." It was only one of about a hundred

questions racing through Matt's brain. What did his dad have to do with the Obsidian Compass? How could he know where the captain was traveling without being on board the *Vermillion*? Maps . . . Maybe his dad's obsession with maps went beyond antiquities. What if some of his maps could show the mark of a certain ship at certain times and locations? He thought of the old map above their dining room table. Matt often saw his dad studying it, tracing his finger over certain markings, as though he were seeing things for the first time. He'd been doing it the morning Matt, Corey, and Ruby had boarded the *Vermillion*, just before he and Mrs. Hudson left. It was like he knew the captain had been coming for them. Maybe his parents had gone to try to stop him, but they must have gone to the wrong location or miscalculated the timing somehow. And that brought to mind a more troublesome question: What were Captain Vincent's real motives in bringing them on board the *Vermillion*? The captain clearly had not been completely honest with them.

"What are you going to do?" Jia asked.

"I don't know yet. I need to talk to Corey and Ruby."

"Talk to us about what?" said Ruby. She and Corey were just now entering the room, Corey with a bag of Doritos and a can of Dr Pepper.

"I think I'll go check on Albert," said Jia, starting to rise.

"No, stay," said Matt, and Jia sat down again.

"Talk to us about what?" Ruby repeated.

Matt unfolded the letter and held it out to them. Corey and Ruby both took it and read it together. He watched their faces go from confusion to wonder and disbelief.

"Jia found it in the captain's office," said Matt. "It's the letter we brought him from Queen Elizabeth."

Ruby looked to Jia. "I don't understand. Dad wrote to the captain? But . . . how? And why?"

"It's obvious, isn't it?" said Corey. "Dad's a time pirate!"

Ruby gasped. "Do you think Dad is the one who got to the queen before us? Could *he* be the maker of the compass?"

"I'm not sure that's what this means," said Matt. It was clear their dad knew something about the *Vermillion* and the Obsidian Compass, but it was difficult to picture him on board the *Vermillion*, going on wild adventures and heists. When Matt thought of his father he always pictured him sitting in a chair, reading, or poring over old maps.

"Well, how else do you explain that letter?" said Corey. "What do you think he stole from the captain?"

"Whatever it was we were supposed to get from Queen Elizabeth, duh," said Ruby. "Probably one of his precious maps or something."

Matt folded up the letter.

Matt doubted this too. The Hudsons weren't poor by any means, but Mr. Hudson had never seemed preoccupied with wealth or treasure. He was far more interested in borders and trade routes, how land and geography shaped culture and civilization. He always said a good map could tell more about ancient civilization than novel-length recorded history, and he loved to collect old maps from all over. But what map could possibly have been so alluring to him that he would steal from Captain Vincent and inspire such rage? It didn't all seem to add up in Matt's mind. "Whatever it is, the captain probably knows where it is now. It's probably at the museum, maybe even in Dad's office, which sort of puts us in an awkward position. It's not like we're going to steal from our own dad, which brings us to another problem. Clearly Dad and the captain know each other, and it doesn't seem like they're very friendly, does it? Which means the captain lied to us. He's been using us against our own father."

They were silent for a few moments as they let this information sink in.

"But the captain has always been so nice to us," said Ruby. "What if he didn't *know* Dad was our dad?"

"But clearly he does," said Matt. "The letter proves that."

"Yeah, but who knows when that letter was written?" said Ruby. "I mean, what if this letter is talking about things from the captain's future? Maybe the captain hasn't even *been* to the Siege of Ascalon yet. What if whatever Dad steals hasn't been stolen yet? What if Dad is trying to steal the compass from the captain!"

Matt thought about this. "But clearly he stole something the captain wants now. Whatever it was that the *Mona Lisa* key unlocks. What if the captain has known all along that Dad is working against him and is using us as ransom and revenge, as tools against our own father?"

The Hudson children all sat in silence. Memories started to flash before Matt, all of them taking on new meaning. Their parents' strict rules, their mom's aversion to transit. They knew the captain would be looking for them.

"I want to go home," said Ruby. "I want Mom and Dad."

A cord seemed to have been snapped with those words. "Me too," said Corey.

Matt nodded. "We need to talk to the captain."

"Please don't show him the letter!" Jia pleaded, her eyes panicked. "He'll know I took it. He'll think I was being disloyal."

Matt nodded. He didn't want to get Jia in trouble. "We won't show him the letter. We don't have to. We'll simply ask him to take us home."

"But will he?" said Corey. "I mean, I know he said he would, but it seems like he wasn't exactly telling us the truth."

They all looked to Jia. She squirmed a little. "I don't know. The captain has never held anyone on board the ship against their will, but . . ."

But they were a different matter, Matt thought. Their father was clearly an enemy to Captain Vincent. "Maybe we can convince him that our dad will give us what he wants if he takes us home."

There was an awkward pause. Jia wouldn't look at any of them, but Matt could see that her eyes were glistening with tears. He had the impulse to reach out and hug her, but she got up quickly.

"I'd better go check on Albert," she said. She picked up her box of medical supplies, hurried to the door, and then stopped. "Please don't leave without saying goodbye. Promise?"

"We promise," said Matt.

Jia shut the door behind her, leaving the Hudsons alone.

"She doesn't seem too happy for us to leave," said Corey.

"Of course not," said Ruby. "When we leave she'll be stuck here with no one but Albert and Pike for company. We'll likely never see her again."

"If the captain takes us home," said Matt.

"He will," said Ruby. "He has to." But her voice was thin, and none of them were certain what the truth was.

They talked a little while longer, discussing what they should say to the captain, how much they should reveal. They decided it would be wise not to mention their father or the letter.

"Our best bet is to simply tell him we think it's time to go home," said Matt.

"And what if he says no?" said Ruby.

"One of us could fake sick," said Corey. "Matt could pretend to have one of his seizures, and we could say he has to go home to get his medicine, or say he needs a hospital."

"I'm not sure that will work," said Ruby. "He could very easily travel back and have another crew member get the medicine or just take him to the hospital himself at some other time and place."

"Maybe we should tell him that our mom is dying," said Corey. "And we just really want to spend some time with her, but we want to come back later?"

"Is it really necessary to lie?" said Ruby.

"Do you really think Captain Vincent will take us home if we tell the truth? I'm just trying to increase our chances here."

But Matt worried their chances were fairly slim no matter what.

"Well, there's no reason to wait, is there?" said Matt. "Should we go talk to him now?"

"I guess," said Ruby.

Ruby and Corey changed into their clothes from home, and they all gathered their backpacks. They didn't see anyone on their way to the captain's cabin. No one was in the dining hall.

Matt lightly knocked on the door of the captain's cabin, but there was no response. He knocked again. "Captain Vincent? It's the Hudsons. We need to talk to you."

He kept knocking until the door finally opened. It was not the captain who opened the door but Santiago. He stuck his nose around the doorframe and sniffed, showing his long teeth.

"Uh . . . Hi, Santiago. We'd like to speak with Captain Vincent, please."

Santiago scurried down the frame and pushed opened the door. He swished his tail, motioning for the children to enter.

The captain's cabin was in quite a bit more disarray than the first time Matt had seen it, when he and the captain had found the *Mona Lisa* key. Clothes were strewn everywhere. Trays of food, much of it untouched, rested in different areas of the room—on a chair, on the bed, on the floor. There were crumpled-up papers all over the desk and floor. The captain was standing in front of all the paintings of the dark-haired woman, his sword in hand. Matt noticed that the paintings had been further slashed, stabbed, and torn. One had a dagger sticking right in the woman's eye. The captain looked a bit sweaty and rumpled. Santiago climbed up onto his shoulder, red eyes glaring suspiciously at the children as they approached.

Captain Vincent seemed a bit surprised to see all three of them, especially in their regular clothes with their backpacks. "Good evening," he said with what Matt felt was forced cheerfulness. "And to what do I owe this honored visit? Mateo, are you feeling all right?"

"Yes, sir," said Matt, then he hesitated, not sure how he should start. He decided diving right in was probably best. "Sir, we want to go home."

Captain Vincent blinked, like he needed a minute to process what Matt had just said. "My dear Mateo, I know you had a close call this last adventure, but you can't let that stop you from fulfilling your grand potential as a time pirate! There is still so much for you to do!"

"It's not that," said Matt. "Well, it sort of is . . . I mean, we've had a great time and everything. It's been amazing, more than we could ever have hoped for, but the truth is we miss our home . . . and our parents. So with respect and, um, much gratitude, we request to go back home to New York."

The captain just stared at them. He said nothing for what felt like a very long time, and it made Matt squirm a little. He looked to Corey and Ruby.

"We could probably come back, though," said Corey. "At some point in time, if you want us to."

The captain slipped his sword back in the scabbard at his side. "Request denied. You may go."

"What?" the children all said together.

"I've other pressing matters of business and don't have time to take you home at the moment."

"Then tomorrow?" said Matt.

"No, I'm afraid my business will take a bit longer than that."

"How long?" Ruby asked. "What pressing matters of business?"

"That is none of your business," said the captain with a tight smile on his face.

"It is if it has anything to do with our father," said Corey in a brazen voice.

"Corey . . . ," growled Ruby, her teeth clenched.

The captain's smile froze on his lips. "And pray, why would my business have anything to do with your father?"

Matt sighed. He glanced at Ruby, who simply shook her head in defeat. They were busted. Matt took out the letter and held it out to the captain. The captain stared down at it.

"Where did you get that?" he said, his voice half whisper, half growl.

Matt thought quickly. How to explain without getting Jia in trouble?

"I took it," said Ruby suddenly.

The captain raised an eyebrow. "You, Miss Ruby?"

Ruby nodded. "I wanted to know what was in that letter, so I snuck into your cabin when Jia was bringing you food. Neither of you saw me, and I took the letter off your desk."

The captain appraised her, searching for the lie. Ruby didn't flinch at all. "You really have become little thieves, haven't you?" he said. "Stealing my private correspondence from my private quarters."

"And you lied to us," said Matt.

"I never lied," said Captain Vincent.

"You withheld the truth from us," said Ruby, "which is pretty much the same thing."

"In that case your father is just as much a liar as I am, isn't he?"

"You kidnapped us!" Ruby shouted.

"I most certainly did *not* kidnap you. You boarded this ship without any force or even bribery. We opened our doors and you stepped aboard, and once you board the *Vermillion* you are bound by its rules. *My* rules. And stealing from my desk is against the rules."

Matt defiantly stuffed the letter back in his pocket. "How do you know our dad?" he asked. "Why was he writing to you?"

"Was he a time pirate?" Corey asked. "He was, wasn't he?"

"Pfft," said Captain Vincent. "Your father could never be a time pirate. Doesn't have the stomach for it. No, your father is nothing more than a common thief."

"What did he take from you?" Corey asked.

Captain Vincent's jaw tightened at this question. "Something that did not belong to him. And believe me when I say he will be *very* sorry that he did."

"And does whatever he took rightfully belong to you?" Ruby asked. "Or did you steal it, too, like you do everything else? Maybe our dad took it with *noble* intentions, to keep it safe from *you*."

The captain gave Ruby a tight smile. "What makes you think your father is the noble one in this situation? Simply because he's your father? Children always think the best of their parents. They always want to believe that they are good and honest and have never done anything wrong, but one day you will grow up and learn otherwise."

"Take us home," said Matt. "Whatever it is you want, you won't get it by keeping us here. If you bring us back, my dad will give you what you want."

"Are you sure about that?" said the captain. "Some people will guard their treasure at any price." He smiled, but his eyes were distant and cold. It made the hair at the back of Matt's neck prickle.

"Not our dad," said Matt. "Whatever it is, he'd never choose it over us. Never."

The captain considered, fingertips beneath his chin. "Perhaps you are right. In any case, I've already made plans to return to New York." He brought out the compass and lightly circled a finger around the dial. "But I'm afraid you three won't be able to join me this time."

"What?" said Matt.

"Why not?" demanded Ruby.

"Leverage, Miss Ruby." The captain turned the inner dial of the compass to the left. "I'm not taking any chances this time. I believe I'll fare better in my bargains with you three out of their reach"—he turned the dial to the right—"and out of my way."

Matt gulped. Ruby and Corey backed away a little, eyeing the compass.

"It's a shame, really. I did enjoy our time together, but I'm afraid I can no longer trust you. When you board the *Vermillion* you are making a very simple choice: loyalty"— Captain

Vincent turned the middle dial—"or nothing. If you're not with me, then you're against me." He turned the third dial to the left.

Matt made a split-second decision. He lunged toward the captain, reaching for the compass. Corey and Ruby must have had the same idea because they all crashed into each other, knocking heads and shoulders, while Captain Vincent quite easily sidestepped them all. And then it was too late. The captain made the final turn of the outer dial, and the compass clicked. The lamps in the captain's cabin flickered, the ship tilted sharply, and they were all thrown to the floor as the ship began to transform.

19

Time Castaways

The *Vermillion* screeched and roared as it transformed, as if it were some kind of monster that had been violently ripped from a deep sleep. The walls pressed in on them, the floors melted beneath their feet, turning to metal. The furniture sank into the walls and floor. The captain's desk became a control panel with buttons and dials, levers and gauges. The roar began to pulse in a steady rhythm. The *Vermillion* was a helicopter.

The captain was flying, though not very steadily. The helicopter swooped and tilted erratically, and Matt was shoved against the side while Ruby and Corey fell to the floor. Out the window Matt could see a hazy spot of land in the distance.

The helicopter tilted sharply to the right, and Matt went sprawling. When he looked up he saw the rest of the crew all huddled together in the back of the helicopter. They all looked at Matt with mixed expressions of pity and surprise. Jia was pale and trembling, her eyes welling with tears.

The helicopter sank suddenly, and Matt's insides smashed up against his ribs. He was going to be sick.

The captain turned around. "Open the gate!" he shouted, and Brocco and Wiley sprang into action. They pulled open the side of the helicopter. The beating roar was deafening. They were hovering just twenty feet above the water, which was rippling furiously outward from the beating rotors. The captain shouted something from behind him, but Matt couldn't tell what. He turned to see what was going on. Brocco was trading places with the captain in the pilot seat. The captain came toward Matt, his dark eyes blazing, yet at the same time, empty. He grabbed Matt by the collar and without a word of warning pushed him out of the helicopter.

He didn't even have the presence of mind to scream before he hit the water. It felt like breaking through a glass ceiling. Icy shards cut into him, cut off his air, seared his lungs. He came to the surface and gasped for breath, taking in a mouthful of seawater at the same time. He saw Corey fall, and then Ruby. She screamed until she was silenced by the water. Wiley shoved a small life raft out of the helicopter, just before the captain slid the door shut.

The *Vermillion* lifted up, flew over their heads and the island, then dipped below the rocks. Matt watched it disappear as he struggled to stay afloat. He slapped at the water and coughed as he swallowed a mouthful. Corey was dog-paddling frantically. Ruby was thrashing and starting to hyperventilate. None of them were strong swimmers. They'd only taken enough lessons to not drown instantly, but they wouldn't last long, especially with their clothes and backpacks weighing them down. Matt had to keep his head together. The life raft. He swam as best he could to the small, inflatable raft and grabbed ahold of the rope. He took off his backpack and swung it over the side, then pulled the raft toward his brother and sister. Ruby went below the surface for a moment, then came back up, coughing and gasping for air. Matt grabbed her hand and forced it onto the rope. "Corey, help me get her up."

Corey dog-paddled over to Matt, and together they hoisted Ruby up until she flopped over to the other side. "You go next," said Matt. Corey didn't argue. He grabbed onto the sides, and Matt pushed him from behind, using his shoulder to get him over. Once Corey was in he leaned back over to help Matt, grasping his wrists and pulling. He slipped and went under. He tried again, and this time swung his leg up and over and rolled into the raft. His legs crashed into Ruby, but she didn't even express annoyance. She was huddled in a ball, shivering violently. Corey's lips were blue, and his dark eyes seemed to be iced over, the usual warmth and laughter in them drained. The wind whipped and went right through Matt's clothes, biting beneath his skin and chilling his very bones. They needed to get to that island.

There were paddles in the boat. Matt forced himself to take one and started to paddle. After a minute of struggling on his own, mostly making the boat go in circles, Ruby grabbed the other oar and they each took a side. It was slow, torturous work, especially as the ocean seemed determined to keep them away from the island, but at last they made it to the shore. They all climbed out of the raft and pulled it farther up the beach. Ruby collapsed on the sand, breathing hard. Matt's brain finally unlocked and allowed his body to do what it had been wanting to do for a while. He fell to his hands and knees and vomited.

Corey put a hand on his back. "You okay, bro?" he asked, teeth chattering.

Matt nodded, even though he knew he wasn't. He was dizzy. His head was pounding. He was freezing. He shook his head, trying to clear his vision, and looked around. The island looked to be just sand and rock, no life at all. He didn't even see any birds. They must truly be in the middle of nowhere, on some forgotten island who knew when. They were hopelessly lost, but he couldn't think about that right now. Right now they just had to survive, get dry and warm.

They removed most of their wet clothes, stripping down to their underwear, and laid them on some rocks. Hopefully the fierce wind would dry them quickly. In the meantime the wind was freezing them to death. They tipped the life raft on its side against a rock and huddled beneath it for shelter. As they tipped the boat, a few supply packets toppled out. They each contained some emergency food bars, bottles of drinking water, and a small first-aid kit. It was the barest of survival kits, it certainly wouldn't help them survive for long, but it was better than nothing.

None of them spoke, only huddled as close together as possible to try to get warm. The only sounds were the waves crashing against the rocks and the chattering of their teeth.

After an hour or so of shivering, Matt inspected one of the survival kits a little more closely, hoping to find one of those emergency blankets or something. He didn't find one, but the first-aid kit did contain a small packet of matches.

"I'm going to go see if I can find some wood," said Matt.

"I'll come with you," said Corey, but Matt shook his head.

"Stay with Ruby." Corey didn't argue. He slumped back down, exhausted. All the shivering had taken its toll. Matt was tired too, and still nauseated, but he forced himself to get up. Soon it would be dark, and they'd be even colder. He needed to find some firewood now.

The island was not what Matt would call a tropical paradise. There were no trees that he could see, and very few plants, mostly seaweed, but he found some dry grassy stuff growing in the sand. It might at least help get a fire started, but what he really needed was wood.

The island was small, probably only a mile long and just a

few city blocks wide, like a miniature version of Manhattan. Matt walked all the way to the other side and found a few pieces of driftwood. They were damp, but he picked them up anyway. A bunch of tiny crabs skittered away when he lifted the wood. If they grew desperate enough, they could eat them, he thought. He saw some small shells scattered along the shore. Maybe they could dig up some clams, or catch some fish somehow. This was as far as his survival instincts took him. He tried to think if his mom or dad had ever taught him anything that might help them now, but as far as he could remember they only taught him how to survive in the city— how to cross streets safely, to not talk to strangers, what to do if you got lost, and to never, ever take any kind of transit without a supervising adult. Well, he'd heeded all but the last, which was ultimately how he'd ended up on a barren island, where none of his parents' lessons would be of any use. Well done, Mateo.

Matt went higher up on the island, climbing the rocks. Between a few larger rocks Matt found what he felt was no small miracle—a pile of dry wood. It was so perfect he almost thought he was hallucinating, but when he lowered himself between the rocks and brushed his hand along the wood it gave him a few splinters and he knew it was real. He started to gather some in his arms and then shouted and dropped it all. He fell back and smacked his head against a rock. There was a skull, a human one, beneath the wood. After his heart stopped hammering he laughed at himself a little. There wasn't anything to be afraid of, was there? Whoever it was, they were clearly dead. Slowly he edged back. His heart calmed enough to allow a bit of curiosity in. He looked between some of the cracks of the wood. There looked to be a full skeleton buried beneath it all. He stood back and observed the wood more closely. It was all flat boards, some of them nailed together, and there was the hint of a shape of a boat. He could see the bow now. He removed a bit more of the wood. The skeleton was mostly buried in sand, but a bit of cloth peeked out and it looked like it was once quite colorful, but now faded from time, salt, and sun. Matt wondered if this could be one of the old crewmates from Captain Bonnaire's time that Captain Vincent had discarded.

Matt picked up as much wood as he could carry and headed back to Corey and Ruby. He decided he wouldn't tell them about the skeleton. It would probably make them panic. Their circumstances were desperate enough, and Matt felt the need to protect his siblings, give them as much hope as possible. Somehow they would get home. They had the raft, at least, and some supplies. He'd figure something out.

It was completely dark by the time they got a fire started. Matt used up nearly an entire packet of matches and all his patience, but finally Ruby stepped in and helped him get it going by blowing on the small embers to keep the flames burning until the wood caught fire. They piled on the wood until they had a blazing fire that was like a balm to their weary, icy bones.

The three children all stared into the flames, and as the heat started to melt away Matt's shock, his hunger set in. They shared one of the bottles of water and an emergency calorie bar. It was dry and tasteless, but it filled their stomachs, and then their brains were able to move on to their next dilemma.

"Where do you think we are," said Corey, still shivering. "And when?"

"I dunno," said Matt. "We came in a helicopter, so we can't be too far in the past."

"Doesn't give us a clue as to where we are though, does it?" said Ruby.

"No, not really," said Matt.

"Wait," said Corey, "what about the phone?"

"What phone?" said Matt.

"*Our* phone? The one Mom and Dad gave us for emergencies?"

Ruby gasped and scrambled for her backpack. She pulled out soggy papers and books and finally found the phone in an inner pocket. "It doesn't look like it got too wet," she said hopefully. She flipped it open and miraculously it switched on.

"Oh please, oh please . . . ," Ruby whispered, and Matt felt his hopes rise just a little until Ruby's shoulders collapsed. She shook her head. "Nothing." She turned the phone off, flipped it shut, and dropped it back inside her backpack.

They fell silent again, staring blankly at the fire. Matt could feel that they were all thinking the same things. How were they going to get home? Would they ever see their parents again? And then Ruby gave voice to the worst fear of all.

"Are we going to die here?" she asked in a small voice.

"No," said Matt, though the image of the skeleton crept into his mind. He shook it off. They couldn't think like that, though he knew their situation was dire. Matt had inspected the emergency supplies already. They had only enough food and water for them all to survive for a few days, a week at most, if they stretched. Matt could sense Corey and Ruby sinking into despair and he couldn't let that happen. He was the oldest. He was an optimist. Hope was key. It was up to him to keep it alive.

"Remember the time when Mom and Dad forgot to pick us up from school?" Matt asked.

"I thought something horrible had happened," said Ruby. "I thought we were orphans."

"Me too," said Corey.

Matt had felt the same, like they were completely alone in the world. And none of them thought to go back inside the school to call. They didn't have the cell phone then. So they waited and waited in front of the school, until it was nearly dark and they were all shivering with cold. It was March and still quite chilly, but they hadn't brought jackets. Matt's mind had been racing about what they would do, where they would go. Would they have to live in an alley? Sleep in a dumpster when it rained or snowed? Would they have to beg on the streets for their food? Then one of the teachers came out. She stopped short when she saw them and exclaimed, "Oh! What are you still doing here?"

She took them to the office and called their parents. Their mom came within ten minutes, mortified and nearly in tears. It turned out that she had simply mixed up her days and thought their dad was supposed to get them. Mrs. Hudson felt so guilty she took them out for hamburgers and milkshakes, which actually gave Matt a stomachache, but he didn't care. It tasted amazing, and he was so relieved he wasn't an orphan.

"Let's just think of it like that," said Matt. "It all seems hopeless, like we're going to be stranded here forever, but we'll find something, think of something, that will get us out. We just have to take this one step at a time."

Their clothes finally dried enough that they could put them back on. Matt added a bit more wood to the fire, and they all lay back in the sand, wiggling around to try to smooth out the lumps and get comfortable. It was almost impossible, but they didn't have the energy to complain about it.

"Maybe Mom and Dad will find us," said Ruby sleepily. "I mean, they *have* to know how to time-travel, don't they? At least Dad does."

"Or the captain might come back for us," said Corey.

"Once Dad gives him what he wants."

"Will he, though?" said Ruby.

"Of course he will," said Corey. "Dad would never leave us here, no matter what. Mom would chop off his head with one of her swords."

"True," said Ruby.

Matt didn't say anything. He decided that his father had some explaining to do once they got home . . . if they ever got home. But they had to get home somehow. His future self is supposed to travel back in time to help the captain. That was proof of survival. But Matt was very confused on that point, maybe even more than after he'd read his father's letter. Why was Matt helping Captain Vincent in the future when the captain was so obviously against them? Is it a ruse, or is his future self actually on the captain's side?

What makes you think your father is the noble one in this situation? Matt shivered as the captain's words ran through his mind. What if his dad *wasn't* the good guy? No. He couldn't believe that. Whatever his dad had taken from the captain, he had good reason.

Matt added more wood to the fire then rummaged through his backpack, searching in vain for anything that might help them. Everything was wet and mostly ruined, his schoolbooks and papers, his notebook with his drawings of the compass, the ink faded and smeared. He found a copy of *El León, La Bruja y El Ropero*. He'd forgotten that he'd borrowed it from

Wiley's library to keep up on his Spanish. He opened it and set it near the fire to let the pages dry. In a way Matt thought they were a little like Lucy, Edmund, Susan, and Peter. They had gone through a sort of portal, and, like Edmund at least, had been hoodwinked and betrayed by someone who acted as a friend. If only they had a great talking lion on their side, or some magical gifts to fight evil. If only they could get back home simply by stepping through a wardrobe.

"Good night, Matt," muttered Ruby.

"Good night, Ruby."

"Don't *even* say good night to me," mumbled Corey.

Matt laughed a little. "Good night, Corey."

"Night-night, knuckleheads," said Corey, and then a few moments later, "I'm sorry I got on the train."

"It's not your fault," said Matt.

"It is," said Corey. "You know it is."

"We know," said Ruby in a sleepy voice. "We forgive you."

"Really?" said Corey.

In answer, Ruby put her fist in the air. Corey met her fist with his own and Matt did the same, making their three-way fist bump.

Corey and Ruby drifted off to sleep within minutes, but Matt stayed awake for quite a while, his mind going in hopeless circles. He anxiously rubbed at his bracelet. Even if they could get off this island, they had nowhere to go, no one to take care of them. Even if their parents were alive at this time, coming in contact with either of them would surely cause some kind of ripple or glitch in the space-time continuum. They could cause a real disaster, maybe even cancel out their own existence.

No, the only way to get home was to time-travel, and in order to do that they needed the Obsidian Compass and the *Vermillion*. But both were gone, probably hundreds of years and thousands of miles away by now.

Matt slept fitfully that night. He had dreams about the compass. He was turning the dials in the direction of home, but every time they began to travel, just as he could see the New York City skyline, they were yanked back to Nowhere in No Time, sudden and violent. It was like he was on a merry-go-round, spinning faster and faster, and every time he tried to jump off, he got whipped back on the ride.

Matt woke to a cold shock rushing up his legs. He sat up abruptly and scrambled up higher on the beach. The tide had come in. He looked around for Corey and Ruby in a panic, fearing that they'd been carried away in the water before waking, but they were safe. They were sleeping a little higher than him, parallel to the water, so it just missed them. Ruby was curled up in a ball, her face covered with the hoodie. Corey was sprawled out on his back with an arm over his eyes. They both looked completely exhausted.

Matt looked out over the waves and his heart sank to

his stomach. The life raft was bobbing upside down at least twenty feet from the beach, and their food, water, and supplies were nowhere to be seen. Matt rushed out into the water and dove toward the life raft. He swam as hard as he could, which wasn't very fast at all, but he managed to reach the life raft. He grabbed ahold of the rope and began to tug it back to shore. When he at last reached the shore he was completely out of breath and his head began to throb dully at his temples. Corey and Ruby were still asleep, which annoyed him for some reason. For a brief moment he thought about kicking water or sand in their faces to wake them up, then immediately chastised himself for feeling so harshly. It wasn't their fault, but if they woke to find they had no food or drinking water they'd be every bit as grumpy as Matt felt.

He searched the shoreline for any of their supplies, hoping some of it might be floating on the surface somewhere or buried in the sand. After searching for about twenty minutes he found one of the water bottles just beneath the ocean, wedged between two rocks, and the packet of matches floating on the surface. He also found one of his shoes half buried in sand beneath the water, but he didn't see the other anywhere. Well, one shoe wasn't much good to him. The water was the only essential thing, but one water bottle . . . They wouldn't last long with that.

He set the bottle of water and matches on a rock above the place where they'd slept. Corey and Ruby were still fast asleep, and he didn't want to sit still and wait for them to wake up. He decided to go for a walk. He'd dry quicker anyway. He'd go collect more firewood.

When he reached the boat he started to pull the wood and got several splinters. The sun rose fully in the sky as he worked and beat down on his head and shoulders. By the time he collected as much wood as he could carry his head was pounding. He was probably dehydrated. He'd have a big long gulp of the water when he returned. He selfishly contemplated drinking it all and telling Corey and Ruby that all the water had floated away. He walked back toward the camp, scraping his bare feet on the rocks, which only darkened his mood further.

When he reached the campsite with his arms full of wood, Ruby and Corey were awake and they were shouting. He couldn't hear what they were saying, but they were definitely upset. Ruby was crying, and Corey was holding one of Matt's wet shoes. Finally they both looked up and saw Matt.

"Where were you?" Corey shouted.

"I went to get more firewood, so we wouldn't, you know, freeze to death."

"You could've woken us!" said Corey. "Ruby thought you'd been eaten by a shark."

"I didn't," said Ruby, drying her tears. "I just thought something bad might have happened."

"I don't think these waters are actually shark infested,"

said Matt. "And anyway, I think it would be a bit difficult for a shark to attack me on the beach."

"Har, har," said Corey. "You scared us half to death, you know! Next time have the decency to at least wake us and let us know where you're going."

Something cold seeped into Matt's veins. The bond he'd felt with his siblings so strongly the night before seemed to suddenly fracture. "I don't have to tell you anything," said Matt. "You're not my mother."

"But Mom and Dad told us to stick together, no matter what," said Ruby. "You can't just leave us like that."

Something snapped inside Matt, and he exploded. "Mom and Dad are not here!" he shouted. "They might not even be born yet! And in case you hadn't noticed, we're stranded on a tiny island in the middle of nowhere. We're about as stuck together as we can get!" He dropped the firewood in the sand and went to the rock where he'd left the matches and water, only to find the water bottle was half empty. He whirled around.

"Who drank all this?" said Matt.

"We were thirsty," said Corey.

"This is our *last* water!" said Matt.

"What do you mean?" said Ruby. "There were at least a dozen in the raft."

"Yeah well, the tide came in last night and carried all of it away, including the raft. While you were sleeping so peacefully, I swam out and saved the raft, and found this water bottle, but that's it."

"You mean . . . we have no food?" said Ruby, her face going pale.

"Go fish," said Matt, gesturing to the ocean. He grabbed the water bottle and walked away, along the shoreline. He plopped down right in the wet sand, opened the water bottle, and took a long drink, taking it down to a quarter. He didn't care. His head pounded even harder and tears burned in his eyes. He pushed them back. He couldn't afford to waste the water. Oh, what did it matter? They were going to die here. They'd become skeletons, just like the guy beneath the boat. The tears spilled over, rolled down his cheeks, and fell to the sand. Their parents would never know what happened to them. No . . . their parents would never even remember them. Corey and Ruby would never have been born to their parents. They would never adopt Matt. Their mom and dad would have other children, completely unaware that they'd ever had any others. They were like the Lost Boys in *Peter Pan*. Two Lost Boys and a Lost Girl.

He stared out at the ocean, focusing on the blue horizon and the water glistening in the sunshine. It would have been a beautiful sight on the *Vermillion*. Now all Matt could think was how the sun would just make him hot and suck up all the water in his body. He was already thirsty.

It had all seemed like such a grand adventure on the

Vermillion, being a time pirate, going on missions. He had felt big and important for a moment, but no more. They were time pirates no longer. They'd been discarded. They were castaways now. Time castaways.

Matt began to draw idly in the sand with his finger. Circles within circles, arrows, symbols, numbers. After a while he realized he was drawing the Obsidian Compass, the details pouring from his memory into his fingers. He brushed his hands over the sand, erasing the drawings. He turned his attention back to the horizon, the sun now lowering in the sky. It must be late afternoon now. His stomach growled with hunger and his head was now throbbing.

"Matt!" Ruby was running toward him. Matt stood abruptly.

"What is it?" Matt said. "Is Corey okay?"

Ruby reached him, completely out of breath. "You have to come see . . . ," she gasped. She didn't seem scared or worried. She seemed excited. "Hurry!"

Matt ran after Ruby. She led him back to their campsite, then around the tip of the island to the other side, near the place where Matt had gathered firewood. Maybe they'd found the skeleton.

Corey was crouched down in the sand, looking at something. When Matt approached, he stood and backed away, as though whatever it was belonged to Matt. Matt understood why when he saw. There were words written in the sand.

YOU KNOW HOW TO CALL THE COMPASS, MATEO.

Matt stared and stared. This had to be some kind of joke. "Did you write this?" he finally asked, looking between Corey and Ruby.

"I swear I didn't," said Corey. "Ruby found it first."

"I think it's from Dad!" said Ruby. "Somehow he found out where we are, and he came and left this message."

Matt bent down in the sand and inspected the message more closely. The sand was wet, and he could still see the finger grooves in the words. "It's not from Dad," he said. "It's from me."

"Oh," said Corey, clearly disappointed. "I guess we got excited for nothing, Ruby. Matt was just talking to himself in the sand."

"I mean it's from future me."

"*Future* you?" said Corey. "How do you know?"

"Look at the M," said Matt. "It's my M, just like the one in the mast." He traced the letters. A wave of dizziness crashed into him. This had to have been done very recently, within hours, otherwise the tide would have washed it out. He could almost sense the forememory of writing the words. He even thought he sensed himself, or the essence of his future self. It was a crazy feeling, like he'd been split in two, and yet each part was the same thing.

"Why didn't you rescue us, then?" said Corey. "If future

you was here, why didn't you get us off of this stinking island?"

"He couldn't do that," said Ruby. "You can't meet yourself, remember? That would have caused a glitch for certain, maybe even a big one, like a hurricane or something, depending on how old he was when he came."

"He could have at least left us some food and water," said Corey. "Seriously, I can't stand you, future Mateo. You send messages to help the captain, who's clearly our enemy, and now you're sending us cryptic messages that don't help us at all! If future Mateo were here, I would punch him in the face. Or should I just do it now as a preemptive strike?"

Matt couldn't blame Corey. He didn't understand his future self at all and even felt quite frustrated with his future self. It was a really bizarre feeling.

"So what does this mean?" Ruby asked. "Why does it say you know how to call the compass?"

Matt reached for his bracelet, his brain doing somersaults. He remembered the Mets game and the strange, glitchy showing of time. He'd convinced himself it had been a figment of his imagination. But now, seeing this message, he began to wonder if it had been something more than even he had imagined.

"My bracelet . . . ," he said, rubbing over the stone. He suddenly felt as though it were warming at his touch. "I think it's connected to the compass somehow."

"How do you know?" Ruby asked.

"Remember the Mets game? Remember how after we saw Dad we caused a glitch and changed the game? I think maybe I saved it somehow, or my bracelet did. It caused that glitch that led to Bill Buckner missing the ball. I think when I was pumping my fist in the air, I somehow triggered something that shifted time and space just enough to cause a ripple."

"Why didn't you tell us this before?" Ruby asked.

"Because I wasn't sure it really happened," said Matt. "I thought I was about to black out. I think I actually might have for a moment. Everything got really slow and weird. It was almost like the whole stadium, or earth, was shifting beneath our feet, right at the moment when Bill Buckner missed the ball, and then the next thing I knew the game was over."

Matt paused for Corey and Ruby's reactions. They were both just staring at him. He couldn't tell what they thought.

"Anyway," he went on. "It might have just been some freaky thing that can't be explained. Even if I did cause it with my bracelet, I'm not sure how this can help us now. I mean, I didn't call the compass to me then, did I?"

"Maybe you did, and you just didn't know it," said Ruby. "The compass was right next to you when it happened, wasn't it? Maybe that's why it only caused a tiny glitch. It wasn't far enough away in time or space to do anything too big. But what if you did the same thing when the compass was a farther distance from you in time and space? What if you could call the compass, wherever it is, and make it come to you?"

Matt's mind raced. Could he have done that before? He thought of Wiley's record book, all the times the *Vermillion* had traveled to New York. What if it hadn't been the captain using the compass to get there? What if Matt had unwittingly been calling the compass to him with his bracelet?

"Well, there's no harm in trying," said Matt, untying his bracelet.

"Wait," said Corey, grabbing onto Matt's wrist. "Say we get the *Vermillion* to come to us? Then what?"

"We have to steal the compass and get ourselves home," said Matt.

"That sounds awesome," said Corey. "Except we don't know how to use the compass, do we?"

"I think I do," said Matt.

"You *think*?" said Ruby.

"I'm pretty sure. I paid attention when we traveled. I really wanted to know how the compass and ship worked, so it's been sort of a hobby to figure it out, I guess. Here, I'll show you."

Matt knelt down in the sand and drew three circles within each other, then the notches and symbols.

"The center of the compass is much like a regular compass," he said, pointing. "North, south, east, west, three hundred and sixty degrees. That's how you determine where you are traveling. You only have to know the coordinates of where you want to go. But the outer dials have to do with time."

"That makes sense," said Ruby. "They have twelve notches, like a clock or the months of the year."

"But which is which?" said Corey. "Probably not gonna help if we mix up our months with our hours or years."

"Right, but there are symbols around the compass too." He drew the Chinese characters he'd seen on the compass. "I didn't know what these meant at first, but I've been studying Chinese with Jia. This character is specific for time as it relates to broader time, like years and centuries, but this character relates to more specific times, like months, days, and hours. It's like a clock, a very sophisticated one. A clock has twelve notches, but they can mean two things at once, depending on the hand that's pointing to it."

"But there's only one needle," said Corey. "It doesn't have two hands like a clock."

"We don't need two hands. The dials work like a combination lock. Each layer turns *both* ways."

"Of course!" said Ruby. "This makes perfect sense."

"So the very center dial determines place; it goes left for latitude, right for longitude. The second layer goes right for the century, then left for the year. The third layer you have to turn three times—left for month, right for day, left for time."

"How do you distinguish between morning and night?" said Ruby. "There's still only twelve numbers."

Matt was stumped for a moment. He hadn't thought of that particular detail.

"Maybe," said Corey, "it's like a locker combination? You know how you have to go a full round on the second number? So going a second round on the last turn of the dial could determine whether it's a.m. or p.m.?"

Matt stared at his brother. "I never would have thought of that," he said.

Corey tried to hide his smile, but Matt could tell he was pleased with himself.

Matt looked back at the drawing of the compass in the sand, going over every detail. "It all makes sense," said Matt. "If we can get to the compass, we can get home."

"Yes," said Ruby, "but how do you expect to get to the compass, exactly? The captain has it chained to his wrist at all times. I doubt he'll hand it over for us to have a look."

"Yeah," said Matt, rubbing at his bracelet. "I don't know how to solve that one." They all sat there, staring at the compass and message in the sand.

"We must figure it out somehow," said Corey. "Future Matt wouldn't have been able to put this message in the sand if we didn't, right? And it's not like we can wait around to figure it out. We've got no food or water."

Matt looked to Ruby. As rash as it sounded, Corey was right. They were going to have to take a leap of faith and trust that they'd be able to get to the compass somehow.

"I guess there's no point in waiting then," said Ruby. "Go ahead, Matt."

Matt took a breath and balled the bracelet up in his hand. At the game, he had been pumping his fist with the bracelet inside. He raised his fist in the air. Ruby and Corey watched Matt closely, which made him feel self-conscious and awkward. He began to punch the air over and over. Nothing happened.

"Maybe you need to do it harder," said Corey.

"And faster," Ruby added.

Matt tried again, trying to simulate the excitement and force he'd had at the game. He felt a slight tremor in the sand. The ocean waves seemed to slow and hush.

"Whoa," said Corey, stumbling to the side a bit. Ruby grabbed Matt's arm and looked around.

That was it. Matt was sure he'd done something, but was it enough to call the compass to them? He looked around for any sign of the captain or the *Vermillion*. Would they just appear?

"I think it needs to go faster," said Ruby. "Maybe try twirling it?"

"Yeah, maybe wind it up tight and let it spin out," said Corey. "Like one of those button spinners we used to make in preschool."

Matt held the bracelet on both ends of the string. He wound it up as far as it would go, twisting each side until the twine was coiled tightly on either side of the stone. He took a breath. "Here goes," he said. He yanked hard on both ends of the string. The stone spun, faster and faster. Even after the twine had all unraveled it continued to spin until it was a blur, until it glowed, and the glow intensified and moved outward.

Matt felt the heat on his face. He felt the ocean pulling and the world spinning beneath him. The sun fell from the sky, the moon shot up, and then they switched again, like some invisible giant were juggling them. The whole galaxy seemed to turn, revolving around Matt and his little stone.

And then it stopped. The light evaporated. The earth stilled. Matt was drained and dizzy. He saw the blurred faces of his brother and sister just before he collapsed in the sand.

"Matt? Wake up."

Someone slapped at Matt's cheeks. His eyes fluttered open. Two dark shapes hovered over him. He took in a breath and immediately choked on sand. He sat up, coughed and dry heaved.

"You okay, bro?" said Corey.

"Yeah," Matt croaked, spitting the sand out of his mouth. He felt terrible. His head ached, and he was nauseated. He wondered if this was time sickness or just a lack of food. Maybe a bit of both.

He looked around. It looked like it was nearly nighttime, even though it had been early afternoon just moments before.

The sun was dipping below the water. "How long was I out?" he asked.

"It seemed like just a few minutes," said Ruby, "but it was crazy. It was like the earth was spinning ten times as fast. The sun fell from the sky and I thought the world was ending."

Matt felt for his bracelet, but of course it wasn't on his wrist. He looked around until he saw just the edge of it sticking out of the sand. He pulled it up. It was warm. It seemed to pulse in his palm. He must have caused an even bigger shift than he had at the Mets game.

"It was seriously way cooler than the solar eclipse we saw a couple years ago," said Corey. "And look!" He pointed out to the water. In the distance, maybe two hundred feet from the shore, a black fin was jutting out of the ocean. It was attached to a much larger body, long and smooth, just barely peeking out of the water.

"A whale?" said Matt.

"That's what Ruby thought too," said Corey, "but look closer."

Matt squinted and then saw that the fin was not a fin at all. It had some smaller spires attached to it, very industrial looking, like radio antennae. Matt breathed out. "It's a submarine."

"I thought it was maybe a Russian spy submarine at first," said Corey, "like in *The Hunt for Red October*?" That was one of their dad's favorite movies. They'd all watched it at one time or another. "But then Ruby spotted the symbol. See?"

Corey pointed to the middle of the submarine, where there was a painted symbol, only half visible, but unmistakable. It was the compass arrows with the red V in the center.

"The *Vermillion*," said Matt. It worked. He had called it back to them. "So . . . what do we do now?" asked Ruby.

"What do you mean?" said Corey. "We row out there and get on board!"

"Yeah, but Captain Vincent probably isn't going to welcome us back on the ship," said Ruby. "If we're caught we'll just get discarded again, and maybe someplace even worse than this."

"He doesn't need to know," said Corey. "We can sneak on board."

"And then what?"

"We don't have time to figure out every little detail," said Matt. "Corey's right. For now we just need to get on board before someone sees us."

"I guess if that's the best we've got, that's the best we've got," said Ruby.

They prepared the raft, tossed in their backpacks, the empty water bottle, and matches, and prepared to row out. But before they left, Matt turned back to the spot where the message was written in the sand. He bent down and erased it. Somehow it felt necessary.

20

Stowaways

They took turns rowing. Two took paddles while the third kept a lookout to make sure no one had spotted them. Matt kept a close eye on the periscope as they rowed. It didn't seem to be pointed toward them, and it was almost full dark, but who knew what other technology or power this submarine had. The captain could be watching them right now. They could be headed straight toward an ambush, but he didn't think so. Somehow, he thought, the *Vermillion* was on their side.

When they reached the submarine, they punctured the raft against one of the sharper metal edges. If the captain did come looking for them, they hoped he'd believe they'd drowned.

When they crawled on top of the submarine, they found there were several hatches. It was a bit of a gamble choosing which one to use, but they decided on a small one on the end.

Or front. They weren't really sure.

Matt pulled on the handle of the hatch, and it opened with a groan that almost sounded like the call of a whale. A ladder descended into the hole and then disappeared in ominous darkness. "I'll go first," Matt said. "I'll whistle if it's safe to come down."

He descended the ladder. It seemed a long way. When he reached the bottom he found himself in a dimly lit, narrow corridor, surrounded by pipes on both sides. He didn't hear or see anyone, but who knew how long that could last. He whistled up. Ruby came down followed closely by Corey, who shut the hatch.

It took a few moments to adjust to the darkness.

"What now?" Ruby whispered.

"We find Jia," said Matt. He was thinking as he went, but that made the most sense. They would need some inside help, and Jia was the only one of the crew they could totally trust.

"But we don't know where anything is when the *Vermillion*'s a submarine," said Corey. "What if we run into another crewmate? Albert, or worse, the captain?"

"We'll just have to risk it," said Matt. "But I think we're on the lower level of the submarine, similar to the hull of the ship, which is the area most of the crew never goes."

They walked down the narrow corridor, listening closely. Every creak and groan, of which there were many, made Matt's heart race just a little faster. They found a door. After he'd pressed his ear against it for several seconds, Matt slowly opened it. It was just a storage closet with stacks of sheets, pillows, and blankets, and an old radio set that looked to be from World War II. The next door revealed a tiny bathroom with a toilet, sink, and narrow shower. "We could all use a shower," said Ruby.

"Not a top priority," said Matt.

"Hey!" Corey whispered. He was farther down the corridor, peeking through another door. He motioned for Matt and Ruby to come. Matt walked over cautiously and peeked through the crack. He instantly knew what had caught Corey's eye. There were trays of dirty dishes and leftover meals sitting on a stainless-steel countertop—a half-eaten loaf of bread, a chunk of cheese, a platter of fruit, and a pot of something. Matt could smell fish and garlic.

"I don't see anyone," whispered Corey. "I think we can grab some if we hurry."

Matt hesitated. It almost seemed like a trap, but it was working very well. He was starving and incredibly thirsty, and he reasoned that their chances of escape would be much better if they had fuel for their brains and bellies. "Quickly then," he whispered.

They opened the door, which creaked a little, and slipped inside. Corey immediately went for the bread, tearing off great chunks and stuffing them in his mouth. Ruby took an apple and bit into it. She closed her eyes as juice ran down her chin.

Matt looked into the pot and found a fish stew. He ladled some up and slurped down the broth first, then devoured the chunks of fish and tomatoes, satisfying his hunger and thirst at once. He offered a ladle of broth to Corey and Ruby. They sucked it up like withered plants.

Matt glanced quickly around the room. It was entirely stainless steel with fluorescent lights. Pots and pans hung above their heads and dishes were piled in a sink.

"We'd better go," Matt whispered. "We don't want to run into . . ."

There was a sudden burst of song in the opposite corner of the kitchen.

Ah! ça ira, ça ira, ça ira,
Les arisocrates à la lanterne!

A door opened. Matt grabbed Corey and Ruby and shoved them to the floor.

Ah! ça ira, ça ira, ça ira,
Les arisocrates, on les pendra!

It was Agnes, the cook. She was singing in French, something about everything being okay because they were going to hang all the aristocrats. It sent a chill down Matt's spine, especially as the sound drew closer and then came to an abrupt stop, midphrase. She must have noticed the missing food. Matt held his breath and then jumped as something came down hard on the counter above them, sending vibrations right down to the floor. Ruby squeaked and covered her mouth.

"*Le rat! Je vais tuer le rat!*" She continued to mutter in French as she shuffled around the kitchen, how her mademoiselle would never have allowed such a creature on the ship, how she hated the ship. She cursed the rat and *le capitan* repeatedly, threatening to chop off both their heads.

She started to sing again, the same song about hanging aristocrats, when again she stopped midphrase. Matt turned his head, just so he could see what she was doing underneath the counter. He jumped as Agnes dropped a knife, lifted her skirt, and hobbled over to a cupboard. She swung the door open and, with more agility than Matt would have thought possible, crammed herself inside and shut the door.

"What is she doing?" whispered Corey.

"No idea. But I think this is our chance to exit." He began to crawl toward the door when Ruby stopped him.

"Wait, what's that sound?"

Matt cocked his ear. The creaks and groans of the submarine seemed to be getting louder. It sounded like twisting metal and the calls of a whale in distress.

"Is it a storm?" asked Corey.

There was a rushing that got louder and louder, like the

sound of a great waterfall as you get nearer to the source.

"I think . . . ," said Matt, but he didn't have the opportunity to say what he thought, for suddenly the floor tilted violently and the children were shoved hard against the metal counter.

Ruby screamed as dishes crashed and knives and utensils flew around as though the kitchen were waging war on them.

They were traveling. Matt grabbed ahold of a pipe in the wall until it stretched out and disappeared and he went flying again. The walls shifted and pressed in on him while he tumbled about. It felt like he was being tossed around in a big drying machine. When the transformation was complete, he was crammed at odd angles in a small, dark space, a little closet or cupboard, he guessed. He fumbled around until he felt a latch. He turned it and a door flew open and he fell out and on something solid, but a bit squishy.

"Oof!" The something was Corey. He was lying in the fetal position, his hands above his head and clutching the handle of a knife that was lodged deeply in the floor. Matt helped him up, and they both observed their new surroundings. They were still in a kitchen, but altered somewhat by the transformation. The stainless-steel walls, counters, and cupboards had been turned to old wood. An old iron woodstove sat against the wall, a brick fireplace next to it. Matt guessed that they had transformed back into the *Vermillion*'s original form as a frigate ship.

"Where's Ruby?" Corey asked.

"Help!" said a small, muffled voice. They looked around but couldn't see any sign of Ruby.

"Talk again, Ruby," said Matt.

"I'm in here, in . . . something small and full of . . . something slimy. I can't get out!"

"The barrel!" said Corey.

Sure enough, Ruby was inside a barrel with a stick coming out the top. Matt pulled the stick, but it didn't budge. Corey tried as well without success.

"We need a lever," said Matt. He looked around and spotted the fire poker leaning against the stove. He grabbed it, wedged it beneath the lid, and pushed down. The wood split and cracked, a few of the metal braces sprang loose, and the lid finally popped off.

Matt and Corey looked inside. Ruby was crammed with her arms pinned at her sides and her head covered in gobs of what looked and smelled like butter. Somehow during the transformation she had managed to get stuck inside an old butter churn.

The boys reached in and tried to help her up, but she was so slippery it was a difficult process. They finally had to tip over the churn so Ruby could slide out like a snail coming out of its shell. She finally emerged and lay on the floor, covered head to foot in butter. She looked sort of monstrous.

"Are you okay?" said Matt.

"I hate this ship," said Ruby.

The cupboard beneath the sink suddenly flew open and out came a pair of arms. Agnes grunted as she tried to wriggle herself out of the cramped space. "*Je déteste ce navire*," she muttered.

Matt motioned for them to go, but Ruby slipped in her buttery mess. Matt and Corey both tried to help her up, and then Corey slipped in the butter too, just as Agnes popped out of the cupboard like a cork and fell onto her hands and knees.

She glanced up, and her eyes widened with fear and surprise as she noticed the three Hudsons, then quickly hardened. Her face twisted into a snarl.

"*Allez-vous-en!*" she shouted. She took a ladle off the ceiling and threw it at them. "*Allez-vous-en, méchants, avant que je vous coupe la tête!*"

A pot came next, followed by a cast-iron frying pan.

"Run! Go!" Matt shouted. Corey and Ruby crawled their way out of the butter, then stood and ran to the door as more pots, pans, and knives came at them like a hailstorm of bullets and spears. Matt was clocked in the ear with a pewter goblet just as he was slipping out the door.

They ran down the corridor, not thinking about what direction they were going or who or what they might run into next, only to get away from the danger behind them.

They came to a set of stairs and stopped. Matt bent over, panting.

"She . . . is . . . crazy!" said Corey, between breaths.

"Shh!" said Ruby. She pulled Matt and Corey behind the stairs as the floorboards above them creaked.

"Crikey, that was a close call!" It was Brocco. "What did you travel so soon for? I was barely through the hatch!"

"I'm sorry, Brocco, but it wasn't my doing," said the captain in a clipped voice. "The *Vermillion* is out of sorts. She wouldn't travel when I wanted her to and then decided to transform without my permission."

"That doesn't sit well, does it?" said Brocco. "I got squeezed so hard my eyeball nearly popped out of my head!"

"Well? Did you find them?" said the captain.

"No, sir. I searched the whole island."

"Hmm," said the captain. "Perhaps we're off on our timing then. Maybe we came before we dropped them."

"I thought of that," said Brocco, "except I found the little life raft all broken and deflated. Looks like they maybe tried to get somewhere, but sprang a leak, or a shark could've gotten 'em."

"These are not shark-infested waters, Brocco," said the captain impatiently.

"Well, I didn't see the kids anywhere in the water," said Brocco. "So I suppose they drowned?"

There was silence for a moment, and then the captain spoke again. "Whatever happened to them we'll sort out later. We can always go back. Right now I want to get to New

York. I've a pressing mission at the Metropolitan Museum of Art."

Matt instinctively reached for something to hold on to, which ended up being Ruby's buttery arm. The captain was going to New York, to the Met! They had boarded the *Vermillion* just in time!

"Perhaps we should wait a day or two?" suggested Brocco.

"For what purpose?"

"Well, I was thinking maybe the *Vermillion*'s energy is a bit low. We've been traveling an awful lot lately, more often than usual. Maybe that's why she's being so temperamental. You know women." Brocco chuckled.

Ruby snorted, then covered her mouth. Matt gave her a sharp warning look, and Corey flicked her in the head.

"You may be right," said the captain.

"You're looking a bit worn out yourself, Captain," said Brocco. "Why don't you go have a lie-down, rest yourself a while?"

"I could use some rest."

"You're working yourself too hard. You go on now. I'll keep my eye out for those children, let you know if I find anything."

"Thank you, Brocco," said Captain Vincent. Their footsteps began to move in opposite directions and then the captain stopped. "Oh, and one more thing, Brocco. Where precisely did you find the raft?"

"Oh, twenty feet from the sub, in the rear, just hovering below the surface."

"Hmm . . . ," the captain mused. "Very good, carry on." Brocco left, but the captain remained above them for a minute, and then his red Converse appeared on the top step. The Hudsons shrank back as the captain descended the stairs and moved down the narrow corridor. He opened a few doors, peered inside, then moved on and disappeared around a corner.

They couldn't hide here any longer. When the captain came back this way, he'd surely notice them. They had to move now. Matt motioned for Corey and Ruby to follow him. He went slowly up the stairs. Matt crouched at the top and peeked his head above the last step to make sure the coast was clear. He neither saw nor heard anyone. They walked as quickly as they could, looking over their shoulders as they went. They turned a corner and finally reached Jia's room.

"Are you sure this is Jia's room?" Ruby asked.

Matt pointed to the little hammer door handle. "I'm sure," he said.

Matt opened the door and stuck his head inside. It was empty. He motioned Corey and Ruby to go inside, then followed behind. He shut the door and leaned against it, allowing himself to finally breathe freely, until a small shuffle and tinkling sound brought him to high alert once again.

Ruby gasped as Pike emerged from behind a stack of

crates. She looked at Matt with her pale eyes. She didn't seem surprised to see him here. Maybe she didn't really understand what the captain had done with them.

"Hi, Pike," said Matt in a gentle voice. "How are you?"

Pike looked past Matt and fixated on Ruby, glancing up and down at her. She came a little closer and swiped a finger at a glob of butter on Ruby's sleeve. She studied it, then rubbed it between her fingers and wiped it on her pillowcase dress. It looked like she had added more pins along the sleeves and side seams.

"Is Jia around?" Matt asked, trying to pull her attention back to him.

Pike looked at him and blinked, then abruptly ran out of the room.

"Wait!" Ruby called, but Pike was gone. Ruby turned back to Matt and Corey, her eyes wide and fearful. "You don't think she'll tell the others, do you?"

"How can she tell?" said Corey. "I've never heard her talk. And it's not like we can go after her to make sure."

"Well, we can't stay here," said Ruby. "Maybe we should hide in our room. No one will be in there."

"I don't know," said Corey. "Albert might have decided to turn it into his second bedroom or something."

"I'm not even sure it's a good idea for us to contact Jia," said Ruby. "How can you be sure she won't tell the captain that we're here?"

"Jia would never betray us," said Matt.

"But what if—" Ruby began, but Matt raised his hand, cutting her off. He cocked his ear toward the door.

"Someone's coming!" he whispered. "Hide!"

They each huddled behind some of the piled-up boxes and crates. Matt's body was starting to feel cramped and stiff with all the crouching and crawling, and he felt his heart might burst if it didn't get a rest from pumping so hard.

A minute later the door cracked open and Jia entered, followed closely by Pike.

"What did you bring me here for, Pike?" said Jia, sounding a little exasperated. There was a click and a buzz and the room was suddenly flooded with light. "There's nothing—Oh!"

Matt stood up from behind the crates.

"Matt?" Jia whispered.

"Hey," he said, and smiled tentatively. Jia looked at him as though she were seeing a ghost. She looked back through the door to make sure no one was nearby, then shut it and pressed her back against it. Pike tottered over to her crate bed and began tying knots in her quilt as though nothing unusual were going on.

Corey and Ruby now stood too.

"You made it back," said Jia. "How . . . ?"

Matt looked down at Pike, not sure how much he should say in front of her.

"It's okay, she won't tell," said Jia. "She came and got me, but it didn't alarm any of the others."

Matt nodded. "We snuck on board the *Vermillion* when it was a submarine. It came back to us."

Jia nodded. "The helicopter malfunctioned for some reason. After he discarded you, the captain didn't seem to be able to get it under control, and then when he tried to travel we didn't go where he wanted, and the ship transformed without warning and then we couldn't travel at all. It was like the *Vermillion* didn't want to leave you behind."

"Bet the captain didn't like that too much," said Matt.

"I've never seen him so angry," said Jia. "I was running all around the submarine, trying to figure out how to fix it, but nothing seemed wrong, and then all of sudden we transformed back to the ship. It was a bit of a mess. Albert got his leg caught in the toilet."

Pike made a sort of choking sound and covered her mouth. Matt realized she was laughing. It was the most sound he'd ever heard out of her.

"Yeah," said Matt. "We got tossed around a bit too. Ruby had a war with some butter."

"So that's what that is," said Jia. "I thought you looked a little . . . shiny."

"It's certainly not my new beauty routine," said Ruby.

"No one else saw you, did they?" Jia asked.

"No," said Matt. "Well, Agnes did, just for a moment, but

that shouldn't be too much of a problem, should it?"

Jia bit her lip. "I don't think so. She never comes out of the kitchen, and the captain avoids her at all costs. I'm the one who sees her the most."

Matt nodded. It was still a risk. He looked around the room and suddenly realized that the light bulbs that had been strung along the ceiling were all glowing. "Hey, you did it! You got the electricity to work!"

Jia beamed. "All we needed was a fuse!"

Matt slapped his forehead. "A fuse! I should have known that. Well, it was fun getting electrocuted anyway."

Jia laughed a little too loud and then covered her mouth. Her smile faded and she grew serious again. "I'm sorry for what the captain did to you all," she said. "You didn't deserve to be discarded."

"Clearly our dad made the captain very angry," said Matt.

Jia nodded. "Whatever he stole must have been extremely important or valuable or both."

"We heard the captain say he's planning to travel back to New York to try to get it back," said Ruby. "Do you know the date?"

Jia shook her head. "He hasn't said, but I imagine it will be close to the time he picked you up, to make sure your father has whatever it is he wants."

Matt breathed out a little. "So all we have to do is wait for the captain to travel back to New York, and then we escape."

"That's a lot simpler than we thought it would be," said Corey.

"Yeah," said Matt. Almost too simple, he thought, but he didn't say it out loud.

Matt wondered how long it would be before the captain decided to travel back to New York. A day or two? Could they remain hidden and undetected on the ship for that long?

A sudden scratching noise made them all jump. Matt swept his gaze around the room and caught a flash of white between the slats of a crate.

"Santiago!" he shouted, and the white rat burst from his hiding place and shot across the floor, heading to escape beneath the door.

21

Thieves in the Night

"Catch him!" shouted Matt. "Don't let him get out!" Matt dove for Santiago. He didn't catch him, but he effectively diverted him from escaping beneath the crack of the door. Santiago ran toward Ruby, who jumped up on one of the crates.

"Ew! Get him out!" screeched Ruby.

"No! We have to catch him!"

"He's just a rat," said Corey. "Do we really need to worry about him?"

"You know he's not a normal rat," said Matt, trying to keep his eyes on Santiago as he skittered along the wall. "He'll let the captain know that we're here!"

Matt chased after Santiago, tripping over wires and boxes and backpacks as Santiago crawled between them. Ruby, Corey, and Jia all surrounded him, backing Santiago into a corner, when suddenly he leaped onto a wall and began to skitter up toward the rafters, where there were plenty of holes for him to escape.

"No!" Matt climbed onto a pile of crates and leaped toward the ceiling. He caught Santiago and dragged him down the wall, but as Matt fell to the ground the rat twisted free of his grasp. He scurried along the wall and slipped beneath the door.

Matt jumped to his feet and ran after him.

"Matt!" cried Ruby. "Stop! You'll be seen!"

"We can't let him get to the captain!" He threw open the door and raced down the dark hallway. Santiago was just ahead of him, squealing as he scurried up the stairs and ran toward the captain's cabin, as though he were trying to sound a warning. He was only ten feet from the door. Desperate, Matt dove just as Santiago stuck his nose beneath the crack and caught him by the tail.

Santiago screeched as Matt dragged him away from the door and lifted him off the ground.

"Nice one, bro," said Corey. He, Ruby, and Jia came to stop before Matt and the writhing Santiago, all of them gasping for breath.

Matt looked around. It was quite dark, but he could see the shape of things and spotted the chest Ruby had gotten herself stuck in during a transformation. He lifted the lid, dropped the squealing rodent inside, and shut it, securing the latch. He sat down on top of his prison and took a deep breath.

They all stood in silence as Santiago squeaked and

scratched madly inside the chest. Matt suddenly realized how exposed they all were. Someone could find them at any moment. It was a miracle the captain didn't wake up with all the commotion.

"What do we do now?" Ruby whispered.

"The captain will notice Santiago's missing before too long," said Jia.

Matt rubbed his fingers over his temples. They were out of time and options. "We have to go tonight," he said. "Right now. We'll have to get the compass and get home ourselves."

"But . . . how will we get it?" said Ruby.

Matt turned to Jia. "Can you help us get into the captain's cabin?"

Jia's eyes widened in alarm. She shook her head. "There's no way I can do that. I can't even get in."

"But you go into the captain's cabin all the time," said Matt.

"When he's awake, and when I have his permission. Otherwise his cabin is always locked. I don't have the keys."

Matt rubbed at his bracelet. "We'll have to pick the lock. You have plenty of tools that could work, don't you? In your pockets?"

Jia pressed her lips together. Matt could see the tension rise in her neck and shoulders. He knew he was asking a lot, maybe too much. It was one thing to hide them in her room, but now he was asking Jia to actively betray the person who had fed and clothed her since she was seven—the closest thing she had to a parent—when she had nothing and no one to care for her. If they were caught, Jia would most certainly be discarded right along with them. He was asking her to risk her own life.

But they needed her. He didn't think they could get inside the captain's cabin on their own. "Please, Jia," Matt pleaded. "We won't be able to get home without your help."

Jia finally nodded. "I'll do what I can."

"Thank you," said Matt.

Jia rummaged through her pockets and pulled out a screwdriver, a wrench, pliers, a little hammer, and some nails. Matt had no experience in picking locks; he'd only ever seen it done in movies, but it seemed like something he could manage if he had the right tools. Matt took a thin file and a nail and approached the captain's cabin slowly. He fiddled around with the lock for a minute, but nothing happened. Santiago hissed and screeched as he ran all around the chest. It made Matt feel uneasy, but he tried to ignore it.

"Let me try." Corey pushed Matt aside and tried to work the lock himself.

"You're being too loud," said Ruby.

"I am not," said Corey. "Back off."

A light suddenly flashed behind them. Matt put his hand up to block the glare. It was Albert, shining a flashlight. He swept it over each face and finally rested on Jia. She winced and turned away from the light.

"I knew it," said Albert. "I knew you'd try to help them, you traitor."

"Albert," Jia whispered. "Please! They just want to go home. You want that too, don't you? You've never wanted them on the *Vermillion*."

"It's not what I want that matters," said Albert. "It's what the captain wants, and I think he'd want to know when someone's trying to break into his cabin." Albert took a step and then suddenly went sprawling to the floor, dropping the flashlight. Matt picked up the flashlight and shined it around the dining hall until he saw Pike standing at Albert's feet. She'd tied up his ankles with her rope!

"You little weasel!" Albert hissed. "The captain will discard you all for this! Cap—!" He started to shout, but Corey pounced on Albert and pressed a hand over his mouth.

"We need to gag him," said Corey.

"Jia, do you have any tape?" Matt asked.

Jia rummaged in her pockets and brought out a roll of black electrical tape.

"Ruby, help me grab his arms." Matt and Ruby rushed over and pinned down Albert's arms while Jia wrapped the tape around his mouth. He struggled mightily and tried to shout for help, but Jia got the tape around enough to cut off most of the sound.

"Tape up his hands," said Jia, handing the tape to Matt.

Matt used almost the entire roll taping Albert's wrists together. "Sorry about this, Al," said Matt. "Or should I call you Bert? Bertie Beans?"

Albert glared at Matt, struggling to free himself.

Matt stood up. "That's two rats down. Now we just need to . . ." Matt trailed off as he turned back to the captain's door, only to see Pike on tiptoe working some of her pins into the lock. Within seconds there was a *click*. Pike turned the knob of the door and it opened with a soft creak.

Matt gaped at the little towheaded girl. Pike simply stared right back at him, though he detected the barest hint of a smile. He suddenly had a pretty good idea of what the captain had been training her for.

Pike very calmly put the pins back onto her pillowcase dress and without so much as a backward glance scampered away and disappeared.

Jia handed Matt the flashlight and nodded. "Good luck," she mouthed.

Matt glanced at Corey and Ruby. Each of them looked a little bewildered, like they weren't really expecting to get this far. Matt wasn't either, if he was being honest.

"We can do this," Matt whispered, trying to convince himself as much as anyone.

Ruby nodded. "We stick together. No matter what."

"You guys are such nerds," whispered Corey, but he stuck his fist out. Matt and Ruby did the same.

"Put your other fists in," said Matt.

"Why?" said Ruby.

"One for Mom and one for Dad. We need them too."

Ruby put in her other fist and then Corey followed. For just a moment, it felt like they were all together, not just the children but their parents too.

With as silent steps as they could manage, the three Hudsons entered the captain's cabin.

It was very dark, only a faint glow from the window on the other side of the captain's bed. It was either a moonless night or cloudy. Matt held the flashlight against his body, blocking the light. He tiptoed slowly to the captain's curtained bed, pausing as the floor creaked. He could hear the captain breathing deeply and loudly, practically snoring. It must have been the only reason he didn't wake at all the commotion outside his door.

Matt found the seam in the bed curtains and parted them slowly. He moved the flashlight carefully over the captain's body, careful not to flash it in his eyes. The captain slept on his back, one arm beneath his head and the other on top of his chest. His left. The one where he kept the compass. Matt flashed the light over his wrist and saw just a glimmer of the gold chain protruding from his cuff. He put the flashlight beneath his arm and reached for the chain, pulling it as gently and slowly as he could until there was a pull on the other end and he knew he'd reached the end of it. Now he needed to pull out the compass itself. He pulled a little harder, but it didn't come. He increased the tension until he felt the compass pull along and then appear at the edge of the captain's cuff. He reached for it and slowly, slowly pulled the compass out. He could see the dials, the numbers and notches. All he had to do was turn them the right way and they could go home. He gave a final tug and the compass slid out of the captain's sleeve.

He was almost paralyzed with fear. He had forgotten what to do now. *Turn the dials*, he told himself. *Get home.* He took hold of it. He looked up at Captain Vincent, and his breath caught in his throat. The captain's black eyes shone in the darkness. He stared right at Matt, glanced at the compass in his hand, then back at Matt. The flashlight fell from Matt's arm, dropped to the floor, and rolled along the rough planks.

"I . . . ," Matt stammered. He wasn't sure what he was going to say. It didn't matter.

The captain grabbed Matt's wrist and twisted. Matt cried out in pain, dropping the compass. The captain tossed aside the bed curtains. Ruby squeaked in fright. Corey had a chair raised above his head and charged the captain, but the captain caught the chair easily and twisted it free, smashing it against the wall. Matt was able to yank himself free of the captain's grasp. He went for the compass again, but the captain gave him a swift punch in the stomach, completely knocking the wind out of him and blurring his vision. Corey made an attempt as well, but before he could even touch it, a white blur suddenly leaped at him. Santiago hissed at Corey and sank his teeth into his hand. Corey screamed and fell back.

"Go, Ruby! Get out!" Matt shouted.

Ruby scrambled to the door, but Santiago was faster. He scurried ahead of her and slammed the door shut, then turned around and hissed at Ruby. She stopped short, lifting her hands in surrender. She slowly backed away until she bumped into Matt. She sank down next to him, and Matt put his arm around her shoulder.

"Well done, Santiago," said the captain. Santiago scurried up the captain's leg and arm and rested on his shoulder, glaring at Matt, Corey, and Ruby now all huddled on the floor. The captain drew his sword and pointed it at them.

"Please," said Matt, breathing hard. "We just want to go home."

"And how were you going to manage that on your own?" said the captain. "Did you think you could use the compass?"

A slim shadow moved behind the captain. Matt's heart leaped in his chest. *Jia.* She was here! She must have snuck inside the door before Santiago shut it. She lifted her finger to her lips and pointed to the compass, still dangling from the captain's left wrist. It took all of Matt's concentration not to look at it or Jia, or show his relief and hope. He looked to the captain. He would have to keep him distracted and talking and Santiago fixated on them.

Jia, crawling on her hands and knees, had reached the compass. She looked to Matt with a question in her eyes, and he realized with a sickening dread that she didn't know how to use it. She didn't even know where or when to take them.

Matt's mind raced. He would have to find a way to communicate to her how to turn the dials without the captain knowing what he was doing.

"I *do* know how to use the compass," said Matt. "I've had it figured out for weeks. For instance, I know that if you turn the very center dial to the left to thirty-nine degrees north and to the right to seventy-two degrees west, it will take us roughly to the place where you picked us up."

Matt tried to keep his eyes on the captain, only looking at Jia out of the corner of his eyes. Her hands were on the compass now. She was turning the center dial.

"Bravo," said the captain. "But that doesn't help you get to the right time, you know. See, that's the tricky part, and perhaps the most important."

"That was difficult," said Matt. "But I've got that figured out too. The second dial is for the century and year. Right for the century, we'd go to twenty-one, and left for the year, nineteen."

The captain raised his eyebrows, clearly impressed. Matt continued on. He needed to keep the captain's focus on him. He needed Jia to hurry. "Finally, the outer dial will determine the month, day, and time," he said. "That was the hardest part to figure out. Corey actually figured out that one. You go to the left for the months. We'd want four for April, to the right for day, we want twenty-six, and finally we'd want to arrive right when we boarded the *Vermillion*, so we'd go one more round to the left for eight a.m."

Jia was slowly turning the dial. *Hurry*, Matt silently pleaded.

"Very goo—" the captain began, but was cut off by a hiss from Santiago. Captain Vincent glanced down and saw Jia with her hands on the Obsidian Compass. Jia looked up, her face horror-struck. She dropped the compass just as the captain shot out a fist and struck Jia hard in the side of the head. She made a sickening *thud* as she fell to the ground. She didn't move.

"Jia!" Matt wanted to rush to her, but the captain began to pull the compass up by the chain. He could not let him change the dials. Matt made a mad dive for the captain and tore at his hands, reaching for the compass. The captain grabbed Matt's hair and pulled so hard he feared his scalp would rip clean off, but he did not let go of his grip on the chain of the compass. He felt the floors begin to shift beneath him. The *Vermillion* was transforming.

What little light was in the cabin suddenly evaporated and the ship gave a violent lurch, throwing Matt and the captain to the floor. The walls pressed in on them. Matt felt metal rise from the floors, and the floors melded into grooved black rubber. There was a sudden roar, a flash of light, and then he was shoved against a pane of glass. They were bouncing over grass, swerving around large trees.

At first Matt had thought they had made a mistake. Jia hadn't turned the dials correctly. They weren't in New York. They were in a forest, probably in the middle of nowhere, but then they broke through to a paved clearing, and Matt's heart skipped a beat as he saw something he recognized. The Alice in Wonderland statue! They were in Central Park, not far from the museum! They had made it!

The bus swerved around the statue and then burst onto Fifth Avenue. A car honked and swerved around them. They were traveling down the wrong side of the road and no one was driving the bus.

"Wiley, the wheel!" the captain shouted.

Wiley was staggering bleary-eyed down the aisle of the bus in a nightshirt. He plopped down in the driver's seat and cranked the wheel violently to the right. The bus swerved and nearly crashed into a taxi. Wiley cranked the wheel in the other direction, nearly tipping the bus on its side and sending everyone crashing to the right side of the bus. The force of it allowed Matt to yank free of the captain's hold.

"Ruby! The phone!" Matt shouted.

Ruby dug into her backpack. She pulled out their cell phone and turned it on. "Come on, come on!" The phone finally beeped to life, and Ruby pushed the button to dial their parents.

Wiley stepped on the gas and jerked the wheel to the left, the right, then left again, weaving in and out of cars as they honked and swerved and slammed on their breaks. Everyone was tossed about like bugs in a jar being shaken by a toddler.

"Wiley!" shouted the captain.

"Sorry, Captain. I've never driven one of these contraptions!" It was usually Brocco or the captain who drove the *Vermillion*, whatever it was.

Ruby dropped the phone. It slid across the bus, and Matt dove for it.

"Hello?" He could hear his mother's voice on the other end.

"Mom!" shouted Matt. "Mom. It's Matt!"

"Mateo? You're breaking up . . . Where are you?"

"We're on the *Vermillion*! We're headed for the museum!"

"The museum? But—"

The captain kicked Matt's hand, and the phone flew down the center of the aisle. He reached for the compass again, but Matt grabbed onto it, swinging from the chain as the bus tipped from side to side.

"Wiley, pull over! Pull over!" shouted the captain. Wiley jerked the wheel to the right, taking the bus up on the sidewalk, miraculously free of pedestrians. The bus was now bumping up the stairs of the museum, making all their teeth rattle.

"Wiley, stop! Stop!" the captain shouted.

"It won't stop, Captain! It only goes faster!" He didn't seem to know there was a brake pedal and continued to pump on the gas. The bus reached the top of the stairs and headed straight for the museum entrance. They were going to crash.

"Hold on!" Matt shouted. He braced himself on a metal pole just as the front of the bus met with the stone pillars. The bus groaned and screamed as if it were in pain, but it didn't stop moving. The *Vermillion*, as if determined to keep going, began to shift. The sides of the bus pressed inward, the ceiling shrank, and the back end of the bus came forward like an accordion, pushing them all between the pillars. The crew was suddenly all mashed together in a glob of arms and hands and faces. Matt was still holding on to some kind of pole, but half his body was hanging outside of whatever the *Vermillion* was now. It seemed to have turned into a golf cart. Ruby was sandwiched between Corey and Brocco. The captain was pressed up against Wiley. He took the wheel into his own hands, but Wiley still had his foot on the pedal. The cart swerved to the left, narrowly missing the marble statue of Athena, then took a sharp turn to the right and headed for the grand staircase.

"Help!" cried a terrified voice. Matt looked backward and saw Albert clinging desperately to the back of the cart. He'd managed to get the electrical tape off his mouth, but he was still bound at the wrists and ankles. The cart swerved to the right of the grand staircase and zoomed down a corridor, zigzagging between sculptures, then took a sharp right into the Arms and Armor exhibit.

"Wiley, you fool," said the captain. "Put your foot down on the other pedal!"

"Sorry, Cap, I'm trying, but it's like she don't want to stop!"

The captain growled. He held the wheel steady, heading straight for the large display of armored knights on metal horses, each of them holding up lances like they were ready to do battle. Matt braced himself as they drove right into them. The knights toppled over like bowling pins, and the *Vermillion*, as if sensing it had reached its destination, came to a sudden and violent stop. Matt was flung forward as though being shot out of a giant slingshot. He landed hard on the floor and rolled until he came to a stop at the bottom of a glass display case full of spears.

Matt lay on the floor, shocked, the wind knocked out of him. The chandelier overhead shook ever so slightly, as though frightened by their sudden and violent arrival.

There were several groans around him and the sounds of clanking metal. Apparently Matt hadn't been the only one to be thrown from the cart. A flurry of footsteps came pounding down one of the corridors. There were a few clicking sounds and the museum was flooded with bright light. Matt lifted his head just enough to see his parents race into the exhibit. They were both in their pajamas and other random attire. Mrs. Hudson was wearing her thick leather combat boots over her plaid flannel pajama bottoms. They skidded to a stop as they surveyed the scene before them, their faces ashen and shocked.

"Mom!" Ruby cried. She picked herself up off the ground and ran to Mrs. Hudson, who caught her in her arms and hugged her fiercely. "Boys! Mateo! Corey!" she shouted in a panicky kind of shriek, searching the bodies strewn all over the floor.

"I'm here," groaned Corey.

"Me too," said Matt. He picked himself up off the floor gingerly, wincing at the sharp pain in his side. He gritted his teeth and limped to his parents. They were both there, holding out their arms to him. He'd never been so happy to see their faces. Matt got to them at the same time as Corey, and they crushed themselves against their parents. Matt ignored the searing pain. He wanted to glue himself right where he was.

His mom released him, though, as someone approached behind them. Matt turned to see Captain Vincent stumble to his feet, wincing. A gash in his eyebrow streamed blood down his face. The compass swung from his shirtsleeve. He looked around and then stopped cold when he saw the Hudsons all clasped together. Matt expected him to charge at them, to attack his dad, but to Matt's surprise, the captain smiled as though greeting a long-lost friend, not at his dad, but at his mom. "Hello, Bel," he purred.

Mrs. Hudson went rigid. "Children," she said in a low voice. "Get behind your father."

"Mom, what—" Matt began.

"Don't argue. No questions. Just go." Her voice was so sharp and quick, none of them dared to argue. They removed themselves from their mother and stood with their dad, who was looking at the captain with a mixture of fear and hatred.

Mrs. Hudson kicked a display case with the heel of her boot, shattering the glass. She pulled a sword from the metal hand of a suit of armor and pointed it at Captain Vincent.

"You," Mrs. Hudson growled.

Captain Vincent's smile broadened. "It is so good to see you, Bel, alive and well, beautiful and savage with a sword in hand, just as I have kept you in my memory these twenty years."

With a sickening horror, Matt realized the thing their father had stolen from Captain Vincent was not any map or treasure. It was his mom.

22

The Fate of Captain Bonnaire

Mrs. Hudson stood like a statue, sword outstretched. She seemed very comfortable with it. "You kidnapped my children, you evil . . ." Matt had never seen his mother so angry. Her face contorted into a feral grimace, teeth bared, body tensed for attack. She was like a fierce lioness protecting her cubs.

None of it seemed to frighten Captain Vincent at all. "Actually, they came quite willingly," he said. "In fact, they were practically starving when I picked them up and rather unsupervised or cared for. You never were the motherly type though. You were much better with swords, but I don't imagine you've kept up your skills all these years?"

Mrs. Hudson roared and charged at Captain Vincent, slashing the sword across his body. The captain jumped back and only narrowly missed the blade. Mrs. Hudson made a sharp turn and pointed the sword at Captain Vincent again.

The captain smiled, completely delighted, then drew his own sword and struck, clashing against Mrs. Hudson's blade. "You've no idea how much I've missed our duels."

"Do you care to explain yourself?" said Mrs. Hudson, circling slowly around Captain Vincent.

"If anyone deserves an explanation, it's me, don't you think?" he said. "Imagine how I felt all those years, believing you were dead. It nearly destroyed me."

"I daresay you recovered well enough," said Mrs. Hudson. "You got the compass, which is what you really wanted all along."

"True," said the captain. "But it's not nearly as *fun* without you, my Bel, my Bonbon."

"Don't call me that!" Mrs. Hudson snapped.

Captain Vincent flashed a roguish grin, clearly delighted by Mrs. Hudson's anger. "But you always liked it when I called you Bonbon."

Mrs. Hudson slashed her sword down. Metal clashed; they danced around each other, stepping over the broken glass and debris.

"Not up to your highest standard, Bel," said Captain Vincent. "Such a pity to let your talent go to waste."

"Don't tell me about waste," said Mrs. Hudson. "I assume your heart has blackened completely since last I saw you, or did you sell it for more power and treasure?"

"I don't know what you're talking about," said the captain.

"My heart always belonged to you. You stole it fair and square."

"If that's the case, you won't think it foul play if I run it through with a blade." Mrs. Hudson crashed her sword into the captain's. The blades hit so hard they emitted sparks and seemed to strike a bit of fear into the captain.

"Get the children!" Captain Vincent shouted. "Get them back on board. Kill the father if you have to."

"No!" shouted Mrs. Hudson. "Matthew, take the kids and run! Get out!"

Wiley and Brocco came toward them. Mr. Hudson backed away, his arms stretched out in an effort to shield his children, but he seemed to hesitate as to what to do under attack. He clearly was not a man of combat. Ruby, however, ducked underneath her father's arm and charged Wiley.

"Ruby, no!" their father shouted. "Corey!" Corey had gone after her. Ruby grabbed the arm of a suit of armor, wrenched it off, and swung it full force at Wiley, hitting him hard in the stomach so he doubled over.

"Nice one, sis!" said Corey.

At the same time Brocco came after Matt and Mr. Hudson. Mr. Hudson was holding tightly to Matt while Brocco drew a gun and pointed it right at Mr. Hudson's chest. "Give me the boy," he said.

Mr. Hudson was breathing very hard, clearly terrified, but he shook his head and said in a resolute voice, "No."

"Very well, if you insist." Brocco cocked the gun.

"Brocco, heads up!" Corey was swinging a metal ball and chain over his head. He released it and it soared right at Brocco, who yelped and crouched down, covering his head with his arms. It was just enough of a distraction for Mr. Hudson to charge Brocco and knock him to the ground. The gun flew out of Brocco's hand and disappeared in the piled-up armor in the middle of the room. Matt made eye contact with Albert. He was standing about the same distance as him from the gun, removing the last bit of tape from his wrists and ankles. They both made a mad dash for it, climbing and stumbling over metal arms and legs. Matt tossed aside a helmet, but just as Matt reached for the gun, Albert yanked him by the hair. Matt tried to grab him by the boots, but Albert kicked him in the mouth. Matt fell back. He tasted blood, and when he looked up, Albert was standing above him, pointing the gun right at him.

"You're actually going to shoot me?" said Matt. "I could have let the captain drop you, you know."

"I never asked you to save me," said Albert. "I don't owe you anything. I'm loyal to the captain. *You're* the traitor." He cocked the gun.

"You wouldn't da—"

There was an explosion and a cloud of black smoke. Matt threw his arms over his face, certain he'd just been shot, but when the smoke cleared and he took stock of himself, he was unharmed. He looked over to where Albert had stood. He was in the driver's seat of the golf cart, his face blackened by gunpowder and his arm bleeding. The gun had backfired. Albert groaned a little. Matt quickly stood, surveying the chaos all around him.

Mrs. Hudson was still fighting the captain. She was incredible with a sword, but Matt could tell it was a strain. Her T-shirt was soaked with sweat, and she grimaced with each stroke of her sword. Still, she fought Captain Vincent with everything she had. Her feet danced around him, her sword clashed powerfully against the captain's. They were very evenly matched.

Mr. Hudson was still fighting Brocco, hand to hand. Brocco wasn't much without a gun, and Mr. Hudson was a good head taller than him, but he was also gentle by nature. He didn't strike Brocco so much as simply try to restrain him. Brocco in turn was trying everything he could to get himself free, including biting Mr. Hudson's nose.

Corey and Ruby were still fighting Wiley, Ruby with a sword in hand and Corey with the dismembered arm of armor. Wiley was defending himself with a copper pot, blocking and dodging Corey and Ruby's attacks.

"Hey now, there's no need for violence," he said. "We can work this out peaceably, can't we? We were always friends, weren't we?"

"Not if you're going to try and kidnap us again!" said Ruby, swiping the sword at him. Wiley blocked it with the pot and moved backward. He was clearly not trained in combat. It was also clear he was reluctant to strike back at Corey and Ruby. They would be fine, Matt determined. It was his dad who seemed to need the most help at this moment.

Matt moved to assist Mr. Hudson, when a metal horse suddenly tipped over and fell onto him, pinning him by the leg. He looked up to see Albert sneering down at him.

"Mateo!" Mrs. Hudson shouted and lunged for Matt, momentarily forgetting that she was supposed to be fighting Captain Vincent.

"Mom! Look out!"

Mrs. Hudson turned back, but it was too late. The captain struck Mrs. Hudson in her upper arm. Mrs. Hudson gasped and dropped her sword. It clattered to the floor, landing only feet from Matt.

"Mom!" Matt shouted. Mrs. Hudson clutched at the wound now flowing blood. Matt struggled to get free of the metal horse, but hot pain shot up his leg. He couldn't move it.

Corey dropped the metal arm he'd been using against Wiley, and Ruby lowered her sword. Mr. Hudson paused with Brocco in a headlock, the skin of his nose bleeding from Brocco's bite. "Belamie." He shoved Brocco to the ground, knocking his head on the hard marble, which probably hurt more than anything else he'd done. Mr. Hudson rushed to his wife.

"Matthew, stay back!" Mrs. Hudson shouted. Mr. Hudson paused, unsure what to do. Captain Vincent pointed his sword at Mrs. Hudson's heart. Her chest rose and fell with fast, heavy breaths.

"You can't have them," said Mrs. Hudson. "You can steal the compass and do whatever you wish, but they're my children and you can't have them."

"They should have been *our* children, Bel, not just yours."

Mrs. Hudson let out a short laugh. "You may think my maternal instincts are lacking, Vince, but as poor a mother as I may be, you'd make a far worse father. What would our children have ever learned from you except to lie, steal, and cheat?"

"You always said the world was ours for the taking, Bel. How can you steal what already belongs to you? Your children show great promise as time pirates. Ruby is quite impressive with the sword. Corey is well on his way to becoming a master of explosives, and Mateo . . ." Captain Vincent smiled wryly. "Why, Mateo is a genius, a true time pirate in the making. Who knows what wonders he'll perform?"

Mrs. Hudson glanced at her daughter, then Corey, and finally Matt. She seemed to be looking at them in a new light, suddenly noticing that they were different than the last time she'd seen them tucked in their beds, asleep. They'd traveled and seen and done many things without her, including lie, steal, and cheat. It seemed to terrify her that her children could have been so far outside her control and protection for so long without her even knowing.

"You see, Bel, your children are destined. They belong on the *Vermillion*. And they know it too."

"Just go," Mrs. Hudson said in a raspy voice. "Please just go and leave us alone."

"You know I can't do that, Bel," said the captain. "But I'll give you a choice. I'll let you come with us if you wish. Come be a time pirate once more. Relive old times. What do you say?"

Mrs. Hudson was shaking now. Matt couldn't bear to see it, his strong, fierce mother, trembling and bleeding. It churned something inside him, a heated rage that made him forget any pain or weakness or doubt. Matt shouted and wrenched his leg with all his might, freeing himself from beneath the armored horse. He stumbled to his feet and grabbed his mother's sword. Before the captain could react, Matt slashed toward the captain. "Get away from my mom!" he shouted.

The captain stumbled back, hand cupping his cheek. When he brought it away it was soaked in blood. Matt dropped the sword, shocked by what he had done, but it also seemed to shock Mrs. Hudson into action and give her the opening she needed. She picked up her sword and swiped at the captain, only narrowly missing his neck.

"My children do not belong to you!" Mrs. Hudson shouted, thrusting her blade toward the captain's chest. He barely had time to block it. "I *never* belonged to you! We are not treasures for you to steal and collect!" She swung again and again. Captain Vincent blocked and parried until Corey and Ruby came charging. Corey swung the metal arm at the captain's legs, and Ruby thrust her sword at his chest. The captain was barely able to block all the blows. "Wiley, start the ship!"

Wiley dropped the copper pot and ran for the golf cart. Brocco crawled on hands and knees toward the cart as it sputtered to life.

Jia, Matt thought. She couldn't stay on the *Vermillion*. He needed to get her off. Matt limped toward the cart. "Jia!" he called. He saw her. She was pulling herself up, looking disoriented. She met eyes with him.

"Jia! Get off! Get out now!"

But it was too late. Captain Vincent dropped his sword and leaped for the cart, and Wiley pressed on the gas. Captain Vincent pulled the compass out from his sleeve and began to move the dials. Mrs. Hudson dropped her sword and lunged for him, readying to leap on to the cart. "Belamie, no!" Mr. Hudson grabbed his wife from behind.

"The compass!" she shouted. "We have to get the compass from him or he'll never leave us alone!" She wrenched herself free, but the cart was out of reach now, driving away through the wreckage of the armory. Mrs. Hudson ran after it, and Mr. Hudson ran after her. Matt tried to run after both of them, after Jia, but he stumbled and fell.

Corey and Ruby each got under one of Matt's arms and supported him while they ran together. They reached the foyer just as the cart went out the doors, screeching as it squeezed between the pillars. It bounced down the steps of the museum. When it reached the bottom, it suddenly stopped. Matt thought maybe the *Vermillion* had broken down, but then he saw someone running down the sidewalk toward the cart. It was Pike. Her white hair bounced up and down as she ran toward the cart as fast as her little legs could carry her. Where had she been in all the commotion? There was a bulge in her pillowcase dress. She was carrying something.

Pike reached an arm out. The captain yanked her into the already overflowing cart and they started to move again just as there was a spark and the cart seemed to flicker. The captain glanced back at the Hudsons once more. His dark eyes rested on Matt for a brief moment and then there was a flash. The *Vermillion* disappeared, leaving behind only a thin vapor of smoke and the faint aroma of peanut butter.

They all ran to the spot where the cart had disappeared. Mrs. Hudson leaned over, resting her hands on her knees. She was breathing very hard, but then she looked up at her family. Her eyes rested on Ruby, Corey, and finally Matt. Her chest caved in, and she fell down to her knees before them.

"Are you all right?" she cried, looking at each of her children. "Did he hurt you? Oh, Mateo, you're bleeding." She took the sleeve of her T-shirt, already splattered with the blood of her own injuries, and pressed gently on Matt's bloody lip. The action seemed to release something inside of him, all the bravery and bravado he'd felt in the heat of the battle seemed to vanish, and he suddenly felt very small and weak.

"Mom?" said Matt.

"What is it, *mon chéri*?"

Hot tears burned in Matt's eyes. He tried to sniff them back, but they spilled over anyway. "I'm so sorry, Mom," he said, pushing down the lump in his throat. "We didn't mean to . . . We shouldn't have . . ." Mrs. Hudson wiped the tears spilling down his cheeks. She brushed her fingers through his hair and pulled him in to her.

"It's okay," she whispered. "You're okay. That's all that matters." She pulled Corey and Ruby in as well and wrapped her arms around all three of her children.

The sound of sirens suddenly blared. Fire trucks, ambulances, and police cars were speeding down Fifth Avenue, screeching to a stop in front of the museum. Matt felt Mrs. Hudson stiffen against him. She turned around and thrust her arms out, blocking her entire family, as though another threat were imminent.

"It's all right, Belamie," said Mr. Hudson, placing a hand gently on her shoulder. "They're here to help."

When the NYPD and FDNY and FBI and all sorts of special agents arrived on the scene, Matt realized that his mother was quite a skilled liar when the situation called for it, and a fine actress to boot. She mixed fact with fiction with ease, weaving a tale about a crazy man who'd been stalking her for ages and just that morning he'd attempted to kidnap her children. Her children, being intelligent and resourceful, called her on the cell phone they always carry and said they were in a bus very near the museum, so she and her husband raced down here just as the bus crashed into the front of the museum.

"Must have been drunk," said the officer. "And how would you describe the man, ma'am?"

"Like the devil," said Mrs. Hudson, and when she offered no further description and didn't appear to be joking, the flummoxed officer turned to Mr. Hudson.

"Tall," said Mr. Hudson. "Black hair, short beard, about my age and build. He was wearing all black."

"Except the shoes," said Ruby. "He wears red Converse."

"He also has a pet rat that lives inside his jacket," said Corey. "A white rat with red eyes."

The officer looked dubious but wrote down the description.

"And your injuries, ma'am?" said the first officer's partner. "You're bleeding pretty heavily. How did you sustain them?"

"I got into a sword fight with the maniac."

The first officer lowered his pen. "A sword fight?"

"Yes," said Mrs. Hudson, as though this were a natural thing.

"She's an expert swordswoman," Ruby said.

"Well, we'd better get a medic to look at that."

"It's nothing serious," said Mrs. Hudson. "It's more important that you find the crazy man who did this before he hurts someone else."

"We've barricaded all exits to the park and set police at every exit to the city. We'll find him," said the officer.

Mrs. Hudson said nothing to this. She would allow them to believe what they would.

It was well over two hours before the Hudsons were all released to go home. The police wanted to interview each of the children separately, but Mrs. Hudson would not allow them to be separated, so they had to be interviewed all together. News trucks flooded the scene, and reporters and camera operators tried to get their way to the Hudsons, but the police thankfully had barricaded the scene and would not permit the family to be interviewed by the media at all.

The medics inspected everyone. Mr. Hudson, Corey, and Ruby had just a few cuts and bruises. Matt's left ribs did appear to be cracked, he had a bloody lip, cuts all over from the glass, and his ankle was badly sprained. Now that they were out of danger and he had started to breathe normally again, sharp pain settled into all parts of his body and he felt completely drained. The medics wrapped an ice pack around his side and ankle, cleaned up his lip, and gave him some pain pills. Mrs. Hudson's arm needed stitches, but she absolutely refused to go to the hospital, so one of the medics cleaned the wound, stitched her up on the scene, and wrapped her arm in gauze. Finally the police drove the Hudsons home. Matt was almost surprised his mom didn't ask to see the police officer's badge, driver's license, and registration, but when Mr. Hudson opened the door, she simply guided the children in and sat down next to them without a word.

As the police arrived at the Hudsons' apartment building, the officer gave them strict instructions that they should not leave town for a while, in case they had more questions.

"We've no plans to travel, Officer. Thank you," said Mr. Hudson.

The policeman nodded and drove away.

The exhausted, bewildered family stood in front of their building, huddled together in a sort of awe-filled silence. Mr. Hudson kept his arms protectively around his wife, while Mrs. Hudson wrapped her arms about her three children, pressing them to her as tightly as she could.

"Ruby, what on earth?" She rubbed Ruby's buttery hair and finally noticed that she was greasy all over. "Did you bathe in a tub of lard?"

"No, butter," said Corey. "It's her new beauty regimen."

"Mom?" Ruby asked, her voice small.

"Yes, *chérie*?"

"Who are you?"

Mrs. Hudson looked down at Ruby with wide eyes, clearly taken off guard by the question. She gaped, then looked to

Mr. Hudson, as though unsure what she should say. He nodded. "It's time, Belamie."

Mrs. Hudson knelt down before all of her children. She took each of their hands in her own, grasping them tightly. Matt felt her trembling slightly. "My name is Belamie Rubi Bonnaire. I was born in 1757 in Asilah, Morocco."

"And so . . . you're Captain Bonnaire," said Matt.

Mrs. Hudson nodded. "Was. That was a long time ago."

"But . . . you were a time pirate," said Matt. "And you used to be with . . . with Captain Vincent."

Mrs. Hudson winced. "I was a very different person then, and I did things that I now regret very much, but I can't go back and change them."

"And Dad?" Corey asked. "Were you a time pirate, too?"

"Me?" said Mr. Hudson, clearly taken aback. "Don't I wish! But I'm afraid I'm just as normal and boring as you always believed me to be. Your mother's the exciting one."

"You mean you've never time-traveled?" Matt asked. "Not once?"

"No, and it's a real shame. I begged your mother to take me to someplace exotic on our honeymoon, like the Battle of Salamis, but she said no."

"But the letter . . ." Matt pulled the letter out of his pocket, now severely torn and faded, and unfolded it. "You wrote this letter to Captain Vincent."

Mr. and Mrs. Hudson bent down and squinted at the letter.

"Huh," said Mr. Hudson. "That's odd."

"The ink is too blurred for me to be certain," said Mrs. Hudson, "but I'm not entirely sure that's your handwriting."

"No," said Mr. Hudson. "Not quite as messy as mine, is it? Though I do have some very interesting maps that tell me where and when the *Vermillion* will strike in certain places."

"It's the map over the dining room table, isn't it?" said Matt. "Where did you get it?"

"At a flea market in London. It wasn't until after I bought it that I started to notice the strange markings appear. When I saw one in Manhattan I decided to investigate. It's how I met your mother, in fact. It's a very romantic story."

"Romantic?" said Ruby. "You told us you met Mom at a convenience store."

"I did," said Mr. Hudson, beaming. "She was robbing it."

"Whaaaaaat?" said Corey. Matt blurted out a laugh, which really hurt his ribs. He winced and clutched at his side.

"All right, that's enough revelations for one day," said Mrs. Hudson, standing up. "Let's get home already."

"But seriously, I don't get it," said Corey. "Why'd you stop being a time pirate? Seems to me like it was a pretty good life."

"I'll admit, it was exciting," said Mrs. Hudson, "and there are some things about it that I miss."

"Then why did you give it all up?" asked Matt.

Mrs. Hudson smiled gently down at him, brushing a hand

through his hair. "I gave it all up for you, of course."

"Me?"

"Yes, and Corey and Ruby, and a little bit your father."

"Only a little?" said Mr. Hudson, pouting.

"Just a little." Mrs. Hudson winked at her husband.

"But you didn't know we'd be your kids then," said Ruby. "I mean you never saw us before, when you were time-traveling, did you?"

"No," said Mrs. Hudson, "but I had this hole in my heart, you see." She pressed her hand to her chest and her eyes grew watery. "I knew something was missing in my life and I searched and searched for the thing that would fill it. I traveled all over time and to the ends of the earth, but it wasn't until you three came along—"

"Four," Mr. Hudson coughed into his fist.

"It wasn't until you *four* came along," said Mrs. Hudson, "that I was finally whole. *You* are my family, and no matter my past, you are my present and future, and I love you more than anything in the entire world."

"Even more than the Obsidian Compass?" said Matt.

Mrs. Hudson wrapped her arms around her three children and pressed them to her. She rested her head on top of Mateo's and whispered, "An infinity times more."

The city was fully awake now, cars, buses, and taxis driving up and down the street, pedestrians with coffee and pastries, walking dogs or hustling to the subway or bus stop. A flock of pigeons pecked at a pile of crumbs around a garbage can. Just a normal morning in New York City. A man walked by with his dog and waved at them. "Morning," he said. He was wearing a Mets hat.

"Hey, Dad, one more question," said Corey. "How come you never told us you were at Game Six?"

Mr. Hudson looked confused at first. "Game Six . . . ," he muttered, and then his eyes widened.

"You . . . ," he said, putting his hand to his mouth. He looked at each of his children as though seeing them in a new light.

"Yeah, remember us?" said Matt. "You told us about that game over and over, and you never once mentioned that you were *there*."

"You had a sweet mullet!" said Corey.

Mr. Hudson's face burned scarlet, and Mrs. Hudson laughed. "Perhaps just one more reveal then. Go on, Matthew," she said, in a slightly goading voice. "It's time."

Mr. Hudson rubbed the back of his head and looked anywhere but at his children. "Well, uh, you see, I didn't exactly have tickets to that particular game . . ."

Ruby gasped, but Corey just laughed. "You snuck in, didn't you? I thought so."

"You could have at least told us you were there!" said Matt.

"Your mother forbade me, actually, in case I slipped up somehow."

"Well, it wasn't the best example for our children," said Mrs. Hudson.

"Well, I think their pirate mother makes up for all my shortcomings," said Mr. Hudson. Mrs. Hudson punched him playfully in the arm.

"Yes, speaking of that," said Ruby. "I have a request. For Mom."

"Oh?" Mrs. Hudson looked to her daughter.

"Will you give me sword lessons? Please?"

Mrs. Hudson opened her mouth, but no words came out.

"It's inevitable, Belamie," said Mr. Hudson. "Sooner or later our children turn into us. We might as well show them the way."

Mrs. Hudson smiled at her daughter and squeezed her hand. "We'll start right away. No time like the present."

"Hey, Mom," said Corey. "Did you know, on the *Vermillion*, we ate *tons* of junk food and it actually made us feel good?"

"Ah, the time-sickness remedy," said Mrs. Hudson. "I hope you enjoyed it while it lasted. Back to couscous and vegetables, *mon chéri*."

Corey groaned.

"Do you get time sickness here?" Ruby asked. "Is that why you never eat any junk food?"

"Partly," said Mrs. Hudson. "I also don't eat it because it's gross. How Americans stand all that junk . . ."

"With great pleasure," said Mr. Hudson, patting his stomach. "Come on, let's go home."

Yes. Home. Matt couldn't believe how much he missed it, how much he missed his parents, his whole family being together. He decided he would never take for granted the time they had together. He would never again wish to be away from them.

Still clinging to each other, limping and tripping over one another's feet, all five of the Hudsons walked into their apartment building and headed home.

23

Full Circle

When the Hudsons reached their floor, they found their apartment door was unlocked and slightly ajar.

"You locked it, didn't you?" said Mr. Hudson.

"I think so," said Mrs. Hudson. "I certainly *closed* it all the way."

Mr. Hudson frowned. He pushed the door open and stepped inside. "Hello?" he called.

No one answered. Then there was a rustling sound, a thump, and a shriek. "Wake up! We're going to be late!"

"Who—" Mrs. Hudson began until Ruby hushed her.

"It's me . . . ," Ruby whispered.

"Why didn't Mom wake us?" said the Ruby in the bedroom. "I'm supposed to give my presentation in first period!"

"Probably slept in themselves," said another voice, a sleepy one that was weirdly familiar to Matt. He looked to Ruby and Corey, then his parents. "We're still here!" he mouthed, pointing to the rooms. They'd come home before their past selves left!

Mrs. Hudson paled. They all knew it would be a disaster if they saw themselves. They couldn't see their parents either because, well, they hadn't seen them before, so if they did in this scenario it might cause a ripple, or worse, they'd get trapped in the space-time continuum.

"Quick! Get into the closet!" whispered Mrs. Hudson. She opened their coat closet by the front door and they all piled in, except Ruby, who was squinting toward the kitchen.

"Ruby!" their mom whispered.

"Hang on." Ruby sprinted silently to the kitchen counter and grabbed something.

"Oh, I give up! You wake him!" came past-Ruby's voice from the bedroom. Now-Ruby made a mad dash for the closet and slipped in just as her past self walked out of the bedroom and trudged to the kitchen.

"What were you doing?" hissed Mrs. Hudson.

"Getting Corey's lunch!" Ruby shoved a lunch bag in front of Corey. "Corey forgot his lunch this morning. If he gets it this time, we could be stuck in this closet forever!"

Understanding dawned on Matt. Corey's hunger was one of the main reasons they'd boarded the *Vermillion* in the first place. If he wasn't desperately hungry and their past selves didn't end up getting on the train, who knows what future they would create, if it would stop Captain Vincent from kidnapping them, or if they'd ever reunite with their parents.

"Good thinking," said Mrs. Hudson.

"But . . . ," said Corey, thoroughly perplexed. "Whatever. If pre-me is going to starve, now-me is going to eat." He opened his lunch and started eating as they listened to themselves argue about breakfast and being late. Finally the past–Hudson children all rushed to the door. They opened the closet and reached for their backpacks. The Hudsons inside the closet all squeezed together as much as they could, trying to hide themselves behind the long coats, but the past–Hudson children weren't looking. They opened the door and were about to close it when past-Ruby said, "Wait! I need a jacket." An arm reached inside the closet again and fumbled around. "Where is my gray jacket? This closet is a disaster." She started tearing bags and coats out of the closet. Matt turned his head, pressing it into his dad's shoulder. If she kept going, she was going to knock right into them. Now-Ruby suddenly tugged on Matt's sleeve. "Your sweater!" she whispered in his ear, and Matt understood. He was wearing the hoodie that Ruby had taken that morning. He quickly pulled it off and chucked it to the front of the closet.

"Oh fine, whatever." Ruby took the hoodie and went out the door.

"Hey, that's mine," Matt heard himself say.

"Well, I'm borrowing it. Ew, it smells. When's the last time you washed this thing?"

"I don't know. Never?"

"Gross."

The door slammed, and the deadbolt clicked. They heard themselves run down the stairs. Then silence.

"That was seriously weird," Corey said. Ruby slowly pushed open the door and crawled out of the closet. Matt followed her, and then Corey and then Mr. Hudson. There was an audible gasp behind him.

"Belamie?" Mr. Hudson asked. Mrs. Hudson turned on her phone flashlight and shifted the contents of the closet, revealing the safe in the wall. It was open. And it was empty.

"Who could have . . . ," Mr. Hudson began to ask, and then trailed off as Ruby reached down and plucked a hair off the sleeve of a black coat—a long white-blond hair.

"Pike," breathed Matt. "I saw her running down Fifth Avenue just before the *Vermillion* disappeared. She was carrying something."

"Who?" Mrs. Hudson asked.

"Creepy rat-girl," said Corey.

"Corey, don't be rude. She helped us get home!"

"Yeah, but it seems like she had a mission of her own," said Matt, "and I guess we underestimated her loyalty to the captain."

"A child couldn't have broken into this safe!" said Mrs. Hudson, growing more panicked by the second. "It's impossible to break into this thing!"

"I'm guessing not for Pike," said Ruby.

Mrs. Hudson stared at the empty safe until Mr. Hudson finally reached in to help her out. "Come on, Belamie," he said. "There's nothing we can do about it now."

Mrs. Hudson crawled out of the closet and stomped into the living room. She paced back and forth in front of her wall display of swords, her hands pressed together at her mouth. Matt just stood there with the rest of his family and watched, all of them unsure what to do. Matt was trying to understand exactly why his mother was so upset just then. Almost as upset, it seemed, as when she realized the captain had kidnapped her children.

"It was a client's artifact, wasn't it?" said Matt. "You have insurance for that sort of thing, don't you?"

But then Ruby gasped.

"The Queen Elizabeth box," she said. "That's what Captain Vincent was after! And *you* had it *here* the whole time?"

Mrs. Hudson didn't answer Ruby. "Okay," she said, pushing her fingers through her hair and pulling at the ends. "It's okay. He doesn't have the key . . ."

Matt swallowed. "You mean the one hidden inside the *Mona Lisa*?"

"What?" Mrs. Hudson said sharply, turning to Matt.

"The *Mona Lisa*," said Matt. "We were there when he stole it from the Louvre in 1911, and I watched him take the key out of the back." Matt didn't have the courage to tell her that he had been the one to direct him to it, or at least his future self did.

What little color was in Mrs. Hudson's face now drained completely. She shakily sat down on the couch. "He has the box and the key . . . ," she said in a bit of a daze.

"Belamie," said Mr. Hudson, sitting next to her. "What does it matter, hon? We're safe now. We have the kids."

"You don't understand," she said, her voice cracking a little. "I was supposed to keep it from Vincent at all costs."

"What's inside it?" Corey asked.

"A letter," said Mrs. Hudson.

"A *letter*?" said Corey. "That's all?"

"Who is the letter from?" Matt asked.

"From the inventor of the Obsidian Compass," said Mrs. Hudson.

"*That's* who your client is?" said Ruby. "Who is he?"

"His name is Marius Quine," said Mrs. Hudson. "I've only met him once and very briefly, with very little contact over the years. He's a strange man, very mysterious and dangerously powerful, but if Vincent is able to gain the same power somehow . . ."

There was a moment of silence.

"Will he come after us again?" Ruby asked in a small voice.

"Maybe *we* should go after *him*," said Corey.

"How are we supposed to do that?" Ruby asked. "We don't have the compass or the *Vermillion*."

Matt instinctively reached for his bracelet. He could call the *Vermillion* back to them! Just like he had when they'd been discarded. They could get the box back and the key and maybe the compass, even. And Jia . . .

But his bracelet was gone. He searched his pockets and the floor, even though he knew it wouldn't be there. It must have come off during the fight at the Met, or before. It could be on the *Vermillion*, long gone.

"What's wrong?" Ruby asked.

Matt shook his head and held out his wrist. "My bracelet . . ."

Ruby's eyes lit up with comprehension. "Oh . . ."

The lump rose in Matt's throat again. Jia would be discarded, and he was powerless to help her.

"It's okay, Matt," said Ruby. "We'll figure something out. It's not over."

Matt nodded. No, it couldn't be over. There was still hope, however small.

"I have a lot of explaining to do, I know," Mrs. Hudson said. "And I will, but for now I need you to simply trust me. Can you do that? I know I don't deserve it, but can you? Wherever we go from now on, we will all stay together. Agreed?"

Matt didn't think he could take any more surprises, no more adventures. He just wanted to crawl into his bed, go to sleep, and wake up tomorrow to plain oatmeal and go to school and never, ever ride on another train or bus or boat. He looked to his brother and sister, dirty, bruised, and ragged. He could tell Corey and Ruby felt the same, but that they also understood the inevitability of their situation. Matt felt a chill come over him, and a deep, down-in-the-gut feeling that this wasn't over. He pictured all three of their names carved into the mast of the ship. They never did that, which meant at some point they would board the *Vermillion* again, face Captain Vincent, perhaps even meet the maker of the Obsidian Compass. And Matt's future self would do things that he still didn't quite understand now. He understood so little. There was only one thing he knew for certain—the love he felt for his family. It rose above his exhaustion and aching body now, surpassed his fears and doubts. It was something that couldn't be broken or dissolved, no matter where they went, or when. This was his family, and they belonged together at all times and all places.

Matt held his fist out in front of him. Ruby and Corey both joined him, then their mom and dad.

"Agreed," said Matt.

It was their first five-way family fist bump.

Acknowledgments

Writing any book is always a big undertaking, like climbing a mountain. Writing a series is like climbing several mountains. Writing a time-travel series is like climbing all the mountains all over the world and throughout all time. It's vast, it's complex, it's daunting. Simply put, no human being can do it without an oxygen mask and a team of experts to help you get where you want to go and (hopefully) not die in the process. To that end, I would like to thank Melissa Miller for believing I could write this series in the first place, and to Alex Arnold and Rebecca Aronson, who jumped on the ship brandishing magic pens. I loved all our brainstorming sessions. I still have fireworks going off in my brain. To my agent, Claire Anderson-Wheeler, always ready to read at the drop of a hat, offer advice and assistance, champion my work, and talk me off the ledge, thank you so much. Thanks to Katie Fitch for a magical, adventurous cover, and to Robby Imfeld and Gina Rizzo for getting my book into the hands of readers who will love it. Gratitude to Katherine Tegen and Kathryn Silsand, and all those at Katherine Tegen Books and HarperCollins who had any part in bringing this series about and making it what it is. Any remaining mistakes or weaknesses are my own. To Erin Cleary, Janet Lefley, Tabitha Olson, and Susan Tarcov, thanks for reading early chapters and giving invaluable feedback that certainly shaped the rest of the story. Thanks to Brianna DuMont, not only for reading this book section by section and providing fantastic input and ideas, but also lending your history expertise. You were there for me at a critical moment! Thank you to Sarah Beer Clemens for helping me with my very rusty, very limited French. Huge thanks to my husband, Scott, for a million things but in particular with this book, all the baseball facts, terms, and history lessons. I feel like I can sit with the cool kids now, or maybe the next table over? And last, but not least, always love and gratitude to my beautiful children, Whitney, Ty, Topher, and Freddy. You inspire me, delight me, challenge me, and ultimately make my life freaking amazing. *Family fist bump*

Keep reading for a sneak peek of
TIME CASTAWAYS #2: THE OBSIDIAN COMPASS

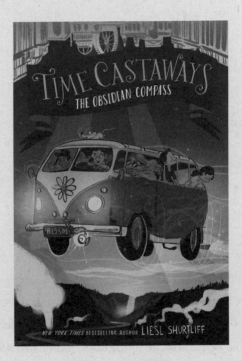

1

The Disappearing Thief

Belamie, Age 5-15
1762-1772
Asilah, Morocco

It was a perfect day. At least in the beginning.

It began with blue skies, not a cloud in sight, and a calm, glassy sea.

No one understood where the storm came from, not even the old fortune-teller, who for decades had been a reliable source for most impending tragedies and doom. Stories abounded of course, as people will always search for answers and reasons. Perhaps some thoughtless sailor had whistled in the wind or stirred his tea with a knife, or maybe an ignorant passenger on a ship had unwittingly cut their nails. Reason or not, the storm blew in, quick and relentless.

The clouds rolled and rumbled into a dark foreboding mass. The first lightning bolt struck just before midday. The wind grew savage and the rain burst from the sky, pelting the water like a thousand arrows every second. The waves swelled to the size of small mountains, rising up and slapping down with brute, merciless force.

The little merchant ship did not stand a chance. The sailors did all they could, followed every order from their captain at the helm, but they knew there was no hope. In less than an hour the ship was sunk and every soul on board was drowned.

All but one.

A tiny girl, no more than five years old, miraculously survived the storm without so much as a scratch. She bobbed along the ocean in a small skiff, wearing only a thin nightgown, soaked and sticking to her like a second skin. The only other possession she had was a small dagger, which she held close to her chest like a talisman. She stared out at the water, now still and calm, as though waiting for something to rise from its depths.

A young sailor on a ship found the girl, floating among the wreckage. He spoke to her in English and then French, and when she didn't respond either time he assumed she couldn't understand him, but she could. The sailor argued with his companions over whether or not to rescue the girl. They seemed to be afraid of her for some reason. Perhaps they thought she had been the cause of the storm, that she would bring them bad luck. She had often heard sailors say that a female, even a little one, was bad luck on board a ship.

They left her in her skiff, lashed it to their ship, and tugged her all the way to the shores of Asilah, where the sunken ship had sailed from the day before. The girl did not speak or cry the entire way. She did not move.

When they had tugged the little skiff onto the beach, the sailors again argued over her, where they should take her, how she would survive. The girl didn't even register their words. She only watched the waves, now calm and gentle, roll upon the shore.

The young sailor gave the girl what little food he had on him, some biscuits and dried fish. He gave her a final look of sympathy and left her on the beach, still sitting inside her little boat, clutching the dagger.

The girl's name was Belamie Rubi Bonnaire. She knew her name as well as she knew that she was now alone in the world. Her parents were gone. Her papa, a French merchant with gentle hands, and her mama, a Moroccan beauty with a quick wit and captivating charm.

Though Belamie had been born in Morocco, her mother's country, she had spent most of her life at sea, sailing the world with her parents and their crew. There was no one to take care of her now. She knew of no other family or friends, no one who cared or even knew of her existence. She once overheard a member of her papa's crew say that her parents' marriage had been a crime, that they'd been disowned by both their families and lived on the sea because no place else would have them.

At the time Belamie thought that was just fine. She preferred the sea to land anyway, and she didn't need anyone besides her parents. And now they were gone. They'd been swallowed by the angry sea, and they would not come back.

Belamie stayed with the boat. It was all she had left, and it would be her home and family now. She slept curled up inside of it that night, then sat in its shade all the next day. She didn't leave the boat until her food was gone and survival instincts kicked in and forced her to get up and seek food and water.

Belamie determined she would not steal. Her religious education had been spotty and vague, but once, when they'd gone to Paris, Belamie had tried to steal a doll from the fancy shop where her father had been doing business. She'd tried to hide it behind her back, but her father had caught her and gave her a long lecture. Stealing was a sin, he had said. It might bring some fleeting pleasure, but then damnation and hellfire. Her mother told her that those who steal get their hands cut off. This frightened Belamie so much she vowed to never steal again. But after a week of eating little more than the dust kicked in her mouth by unsympathetic passersby, she decided a radical change was in order. Damnation be damned, it was steal or starve.

It was painful at first. She got a stomachache after eating her first stolen melon, but eventually she developed a callus on her conscience, and it got easier. By the age of ten she wasn't ashamed to admit she found thieving to be quite fun, though she was always cautious. She learned it was best to steal from foreigners. Not only was it easier, it was safer too. The guards and soldiers were not concerned with protecting visitors. Even if she were caught, she'd likely only be made to give back what she'd stolen, perhaps spend a night or two in jail. That was far preferable to getting her hands chopped off. She'd seen it happen to thieves younger than her. She didn't relish the idea of eating like a dog.

Day after day, year after year, she carved out a meager existence as a thief. She slept and ate and lived in her little boat on the beach. Occasionally thieves tried to steal her boat, but Belamie had her dagger and, despite her smallness, she was alarmingly dexterous and skilled with a blade. Thieves soon learned to leave her and her little boat alone, and Belamie was quite content to remain alone, a petty thief until the end of her days. But fate, as it seemed, had other ideas, as it often does.

She was about fifteen when the strange man who would change the course of her life came to Asilah. The whole village was talking about him. The guard keeping watch from the ramparts (the great white wall that bordered the city along the sea) reported that he'd appeared on the beach out of thin air. They all swore it was true.

The man was a spirit, everyone said. One of the mysterious and powerful jinn. Some said he was a good jinni come to grant wishes. Others said he was evil, come to possess their spirits. Good or evil, there was one thing everyone could agree upon. The man was rich as a king. Gold and silver seemed to flow from his fingers.

That got Belamie's attention more than anything. She had little interest in the jinn, good or evil. Even if they were real, they would not fill her belly. But gold and silver could, and Belamie could steal from anyone.

She found him the next market day. He stood out like a fish on land. He was very different, even from all the sailors and foreigners she saw year after year. Belamie could not confidently discern where he was from. He wore loose trousers and a shirt with many buttons, and nothing around his neck. His head was bare, revealing dark hair streaked with silver. His back was to her, so she couldn't see his face.

Belamie moved a little closer, just enough to hear the man speak. She'd know where he was from based on his accent. She'd traveled the world with her parents before they'd died, and after so many years stealing from foreigners she could accurately detect most accents.

"Would you like some cinnamon, sir?" said the merchant. "There is no better cinnamon in the world." He held out a tiny sack, clearly eager to get some of the foreigner's famed gold.

"Oh, I don't know about that," said the foreigner. "I've had some delicious cinnamon in Brazil, but the cinnamon in Sri Lanka is very nice as well, though I suppose at this time it's not Sri Lanka, but Ceylon? What year is this again? 1772? Yes, it should be Ceylon now."

The merchant blinked at the man, still holding out the pouch of cinnamon. Belamie was utterly perplexed. The man spoke flawless Arabic, only the barest hint of an accent that she couldn't quite detect. It seemed to alter every other word. At first she thought maybe he was French, then English, then Russian.

"Some people think Ceylon cinnamon is the only real cinnamon," the man continued, "but then they probably haven't traveled to India. There, the spices are so pungent you can taste them in the air. Unfortunately, you can taste other less savory things in the air as well, so I don't recommend eating Indian air, but Indian cinnamon is divine."

The merchant nodded, his brow furrowed. He looked as though he didn't know whether to be impressed or offended by the man. "You have traveled very far, it seems. From what country do you hail?"

Belamie leaned in a little closer to hear.

"I don't claim any particular country of origin," the man replied. "I find such labels to be a bit confining and, quite frankly, misleading and unfair to everyone. If I say I'm a Spaniard, you'll instantly think me clever but haughty. On the other hand, if I tell you that I'm French, you'll find me an amiable fellow, but you won't trust me an inch. And yet, if I tell you I'm English, you'll think me a self-aggrandizing snob, though a fashionable one. But there is a real chance that all these things might be true, and so I prefer to give us both the benefit of the doubt and say I am from nowhere and everywhere. It's more accurate anyway. I'll take some cinnamon, since you say it is the best in the world." He pulled a thick silver coin seemingly out of thin air. The merchant didn't move. He stared, blank as a dead fish, until the strange man placed the coin on the table and took the cinnamon out of his hand. "I'll compare your cinnamon to the others and let you know if it is the best, if you like, so you can claim the title with complete confidence. Or drop it altogether. I always like to be accurate. Good day!" He turned away from the spice merchant. He tossed the little sack of cinnamon in the air, tucked it in his pocket, and walked right past Belamie, who was so lost in studying the odd stranger she almost forgot what she was about. She was supposed to be robbing him. Who cared where the man was from!

Belamie picked her way through the crowd toward the man. He was almost to the chicken merchant. That was perfect.

Belamie moved quickly and with purpose. She was just behind the man now, and she slipped her hand into his pocket, when without any warning he stepped out of her path. Belamie pitched forward, crashing into the stacked crates of chickens. The crates toppled onto her. The chickens exploded in angry squawks and a cloudburst of feathers.

Belamie tried to get up, run away, but again she tripped over one of the crates and went down in the dirt, knocking her mouth and chin on the ground.

"*Majnun!* Fool! Get away from my chickens!" cried a voice.

Belamie cursed herself for being so clumsy. She quickly stood, ready to run, but found herself face-to-face with the mysterious man, the very man whom she'd been trying to rob. For the rest of her life Belamie would think about the man's face. She would try to bring it to the surface of her mind over and over and she wouldn't be able to. His features were somehow indistinguishable, blurred, like a smeared painting. She blinked. A bit of dust or sand must have gotten in her eyes.

"Are you all right?" said the man.

He smiled at her, or at least she thought he did. There was a smear of white in the general area of his mouth.

"You must pay for damages!" shouted the chicken man, waving a fist in Belamie's face. "My hens will not lay, and you have created more work for me!"

"It was my fault," said the foreigner. "I was in this young lady's way. Allow me." Coins appeared in his gloved hand. Belamie could not explain it logically. One moment they were not there, and the next they were.

He dropped the coins in one of the chicken cages. The chicken squawked and flapped again as gold and silver rained down on it. The merchant did not complain. In fact, he thrust the chicken out of its crate, so he could gather the coins. It was more money than he could ever make in a lifetime selling eggs and chickens.

Meanwhile, the foreigner had his back turned to her. Belamie was in a most advantageous position. She could see a lump in his pocket, a purse with a tiny glint of gold. She deftly reached into his pocket and pulled out his purse, smooth as a fish swimming through water.

She turned to run but was violently pulled back. The man had chained his purse to him!

"Thief!" shouted the chicken merchant. "She is robbing you, sir!"

Belamie dropped the purse and tried to run, but before she could take two steps, she was faced by the guards. One was pointing a spear right at her neck. Belamie pulled out her dagger, ducked and swiped at the guard, but another one was right behind him. He grabbed her wrist and twisted, forcing her to drop her dagger. She struggled against the guard, tried to step on his foot, jam her elbow into his gut, but he shoved her to the ground, yanked her arms behind her back.

"Thief," growled the guard as he tied a rope around her wrists.

Belamie struggled once more until the guard kicked her in the gut and yanked her to her feet. A crowd had gathered to watch, all of them staring at her, some with expressions of shock, others with gloating glares, clearly glad to see she'd finally gotten what she deserved. The guard grasped her under both arms and began to lead her away. But the strange man, the jinni, was standing right in their path.

He was still blurry. Belamie could not read his expression, but he must be angry. Perhaps he wanted to punish her himself. Spit on her, smack her across the face. Turn her into a mouse and feed her to the chickens. He was holding something in his gloved hands. Her dagger. Perhaps he wanted to cut her hands off himself. The guards would probably let him, if he paid them enough gold.

"Release her," said the man.

"But, sir," said one of the guards. "She was stealing your gold, was she not?"

"No, no, no. This is all a big misunderstanding. We were in the midst of a trade. I wanted this knife. It's a very fine knife, and I took it, but then she never got her end of the bargain because we were attacked by chickens! Untie her at once!"

The guard quickly untied her hands while the man detached the pouch from the chain in his pocket. He held it out to Belamie. She looked down at the pouch, then at the dagger. Her father's dagger. It was all she had left of him in the world. The boat was more of a practical thing. The dagger was precious to her. She did not want to part with it. But she also did not want to part with her hands or her freedom.

She looked at the man. His face flickered and became clear, just for a moment. He looked at Belamie with a curious expression, a smile she couldn't quite read. Amusement? Fondness? It was almost like he knew her, but she couldn't think how. She had no family, no friends. No one in the world who cared about her at all.

The man pressed something into her hand, a small purse, the one she'd tried to steal from him just minutes ago. "See you soon," he said, and then he dissolved, like a pillar of salt in water.

The crowd gasped, a few screamed. The guards lifted their spears, though what good would they do against an invisible man? He was gone, nowhere to be seen.

Belamie knew that if she waited long enough, the crowd would take their fear out on her. They'd say she was connected to the man somehow, believe her full of evil and witchcraft, and throw her in prison, or worse, stone her to death. She took this moment to disappear herself.

She slipped through the crowd and ran all the way to the ramparts. She put the purse in her teeth and grabbed on to a rope, swung herself over and scaled down, jumping the last ten feet to the rocky beach and her little skiff tucked between the rocks.

Belamie pulled the skiff into the water, hopped in, and began to row. She rowed for maybe a quarter hour, then rested the oars and picked up the purse, weighing it in her hand and trying to make sense of what had just happened. Everyone would be talking about how he had disappeared, but that was the less confusing part of the story to Belamie. Why had the man saved her like that? He didn't know her. She guessed there must be at least ten pieces of silver, based on the weight. She could start a new life with that kind of money, maybe even leave Asilah, sail to the Americas where she'd heard fascinating tales from sailors and merchants of work and land and food, more than could be consumed.

Belamie opened the purse and reached inside. She frowned. It was not full of coins as she had assumed. She pulled out what looked like a strange watch or compass, or some combination of the two. Her initial disappointment was softened when she saw how beautiful it was. It was made of shiny black stone and had numerals, letters, and symbols etched and inlaid with gold in three layers of circles. She could get a good price for it from the jeweler in the market. Or the clockmaker. Or maybe she'd get a better price if she sold it directly to one of the sailors on the docks. It was a piece worthy of a captain. Her father would have loved it.

Memories suddenly rushed upon her, one after the other. Her father, holding his own compass, navigating at the helm of his ship. He told Belamie that one day she would be captain and his ship and compass would be hers. She had believed him, had looked forward to the day. Now it was all at the bottom of the ocean—the ship, the compass, and her parents. Try as she might, she could never quite remember how she'd survived or how she'd gotten inside the skiff. Did her father put her inside of it? Her mother? Why didn't they come with her?

Belamie shivered as a sudden cool wind gusted. A small

wave rocked the boat. She studied the compass again. Such a strange thing. She wondered what the dials were for, what the symbols meant. She turned the outer dial. It made a soft clicking noise. Then turned the other dials, too, back and forth. The compass suddenly grew warm in her hands. The skiff plummeted at least a foot and the water around her began to hiss and bubble. Belamie dropped the compass. It fell to the bottom of the boat as she reached for the oars, but they were no help. She was already traveling far faster than she could possibly row.

Marius Quine, the so-called jinni, watched from the beach as Belamie Bonnaire and her little boat disappeared. His heart skipped a beat when it happened, even though he knew it would happen. He'd known this moment would come for years, and yet he couldn't help the rock that formed in his throat, the mixture of excitement and panic. He almost wanted to go after her, make sure she would be all right. But he knew she would be fine. For a time anyway. The danger, and the sorrow, would come later.

He wiped a bit of sweat off his forehead and removed his gloves like a farmer who had just finished sowing the seed in his fields and now only needed to wait until harvest. It had not been simple or easy, getting to this moment. There were so many threads, so many years and places and lives all circling and spiraling around each other. There were so many opportunities for mistakes, and so little room to get it right, but he knew this was how it all began.

"Mr. Quine?" a voice called behind him. It sent prickles up his neck, and he felt his features begin to sharpen and pull into focus. He fought against it, felt his face flicker in and out, like an intermittent radio signal. He was getting interference from present company.

Slowly, he turned around and faced the boy.

And this was how it all would end.